A House with Seven Windows

Judaic Traditions in Literature, Music, and Art
Ken Frieden *and* Harold Bloom, *Series Editors*

A House with Seven Windows

S H O R T S T O R I E S

∙ ∙ ∙ ∙ ∙ ∙ ∙

Kadya Molodowsky

Translated from the Yiddish by Leah Schoolnik

SYRACUSE UNIVERSITY PRESS

English translation copyright © 2006 by Syracuse University Press

Syracuse, New York 13244–5160

All Rights Reserved

First Edition 2006

06   07   08   09   10   11   6   5   4   3   2   1

This collection of stories was previously published in Yiddish as
A shtub mit zibn fenster (New York: Farlag Matones, 1957).

The paper used in this publication meets the minimum requirements
of American National Standard of Information Sciences—Permanence
of Paper of Printed Library Materials, ANSI Z39.48–1984©™

Library of Congress Cataloging-in-Publication Data

Molodowsky, Kadia, 1894–1975.

[Shtub mit zibn fenster. English]

A house with seven windows : short stories / Kadya Molodowsky ;
translated by Leah Schoolnik.— 1st ed.

p. cm.—(Judaic traditions in literature, music, and art)

ISBN 0–8156–0845–4 (pbk. : alk. paper)

I. Schoolnik, Leah. II. Title. III. Series.

PJ5129.M7S513 2006

839'.133—dc22   2005033513

Manufactured in the United States of America

To Gary Schoolnik and Ben Litman

The late **Kadya Molodowsky** was an eminent Yiddish poet. Born in 1894 in what is now Belarus, she received an education unusual for a girl at that time and later became active in Yiddish literary circles in Poland and the Ukraine. In 1935, she emigrated to the United States, where she once again found her place at the center of the Yiddish literary world, publishing poetry, essays, and a novel. In 1949, she and her husband moved to Israel for three years, returning to the United States in 1952. She continued writing prolifically, producing poetry, another novel, and this collection of short stories. She also founded the critical literary journal *Svive*, becoming its editor as well as a contributor. She died in 1975.

Leah Schoolnik has translated other prose works by Kadya Molodowsky and short stories by Yossl Birstein, Avrom Dubleman, Pincas Berniker, and Osher Schuchinsky.

Contents

. . . .

IN A BROWNSVILLE KRETCHMA

Preface to the Original Yiddish Edition

· · · · · · · ·

I wrote the stories included in this book in the last fifteen years. From a world that vanished most dreadfully, and that lives on in our memories, images of piety, virtue, and Jewish morals awaken. There people stood with feet on poor soil, but with their souls in a higher world of good works and good deeds. These very images live in me, and they emerge in a large number of the stories in this book.

A Jew was never concerned with the appearance of the walls of his house. He would never call an interior decorator when he needed to whitewash these walls for Passover. He merely hung a picture of the Vilna Gaon on the wall, and that was embellishment enough. He wasn't concerned about what kind of bookcases he had, as long as they contained the Talmud. It didn't matter to him if the windows of his house weren't in the latest style, because he still knew where the eastern wall was. When he gave to charity, he certainly didn't look in the newspapers to see if his name was there, and if the letters were big enough.

In our time, people have moved from an inner, spiritual world to a life of externals, to things that flaunt themselves in one's face, that have more glitter than warmth, more talk than thought; more outward show than introspection.

And as a Jew advanced from an inner to an outer station, as usual, in that advance, he lost those possessions he had, and had to go back, look for, and find them. These losses and gains are both tragic and comic. A good number of the stories in the book are dedicated to this significant phenomenon in our lives.

Perhaps that was why I wanted to call the book *A House with Seven Windows*: light and shadows enter into each window.

. . . .

I want to give my sincere thanks to the Matones Publishers for publishing this book, and to its director, my good friend Lippe Lehrer, for seeing the manuscript through with me and for his good advice.

Kadya Molodowsky

Translator's Note

. . . .

In those stories set in the United States, Kadya Molodowsky made use of many English words in her original Yiddish text, often (but not always) signalling these words with quotation marks. In this translation, I have deleted those quotation marks in the belief that setting off English words within an English text would give them an artificial emphasis and interfere with the flow of Molodowsky's prose. However, I have listed most of these English words (excepting such words as articles and conjunctions) in an appendix, because I feel her use of them demonstrates the flexibility and adaptability of the Yiddish language, and, further, adds depth to our understanding of individual characters. To avoid a possible unintended comic effect, however, I have not included the Yiddish pronunciations of these words.

Those Yiddish and Hebrew words that are familiar to readers and have entered the English vocabulary are not italicized; other less familiar words and expresions are italicized. All are defined in the glossary.

For Yiddish names and places, I have used the customary—but not necessarily standard—spellings; for lesser-known names and words, I've referred to Uriel Weinreich's *Modern English-Yiddish Yiddish-English Dictionary* (New York: Schocken Books, 1997).

. . . .

For their warm generosity, giving of their time and knowledge, I give my equally warm and profoundly grateful thanks to the following people:

Zachary Baker, Arlen Brownstein, John Felstiner, Fanya Glazer, Ellen Goodman, Kathryn Hellerstein, Ben Litman, Mordkhe Schaechter, Sylvia Schildt, Frank and LaRhee Webster; Hannah Berman, Hebrew teacher beyond compare; Iosif Gavartin and Layah Laks, the dearest and best Yiddish teachers; Lois Ouse; Sheva Zucker; and Gary, David, and Joel Schoolnik.

Sheva Zucker and I have worked together at length. She is the perfect editor, having good taste, a knowledge and love of Yiddish, and a sense of humor.

A House with Seven Windows

A House with Seven Windows

· · · · · · · ·

B ashke was the only girl in Grodno Province who could take the reins of a horse as well as a landowner. Her father was a rich country tenant [1] who leased the fields, meadows, and a herd of a hundred cows from the nearby landowners.

When she traveled to the nearest town, Brisk, [2] it was in nothing less than a britzka with a pair of horses. Her coachman, Yankl, held a whip with a red tassel and sat up proudly, head high, on the upholstered coachbox of the carriage exactly as if he were driving the emperor's daughter herself. He polished his boots for a whole half-hour before he drove Bashke into town.

Bashke's blue eyes and haughty, upturned little chin had a stubborn beauty, as if she were teasing the world all day long, saying: Well, who can outdo me?

When the landowner, driving in the middle of the forest, happened to

1. Three terms define an important relationship between Jews and Gentiles in Poland in the late 1800s. A *yishuvnik,* a country person and often considered ill-educated, could become well-to-do if he held the lease to a landowner's estate. The lease, an *arende,* entitled its holder to administer all the business of an estate and often was good for the lifetime of its holder, after which it was then up for bidding. A *poritz,* a Gentile landowner and usually an aristocrat, owned a large estate and was often abroad in France or Italy. See Yaffa Eliach's description in *There Once Was a World: A 900-Year Chronicle of the Shtetl of Eishyshok* (Boston: Little, Brown, 1998).

2. Brisk is the Yiddish name for present-day Brest-Litovsk, a city about 150 kilometers southwest of Grodno, which is both a city and a province in Belarus.

1

meet Bashke's britzka, he always stopped his carriage, and always had something to say to her: "Where are you off to, Bashke? Why are you so pretty, Bashke?" And once he said, "It would suit you to be a landowner's wife, Bashke."

Bashke's eyes gleamed, her stubborn chin teased him, and she replied, "It suits me to be Mendl Shapiro's daughter, too, sir."

The two coachmen, Vasil and Yankl, sat stiffly on their coachboxes, not uttering a single word to each other, Yankl's wide shoulders clearly taunting Vasil: Indeed, you're driving the landowner, but I'm driving Bashke.

In the province, people talked, wondering: Whom would a girl like Bashke marry?

She married a young timber merchant,[3] a learned man, and she loved him. In Brisk, where she moved with her husband, Bashke ran her house on a generous scale. She brought Yankl and the britzka along with her, and in town she was always driven, never seen on foot—except for Sabbath. On Sabbath, she could be seen walking to the synagogue, and going to visit her husband's family. When she walked with her husband, Reb Iser Paperno— it was grandeur and wealth. She was Bashke Shapiro, and he, from a golden background in Brisk himself, had the makings of a very rich man.

There were always guests at Bashke's table: merchants who had business with her husband, emissaries collecting money for a yeshiva, a visiting rabbi who had come to town, preachers and ordinary Jews, passers-by and paupers. Bashke treated each guest with great respect, and her house was famous in town. Jews said, "It is Jerusalem."

Once a merchant from Warsaw came to see Iser Paperno. Friday evening, after they had sung the Sabbath melodies, the merchant told them that in Warsaw, some Jews had established a society to buy land in Erets Isroel, and they were going there to build a city.

Bashke's eyes turned bluer, as if a light had been kindled in them. She asked the merchant, "What kind of Jews are they?"

---

3. Forests were more accessible to Jews than agricultural land, and a timber merchant was a man who brokered the business of standing timber and lumber. See Eliach, *There Once Was a World*, 275–76.

"Jews, like all Jews," he answered. "My brother-in-law is one of them. He's traveling there with his wife and children."

"How old is he?" Bashke asked.

"He's twenty-eight years old and has four children."

Bashke served tea with cherry syrup and cookies, and when the merchant was getting ready to leave, she said to him, "You've brought us good news—let it count as a mitzvah for you." Surprised, her husband Reb Iser Paperno stared at her, but with a care for respect, added, "May God grant us ever good tidings from Jews."

The business he conducted with the merchant from Warsaw was successful. In one year, Iser Paperno doubled his wealth, but he had no pleasure from it. Bashke had been transformed, mentioning more often than not the society in Warsaw that was buying land in Erets Isroel.

Late one Saturday evening, after the sun had set, Bashke lit their brightest lamp as if for a holiday and sat down to write a letter to the society that was buying land in Erets Isroel.

The next morning she went out in her britzka to Yakov Rabinovitch the Postmaster to ask that the letter be delivered to Warsaw as soon as possible.

Yakov the Postmaster[4] knew all the secrets of the town. When he was curious to know what was in a letter, he opened it, read it, pasted it up again, and sent it on its way. His curiosity never, God forbid, hurt anyone. He read Bashke's letter, too. It gave him so much pleasure to learn that Jews were buying land in Erets Isroel that he actually rubbed his hands together, and reveled, "Listen to this, a remarkable thing! They'll get there before the Messiah, and that's no joke!"

A couple of weeks later, people in Brisk began talking, saying the Papernos were buying land in Erets Isroel. "Rich people! What don't they have?" everyone said. Later, when the rumor was spread that the Papernos were going to Erets Isroel, not a single person dared to ask Iser or Bashke

4. Ordinary people like Yakov the Postmaster were often known by a combination of their first name and the name of their craft or job. A man of higher status was accorded the honorific "Reb."

about it, but they fell like flies on Yankl: "They're really buying land? They're really going?"

Either Yankl didn't know, or he played dumb, and answered: "It's not *my* problem. If the master wants to go, I'll be driving the horses."

A year passed. The town was cooking like a tsimmes: "Reb Iser doesn't want to go, but Bashke—she's steel and iron!" People were curious to know who would prevail—Reb Iser or Bashke?

Many families in Brisk earned their living from Reb Iser Paperno's timber business. Agents, accountants, appraisers, coachmen, guards—they were the town's stronger side, and they maintained that this was all a fantasy of Bashke's, and, God willing, it would fade—the way all rich women's fantasies fade away.

The other side, the neighbors and relatives, said that if it occurred to Bashke to build a city in Erets Isroel, she would build a city. Bashke was Bashke. And on one fine day, just before Passover, she left for Warsaw. She didn't take the diligence, the way merchants traveled—no, she'd race off by train, the way Reb Iser Paperno, her husband, traveled. And although Bashke came to the station in her own britzka with her own coachman, Yankl, all the other coachmen in town came to see if Bashke would actually set foot on the train. Even those who had no passengers, they, too, lashed their horses and hurried over to the train station.

When Bashke returned from Warsaw, it was no longer a secret. She had bought land in Erets Isroel. Reb Iser Paperno was to remain in Brisk, and Bashke was to ascend.[5] People began to say, describing her journey, "She is ascending."

After Passover, Reb Iser Paperno and Bashke went to the rabbi. They sat there from the close of evening prayers until late at night, arbitrating an agreement for the children. Reb Iser was prepared to make a gift of the purchased land for a yeshiva, and to promise to send his elder son there to study when he became bar mitzvah. Bashke argued: Jews were going there to build a city, and she with her children wanted to be among them.

---

5. *Aliyah* means "to ascend" or "to go up" to Jerusalem, or to settle in Erets Isroel.

Reb Iser's mother, the rich Eydl Paperno, wrapped in a shawl, rushed into the rabbi's room, lamenting loudly: "Rabbi, they're taking my children from me!"

"I'm not, God forbid, leading them into idolatry," Bashke answered her. She got up from her chair and said, "Sit down, mother-in-law."

Bashke remained standing. Her blue eyes glowed, and she said quietly, "Who can tell me that I'm, God forbid, leading my children on the wrong path?"

No one answered her.

Throughout the Papernos' house and in their large courtyard there was turmoil, as if on the eve of a wedding. Chests, reinforced with iron bands, stood waiting. Bales of straw lay in the courtyard, and Yankl carried sacks stuffed full of straw into the house. They packed up the meat, milk, and pareve utensils—those for everyday use, and those for Passover. Pots and pans, linen and bedding.

Reb Iser Paperno worked at his business as if nothing were happening in his house. When his people came in, he did the accounts with them, gave them letters, and entrusted them with messages.

The neighbor women, gesturing more with their eyes than with words, talked this over among themselves: "May God help her, and of course, may God help him, staying here all alone, poor thing! He's a saint to let her take the children."

The chests were already loaded on one wagon. The linens and food (dry bread and cookies, cheeses, and cured meats, and brandy) were on another. The children, the ten-year-old son and four-year-old girl, were sitting on this one.

Reb Iser stood next to the wagon where his children were sitting. His eyes were wide open, but he looked like a blind man who no longer sees the light of day. Next to him, almost shoulder to shoulder, stood Yankl, bewildered, his face, brick red, as if he had just come from a fight.

"We're going," Bashke pronounced quietly, as if she were pleading with someone.

Yankl didn't budge.

"Yankl!" Bashke called, "Yankl!" And when Yankl didn't respond, as if his wits no longer served him, Bashke looked around, pressed her lips together, and said, as if to herself, "The horses will obey me, too."

She got up on the wagon, sat down on the coachbox, and prompted the horses. She leaned down from the coachbox and said, "Iser, let us have great joy from our children, Iser!" and she drove out of the courtyard.

From their windows, the neighbors saw how Bashke drove the horses herself, leading her children. They pinched their cheeks and covered their faces with their hands: "May God protect her. Such valor!"

Some ran outside and cried after her: "May you be granted great success! May you arrive in good health!"

When the wagon had driven off a little way, Yankl recovered his wits. It was the first time in his life he had not obeyed Bashke. Like one possessed, he tore himself from his place and ran after the wagon, calling, "Mistress! . . . Bashke!"

· · · · · · ·

Bashke Paperno's house with seven windows stands in Rosh Pinah.[6] The courtyard is surrounded by tall eucalyptus trees. People call it Bashke's courtyard. Her grandchildren and great-grandchildren, all with blue eyes and upturned little chins, will not sell the house and will not rebuild it. If a wall begins to sag, they have it repaired so that the house looks just the way Bashke built it.

---

6. Rosh Pinah was the first town built by Jewish settlers from Russia and Romania in Erets Isroel in the late 1800s. They planned to combine the study of Torah with agricultural work, and to use Hebrew, not Yiddish, as their spoken language. According to *Israel and the Palestinian Territories* (London: Rough Guides, 1998), "some of the houses of the original settlement . . . have been renovated" (250).

On a Day of Rest

. . . .

It is an early Sabbath morning. God created this day for rest, and on this day, the shrill hoarseness of Sarah Meyukhes's [1] weekday voice disappears.

"Morrisl, will you button my collar for me, please?" She begins every Sabbath morning with these words. She puts on her silk blouse, indeed the one with the collar that is so hard to button, and the full grace of Sabbath begins to rest on her. Her shoes are shining, her stockings are pulled up, her hair is curled.

Pleased as if going on holiday, she puts the two small, brown bankbooks, hers and her husband's, into her purse, having checked them earlier to see the last totals of their savings; then both husband and wife leave their house.

Sabbath is the only day that Sarah Meyukhes calls her husband "Morrisl" and sweetens it with a "please." Sabbath, there's time for it.

Both of them walk very slowly down the street. Sarah Meyukhes is in good spirits. This is her favorite walk. She says a few words to the neighbors whom she meets, praises their children, and remarks that it's a beautiful day, or a windy one. If someone isn't feeling too well, she gives a little medical advice, and, walking in this manner, Sarah Meyukhes and her husband arrive at the big bank building, a building with tall windows and a brass door.

---

1. Sarah is the name of one of the four Jewish matriarchs: Sarah, Rebeccah, Rachel and Leah. Meyukhes, in Hebrew, means a person of aristocratic descent.

7

Inside, she gets in line. She feels herself to be among her own. Everyone is standing, brown bankbooks in hand, and Sarah Meyukhes joins the community. She is cheerful. She moves slowly in line to the small window, where the last act of a week's hard work, hers and her husband's, must take place.

The line is quiet, almost happy. The walls of the bank are as tall as those of a temple. The windows are shining. The guards are in uniforms.

Mr. Meyukhes stands on the side and smokes a cigar like a man who finds it convenient to stand there and agreeable to smoke. His coat is pressed, his hat on straight, and the smoke from his cigar, carefree.

Moving in the line, Sarah Meyukhes calculates how much there will be afterward, when she has counted out into the small window the green bills she has in her purse in an envelope. She is filled with calm and feels like doing something good. Simply, she is longing to do a good deed. She offers to let an older woman in the line go ahead of her: "You go before me," Mrs. Meyukhes says, and smiles.

This done, she feels it will now be a full Sabbath, a good Sabbath, a day of rest and meaning.

The procession to the little window is more cheerful than what takes place when that window is finally reached. The clerk counts her bills in a flash with no appreciation of how much effort each one represents. He pens a circle in her bankbook quickly, stamps it, and his eyes are already looking at the next person in line. The clerk in the bank is the only person who makes Sarah Meyukhes's Sabbath morning seem ordinary. He works in a hurry. He doesn't begin to appreciate the solemnity of the bank-temple Sabbath morning.

It seems more like an ordinary day walking back home. Sarah Meyukhes knows that her husband's brother, Jack, will be coming over to play cards, as he does every week, and that he will win three dollars. They meet him on the front stairs of their house. Sabbath never rests on him. Ever since a sewing machine needle pierced one of his fingers, he says, his blood has gotten rusty. He works carelessly, earns little, and has acquired a contempt for money. Jack greets his brother and sister-in-law with a smile. He knows where they have come from, and he says, "Made your deposits already?"

The skin on his cheeks, dark from the rusty blood, has become mockingly pitted. Sarah Meyukhes calms him with kindness. She will not upset the Sabbath that resides so delightfully in her silk blouse and curled hair. She serves her brother-in-law apples and cake, but after the brothers sit down to play cards, she grows restless. She knows that three dollars will be played away just like that and won't even count as a mitzvah.

Sarah Meyukhes calls her husband into the kitchen to help her serve tea and says to him, strengthening her words with a sharp movement of her elbow that makes her hand, for a moment, seem as sharp as a crack: "Morris, if you want to give Jack money, give it to him! Why do you have to lose it? My ambition can't stand it!"

Mr. Meyukhes looks at the glasses of tea, and answers, "Who wants to lose? If the cards aren't right, you lose."

Two smiling sparks are playing in his eyes. He carries out two glasses of tea, not looking at his wife.

Sarah Meyukhes remains standing in the middle of her kitchen. She is flushed with anger. Her silk blouse is too tight, and her skirt is so stiff in the back, that it pinches sharply into her full flesh. She feels a need to pour off her anger. She walks into the room, a third glass of tea in her hand, sits down next to her brother-in-law, and says, "Jack, how long can a man looking like you do keep working? Is it some kind of trick to drive yourself until you drop? You have to be careful. In our shop, may it never happen to anyone, an operator passed away at his machine. Just like that, sitting at his machine, and he was gone. You remember, Morris? How many years ago was that?"

Her voice has acquired its weekday hoarseness.

Her brother-in-law's cheeks turn even darker red. He answers her offhandedly, looking at his cards: "Every Sabbath she worries about my health! What should I do the rest of the week? Hah?"

He drains his glass of tea, finishes playing his hand of cards, gathers up his winnings in a hurry, not counting, and says to his brother, "Come, Mendel, let's take a little walk."

The brothers go out. Sarah Meyukhes cries after her brother-in-law, in her hoarse, workaday voice, "Jack, take care of yourself."

He shakes his head, not looking back. Mrs. Meyukhes closes the door.

Hot waves of anger surge through her. Her face tinder red, she takes off her silk blouse, struggling with the difficult buttons on her collar, and mutters, "Say good-bye to three dollars. And it doesn't even count as a mitzvah. Every Sabbath."

Across from her stands the table covered with empty glasses, apple peels, and cake crumbs, and with the long, difficult week that is drawing near.

October 11, 1946

The Queen

· · · · · · · ·

Fischel married Eydele because she was a "golden ring."[1] Eydele had black, laughing eyes and the face of a child, although at Hunting Point, the summer place where she worked, people said she was already more than twenty. She was short, had little round hands like small rolling pins, and she was quick to earn a couple of dollars, just as if she could pluck them out of the sky.

Eydele worked in the kitchen of a restaurant, and Fischel drove its produce truck.

Eydele trembled every morning when Fischel drove up to the kitchen door, and called out for her to help unload the vegetables, each time with the same words: "Eydele, honey. So, let's have a look at you!"

Her face bright red, Eydele ran over to his truck. Fischel was two heads taller than she was, and he looked down at her with roguish eyes, as though he could be a prince in disguise, just hiring himself out as a truck driver.

Eydele brought Fischel a glass of lemonade and served it to him with a radiant smile, as if his drinking it would bring her good fortune. Another time she brought him a chicken sandwich as a snack. Fischel took it as though he were doing her a favor, and Eydele was delighted that he smiled.

Every Friday, she gave him her bankbook and her earnings for the

---

1. A golden ring is a Yiddish metaphor for something of great value or that is worth a lot of money.

week, and asked him, "Fischel, I don't have any time, just drop off the deposit in the bank."

"Are you saving for a dowry?" he joked.

"Yes, for a dowry, what else?"

The bankbook meant more to Eydele than the money because each Friday Fischel held it in his pocket; she knew that the week would fly by and soon the bankbook would be in his hands again. "Gold attracts like a magnet," she thought. "It's a good thing that Fischel carries the bankbook around with him."

After working in the restaurant, Eydele didn't sit around with idle hands. She provided several housewives with meat and chicken, delivering it herself. She found a room for a guest at the summer place. She sent a girl to clean up for a housewife, and with each job, she made several dollars.

Eydele moved around the summer place like a nimble squirrel; she knew each person, and did something of service, or a favor, for everyone. "Just being able to do something for you," she told each of the housewives, "gives me the greatest pleasure." At this, her black, laughing eyes sparkled with real happiness and affection.

In the winter, Eydele worked in a rest home. She went around in a white smock and wore a little white hat on her head as though she had been born in these white clothes. She was like a sister to each guest. She glided from one room to the next, bringing something to one, asking a second if he needed anything, bringing a newspaper, bringing a hot-water bottle. Eydele belonged to everyone. And all the guests were her friends, almost brothers and sisters. Eydele's tips were sizable; people gave from the heart. Each one felt that she deserved more than a few dollars.

But Eydele really came to life in summer, when she worked in the restaurant in Hunting Point, and Fischel made her bank deposits each Friday.

One summer, in fact on a Friday, when Eydele had given Fischel a glass of lemonade, a chicken sandwich, and her deposit for the bank, she asked him, "Fischel, would you like to go into business with me?"

Her heart stopped beating while she waited for his answer.

"What kind of a business?" he asked, and he smiled like a rogue with his prince-disguised-as-chauffeur eyes.

"I've been looking at a small hotel to buy on installments here. . . . I'll buy it on installments. . . . I . . . I can. . ."

Fischel looked at her little round hands like small rolling pins, and thought: she'll buy it on installments. She could turn this whole summer place over with those little hands.

"A business is a business. Why not?" Fischel answered, turning the wheel of his truck, as if he didn't know whether to turn it right or left. Eydele's black, laughing eyes noticed his movements. She said, "You'll see, Fischel, five years from now we'll be laughing at this restaurant . . . a restaurant is not a business for us!" And she flew into the kitchen with such force it seemed as if she were running to tear the building open.

Fischel drove away and thought, she'll be a good partner, Eydele. She knows how to get things done . . . she knows how. She'll be a *partnerke*,[2] worth her weight in gold . . . and later on we'll see. . . .

Thinking about a hotel of his own, Fischel felt that he'd be rid of the truck's wheel, of the baskets of vegetables and the crates of bottles he had to carry around, and of the resturant's back door, where he had to stand for a long time each day. "In five years, we'll be laughing at this restaurant; a restaurant is not a business for us!" he recounted Eydele's words. The truck set off faster and easier than ever before.

Fischel barely recognized Eydele when he went with her to make the deposit on the hotel. She spoke about the terms like a businessman. A couple of times, she said to him, to Fischel, "What do you think, Philip?"

Fischel, a little startled that she had called him Philip, smiled and pushed his hand deeper into his pocket, as if this were where he should put his new name. Eydele saw his smile, and on the way back she said to him: "You know, for these people here, Philip is more of a name than Fischel . . . it's more . . . more of a name."

For several days, Eydele and Fischel thought about what they should call the hotel. She didn't want the old name, Olympia. "A new management needs a new name," she said.

---

2. *Partnerke* combines the English word "partner" and the Yiddish/Russian feminine ending "-ke."

"Maybe Hotel Rome," Fischel offered.

"What does Rome mean?"

"Rome is the capital city of Italy."

"What does Italy have to do with us?"

Eyedele soon began referring to Fischel and herself as "we," as if they had been partners for a hundred years.

"Maybe Hotel Mississippi," he suggested, still trying to find names for the hotel.

"What does Mississippi mean?" Eydele asked, marveling that Fischel knew so many things.

"Mississippi is the name of a river here in America."

"I never heard of such a thing. . ."

Eydele thought a little longer and said, "Listen, Fischel, for the time being, we won't be flying to Italy, or going on the Mississippi River; we'll simply call the hotel The Queen because we'll provide only the best, fit for kings. . ."

Fischel smiled and looked at little Eydele with her big undertaking, The Queen. . . .

The Queen, with its owner, Eydele, soon occupied a special place among the hotels in Hunting Point. The Queen was a home. It was comfortable in The Queen; no one felt strange there or alone. Hundreds of people knew Eydele: people from the rest home, from the restaurant, and all those people she had done favors for. There were always guests at Eydele's. Guests? No, they were her countless brothers and sisters.

Eydele hovered over the rooms. All of a sudden, she'd knock on a door, come in with a glass of milk, and say, "Mr. Piltz, please, drink it up. It's good for you."

Eydele worked from four o'clock in the morning on: cooking, baking, and cleaning. About ten or eleven, she'd put on a light silk dress and a blue brooch of shining stones. She wore two bracelets with charms on her little round hands, and she looked like the monarch of the small hotel, The Queen.

Although Eydele herself never rested, she said to Fischel, "Not working can pay off better than working. Take my advice! I already have a driver for our station wagon. It's not your work, Philip. It's enough for you to chat with the guests and listen to their stories. You don't know how much a person loves it when people listen to him. I learned this at the rest home."

Fischel chatted with the guests. He wore fine silk shirts that Eydele had given him for his birthday, and he smiled like a prince disguised as a hotel manager. Eydele's heart welled up when she looked at him. She would bring him a small dish of ice cream, as if he were the most distinguished guest at the hotel, and say, "It's a hot day, Philip. It's good for you."

Fischel thought about Eydele, thought that she was a golden ring, and he grew to love her with an exasperating affection that was more sad than happy.

From time to time, Fischel would commandeer the station wagon and drive like the devil into the city. It was understood that he was going to bring beverages back to the hotel. Eydele knew that he'd be seeing Yetta in the city. Let him see Yetta, Eydle thought, he can fool around with her, but he'll never leave The Queen.

Sometimes it happened that Fischel would stay overnight in the city. Then he'd call Eydele on the telephone with the excuse: "My sister doesn't feel too good—I have to stay with her in Brooklyn."

"Give her my regards," Eydele would answer, playing along with him, as if she believed his every word.

Patiently, she endured each trip that Fischel made to the city in the station wagon the way one endures a fever, a toothache, or some other affliction. Patiently she waited for his return, and joyfully she welcomed him back.

When Eydele worked at the restaurant, she had once seen Yetta. Yetta had been standing next to the glass door of the restaurant, talking with Fischel. Her hand had rested on his shoulder. Eydele remembered the sharp pieces of red coral Yetta had worn around her neck, and her long painted fingernails on Fischel's shoulder.

"Who was the pin-up girl talking to you? Your bride?" Eydele had asked Fischel then.

"Oh, that's Yetta," and he laughed like a rogue.

When summer was over, The Queen paid off the first of the terms. Eydele didn't close the hotel for winter. "The Queen is also a rest home," she said. She wrote letters to her scores of "brothers and sisters" and signed them "with loving devotion, Ida Karash, manager of The Queen hotel."

Summer and winter seasons were moneymakers. The Queen boiled over with checks and tips and the green magic of dollars. Eydele paid the terms, and they had a new wing with a sun parlor built onto The Queen.

Eydele saw to it that Fischel always had money in his pocket, and before one of his trips to the city, she gave him an order: "Don't forget to buy a coat for yourself, a camelhair. You hear, Philip? The best!"

Just as Fischel accepted his new name, Philip, as necessary for the hotel, The Queen, so he accepted the new camelhair coat: it belonged to The Queen, and Eydele belonged to The Queen.

Eydele, her heart heavy, suffered through each trip Fischel took to the city. She thought: you have to pay the terms with your money, and you have to pay the terms with your health; what else can you do? When Fischel returned, she always greeted him as if she would meet with good fortune, and announced some good news for the hotel: "Two new guests arrived today; they're paying me good rates." And Philip went to chit-chat with the new guests.

Eydele was overjoyed the time Fischel brought a Chinese vase back from the city for the new sun parlor. He carried the vase carefully with both hands, and called to her, "Eydele, honey, where should I put it?"

Eydele didn't look at the vase, just at Fischel.

"You see this vase?" Fischel crowed, "Confucius, I'm telling you, Confucius! And I bought it for nothing," Fischel laughed with roguish delight, like the time he had mentioned Yetta. Eydele's heart was filled with the sweet anguish of joy. The Queen has conquered him, she thought, and she asked him, "Who is Confucius?"

"Confucius is a Chinese philosopher, and this vase, I'm telling you, is Confucius."

Eydele patted the vase with such tenderness one would have thought that the cold, stony porcelain was her deepest love. "The Queen has conquered him," and she thought that in order to make Fischel happy now, she'd have to give in completely to his broad learning: "But he isn't a priest, this 'Tsanfukius,' hah, Philip? We have pious guests, you know . . . and if such a story . . . we don't need that. . ."

Philip laughed. He busied himself with the vase for an entire day. He polished it, poured in some dirt, and planted a seedling in it. He didn't let Eydele touch the vase.

"Don't touch . . . it's a delicate color. It's Confucius!"

Late one evening, in a gas station where Fischel had stopped on his way home from the city, he happened to meet an old friend, a truck driver.

"Fischel! Haven't seen you for a long time!" he greeted him with open arms. "They say you've become a rich guy, a valet at The Queen!" And they chatted for a while.

"Listen, Fischel, you have to be strict with money . . . listen to a good old brother. . ."

"What does strict mean?" Fischel asked him.

"It means . . . you have to be strict with money . . . you have to be a real boss and not a little valet. . . . Money! Ha! Money! Your own mother would throw you out for money! Ha! Money!"

Fischel hugged him like a brother and said, "It's all right, Bernard!" and left.

The words "a valet at The Queen" stayed with Fischel, and like a cloud, they flew ahead of his car as he drove off.

It was already night when Fischel got back to The Queen. All the windows were dark. Only a green glow from the night lights in the corridor filtered through the glass door at the entrance. The electric lights on the sign were blinking on and off. "The Queen," "The Queen," "The Queen."

For a while, Fischel stood looking at the sign. Then he walked quickly up the six wide steps to the entrance. He unlocked the door and thought: For the time being, I'll be the boss and not a valet. He walked over to the door of Eydele's small, narrow room at the end of the corridor. Eydele had felt his steps and, beaming, opened the door for him, as if the greatest good fortune were to meet her.

"Philip!" and she began to tell him some good news.

'Eydele, honey," he interrupted her, "Eydele, honey. . ."

Her heart missed a beat. What did he mean to tell her now, returning so late from the city?

"Eydele, honey. You know, people are talking about us. It's not good for the business. We should arrange things differently . . . better . . . the way all people live, and get married."

Eydele felt good fortune's greatest dilemma, the one that opens all the doors to the heart. She couldn't find a single word to say to him. She was silent for a while. Then she said, with trembling lips: "I prepared some orange juice for you, Philip. Drink. It's good for you. . . . I was waiting for you." And tears filled her eyes—big, full, warm tears.

The electric lights of the sign on the roof blinked on and off: "The Queen," "The Queen," "The Queen."

New York, 1955

The White Wedding Dress

· · · · · · · ·

On Tuesday, at the Greenberg's big house, a little before Shavuos, they stretched fresh curtains in the windows and set down flower pots with pink blossoms. They scrubbed the porch with sand and washed it with vinegar so it would shine like an egg yolk. The bridegroom and the in-laws of Arke the Miller's daughter, Hannah-Beyle, would stay there on the day of her wedding.

The bridegroom was a learned young man, a bookkeeper, who worked in a large whiskey distillery.

Arke the Miller sent six wagons to bring the bridegroom and the in-laws over from Ostrovkeh, two miles away.

Because the bridegroom was a worldly person, the bride's wedding dress was ordered all the way from Slonim,[1] from a Petersburg tailor. Why he was called a Petersburg tailor, nobody knew, but it increased his prestige and fame in the tailoring profession.

When they brought Hannah-Beyle's dress from Slonim, all the young girls in town went to look at it. The dress was decorated with seven pink and white ribbons. It was some wedding dress! Each time Hannah-Beyle showed the girls her wedding dress, her mother, Esther, said: "Hannah-Beyle, wash your hands, don't let the ribbons get stained."

---

1. Slonim is a city about two hundred kilometers southwest of Minsk, in present-day Belarus.

By this, she implied that the other girls shouldn't touch the ribbons with their hands.

"Such a dress brings one good luck!" they predicted, with a flash of envy in their eyes.

The bridegroom and his family were late in arriving. It was already four o'clock in the afternoon, and the six wagons hadn't yet returned.

The klezmers hadn't waited for the in-laws. They went to the bride's house, had a drink of whiskey, and began tuning the fiddles, strumming the bandura, and rolling the drum. The house was fragrant with sponge cake and wine.

Hannah-Beyle's friends arrived to help arrange her hair and put on the wedding dress. In a corner of the big dining room, a wide armchair was already placed, covered with an embroidered white cloth—the chair where the bride would be seated.[2]

The hands of the brown, four-cornered wall clock moved slowly. They were approaching five o'clock. The bridegroom and his family still hadn't come.

Arke the Miller, dressed in a black frockcoat and ready to lead his daughter to the chuppah, stood at the window and watched for the wagons with the in-laws.

Except for the klezmers' strumming, only one sound could be heard in the house—the tick-tock from the wall clock. Tick-tock, tick-tock. Now no one looked at the clock willingly, as if that might set Hannah-Beyle's luck rocking—back and forth, back and forth.

Berl the Klezmer, skinny and short, leaned his fiddle on the wall, and just as though he were near-sighted, walked right up to the front of the clock to take a look at it. Arke the Miller turned away from the window and pierced the klezmer with a sharp look. Berl the Klezmer picked up his fiddle and began strumming hastily. It was six o'clock.

Like a bolt of lightning, a rumor spread through the town: Hannah-Beyle was already wearing her Slonim wedding dress, but there was no

2. Traditionally, the bride is seated, before she is veiled, as part of the wedding ceremony. The custom largely disappeared in America, but it has been rediscovered, as it were, and occasionally is a part of even nontraditional Jewish weddings.

sign of the bridegroom. One hundred and thirty rubles were missing from the eight-hundred-ruble dowry, and the bridegroom didn't want to go to the chuppah. He and his family were avoiding the Greenbergs' house, where they were supposed to stay, had put up at Mirtshik's inn, and were waiting. . . .

People, good friends of Arke the Miller, began closing up their shops to go find out what was happening.

Children jumped on the porch, got up on the benches, and peered in through the windows to see how the bride looked. They spread the word: "It's true, she's sitting in her wedding dress and waiting."

Hannah-Beyle sat and remembered how her bridegroom had walked with her in back of the church orchard. He had embraced her and kissed her. He'd held her tightly in his arms and persuaded her with sweet words: "You think all I want is your dowry? No, it's just that I want to build my own distillery, for both of us. I want this more for you than for me." And he stroked her black eyebrows.

When Hannah-Beyle got home from that walk, she went up to the mirror and looked at the eyebrows her bridegroom had stroked so lovingly. Like two black, slender magic wands, they twitched happily over her smiling eyes.

Hannah-Beyle didn't care that the children were peering in through the window. She saved the memory of that walk behind the church orchard, that was in danger of disappearing from her now because of the hundred and thirty rubles.

The festiveness of the chair she was sitting on and the whiteness of her wedding dress now seemed ordinary. The klezmers had gotten hold a bottle of whiskey and were sipping from it, one after the other, as if they were in a tavern, not at a wedding. Hannah-Beyle closed her eyes so as not to see any of it.

Arke the Miller and his wife stood in a corner of their bedroom and looked at each other, ashamed.

"Where can a person get a hundred and thirty rubles just like that? Ten, you can get, twenty-five—maybe, but such a fortune?!"

Arke had turned pale yellow. The wrinkles on his forehead were heavy and deep, and his face looked like an old, wilted cabbage leaf. The skin on

Esther's neck quivered, and her veins were ready to burst. Their mouths were both open, as if they wanted to ask each other: Say something. Give me some advice.

Suddenly, Esther began pulling off her jewelry: the gold watch, the earrings, pearls, and rings.

"I know what to do, I know what to do!" she said, as though she were ready to jump into the fire to save her child. "I'll go to Velvel the Pawnbroker, and I'll fall at his feet. . ."

She had just pronounced these words when the door to their room opened, and in walked Tsirl the Rich Woman.[3]

"Mazel tov!" she said. "I have sent my Dovid-Meylekh to bring this loafer to the chuppah! For me, Arke the Miller is still good for a hundred and thirty rubles. An end to all this!"

Because of this unexpected good luck, Arke the Miller and his wife were speechless for a while. Esther's lips trembled; she couldn't get a word out. Arke grabbed Tsirl the Rich Woman by the hand and gasped: "God . . . God grant you. . ." Tears came into his eyes and his voice was muffled. Then, his voice hoarse, he managed a few words: "You have pulled me from the lion's den. . ."

Tsirl the Rich Woman, as they called her in town, lived with her husband, Dovid-Meylekh,[4] and their maid, Malkele, in a big, six-room house that was surrounded by a cherry orchard. She was friendly with no one in the town and never went anywhere. For days on end, Tsirl the Rich Woman sat by her window and looked at the street; but all the neighbors, even those from afar, passed by her window on their way to draw water from her

3. In the original Yiddish, *Tsirl di negideste. Nogid* means "a rich man" in Hebrew, and *negideste* is a Yiddish variation meaning "a rich woman." The connotation is that the person is not only rich but often wise and good.

4. The names Dovid-Meylekh and Malkele probably represent a subtle joke. In Hebrew, *melekh* means "king" and *malka*, "queen." Dovid-Meylekh wears a "hat with a visor" (a mock crown) and is the only person in town to ride a bicycle: like a king, he rides and doesn't walk. In addition, when he rides his bicycle, he is referred to by the townspeople as *Pani*, the Polish term of respect, according him even more ironic honor than the Jewish term *Reb*. The name Malkele, means, literally, "dear, sweet little queen," or Queenie.

well. Malkele did the everyday work in the house, but Tsirl herself took care of the well. From time to time, she'd take a broom and sweep up around her well. This was her work.

Her husband, Dovid-Meylekh, wore a hat with a visor, and because he rode a bicycle, people didn't call him Reb Dovid-Meylekh, but Pani Dovid-Meylekh. He mixed with everyone in town: men, women, even children— it didn't make any difference. Riding his bicycle, he'd stop frequently and snatch a quick conversation with them, with this one and that one, about everything that was going on in the town.

Tsirl the Rich Woman and Dovid-Meylekh were wealthy. They were partners in different businesses in other towns, and they had an iron chest standing in their house, to foil thieves or a fire. Dovid-Meylekh gave small donations, but for really large ones, people had to come to Tsirl the Rich Woman through her husband, Dovid-Meylekh.

"Pani Dovid-Meylekh, have a talk with Tsirl so that she might give some money to the Loan-without-Interest Fund;[5] the Fund is destitute."

Dovid-Meylekh wasn't offended that Tsirl, not he, was the real boss. Just the opposite; he joked about it, and he, too, called his wife Tsirl the Rich Woman.

"For the Loan-without-Interest Fund, indeed, you must go to Tsirl the Rich Woman."

On Tuesday, the day of Hannah-Beyle's wedding, in the evening when the whole town was running in circles, several neighbors, carrying their buckets, stopped by Tsirl the Rich Woman's window and said, "Have you heard what's happening to Arke the Miller and the wedding?"

One woman added, "The bride wanted to take off her wedding dress, but her friends wouldn't let her."

One of Tsirl's eyebrows quivered, as though dust had fallen in her eye. She called her husband and said to him, "Dovid-Meylekh, go to Mirtshik,

---

5. The *Gmiles-khsodim* (Loan-without-Interest Society or simply Loan Fund) was a community-based loan society. It was one of the many benevolent institutions in Eastern European Jewish life, often brought along to America, where it was then run by the various *landsleit* organizations.

to his inn, and whip them with the hundred and thirty rubles." She gave him the money, and she herself went to deliver mazel tov to Arke the Miller and Esther.

When Hannah-Beyle walked to the chuppah her knees were trembling. She didn't hear the playing of the klezmers, but under the chuppah the bridegroom looked at her exactly as he had in back of the church orchard. His look said to her: "I didn't do this for myself, but for both of us, more for you than for me." And she believed him. Her wedding dress with its pink and white ribbons radiated festivity and joy again.

A Fur Coat

. . . .

For two straight hours, Tsilie Belkin stood in front of her mirror, choosing a dress to wear to the annual Poritshe *landsleit's* ball. Although Poritshe[1] was a town about half the size of an eggshell, the Poritsher women were fancy dressers in New York, and the most beautiful models could have come to the Poritshe ball to learn the latest styles. The hall where the ball was held was adorned with small blue, green, and pink lights; the light was shadowy, colorful, and mysterious.

Jack Mandel, who in Poritshe was called Yankel Mandelbaum, the cantor's grandson, was standing at the entryway of the hall, welcoming the *landsleit*.

He still remembered a few verses[2] he had learned as a child in the Poritshe cheder, using and interpreting them at *landsleit* meetings. The Poritshers thought him something of a scholar and took pride in him, although some people muttered that Jack was tight with a dollar, and that he had divorced his wife because a wife was expensive.

When Tsilie entered the hall wearing a blue velvet dress with a rose in

---

1. Poritshe is probably present-day Porecje, a town thirty kilometers northwest of Grodno in Belarus.

2. The author used the Hebrew word *psukim*, the plural of *posek*, which means "a verse from a sacred text." In other words, Jack still knows a few verses or sayings learned as a child in *cheder*.

her brown hair, Jack liked her immediately. He took her by both hands and led her over to a small table. "You'll sit next to me," he said to her, indicating a place.

Tsilie enjoyed herself at the ball. Jack brought her a drink and danced with her. In the middle of dancing he asked, "How much did you pay for your dress?"

Tsilie was astonished at his question, but then took it as a joke and answered: "Who pays for a dress? You get them for free."

The Poritsher *landsleit* saw Tsilie dancing with Jack and bandied words with each other, saying, "A good couple. Maybe they'll give us a reason to be happy."

Tsilie lived in a big apartment building in Manhattan, a building that hummed like a hive. Women with baby buggies stood on the sidewalk, catching a ray of sun and fresh air, gleaning pearls from all kinds of gossip and stories about the neighbors' goings-on. The stairs swarmed with children licking lollipops, laughing, and making a racket. Even the watchman, Mr. Kartshik, was busy on every floor—sweeping stairs, carrying window frames, mending doors, and scraping boards. He seemed to be a hardworking soul who kept the stone building alive from its roof to the depths of the cellar.

There was only one quiet corner in the building—the room where Tsilie Belkin lived. With the flower-patterned curtains and two freshly watered flowerpots in her window, one might have thought it a garden.

Winter and summer slippers always stood in the same place in Tsilie's closet; her summer and winter housecoats, each on its own hanger, hung on an iron clothes rod; wire hangers held her blouses, dresses and suits all clean and starched, in order, like soldiers on parade.

When Tsilie came back from her shop, where she was a well-paid necktie designer, already ten years in the same factory,[3] she sat down on her soft chair, that stood in the middle of the room, and read the newspaper. Whenever she came across some surprising news, she called Mrs. Shapiro, with whom she had lived for seven years now.

---

3. The original text, *shoyn tser in der zelber fabrique,* probably represents a problem in typesetting. Sheva Zucker suggests this should read *tsen yor,* meaning "ten years."

"Mrs. Shapiro! You hear? They've invented a car that can fly like an airplane and swim like a motorboat! Have you heard about this?"

Mrs. Shapiro answered her pessimistically. "They can think up everything, but not how to keep a person from being tormented."

The clock on Tsilie's table was accurate to the dot. It didn't run too fast and never lost time—it was as good as the best town clock. Its tick-tock was as steady as any clock's in the world. It measured the time and rang on the hour. No more, no less.

The neighbors in the building chatted about Tsilie and wondered to themselves: Such a young woman, a good wage earner; she dresses like a countess and has all the virtues—why isn't she married? Any nothing or no-good can catch a man, but she's surely in her thirties already. How long can she wait?

A week after the ball, Jack Mandel dropped by Tsilie's room, just as she was telling Mrs. Shapiro some surprising news from the newspaper. "Look, he was passing by and drops in."

Tsilie's face reddened at Mandel's unexpected visit, and Mrs. Shapiro served coffee and cookies.

The tranquility of a home embraced Jack. The flowerpots at the windows, the soft chair, the spotless linen on the corner tables, Tsilie's deep wine-colored satin housecoat—everything was warm, feminine, familiar.

Jack was sitting on the soft chair in the middle of the room when suddenly he asked, "How much did you pay for this chair?"

As if she had been waiting for just such an opportunity, Mrs. Shapiro eagerly told how she had ordered the chair from a Turkish man in Brooklyn, who was like all the other Turks, but he could make chairs like no else in the world could do.

When Jack left, Mrs. Shapiro, with all the warm-hearted sincerity of a Jewish woman, said to Tsilie, "It's good that he asked about the chair. If he didn't like you, he wouldn't have thought to ask such a question."

Tsilie was grateful to her, and smiled. But as she lay in bed trying to sleep, the street light shining through the darkness of her room onto the Turkish chair, she thought that during the seven years she had lived in this room, Marvin and Bernie had also sat in that chair, and she had parted with them before anything had come of it.

The neighbors in the building saw Jack come to Tsilie's several times, and they chatted about it. "That's that." They wished with all their hearts that Tsilie would get on with it and do as all women did: be a Mrs. Mandel. Just as if this were necessary to the harmony of everyone in the building. Even the watchman, once passing Tsilie on the staircase, said to her, "He's a fine young man, the one who comes over to see you, a very likeable gentleman."

Perhaps more than Tsilie herself, they all longed for her to get married.

In the summer, when Tsilie had her vacation, she sat with Jack making an inventory of what he owned, what she owned, and what kind of an apartment they should get.

"Tsilkele," he said, "you're my treasure," and he held her tightly.

She was overjoyed that he softened her name so tenderly—Tsilkele.

The wedding was happy. All the Poritsher *landsleit* danced.

Three weeks later, Tsilie invited several friends over to the new apartment for dinner. She and Jack stood by the door and greeted the guests, taking their coats and hats.

The table was decorated with precision and beauty, as only Tsilie knew how to do—with flowers, the salads on small plates garnished with greens. The table looked like a picture.

The guests praised Tsilie for her housekeeping, congratulated her, and wished her all the generous praise she deserved. Tsilie and Jack were happy.

After the guests had gone, Tsilie was joyfully tipsy from the new feeling of having her own home and running her household in her own way. Here, at last, in God's great world, she had made her notch in the fast-moving cycle of life. She patted Jack's smooth-shaven cheeks and smiled at him. She went in to clear the table and wash the dishes. Lovingly, she held each spoon and knife in her hand, as though they were partners in her happiness.

Jack walked back into the room, his shoes squeaking. Tsilie was pleased. She'd just had guests over for dinner, she was washing the dishes, her husband was walking around; life was taking shape around her, a family life. Suddenly Jack called to her: "Tsilke, how much did you pay for the goose?"

"For which goose?" She didn't quite catch what he was asking her.

Jack pointed his hand at the table, indicating the leftovers from the meal. Tsilie shrugged her shoulders: "Tut, tut . . . a husband doesn't bother himself with goose matters."

"I have to know how much it cost," he muttered.

Tsilie didn't answer him. She was almost happy to have an argument with Jack, just as there should be in a family.

During the day, Jack was busy in his lunchroom, and in the evenings at home, he counted the money he had taken in. He counted it once, then again, and then a third time. Counting money was heaven and earth for him.

When friends called to say they should get together, he waved them off with both hands: "Tsilke, tell them we're busy."

When their "till" was growing and Jack was in a good mood, he'd say to Tsilie, "Tsilke, count the money in the envelope again. I think I may have made a mistake."

On Fridays when Tsilie brought home her week's earnings from the shop, Jack counted the money with a special pleasure. He counted his money first, and then counted hers, and gave her an extra kiss. Tsilie was shocked by this "payday kiss"; she delicately called it "the Sabbath-eve kiss."

The young couple established a daily routine. During the day they both worked, and in the evening Jack did the accounts and added up all the money: "twenty-one, twenty-two, twenty-three" . . . and Tsilie read the newspaper. A few times, she wanted to tell Jack some surprising news, but he put a halt to that: "What's it to do with me? Let them think up what they will, they're not telling me what to do." And he went back to recounting monotonously, "twenty-four, twenty-five, twenty-six. . ."

The clock that Tsilie had brought with her from her old apartment counted with him, "tick-tock, tick-tock." Both Jack and the clock were very serious, and it was impossible to interrupt them.

The time for the annual Poritshe *landsleit*'s ball grew closer. The Poritshe women phoned each other to talk over their wardrobes for the ball. Tsilie ordered a fur coat and said to Jack, "You'll see how beautiful it will be! I'll surprise our *landsleit*."

Jack was silent. Little swellings formed on both sides of his mouth, and his lips seemed to have grown wider.

Tsilie didn't mention the coat to him again; he walked around, his face beclouded, for several days. Because of the coat, the mood hanging over the young couple in the apartment was as tense as it is on the brink of a real fight. Then one evening, before dinner, Jack said, "I called your furrier and told him not to make your coat. It's too much money all at once . . . too much all at once. . ."

Tsilie was so surprised she couldn't find anything to say.

Jack's eyes were serious, without a drop of tenderness, and his mouth was swollen and strained.

They ate dinner quietly and chewed slowly, the way people try to avoid swallowing a bone. And although they said nothing to each other, the quarrel deepened, grew harder and full of resentment.

After dinner, Tsilie went to the telephone and called her furrier. "It was a misunderstanding," she told him. "Everything stays just as I arranged with you."

Jack ran over to her. "I'm warning you . . . I'm warning you," he said to her, and would have taken the receiver out of her hand.

Calmly, she turned her back to him, took a step away, and concluded her conversation: "Yes, everything that we arranged . . . bye-bye." She hung up calmly, as though nothing had happened.

"What were you warning me about?" she asked Jack, looking him right in the eye.

He searched for the words to insult her. He stepped back and said: "Well, that's what happens when you marry an old maid . . . all of a sudden, a coat!"

An enormous sorrow poured over Tsilie and wiped away her anger. She replied quietly, without any sharpness, "Well, I can't help that. . . . I can't get any younger." There was a hard lump in her throat, but she didn't want to cry in front of Jack, so strange had he become to her. She got dressed and left the house.

. . . .

Tsilie separated from Jack without any malice. She felt like a person who had fallen into a pit, climbed out, and was taking pains not to travel the same path.

From her new apartment, she took only her clock, and placed it on its table in her room with Mrs. Shapiro, with whom she was living again.

New York, 1954

The Daughter-in-law

· · · · · · · ·

Taibl, Yosl the Kettlemaker's daughter, in the space of one year, grew up into a tall, beautiful young girl. Somewhat light complexioned, she had become a young woman. The straight part in her dark-blond hair and the quiet smile around her small mouth made her seem like an exalted guest on the low porch of her father, Yosl the Kettlemaker's house.

The clanging of a hammer and the peal from the pans that rang out from the sooty-walled kettlemaker's shop, deafened that part of the street, as if their noise wanted to compete with the town's church bells, let us distinguish between them.[1] But this in no way hindered Yisrolik Pomerantz, Reb Shayeh the Brickmaker's son, from often coming to see Taibl, and to sit with her for hours at a time. People had already seen them walking together on the main road, and they began to say that Taibl would be really lucky were she to become Reb Shayeh the Brickmaker's daughter-in-law.

People soon began calculating what kind of an inheritance she would have from the brickmaker (may he live one hundred and twenty years)[2] who was a golden ring and who was worth a good couple of thousand rubles: he had a two-story brick house, the only such one in town, two

1. *Lehavdl* means "to distinguish," the entire phrase being, "Let us distinguish between the sacred and the profane." *Lehavdl* is said when differences, usually between Jewish and Christian subjects, occur in the same sentence.

2. "May you live one hundred and twenty years" is a traditional wish made to a person on a special occasion such as a birthday.

shops rented out in the market, and of course, how much was Reb Shayeh's *yikhes* worth?

That her Yisrolik went around with the kettlemaker's daughter made Reb Shayeh's wife, Etel the Brickmaker's,[3] heartsick, and her face grew haggard. When she walked past Yosl the Kettlemaker's house she turned her head away, but the clang of his hammer followed her and fell heavily on her heart.

At home, she said her real concern was for Reb Itzkhokl Vinitser, the father-in-law of their oldest daughter, Tsipkele.

"For me, it doesn't matter that Yisrolik creeps into Yosl the Kettlemaker's 'shamily,' but it's a slap in the face for our in-law, Reb Itzkhokl Vinitser. We'll be dragging him into a bad *yikhes*, and if God helps and there'd be a celebration, Reb Itzkhokl would be sitting on one side of the table and on the other side, exactly opposite him, Yosl the Kettlemaker! Silk and burlap!"

And here, Etel the Brickmaker's seizes her face in both hands and adds, as one says when, God forbid, a person is dying: "Now, Khaye-Gitl Vinitser, a somebody with seven strings of pearls around her neck, will have to wish a gut yom-tov or a mazel tov to Peshke the Kettlemaker's! She's a no-account woman, and as small as a peppercorn! And those manners of hers! Oy, it's a heartache and humiliation! A misfortune!"

When she gets to the "seven strings of pearls" and the "heartache" and the "misfortune," her son, Yisrolik, slams the door and leaves the house.

Reb Shayeh would listen and say nothing; he'd pray a little longer than usual, say the blessings after eating with more energy, and translate a few of the words into Yiddish—as a reproof for his wife, and nothing more.

But once, when he got tired of hearing the same story, time after time, about Reb Itzkhokl Vinitser's *yikhes* and about Yosl the Kettlemaker's "shamily," he got up, and said to his wife, not mentioning any names: "What's all this? He's not an apostate, is he? He recites the prayers, doesn't he? He's an observant Jew, isn't he? What's all this? You think that Torah was given only

---

3. "Etel the Brickmaker's" is the name everyone knows her by. A woman was frequently referred to as belonging to her husband by way of his profession.

to the privileged? No, it was given to all Jews!" and he let out a cry: "Leave me alone!"

His wife stood quivering, exactly like a wet hen shaking water from her feathers.

After this, Etel the Brickmaker's, stopped talking about the "misfortune," but whenever she felt her anger returning, she'd walk around all day with a wet cloth tied to her head.

When people told Yosl the Kettlemaker that the brickmaker's wife walked around wearing a wet towel for her headache because she didn't want Taibl for a daughter-in-law, he banged his hammer and said, "Why should I worry? I don't run after them! If my Taibl is meant for riches, they won't avoid her."

Because they envied Taibl, people in the town called her "Reb Shayeh's daughter-in-law" even before the wedding.

Taibl acted as though she knew nothing about all this talk. She carried buckets of water to her father in the kettleworks and helped her mother bake bread to sell, always with a quiet smile around her small mouth.

Taibl never went into Reb Shayeh's house, as if their *yikhes* had made it a fortress, impossible to break into. Sometimes she stood for a while near their porch when she was waiting for Yisrolik.

Once at dusk, when Reb Shayeh was leaving to say the afternoon prayers, Taibl was standing next to the staircase of their house. She saw Reb Shayeh, quickly took a step backward as if to make way for him on the street, and blushed. The straight part in her blond hair and her small flower print dress made her seem almost childlike. She looked at Reb Shayeh as if he were a judge, and she was waiting to hear his first question.

Reb Shayeh sensed her unease. He stopped, was silent for a while, and then said: "Well . . . why are you standing there? You can sit down on the bench . . . two empty benches on the porch . . . Well. . ."

Taibl dared not disobey him. She moved from her spot, as though it were hard to pry herself away from the ground. She stepped up the four high stairs and sat down on a bench.

"There, you see, why do you have to wait standing up?" he said, and went on his way.

His gentle, simple words took Taibl so by surprise that she forgot she was waiting for Yisrolik. She watched as Reb Shayeh walked quietly away, and she felt the warm, blue heaven above the world.

Taibl's mother, Peshke, was short and stumpy, had deep-set little eyes and had turned down two marriage proposals before she'd married Yosl the Kettlemaker. Because of her long experience, she was very wise, like an old Talmudic scholar, and she said to her daughter, while they were busy together taking the big loaves of bread out of the oven: "I don't like your running after rich folks' fortune. God gives each person his own destiny. You'll always be like an uninvited guest among rich people."

And on a very beautiful summer evening, when Yisrolik was accompanying Taibl home, Peshke stood at the door of the kettleworks. She looked like a shadow that had come down from the black, sooty walls. She spoke to her daughter, as if Yisrolik weren't there: "How much longer are you going to go around with the rich man's son? Hmm, Taibl? A winter, a summer, what's the limit? I have enough, thank God, to make a wedding for my daughter, but I don't have what it takes to cover a disgrace. You hear me, Taibl?"

Taibl wanted to quiet her mother and ask her to go back into the house, but Peshke stood there like she had grown onto the doorstep and added, "A young girl who loses her luster is just like a shoe that has lost its sole. Try walking on that! No one can buy a new life, you hear me, Taibl?"

Yisrolik stood there, frightened by her words—heavy, dark, and callous—that spread like a threatening cloud and fell over the young, blue, pleasant evening.

He didn't sleep at home, but rambled about in the brickworks, and, like the watchman in a prayer house, spent the night on the floor.

Yisrolik barely spoke to his mother. He would drop by his home as if it were an inn, change his clothes, sleep, and then, just as quickly, be out the door. In the middle of winter, he left for America.

He asked Taibl if she'd swear to follow. The little smile around Taibl's small mouth disappeared, and she said to him, "If we have to run away from town to get married—well, it won't do, Yisrolik. Travel safely."

She didn't want to kiss him at their leavetaking, not wanting to taste the bitterness of a last kiss.

Six months later, Taibl married Nakhum, the butcher's son. Nakhum knew that to show great love for a bride, a man should fall on his knees. He fell on one knee for Taibl, because a Jew cannot kneel on both knees, and said to her, "I'll build a brick house for you, bigger than Reb Shayeh the Brickmaker's. You can depend on me."

And Nakhum kept his word. He began supplying meat for the army, and thus became, Nakhum the Contractor; and when he grew rich: The Contractor, Nakhum Spiegl.

Each summer, Taibl went to a dacha, and later on "to the foreign spas." In town, they said "she was born with a caul."[4] Taibl wanted to rebuild her father's house, raise the front stairs, and put on a new roof, but Yosl the Kettlemaker wouldn't allow it. He banged his hammer and said, "My roof has never leaked, why should I tear it down? A man shouldn't shame his own roof," and he continued to live in his small house.

Then, just as if Reb Shayeh's good fortune had departed with his son, his brickworks lost their golden touch. The new clay pits weren't good, and the bricks cracked in the kiln.

For the first couple of years, Reb Shayeh covered up the trouble. He borrowed money and continued making bricks. He sold his two shops in the market; his beard became striped with gray. In the dining room, they no longer lit the brightest lamp, but used cheaper lights. Reb Shayeh's windows were dark. His in-law, Reb Itzkhokl Vinitser, seldom came to visit. In town, people murmured that Reb Shayeh would soon go bankrupt. Creditors, like annoying flies, beset his home, coming in the morning and at night, to demand, and demand, and demand . . .

Reb Shayeh no longer slept at night, but would get up and pace for hours in the darkened dining room. People show off their good luck, and hide their misfortune. Reb Shayeh didn't light the lamp at night; no one should be able to say that he couldn't sleep.

More than any of his other creditors, two people clamored at him—Dinke the Widow, and Hershl the Peddler. Dinke cried out he'd be killing

4. A caul is a membrane that some babies are born with. It was considered to be lucky and was often dried and sold—to sailors, for example, who thought of it as a good-luck charm that would save them from drowning. Charles Dickens's character David Copperfield was born with a caul.

her "without a knife" unless he gave back the seventy rubles he was holding for her. Dinke the Widow, her hand so skinny you could count the bones, banged on his table, and grew hoarse from crying: "You won't slaughter a poor widow, Reb Shayeh." Hershl the Peddler kept repeating the same few words: "Give me my money. I'll break the walls apart. Give me my money!"

Reb Shayeh staved off his creditors week after week, week after week. The anguish they brought into his house caused a darkness to fall on Reb Shayeh's eyes, and it seemed to him that even the walls of his house had dimmed. In the corners, stains flourished on the faded wall paper. It had been two years already since his home had been caulked or limed. Reb Shayeh looked for someone to buy his brick house. "Better to live without a roof, than be a bankrupt," he said to his wife, and felt the poverty coming on like a flood, wanting to throw him out of his position.

The continual worries bent Reb Shayeh's head down, and he stopped looking at the passers-by to say "good morning" or "good evening."

Early one evening, as he was leaving his house to go to the late afternoon prayers, he heard a "good evening, Reb Shayeh." Yosl the Kettelmaker was standing across from him.

"I was, in fact, coming to see you, Reb Shayeh, to talk something over."

Reb Shayeh's heart began pounding: I don't think I owe him anything. I didn't borrow any money from him. What can he want from me?

They walked over to the front stairs of Reb Shayeh's house.

"Things are good, *keyn eyn hore,*[5] for my daughter, Taibl." To show how good things were for his daughter, Yosl the Kettlemaker spread his hands out wide. "She heard that you were looking for someone to buy your brick house. She stopped here last night on her way to the spas. Things are good for her, *keyn eyn hore.* She wanted me to give you money for the house. That is to say, if you want to sell it, this is from her. That is to say, you understand, she isn't in a hurry, and she said . . . But meanwhile, until she comes back from the spas, she's giving you this for the building. That is to say . . . and she sent you a note."

Yosl the Kettlemaker gave him Taibl's letter and left. With difficulty,

---

5. Literally, "No evil eye!" An exclamation used to ward off the evil eye, especially after good news has been spoken of or praise given.

Reb Shayeh remained seated on the bench. He opened the envelope, and there was a draft for the money, and several words from Taibl: "Reb Shayeh, I am younger than you, but my wheel, too, has already turned, down and up, and I know the taste of sorrow. You were like one of my own when I didn't have the courage to walk up your front stairs. Now, because God has helped me, I want to help you, so that you don't have to fall from the stairs of your home, God forbid. I do this with my whole heart, believe me."

The letter was signed Taibl Spiegl.

Her letter was so completely unexpected, that Reb Shayeh was able to forget his creditors for a while, and was filled with the gentle, simple words of Taibl's note. He went to say the afternoon prayers, and felt the warm, blue heaven over the world.

After Reb Shayeh paid the seventy rubles back to Dinke the Widow, and his debt to Hershl the Peddler, both with interest, the other creditors forgot what street Reb Shayeh lived on, and no longer came to his house demanding their due. He sent for them, but they were in no hurry. Never mind, he is still a trustworthy person, is Reb Shayeh.

And as the wheels of his business rolled heavily on, between worries and bills, a sweet regret would often come to Reb Shayeh—Taibl, his good "daughter-in-law," Taibl.

New York, 1954

Hinde the Gardener

. . . .

Pelte, Reb Chaim the Scribe's wife, didn't lose heart even when they no longer had money enough to buy a cartload of wood for winter. When her husband finished writing a Torah scroll for the main synagogue,[1] all the doors to making a living closed up. The three village boys, who were taught by Reb Chaim and who boarded and roomed with his wife Pelte, crept back to their homes at Hannukah time: it was cold, one of them was sick, and another just didn't want to study. The last few coins were almost gone. No door opened for them, and it seemed it was the end of the world.

Reb Chaim the Scribe wrung out whole days at the house of study.[2] Pelte tried with all her strength to drive away their poverty; let it not be visible in her house. She whitewashed the oven, scoured the benches, washed and rolled the window curtains. Her house was shining with cleanliness, but it brought no happiness. Just the opposite. The emptier the house became, the more space there was for the gloom to spread itself around. In the evenings, Pelte turned the lamp on a little later, to burn less kerosene, and she saved the potatoes that had been meant for the village students. Close to Purim, she went to Shakhne the Matzo Baker, hoping he would hire her to roll matzos so that she could earn a few coins for the holidays. Pelte, Reb

---

1. In Yiddish, *kalter shul* means "the cold synagogue." This was the main and larger synagogue. It was not used every day, and therefore was unheated for most of the time.

2. The author used *beit midrash*, a term meaning "a house or place of study." This was often a smaller room, attached to the main synagogue, where men could study every day.

Chaim the Scribe's wife, was treated almost like a rebbetzin in the town. When she arrived at Shakhne's and he greeted her with a broad good morning and moved as if to stand up for her, she lost her courage to ask him if he would hire her as a roller.

"When do you begin the Passover baking?"[3] she asked him, and faltering, added, "I want to bake matzo a little earlier, it will cost me a little less. . . . It's not such a good time. . ."

Shakhne promised that he would take her matzos from the first batch, and they would come to an understanding about the money. Troubled, she left, regretting on the way home that she'd been ashamed to tell the truth. When she got home, she began wiping the lamp glass until it sparkled like crystal. When Reb Chaim returned from the evening prayers, Pelte lit the lamp. They didn't talk to each other. What could they say? Each thought to himself that things weren't good.

When they were halfway through supper, Hinde the Gardener arrived. Neither Reb Chaim nor Pelte recognized her at first. It was Hinde, yet it wasn't Hinde. She wasn't wearing the muddy boots she always had on, but polished shoes; she wasn't wearing her old shawl, but the black jacket she wore only for Sabbath when she went to the synagogue, and on her head, her fine black wool shawl. She was dressed for a holiday. From her generous good evening and her shining face, Reb Chaim and Pelte saw that she had not come without a reason. But what could Hinde the Gardener need?

Because of her stinginess, Hinde shouldered the greatest share of the women's spiteful gossip. Thursdays, when they came to Velvel the Butcher for meat, they would wait on purpose until Hinde left with the pound of lung, liver, and tripe that she bought for Sabbath, and then they would begin their backbiting: "There's a woman for you! There's stinginess for you! She's a fountain of money! She has her own garden, and the two she rents out! Every carrot and each little poppy seed she sells is the same as gold for her! She doesn't need any shoes; she tramps around in boots! No meat for Sabbath either! A yeshiva student has never eaten even once at her

3. Baking for Passover was done in a *podriad,* a special oven for baking matzo. Matzo baking is a complex procedure that involves many people—from grain growers to guardians of the grain, rollers and hole punchers, bakers, and rabbis.

house![4] You should be protected from such stinginess. It's worse than an illness, may it never happen to you! She has a fortune, but what comes of it?"

And when the women were satisfied with their gossip, they went their separate ways, each one feeling that she was a better person than Hinde.

Reb Chaim and Pelte asked Hinde to sit down. Reb Chaim drew up the wick of the lamp to make more light. Pelte noticed that Hinde was wearing the string of pearls around her neck that she wore only for holidays. Pelte's heart lightened. It was not for nothing that Hinde was dressed up; she was bringing some good tidings. Pelte went out to pour a glass of tea from the hot kettle for Hinde.

Hinde took a knotted handkerchief out of her purse, laid it on the table, and covered it with her heavy, work-worn hands. She licked her dry lips and said to Reb Chaim, "Reb Chaim, here you have twenty-five silver rubles. I am all alone, a widow; I have no son, no kaddish. I've married off my daughter, thank God. She doesn't need me, God forbid. You will write a Torah scroll for me, and with God's help, I will pay you every last penny. I won't bargain with you. It's hard earned money. It's my mitzvah and yours."

Reb Chaim actually stood up.

"A . . . a . . . a Torah scroll? That can't be. . . . Well, not even a rich person . . . what do you mean? A Torah scroll?"

With great purpose, Hinde untied the handkerchief and in a high voice, like one making a blessing, counted out the twenty-five rubles. One, two, three . . . and on and on, and so to the end.

"This is a down payment," she said, "and when I hear from you, I will pay you the rest."

When Hinde got up to leave, Pelte took the lamp from the table to light the way for her to the other side of the doorstep, the way people accompany an important guest, paying them the greatest honor. Hinde turned around and said to Reb Chaim, "Reb Chaim, in the meantime, don't tell anyone about this. What do I need to set tongues wagging for?"

· · · · · · ·

4. It was the custom, and considered to be a mitzvah, for housewives to have a yeshiva student for dinner, especially for Sabbath.

Once again, Hinde put on her well-trodden boots and her old shawl. Thursdays, she went to the butcher and bought a pound of lung, liver, and tripe. The women spread their share of spiteful gossip about her as they did each week, and pleased with themselves, went home.

Reb Chaim no longer sat for whole days in the house of study. Piously, and in awe of God, he wrote the Torah scroll for Hinde. And, indeed, he kept his word. No one in town knew anything about the story.

But it happened just then that Reb Itshe Sosnovetsky, a rich man with a generous hand, took sick, and it occurred to him to vow that when he got better, he would have a new Torah scroll written for the house of study.

The town's rabbi came to pay the rich man a visit.[5] Reb Itshe told the rabbi what he had promised, and the rabbi said to him, "The new Torah scroll should be written right away. God willing, you will get better. The Almighty is to be trusted, and Reb Chaim, the Scribe is, is. . ." The rabbi didn't want to say to the rich man that Reb Chaim the Scribe was a poor man. Why say something so rude about Reb Chaim the Scribe, a poor man? The rabbi turned the wagon shaft and continued, "is a virtuous Jew . . . and he will indeed write a Torah scroll for you. A mitzvah should not be put off. Indeed, not put off."

Early the next day, the rich woman, Rashele Sosnovetsky, sent her maid, Shprintzl, to call on Reb Chaim the Scribe and tell him to come quickly. When Shprintzl heard "come quickly," she took to her feet as if she were a pot on the stove ready to boil and rushed over to Reb Chaim the Scribe's.

"Reb Chaim, my mistress, Rashele, says you should come quickly."

Reb Chaim raised his head from his work. He was just then writing the words: "and Moses spake." Reb Chaim was now far away at Mt. Sinai, where Moses spoke to the Jews. Reb Chaim the Scribe was sitting in his little house just then, and was bringing the words of Moses our Teacher to the Jews of Guralke. At this moment, no one would have recognized Reb Chaim the Scribe. He was Moses our Teacher's helper, his face lit up, and his fingers, holding the goose feather quill, moved slowly over the white

---

5. Molodowsky used the phrase *mevaker khoyle*, meaning "the duty or mitzvah to visit a sick person."

parchment. Reb Chaim looked at Shprintzl for a while and wondered what she was doing here at Mt. Sinai.

Reb Chaim's wondering gaze cooled Shprintzl down; she was no longer in such a rush, and a little quieter, she said: "Reb Chaim, my mistress Rashele asked you to come quickly."

"What's the hurry?" Reb Chaim asked.

Shprintzl knew what was happening under the very fingernails of her mistress; it didn't matter if people told her things or concealed them from her. In any event, she knew everything that was happening in the house, from the greatest to the smallest. Shprintzl's black-cherry eyes read every little wrinkle on the faces of her master and her mistress. Her small pink ears, with little silver earrings, a gift from her grandmother, could hear through the walls. Shprintzl said to Reb Chaim and to Pelte, who stood, curious to hear, "I don't know why they need you, but I know when the master wants a Torah scroll written, whom should he send me to, a shoemaker? He sends me to you."

Pelte saw that the Almighty had taken pity on her and her husband, and was sending them a livelihood. With a full heart, she served Shprintzl egg cookies left over from Sabbath. She brought her husband his coat and cane, and said to him, "When Reb Itshe Sosnovetsky calls for you—you go to him."

The pain under Reb Itshe's shoulder blade let up, and he felt better.

He sat on his bed, wearing a blue flannel robe and leather bed slippers, and spoke to Reb Chaim the Scribe. The most important thing for Reb Itshe was that Reb Chaim not delay, and begin to write a new Torah scroll at once.

For the first time in his life, Reb Chaim felt that a person didn't have always to give in to a rich man. Deep in his heart, he was pleased that just now he was writing a Torah scroll for Hinde the Gardener, and that Hinde had come before Reb Itshe Sosnovetsky. Indeed, for once let it be so, let Hinde come before. Indeed, for once let it be so . . . and he said to Reb Itshe, "If you're in a hurry, Reb Itshe, for me to start writing your Torah scroll right now, I must ask Hinde the Gardener first."

Reb Itshe raised his eyebrows up high in astonishment, and asked: "What possible decoration could Hinde the Gardener afford to put on my Torah scroll?"

"Hinde the Gardener ordered hers first, you understand, Reb Itshe, she ordered hers first, she comes first. You understand, Reb Itshe, she has already . . . "Reb Itshe tightened the lap of his robe over his knees and murmured, "Well, well, we'll have to, as they say, talk to her."

Hinde the Gardener allowed that a Torah scroll should be written for Reb Itshe first, but when the scrolls were to be carried to the synagogue, they should be carried together, so as not to shame her. And so it was.

On Thursday, Shprintzl went to Velvel the Butcher to get an order of meat for her mistress. The women were in full fever, gossiping about Hinde who had just left with her pound of lung, liver, and tripe. They were about to mention Hinde's garden, and the two she rented out, when along came Shprintzl and told them that Hinde had ordered a Torah scroll to be written.

The wives stood there, unfinished words in their mouths. One ventured to ask again, "Hinde? You mean that Hinde?"

No one said a single word; they just shook their heads piously, as if words might be sinful, and it was better now not to use them.

At the end of summer, both Torah scrolls were carried into the synagogue. Hinde was wearing her polished shoes, her fine black wool shawl on her head, and the string of pearls around her neck, exactly what she had worn when she had gone to see Reb Chaim and brought him her deposit, the twenty-five silver rubles. In the street, people told her mazel tov. She was the most important mother-in-law[6] at the most important town celebration.

The Torah scrolls were carried under a chuppah.

The klezmers walked in front, they played, and Hinde danced opposite the chuppah-Torah. She clapped her heavy, work-worn hands, overflowing with a joy she had denied herself all her life: the meager Sabbath meals, the old holiday clothes, the crooked looks people threw at her for her stinginess. Everything opposite her now shone like a thousand lights. Reb Chaim the Scribe and his wife Pelte danced with her; Velvel the Butcher who had listened to the spiteful gossip about Hinde, now came to dance with her,

---

6. The original Yiddish text used the term *mekhutoneste*, which means "the mother of one's son-in-law or daughter-in-law." The overtones of carrying a Torah scroll to the synagogue are those of a joyful wedding—hence, the Torah scroll is carried under a chuppah.

and the women who had gossiped about her, now danced with her, so as to ease their remorse; and the resounding mazel tovs were enough for a hundred weddings.

Compared to her celebration, Reb Itshe's celebration in the chuppah-Torah was like that of a seven-year-old boy next to a bar mitzvah boy. The klezmers played for him, too, and the town accompanied him, but how could this even come close to Hinde's dancing?!

People stopped calling her Hinde the Gardener, as if the whole town had gotten together and agreed to forget her former name. People called her by one name only: "Hinde" and when people said Hinde, they meant *this* Hinde and none other.

December, 1954

The Meeting

. . . .

M r. Altmann was one of the less successful traveling salesmen in the
clothing firm of Samuel Fink. He didn't sell very much, he didn't
earn very much, and people in the firm didn't pay much attention to him.
Blanche, Samuel Fink's secretary, didn't answer Mr. Altmann's good morning. Her mouth was frozen when he came in, and her eyelids seemed to be
half asleep; she didn't see and she didn't hear and she didn't know that he
was there in the waiting room. In his heart of hearts, Mr. Altmann called her
"the dolly" and when he saw that "the dolly" was completely frozen, he
knew that his business with Samuel Fink was not in good order.

Blanche was a reliable mirror of her boss, Samuel Fink. She welcomed
Robert, the most adroit of the firm's salesmen, with outstretched hands and
would run to offer him a chair. On a hot summer day, she even went down
and brought back a cold drink for him: "I can't let you die of thirst, Rob," she
said, with a sea of smiles in her blue eyes.

When her boss, Samuel Fink, caught a cold, she coughed all day in
sympathy for him, and wiped her eyes with a paper tissue.

"The whole city has a cold," she consoled him, and to demonstrate, immediately took out a paper tissue and wiped the tip of her nose.

Close to twenty, Blanche was already a fully grown adult, complete in
every detail, and no one could outdo her in running the office of the firm of
Samuel Fink. Samuel Fink was pleased with Blanche. A couple of times a
year, in a good moment, he would ask her, "How old are you, Blanche?"

At her precise answer, that she was eighteen years and four months old, he would shake his head back and forth, so that it was hard to know whether he was marveling at her success, or he didn't believe she had told him her real age. At any rate, his question, "How old are you, Blanche?" was always a good sign that she would be receiving a gift: a pair of gloves, a shawl, a dozen stockings. Both of them, Samuel Fink and Blanche, enjoyed this.

Once Blanche heard her boss, Samuel Fink, who happened to be in a good mood, say to Mr. Altmann, clapping him on the shoulder, "If you were a rabbi on the lower East Side, you'd be making more money." And Samuel Fink laughed, enjoying this idea; even Mr. Altmann smiled, too.

After that, Blanche at least looked at Altmann when he came into the firm's waiting room. More expressive than words, the look in her marveling blue eyes would tell him: Why are you hanging around here in the waiting room? Wouldn't it be better if you were a rabbi on the lower East Side?

One Friday, when several salesmen were in the waiting room and all the chairs were taken, Altmann was standing, looking out a window, waiting for Samuel Fink to be free to talk with him. He'd been waiting for a considerable time. There was an empty chair next to Blanche where her purse, paper tissues inside, was lying, because just then Samuel Fink had caught a cold, and Blanche, in sympathy for him, had been wiping the tip of her nose all day. Blanche didn't pick up her purse and didn't free the chair for Mr. Altmann. Both of them, Blanche and Mr. Altmann, looked at the chair where her purse was lying, as if that very spot were on fire. Blanche didn't pick up the purse, and Altmann stood next to the window, barely able to control himself, all the while, looking at Blanche's purse.

Their eyes met once. Blanche's were as unconcerned as those of a newborn child. Just eyes, nothing more than that. And Altmann's look was weary, like that of a person who's been looking at water running in a river for too long: Run, you can run, but what am I doing here looking at you? Nevertheless, he strongly resented it. And when, after settling his business with Samuel Fink, while walking back through the waiting room, he said to Blanche without any special expression of emotion, as though he were talking only to himself: "Blanche, I don't like it."

His words, that fell as if from the middle of the sky, were so unexpected that Blanche actually rose from her chair. But Mr. Altmann was already on the other side of the door. He had closed the door behind him as usual and was gone. If she hadn't heard her name, "Blanche," so clearly, she'd have thought that the good-for-nothing had just been jabbering to himself. But she had explicitly heard her name: Blanche.

She sat down, shrugged her shoulders and looked around at the people in the waiting room. She didn't meet anyone's eyes. It seemed they hadn't heard the strange thing Altmann had said to her. She picked up her purse from the chair as though its being there bothered her, and began pecking on the typewriter, peck, peck, peck, as if nothing had happened.

Altmann thought: A dolly, some dolly, a fickle woman.

When he got home, his wife, Eydl, met him with an alarm. "I just can't stand your crazy ideas! You're in love with these old chairs, with these broken down old things! Ben called; he wants to come over today with his girl, and I'm so ashamed of this furniture. I've already dusted and plumped and brushed your chairs, which helps about as much as a bonnet on a bubbe. Ben's making good money, Ben. . . . Why does he have to feel ashamed?"

The furniture in Mr. Altmann's home was quite old-fashioned. The chairs stood, well established and proper, with high backs, and were upholstered in a large flowered fabric that had already been eating up the dust for fifteen years. Everything was faded, but it was weighty, dignified, and proper. Respectable chairs in a respectable home.

Eydl had been asking her husband to change the furniture for a couple of years. She could no longer stand look at it. But he didn't want to. He hated to throw "healthy" chairs out of the house, just like that, because it was the fashion to change things. He didn't want to hear about it.

"Why should they be thrown out?" he tried to explain to his wife, "just because they're old? Well, and what about us? We're new? Leave them alone. . . . Changes. . . . For me it's enough that my son changed his name. Changes, everything changes. Altmann doesn't suit him, only Mr. Mann will do!"

Mr. Altmann sat down on a dusted-off chair, leaned against its high, respectable back, and felt his legs relax. He said to his wife, "It's a real pleasure to sit in such a chair. And why not?"

Mr. Altmann never brought his troubles at work home, didn't mention the grief, or the insults. When he was really downhearted, he would say to his wife Eydl, "It would be nice to have a cold drink."

Eydl knew that when her husband wanted a cold drink things were not so good. But one didn't talk about that. She'd serve him a cold drink and say soothingly, "Drink, yes, drink, don't worry about it, not one of them is worth the soles of your shoes." By this, she meant the adroit salesmen.

Because of the guest Ben happened to be bringing home, Eydl told her husband to put on another necktie: "A beautiful tie makes a man seem altogether different."

He changed his tie and muttered: "More changes, everything changes . . . a world of changes. Who is she, this girl he's supposed to bring over here?"

The lock on the door of the Altmanns' apartment opened with a couple of loud clicks that sounded like shots. The lock would spring back twice, and only then would the door open. The Altmanns heard the door open and then, in the corridor, the happy voices of Ben and his guest.

Mr. Altmann raised his head—a familiar voice, a very familiar voice. Mrs. Altmann went to the door and said warmly, "Come in, come in."

Ben and Blanche came into the room. There was a sea of smiles in Blanche's blue eyes. She caught sight of Altmann, and in one moment her blue eyes turned blank white, as if they had been burned by a sunbeam. Then they were once again full of blue smiles, and Blanche said: "Mr. Altmann! What an agreeable surprise! Isn't it a pleasure that people can meet outside the office for once? Ah, the office!" and she shook her head of permed hair, and even sighed.

Mr. Altmann said something in a voice like that of a person swallowing a hot potato when it gets stuck in the throat and is neither up nor down. He wasn't silent, but people couldn't hear what he said.

They drank tea. Blanche was utterly delighted with the living room.

"You have a very pleasant living room," she said, looking at the old furniture, and the sea of smiles in her blue eyes confirmed what she said. "You can't get such furniture now! Real antiques—you'd pay out a fortune to get such things now."

Mr. Altmann looked at her, and didn't believe a single word. But he was touched by the compliment to his furniture. She had hit the spot for him with that. And Eydl said, like a comfortable housewife, "And we paid a lot for it then—ay, ay—we spent so much for it, all those long years ago!"

Blanche didn't stay long at the Altmann's. Discomfort lay under the smiles in her blue eyes, as if a piece of the ceiling were on the verge of falling down, but no one knew when it would happen. She said that her sister had sprained her ankle, and she had to go home to find out what the doctor had ordered.

Ben accompanied her. When they were gone, Eydl said to her husband, "Well, what do you have to say? You know her already? She's pretty, very pretty. . ."

Mr. Altmann had a weary look, like someone who'd been looking the water running in a river for a long time. He said to his wife in a clear voice—the hot potato having been swallowed—"They don't come as nasty as she is. But it doesn't matter, she could be a very good wife."

Eydl smiled.

"They don't come as two-faced as she is. But that doesn't matter, it might not be such a bad match."

Eydl twisted her fingers like someone hearing a loud clap of thunder.

"God doesn't make them as bitchy as she is, but it doesn't matter, she can run a business all by herself . . . and did you see? She never even once, the whole time she was here, took out a tissue for her nose, not even once."

Eydl looked at her husband as if at a person who's talking nonsense, and she got busy and cleared the table.

The next Friday, when Mr. Altmann walked into the waiting room of the firm of Samuel Fink, Blanche welcomed him exactly the way she welcomed the best salesman, Robert. She stretched out her hands, brought him a chair and even ordered a cup of coffee for him.

"It was such a pleasure to be in your home that I don't know how I can best welcome you," and a sea of smiles was in her blue eyes.

The Rich Man from Azherkov

. . . .

P eople said that Marcus Applebaum had grown hoarse because of his
stinginess. He had been hoarse ever since Charlie, the synagogue's
gabbai, had come and asked him for a thousand dollars to repair the building and to bring the cantor Mendele Borukhson for the High Holidays.

Charlie, in fact a neighbor of Marcus's, had narrow little eyes that never
stopped smiling. He knew how to stick words right into a person's gut—
and smile, and smile.

"You're still, *keyn eyn hore*, loaded with money," so he spoke to Marcus
Applebaum, "money in the bank, in houses that you own, in the stock market, and a partner in a liquor business. If you don't write me a little check for
a thousand dollars, I won't leave. When we figured out this year's budget for
the synagogue, we put you down for a thousand dollars. Where will I get it,
if you won't give it to us?"

Marcus Applebaum resented Charlie talking about the synagogue as if
it were his own business. "Thinks he has God under lease, and talks so
smoothly you'd think a machine was working inside him." He never took
his eyes off Charlie: Just look how eagerly he talks, just look at his fire. . . .

Meanwhile, Charlie was already talking about the cantor Mendele
Borukhson: "When he sings—it melts your very limbs. Just looking at
him when he's losing himself in a *yoale-ve-yavo'le*[1] is worth a thousand
dollars."

---

1. "May it rise and come," the name of a prayer said at the new moon and on holidays.

Charlie's little eyes were beaming with smiles, as though he were in fact hearing Mendele Borukhson's singing just now.

Marcus Applebaum, the very rich man, was sitting bent over as though Charlie's words were falling on him like a cold rain. He wanted to knock Charlie out of his delighted smiling, and asked him abruptly: "Charlie, how much do you make a year, hah?"

Charlie motioned with his hand, the way people flick away a fly, and answered, in an easy manner, without a drop of envy: "I know . . . I can make in a year, let's say . . . as much as you make in a month . . . but what's the difference? Shrouds don't have pockets."

Marcus Applebaum shook his head, as though he'd been reminded of something, and laughed hoarsely.

Marcus's wife, Evelyn, was listening to the conversation through the open door of another room. She heard her husband's hoarse laughter, and winced inwardly. She went into the living room where her husband and Charlie were sitting.

She was seized with pity for her husband. He looked a pauper waiting for a donation. He was bent over, his face shriveled.

"You'll get the thousand dollars, Charlie," she said to the gabbai. "My husband loves to bargain, but he gives, *keyn eyn hore*, . . . he gives, *keyn eyn hore.*"

Marcus Applebaum wrote out the check, and said with a sigh: "Mendele Borukhson . . . we could do without Mendele Borukhson. *Yoale-ve-yavo'le, schmovele. . .*"

But when it came to signing the check, Marcus Applebaum hastily put the pen down to the side, as though someone else should guide his hand, and said with fire in his eyes: "I won't give . . . I won't give. . ."

His voice had become hoarse, and his words ran together so that it sounded like he was hissing.

The smile disappeared from Charlie's eyes. He stood up, moved slowly to the door, and said, as though nothing would come of it, "Well, well. Nothing's on fire. Another time . . . well, well. . ."

Charlie left, carefully closing the door so that it wouldn't slam. Evelyn remained standing, gazed for a while at her husband, and burst into tears.

Through her tears, she spoke brokenly: "No shame . . . and no conscience. Eat your check . . . eat it up, maybe that will satisfy you."

Marcus Applebaum bent his neck, as if he were swallowing a fly, and replied, "She'd throw a thousand dollars away! You think *you* earned them?"

"I worked just like you did in the junk shop," Evelyn murmured, but as she saw her husband to be pitiable, she stopped talking and left the room.

Ever since Marcus Applebaum had grown rich, and started buying up buildings, one after the other, the seven rooms of their residence had become dead quiet. Only the clocks on the walls tick-tocked monotonously. Guests seldom came. Marcus Applebaum was busy. He was always talking about tenants, mortgages, and money.

"In Long Island I need two tenants. Two tenants are three hundred dollars a month, seventy-five dollars a week, more than ten dollars a day. . . . You have to know how to survive such losses."

Her husband's constant calculations made Evelyn's eyes stick together as though she were getting sleepy. She grew especially sleepy when he talked about his building in Long Island. "Long Island" was the pride of his property, a ten-story brick building with an elevator and a guard at the door.

Because of the building in Long Island, Marcus Applebaum quarreled with his Azherkov *landsleit.* When the secretary of the Azherkovers, Israel Shokhet, came to Marcus Applebaum for a hundred dollars to send packages to the *landsleit* abroad, Marcus laughed and said to him, "Maybe you can offer *me* a loan. I need to pay off my mortgage on Long Island right now; I'm being strangled . . . st . . . st . . . st . . . strangled."

Israel Shokhet coughed, as though he might catch a cold from Marcus' words, and answered, "Well, well. I'll propose to our committee that we should offer you a loan."

Israel Shokhet put the apple he was holding in his hand back on the wide crystal plate that was standing in the middle of the table, and pinged the gleaming crystal with his finger. The plate resounded in a thin, silvery tune, as if it might burst out crying.

When Israel Shokhet had gone, Marcus Applebaum said to Evelyn, "Wouldn't I look good if I had to go to them for a loan! Oh, dear me! They know only one thing: give and give and give. . ."

Marcus pronounced the words through tightly pressed lips, and Evelyn thought he was saying: hipf, hipf, hipf!

More than anything else, it hurt Evelyn that the richer her husband Marcus became, the poorer he looked. It didn't help that he bought the most expensive suits and coats of the best fabrics. They looked like borrowed clothes on him, a rich man's castoffs. The doorman at his Long Island building, a tall, happy young man in a green uniform with brass buttons, looked like a millionaire next to his boss, Marcus Applebaum.

The Azherkov *landsleit* almost stopped coming over to the Applebaums, seldom even calling them on the telephone. Mrs. Shokhet, a friend of Evelyn's, who all too readily spoke her mind, once said to Evelyn on the telephone, with a little laugh, "So, Marcus is still hard up for money? We need money."

After this conversation, Evelyn remained sitting by the telephone like someone utterly depleted. When she told her husband about it, he clamped his lips together and pronounced hoarsely, "When I was sitting in the junk shop, no one bothered to come my way because I was poor. And now? I need to buy them off? Give and give and give. . . . I don't want to!"

Angrily, he went to call his superintendent in Long Island. He notified him that the rents from all the apartments had to be paid up by the fifth of the month. "Give them a dispossess notice if they don't give you a check! Better the apartments stand empty than a tenant give me trouble."

The superintendent knew that first thing in the morning his boss would call up and tell him to be polite to the renters. No one had ever been thrown out of his apartment there. Nevertheless, he answered him subserviently, "As you wish, Mr. Applebaum."

Mr. Applebaum put down the receiver and angrily figured out the losses he would have from ten renters who were ten days late with their payments: "Ten times ten is a hundred . . . a hundred days is more than three months . . . three months at a hundred and fifty dollars a month is a total of. . ."

Marcus Applebaum reckoned to the penny how much he had lost on that. Evelyn's eyes were glued shut as though she really wanted to sleep and she couldn't overcome the heaviness of her eyebrows.

Their married daughter, Irene, used to drop by once a week to see her mother and father. Many times, she didn't even take off her coat. Their son-in-law, an unassuming eye doctor, was on bad terms with his father-in-law because he would never give him any money for expanding his business.

Evelyn talked with her husband about it several times, even quarreled with him: "Who are you saving the money for? The children will hate us!"

Marcus Applebaum, never raising his eyes, would answer, "A young man has to get ahead on his own! You can't ride on someone else's wheels! No one can ride on someone else's wheels! You have to have your own!"

And he would conclude with his usual refrain: "Just give and give and give . . . spare me their love . . . I don't want to buy it even for a few dollars. No thanks!"

The Azherkov *landsleit* were getting ready for their annual ball. No one called the Applebaums.

"Oh, he keeps all his money for himself, so let him be happy by himself." They brushed him off and forgot to write him a letter.

Evelyn's friend, Mrs. Shokhet, who spoke all too readily, told Evelyn, "You know, if they thought they were getting a big check, maybe they wouldn't have forgotten, but as it is . . . you know . . . they've forgotten. . ."

When Evelyn told her husband, he laughed hoarsely and said, "Is that so? If I showed them a couple of dollars, they'd come running. . . . Charlie would be here with his near-sighted wife who can't even see where she should wipe her own nose, and Israel Shokhet, and my daughter, and my son-in-law. They'd clap their hands for me, sing my praises, and give me surprise parties. I could buy anything I want from them. But what's it worth to me? I say, what's it worth to me? I don't begrudge them the money, but I hate their rotten game. What do you mean, they're angry? They shouldn't envy me! They just want me to sit in a junk shop!"

The Applebaums' seven decorated rooms seemed like an abandoned station where the train never stops. The train clacks away on its noisy wheels, and the depot remains engulfed in silence.

Mr. Applebaum bought a house with a roof garden. Every evening he made his calculations: how much income there would be, how much return, how much overhead, and what his profits would be. In the living room, on the table where he loved to make his calculations, there were pieces of paper with long columns of numbers. There were notes, receipts, suggestions, plans, contracts, memorandums, and offers—scraps of paper in different colors like confetti.

His eyes squinting, Marcus placed the pieces of paper down, one after the other, and accompanied each one with a couple of words out loud: "This one's a disaster." "This one's capable." "This one's so-so." "This one's always a misery." "This one's all right." "This one's perfect."

Sometimes it happened that, out of the blue, Marcus would laugh happily, as though he were talking with someone who had just given him good news.

Because of his house with the roof garden, Marcus Applebaum didn't go to the wedding of his sister's daughter. He sent a present, a hundred-dollar bill, and called his sister on the phone: "I can't leave, Chankele! The roof garden has to be taken care of at the right time. It's the season for it. It's just like a field, it's just like a forest! It's just like grandfather's garden in Azherkov! You understand? It's the season for it."

His sister, on the telephone, didn't understand how the grandfather's garden mattered here. She was angry, and she sent back her brother's hundred dollars with a little note: "Since you're the kind of brother who doesn't have the time to come when I'm leading my only daughter to the chuppah, then I don't need your schmundred dollars."

Marcus Applebaum read over his sister's note, boiled over, and said to Evelyn, "You know why she's so angry? She's waiting for five hundred! A schmundred she sent back! Just give, give, give . . . to them, to all of them! Even my own sister. . ."

Marcus Applebaum was standing with his sister's note in his hand. The wrinkles around his eyes were sagging and looked like dark threads.

After the quarrel with his sister, Marcus Applebaum walked around for several days as if he had shriveled up. Evelyn pitied him and said, "Maybe you could send her the five hundred and make it up with your sister."

Marcus Applebaum hurled himself around to her, and shouted out in a hoarse voice, "She'd just squander five hundred! You think you earned it? You want to go back to the junk shop? Hmm? Back to the junk shop? What do they all want from me? Just that I should go back to the junk shop!"

Early one morning, one of Evelyn's eyebrows began to twitch. She looked in the mirror, and saw that her eye twitched all the time, as if it were winking at someone. Evelyn didn't know how to keep the eye from winking. She looked in the mirror for hours, and from the anxiety, lost her appetite. The doctor who came over to see Evelyn advised a change of climate. At this, he gestured with his hand at the walls and said, "You need to get away from here."

And Evelyn left for California.

Before her departure, her friend, Mrs. Shokhet, came over to say goodbye. She sympathized heartily with Evelyn, whose eye was twitching. With wide, brightly colored lips, she talked to Evelyn about the Azherkov Society, telling how many packages they had already sent off, and how many they would still send. With a healthy appetite, she ate an apple, then a pear, and then a bunch of grapes. Her wide lusty lips expressed satisfaction: satisfaction with eating, satisfaction with sending packages, satisfaction with living.

Helplessly, Evelyn winked her twitching eye, feeling both grief and distaste.

Marcus Applebaum accompanied his wife to the train. Several times he told her, "Take care of yourself, Evelyn. Take care of yourself. Take advantage of the climate, take advantage of it."

A tear danced out of Evelyn's twitching eye.

Marcus Applebaum returned to the silent, decorated rooms of his residence. The clock, more clearly than ever, tick-tocked monotonously. Loneliness took hold of him, and indignation: Always something new, the climate, the climate of all things! Angrily, he went to the telephone and called his superintendent in Long Island: "Give them a dispossess notice if they don't give you a check on time!"

"As you wish, Mr. Applebaum," the superintendent answered subserviently.

Marcus Applebaum put down the receiver.

Shriveled up, dark wrinkles under his eyes, he looked like a poor watchman who is guarding a stranger's possessions.

New York, 1956

The Son-in-Law

. . . .

Carrying a large basket packed with food—a roast chicken, a Swiss cheese, baked apples in a small bowl wrapped up in wax paper, pickled herring in a glass jar, and various other good things—Mrs. Potok got off the subway and started to climb the stairs to the street. Her cheeks and lips were brightly colored and the elegant white summer hat with blue flowers that she wore looked as though it should be going somewhere else, and didn't belong at all to the woman who walked a little stooped over, a heavy basket in her hand.

Mrs. Potok approached a new two-story house where Irene, her daughter who had gotten married a year ago, lived. Mrs. Potok looked at the brass nameplate with her son-in-law's name, Dr. Robert Nassau, with pleasure, but she didn't ring the bell. She put her basket down on the ground, took a mirror out of her purse, looked at herself, straightened the hat on her head, applied lipstick, powdered her nose, put on a pair of white gloves, and then rang the bell.

Her son-in-law, Robert, opened the door for her. He said, "Hello, Mom!" and called out, matter-of-factly, like a waiter placing an order at the kitchen window of a restaurant, "Irene, your mother!" and disappeared without saying a word to his mother-in-law. Went into a second room and closed the door behind him.

Irene kissed her mother. She asked how her father was doing, if he was working, and then both women began to unpack the basket. In order to thank her mother for the food that she had carried from such a distance, Irene praised all the good things, and spoke to her mother in Yiddish: "A chicken, *keyn eyn hore,* as big as a turkey! And your apples—the taste of paradise!" Irene tasted a bit of apple, and licked her fingers.

Mrs. Potok glowed with happiness. Her sharp, work-worn elbows moved busily as she unpacked plates, and jars, and glasses. The basket could not be emptied, and she continued to bring one treasure after another out of it. Not even a jar of small pickled cucumbers was missing. Irene was delighted: "This will be a real surprise for Robert. He loves pickled cucumbers!"

With exaggerated cheerfulness, she called her husband, "Dr. Robert! Come in here, there's a treat for you!"

Robert came bouncing in nimbly, glanced at the table, and began chewing right away, starting with a chicken wing; and then taking a baked apple, he said to his mother-in-law, matter-of-factly: "Mom, please, don't talk to the neighbors when you come here."

Under the red of her rouged cheeks, another red leaped out and filled Mrs. Potok's entire face. Irene turned exactly as red as her mother. Now they resembled each other—both with full, slightly up-turned lips, and both with dejection in their round, black eyes. A mother and a daughter.

"Who talks with your neighbors, Robby? I don't even see anyone!" Mrs. Potok gestured with her hand.

Each week, on Sabbath, when Mrs. Potok was free from the shop, she brought a fully packed basket to her daughter, and each week she quarreled with her son-in-law, and Irene always took her husband's side. "He's right— he's right," she said. But in all her movements, in her blushing face and her dejected eyes, she was on her mother's side. It seemed that any moment Irene would be torn in two: her body would remain with her mother, and her words would run after her husband. Now too, Irene sided with her husband: "Yes, Mama, you did speak with the neighbors," Irene said, "you talked with Mrs. Lawrence."

Mrs. Potok actually grabbed her head with both hands. "I don't even know who Mrs. Lawrence is. Maybe it was the tall woman who met me by the door. She said to me, 'Nice day, today, isn't it?' Shouldn't I answer her?

What am I, God forbid, a mute? So I answered her: 'Yes, it is a nice climate today.' How was that worshipping the Golden Calf?[1] How was that a sin?"

Robert burst out laughing, and Irene winced as though someone were trying to hit her on the head. With tears in her voice, she said to her mother, "You don't say it that way, Mama . . . you can understand. Intelligent people live in this building . . . people don't say it. . ."

Her voiced trembled, torn deep inside, as though some kind of misfortune might happen in the house, and no one knew how to prevent it.

Robert twisted his beautifully formed lips and said to Irene, "Explain to her, go ahead, you explain to her!"

But he couldn't resist saying to Mrs. Potok in his elaborate college English, "A climate is a permanent atmospheric condition of the temperatures in different zones. . ."

He spoke in strange words that Mrs. Potok didn't understand and had never heard. But she knew that each word was an accusation against her, and she felt as if she were in a court where she had been brought up on false charges.

Robert kept on talking for a while, pleased that his mother-in-law was confused and that he was so much smarter than she was. Irene could no longer stand to see her mother's suffering, and spoke up bitterly: "Rob, enough already with giving your atmospheric lecture. . . . I swear even your own father wouldn't understand what you're talking about!"

Now Robert flared up because she had compared his father (a bookkeeper, person who read newspapers) to her mother, that Mrs. Potok. Eyes blazing, he said, "You can't understand it yourself either . . . you couldn't even get through college! You made it as far as the third year, and then you ran out of steam! You're a never-made-it yourself!"

His body arched itself angrily, making him look like a dancer. He jumped up high, as if over a puddle, went into the next room and slammed the door.

---

1. Golden Calf (in Hebrew *khute begl*) is a reference to the idol of the golden calf that Aaron, Moses' brother, caused to be made in a time of doubt and trouble while wandering in the desert after the exodus from Egypt. See Exodus 32. Mrs. Potok can't see how she's offending anyone by trying to speak English.

For many years, Mrs. Potok and her husband, Max, worked in a shop. Once a month, they went to the movies. And once a week, on Saturday evening, Max played cards with his friends at his house, and Mrs. Potok served tea and cookies. Every now and then when Max lost half a dollar, his wife, a little upset, would say to him: "You know, cards can impoverish a person."

Mrs. Potok had sent their only daughter, Irene, to college. "Don't let her suffer in a shop and blind her eyes at the needle like we've had to," she had said to her husband, and on her own, she began to work overtime to pay for college.

The house came to life. College opened up a wide world for Mrs. Potok. On Sundays, she would tell all the neighbors that the college was having examinations, and that her Irene was very busy; she had to pass the exams. Summers, when Irene had vacations, her friends, the college girls, came over. Mrs. Potok began to speak English with her daughter and had a telephone installed in the house. "A college girl needs a telephone." They bought a glass cabinet where all of Irene's college books were arranged. The cabinet and the books were guarded like the holy ark itself. Early Sunday mornings, Mrs. Potok polished the glass panes of the cabinet and wiped off the dust. She worked with a special pleasure. They had new furniture moved into Irene's room, and they hung a picture of a hunter pursuing game on the wall.

When Robert, a student in medical school, started coming over to see Irene, Mrs. Potok bought a pair of shoes with rubber soles. It's more refined when a person walks quietly, and doesn't clomp around, she thought. On her silent rubber soles, she would approach Irene's door, knock and ask: "Maybe you young people would like Coca-cola?" and she brought them Coca-cola.

Another time, she asked if they didn't want hot dogs, or if they didn't want a cigarette. Nothing was too hard or too expensive for Irene and Robert.

Max reproached his wife: "Don't be a rag for them! People tramp all over rags with their feet!"

Max couldn't stand to see how his wife danced attendance on college. When Robert came over, Max would leave the house and go over to a friend's to play pinochle. Before leaving, he always had the same line for his wife: "You're welcome to your college, but I won't wear rubber soles."

Irene accompanied her mother to the subway. As they were walking, she said to her: "When Robert goes crazy, it takes a couple of days . . . he curses . . . then he comes to make up . . . kisses my hand . . . what can you do to him?"

Irene sighed and tears appeared in her eyes. Mrs. Potok felt anguish in her heart, and pity for her Irene.

Silently, they walked to the subway. Irene didn't want to return home with a tear-stained face, and said to her mother: "Let's go have a cup of coffee; in the meantime, he'll get over being mad."

Sitting with her mother, Irene said, "We need to pay the rent now . . . with Robert's earnings . . . and with his fine silk shirts that he loves. . ."

Mrs. Potok shook her head. A forlorn sadness was in her eyes.

"I always have a couple of dollars when I come to see you . . . you think . . . I would worry about him? I don't want you to suffer. You don't look good, Khanele. Even before a year is gone a child can change so much . . . don't skimp on yourself, Irene. I've saved a few dollars . . . you won't be short of anything, Khanele. . ."

Mrs. Potok bent her head down, hiding her bosom under her white hat, pulled out a tied-up handkerchief and gave it to her daughter.

"What am I working for, if not for your sake? Take it, Khanele, take it, Irene—you'll give it back to me, you'll give it back later on."

Irene shook her head playfully. Her short light brown hair danced around her ears. She looked young, almost childlike, as she had when her mother used to give her money for ice cream.

"I just want you to be well, Khanele," Mrs. Potok said to her daughter. "Let him worry, he's the man. He's cost us enough! We set up an office for him. Let him worry!"

Mrs. Potok came back home tired from the long ordeal of the subway, and from the quarrel with her son-in-law. Her husband, Max, was already back from his job ("working on a Saturday even," he said) and was waiting for her. He met her with his ever biting words when she returned from their daughter: "So, did the doctor roll out the carpet for you?"

Mrs. Potok didn't answer him. Her face cloudy, she got things ready for dinner. Her sharp elbows moved quickly. She banged the pots, the spoons and forks clattered, the chairs scraped; the kitchen was storming, but she herself, Mrs. Potok, didn't utter a single word.

Max winked at her, and said very calmly, and good-naturedly, "Say something, otherwise I'll think our son-in-law bit off your tongue. So, why are you mad at me? Why?"

"Full of jokes, he's always joking!"

"Why not? I finish my twelve hours of work on Saturday like a Gentile, ripping open a couple of hundred seams, so people don't have to go without pants. What don't I have? What? My daughter is a doctor's wife. What don't I have?"

Mrs. Potok couldn't stand it any longer. She took out a handkerchief, wiped her eyes and nose, and said to her husband: "Eat already, eat! He's starting again with the doctor's wife! I didn't want my daughter to marry a tailor, what's wrong with that? I sent her to college. Should I be punished for this?"

"A tailor isn't good enough for her, a doctor is more genteel. He threw you out, hah? Tell the truth, don't be ashamed. He'll milk us out of whatever we have, become a real doctor, and send your daughter back to you! You'll see! College, just college, nothing will do for her but college, so you can boast to the neighbors, psssss! So—it's better I catch a game of pinochle and talk with my fellow man."

He picked up his hat and left the house.

Mrs. Potok shook her head after him: "He's to be envied—a man who doesn't worry!"

Her legs felt tired; she picked up the newspaper Max had left on the table, and went to lie down for a rest. While reading, she dozed off. The telephone woke her up.

"Oy, it's Irene," Mrs. Potok thought, and with a trembling hand, she picked up the receiver.

Irene spoke with tears in her voice: "Mom, I'm coming to stay with you tonight. Robert's gone crazy, I haven't the strength to fight with him, Mom!"

Mrs. Potok answered her daughter in a hoarse voice: "You stay in your home, Irene! Don't let him get used to the idea of your leaving home. Give him the money I just gave you! He's cost us plenty! But no leaving, no! No! No!"

Because of the excitement, Mrs. Potok's weariness vanished. She got up and went in to clean the kitchen. The pots crashed. She scrubbed and scoured. She worked quickly with her sharp, work-worn elbows, and spoke loudly, "There's pleasure from children for you! Worked hard all my life, saved and shouldered the burden, and this is the pleasure you get from children."

When the kitchen was already gleaming with cleanliness, and all the aluminum lids were hanging on the wall, shining like mirrors, a calmed down Mrs. Potok said to herself:

"Never mind. They'll quarrel, they'll make up, and indeed I'll still have a son-in-law, a doctor. . ."

Mrs. Potok shook her head. Her face was reflected in all the shining aluminum lids, and they were all shaking their heads: a son-in-law, a doctor.

She stood there lost in dreams, and whispered quietly: "And the grand-children won't be just anybodies, and the great-grandchildren. . ."

Her face, dreamy-eyed, was reflected on the wall.

New York, 1954

Gone . . .

. . . .

Seymour Shtuker stopped shaving when he realized that his greatest pleasure in life—his trips to Europe—had ended.

Selling and repairing watches, chains and wrist bands in his narrow, little shop in a small town in New Jersey was just a way for Seymour Shtuker to pass the time between one trip and the others that he used to make every three or four years to Europe. His real life was getting ready for a trip, buying presents for his sister, for a half-town of aunts, uncles, cousins, and their families. In addition to them in Ogrodovke, his hometown, there was a school for children, and a library next to the school; and in these institutions, Seymour Shtuker was a very welcome guest, an American who left behind a whole hundred dollars each time; and because of this, the school was richer than all the other schools in the neighboring towns. People called it the "American foster-child."[1] What town could compare itself to Ogrodovke?

After shopping for the presents, Seymour Shtuker packed them up himself in large leather suitcases, clothing in one, dishes in another, repaired watches placed separately in a little box. In short, he was a specialist

---

1. The Yiddish term *kest-kind* means "a ward, orphan, or foster child." However, *kest* refers to the custom of offering one's son-in-law room and board for a given time so that he could study Torah and not have to worry about earning a living. It was a badge of honor for the father-in-law, indicating that he was rich enough to take care of his son-in-law. Thus Ogradovke is, in effect, Seymour Shtuker's ward.

in packing gifts for Europe. Everything arrived intact, not even wrinkled. Packing the gifts took up a good couple of weeks, and Seymour Shtuker's house looked like a train station, but who cared? In fact, it was part of the pleasure; a kind of special holiday preparation.

He usually set off on a journey in summer, when the watches weren't in such demand, when the crowds lolled about on the grass on vacations and didn't bother to see how late it was.

His assistant in the shop, Jack, had besides watchmaking, another occupation, an additional job—singing with a cantor for the holidays, and thereby earned an extra $150 a year.

Getting ready to leave for one of his trips, Seymour said to Jack, "Don't sing away the business; it's not a holiday the whole year long."

During the time when he was packing up the suitcases to take to Ogrodovke, and his house looked like a train station, in his store Seymour was especially well-disposed. When a "bitter customer" came in, twisted the watches, tested the chains, bargained over a price, and who normally would have irritated him, Seymour Shtuker, excited about his trip, didn't let it bother him. With all his might and half his soul, he was already on his way to Europe. He'd smoke a cigarette and answer the bitter customer with a few short words, and suddenly, because he was in fact more on his way than in the shop, he'd ask him a question: "Where do you come from? Where were you born? Perhaps you're getting ready to go to Europe?"

Sometimes, it happened that the bitter customer was part of Seymour Shtuker's large extended family. Sometimes, it happened that they were *landsleit* or were students from the same yeshiva, or somehow distantly related, and then they could make a deal—a penny more, a penny less—and it was done.

When the bitter customer was a Gentile, if he looked at the extraordinary salesman and saw the obvious (that the sale didn't matter to him: buy, or don't buy) that customer would buy.

In the weeks before a trip, selling watches became easier. And because of that, while he was "playing," Seymour Shtuker learned a principle of psychology: A customer likes it when no one pays attention to him. A customer likes it when no one needs him. It's then that he does what a customer is supposed to do—he buys.

Seymour Shtuker's arrival in Ogrodovke was a huge event, for himself, for his sister, and for the entire town. Only then in Ogrodovke did he feel that America was a great and powerful country, a country the whole world respected.

Driving him home from the train station was the privilege of Sholem Moishe, the oldest coachman of the town. He used to call Seymour "you"[2] familiarly, as he did in those years when Seymour Shtuker as a boy had tried to hitch a ride on the back of his wagon, and he would chase him away with his whip. Sholem Moishe, the first person to have the honor of meeting the American, asked about the president, whether he was still good for the Jews, and hearing the answer, that in America everyone was equal, he'd both guess and conclude: "Yes, people are equal, but they still haven't made *you* their president, Shimondl. All people are equal, but a lame man still limps."

If Sholem Moishe the Coachman was somewhat skeptical about America, then Seymour Shtuker's aunts, the uncles, the sister, and his entire family were more credulous. Seymour Shtuker told them that in America everything was automated, made by a machine. Matzo was baked in a machine, challah was braided by a machine, butter—another machine, cheese was dried in a machine, laundry was washed in a machine, ice was frozen in a machine, and so on. Each time he arrived in Ogrodovke, Seymour Shtuker brought a new machine. The aunts, dressed up in their Sabbath-day clothes, in honor of the guest, wiped the corners of their mouths, and wondered what kind of a land this was where absolutely no one did a crumb of work, because everything was done by a machine. In order to find merit for Ogrodovke, one aunt dismissed the machines with a saying: "Nevertheless, they say people don't know how to keep the Sabbath in America, so what's the use of machines?"

Seymour Shtuker swallowed such trifling remarks from Ogrodovke without the least aggravation and responded with his own generalization: "There's not a thing in the world without its fault."

2. The Yiddish terms *du* and *ir* mean "you." Along with French, Spanish, and many other languages, Yiddish has a familiar "you" (*du*) and a formal "you" (*ir*). Molodowsky used *du* here.

In the study house, the American guest was accorded the best aliyah, in fact the sixth, and because of this, he looked around the study house like an owner. Left money to repair the roof, or to repaint the windows, to reinforce the oven perhaps, and at some point to buy a new hand-basin by the door.

In the school, "the American foster-child," the children's chorus sang a song for him, and the teacher held an evening tea where he spoke about the unity of Jews throughout the world.

During the three weeks that Seymour Shtuker would enjoy in Ogrodovke, he felt he had a secure place in the world: he had two homes, one here and one in New Jersey. What was missing to him in one home was made up for in the second. True, the distance between them was a little too far, but a man is a more important guest when he's made a longer journey.

When, in the middle of the war, information arrived that the Germans had burned Ogrodovke, and of the entire town only a mountain of ash remained, and not a living soul, Seymour Shtuker did not believe it, and did not want to believe it. Then in the newspaper, he saw for himself a list of the few people from his town who were still alive. He could not find a single name of his family; somewhere faraway in the world he felt an emptiness that extended itself to him over towns and oceans, and came to an end with a painful gnawing in his heart. Seymour Shtuker now noticed that many things in his home had become redundant. He carried the large leather suitcases down to the basement, and their empty hollowness was a sign of the desolate emptiness in Ogrodovke. Seymour Shtuker stopped shaving, as he'd been accustomed to doing for many years. One could say, he had lost the measure of his life.

His wife, Gossie, reminds him from time to time: "Have a shave. Shave yourself. People are coming to the store after all."

Seymour Shtuker stands in front of the mirror and shaves. He does this only because people come to his store. It is a part of his work, of selling the watches with the small straps, a part of his narrow, little shop in the small town in New Jersey. In his memory, a name is still dangling, a name he doesn't know where to put: Ogrodovke.

The word floods into his thoughts for no apparent reason when he goes to work. It slips into him with a gnawing emptiness in the narrow little store, where Seymour Shtuker sits at a table with his watchmaker's eye-glasses, loupes, and dials. He rotates, repairs, and blows through thin metal springs; the watches begin to live, beating away, tick-tock. The hands of the watches rotate, pretending that there is a measure to their ticking, but Seymour Shtuker knows—it means nothing. He and they will not be arriving anywhere any more. It's an illusion.

Other times, sitting at his work, he remembers Sholem Moishe, the old coachman, with his creaking wagon. He is also gone. And even if Seymour Shtuker were to take a trip to Europe, upon arriving at the train station, there would be no one who could lead him on to the ruins.

November 3, 1946

The Fourth Mitzvah

. . . .

A person couldn't live in this world if it weren't for the bit of goodness he has seen with his own eyes—so Tulia Shor told me. She was sitting on the steps of a large building the way people used to sit on the earthen seats outside their houses in Frampolieh: she looked at the noisy street, at the cars—with the kind of eyes that weren't seeing cars, but sheep coming back from the field; sheep hurrying home because a storm was approaching. She was gray and I thought this meant she was old. And I had probably looked puzzled when I saw her, but she said to me as if I had been an old acquaintance of hers: "Sit down here, what's the big hurry?"

This was the first time in my life that an utter stranger had started speaking to me right out of the blue, and then invited me to sit down.

I sat down next to her.

"Where do you come from?" I asked her.

"I know. But does it matter where a person comes from? From the world. From Frampolieh. I was meant to see America, and it's exactly the same, exactly the same."

"You came to someone here?"

"Came to a son, he took me off the ship, dressed me up like an empress and gave me some dollars. 'I'll give you the same each week,' he said, and he gives."

The dressed-up-like-an-empress was sitting on the steps wearing a red and white checkered cretonne dress.

70

"You're looking at my dress? This is just an old-country dress. I like things from the old country. These shoes are from there, too."

I looked at her shoes. Black, thick shoes.

"He gives me ten dollars a week, my son, every Thursday. Thursday evenings he comes, gives me the money, gives me a kiss, and goes away until next Thursday. I live this way, with his money and a kiss. If it weren't for this goodness I see with my own eyes, I couldn't live."

"Does your son have children?"

She moved her head in a way that didn't mean yes or no. It did mean one thing, however: she didn't want to talk about it.

"And your husband?"

"My husband?"—she pronounced these words with resigned indifference—"and how did I come here? Right after the wedding, my husband left for America. He left; I got letters from him for half a year, and then it was as if he had vanished like a stone in water. I used to spend entire nights not sleeping, just lying in bed and thinking: Where is he? Where in the world was I? What was I to do? My son was born then . . . enough thinking."

She ran both hands over her gray hair.

"Ever since then, I've been gray, not from now. When I was twenty-four, this snow fell . . . until I was helped."

"Helped?"

"Yes, we had a little Tartar in Frampolieh, or so people called him. A Jew; he had a small soap factory. Made soap. The whole town and the nearby villages bought from him. Became rich, the little Tartar. A shortie, he always went around wearing a green jacket and raked in money from the town. Who ever thought about him? Once a year, and sometimes not even that.

"One time at daybreak, I was lying in bed, the child sleeping next to me in his cradle. It was already turning gray—when someone pounded on my window. My window faced the street. Made my heart pound. Maybe my husband had remembered me . . . maybe sent a telegram. I looked at the window. The little Tartar in his green jacket was standing there. I almost spat.[1] What was he doing here? He said to me, the little Tartar: 'Tulia, come over later, I need to talk to you.' And he walked away."

---

1. To spit three times (ptfu, ptfu, ptfu) was a folk custom used to ward off evil.

"I couldn't lie still anymore. I got up, cooked something for the child, cleaned the house, and could barely wait for the sun to come up so I could go over to the little Tartar. His factory stood on a small, narrow street. I arrived; he was wearing his green jacket and was standing on the doorstep.

" 'Good morning,' I say to him, and wait.

" 'Good morning, good year,' he answers, and asks me, 'What do you live on, Tulia?'

" 'Why?' I answer and say no more. Why should I tell the little Tartar a story?

" 'A person has to live on something,' he says to me. 'You can collect money from the shopkeepers for me, and I'll pay you by the week . . . '

"And he handed me a list of his customers, the shopkeepers. I earned the kind of money from him that a fine householder in town would make from a good livelihood. I sewed a dress for myself, and used to go out every day to collect the money. I walked about town like a fine lady, and as for the child—I raised my son. I used to give big donations; supported the Orphan Bride's Society.[2] Was like a cash collector for them. All the money would pass through my hands. I was restored. I tried so many times to find out from the little Tartar why it occurred to him to knock on my window at daybreak, so that I would be restored, but I never could get an answer from him. It was his nature to smoke a pipe. He used to smoke his pipe like a Gentile, and ask me again and again: 'Is it bad working for me?'

" 'God forbid. As good as in paradise, but I'd like to know.'

"Once, nevertheless, I found out. The little Tartar—Kabaner, people called him—took sick. He had a wife somewhere in Galicia, but he lived with his old mother. When he got sick I went over to cook for him, to serve him something, to put a cloth on his head. What wouldn't I have done for him? He like a Messiah for me. He was lying there, feverish, doing the accounts from his soap factory. I asked him with a laugh: 'Pani Kabaner, why did it occur to you to come at daybreak and knock on my window?'

" 'You really want to know, hmm?'

---

2. Hebrew words in Yiddish, this was *khevre hakhnoses kale*, the benevolent society that provided dowries and other monies for orphaned or poor girls.

"When a person is feverish, he can no longer hide things. When a person's head is burning, his tongue is loosened.

"I changed the wet cloth on his head.

" 'Good,' he said, 'good' . . . and he told me a story.

"His mother had had four young sons. He was the fourth. His three brothers all died by the age of thirteen. When he turned twelve, his mother was so afraid, she almost lost her senses. Terrified that something would happen to him. There was a Jewish shoemaker, a jokester, in their town. His mother, Kabaner's mother, goes to the shoemaker to order a pair of shoes for her child for Passover.

" 'At least he should wear them in good health,' she says.

" 'Why not?' says the shoemaker.

" 'At least he should be healthy,' she answers.

" 'Why not, who would prevent him?' the shoemaker says, the way a jokester speaks.

" 'At least he should have a long life.'

" 'Why not?' says the jokester. 'Since when is it a trick to live a long time? It's not a trick at all. You have only to drink a schnapps each day, and do a mitzvah without thanks for it every ten years.' So the shoemaker says, and licks his cobbler's thread. 'Nothing more,' he says, 'there are no tricks in the world. Whoever wants to can live a long life.'

" 'When she got home, my mother made me swear that every ten years I would do a mitzvah without thanks for it. The fourth decade was ending when I knocked on your window. My eyes were opened,' the little Tartar finished, 'and I saved my own feet clomping around collecting money from the stores. It's worth it to me however much I pay you, Tulia.'

"When the little Tartar was better, he asked me once: 'Tulia, perhaps I said something when I was feverish, hmm?'

" 'No, you didn't say anything,' I told him.

" 'Didn't tell you about a little shoemaker?'

" 'What little shoemaker? I don't know anything about that.'

" 'I know that when a person is feverish,' and he smoked his pipe, utterly happy.

"But I had found out the story." Then she gave a start. "Today's Thursday. I have to go. My son will be coming soon, it's Thursday."

I was sorry she was leaving, and just managed to ask, "And what were the three mitzvahs that he did, the little Tartar?"

"What do I need his stories for when I have my own? A person has plenty about himself to tell . . . and Tulia Shor especially so . . . I've seen plenty in my life."

When Tulia Shor stood up, I saw that her red and white checkered dress was not new at all. A little patch was carefully sewn in the pleats, in fine stitches. She noticed that I was looking at her dress and said: "You think I don't have nice dresses. I could be dressed like an empress. It's just that I like things from the old country."

King Solomon's Bride

. . . .

Once when I walking through a small park on the lower East Side, a red and white checkered dress caught my eye. Tulia Shor, I thought. She was standing there, throwing crumbs to the pigeons. I walked over to her.

"My best friends," she said, pointing to the pigeons. "They know me now and even will sit on my hand."

When she had finished tossing all the crumbs, she sat down on a bench, and I sat next to her, not waiting to be asked. She looked at me slyly and said: "The first time we met, I had to ask you to sit down next to me; now you just seat yourself. . ."

"I didn't know you then," I explained.

"Didn't know me, you say? And I know everyone. I see a person, and I know he's either carrying his bundle of worries or they're waiting for him."

"Are you here alone in the park, or with someone?"

"I'm always alone. Already so used to it that it seems to me I'll be sitting alone in Paradise, too. When my son turned fifteen, I rejoiced. I thought that I'd have my son close by me. One time he came up to me—yes, my son, Nakhum—and said, 'The rabbi is calling for you.'

" 'The rabbi?'

" 'Yes, the rebbetzin said to tell you that the rabbi is calling for you.'

"A letter had arrived just then from 'him,' from America, saying that the boy should be sent to him.

"People advised me to do it. One has to do everything for a child—

even cutting a piece of flesh out is not too hard. So I sent him away. After he left, all that remained were heaven, God, and Tulia. Alone. I began spitting blood and went to live in the forest to heal myself. Rented a tiny house, cooked broth for myself, and thought that even that was useless. A person can die only once.

"One time when I was lying down in the evening, there was a storm so bad the house could barely withstand it. The whole forest was moving. The windows, the doors, everything was hanging by a hair. I was lying in bed and thinking just one thing: what's there to fear from a storm? It will carry everything off, and that will be a fine end to it all. That's what I was thinking, when the little house shook and the light went out. I was terrified, nevertheless. I didn't have any matches. It was dark; demons were running over the house so that the blankets were hopping. Suddenly, I heard someone knocking on the door, hard knocks, so one could hear it. Who could've gotten the idea to come on such a ghost-ridden night? Unless he, the culprit himself, may it never happen to you, had come. But someone was knocking; I get up from bed and open the door. Two corners of a head scarf blow in and fly right into my face, and a woman says: 'Good evening.'

" 'Who is it?'

" 'You'll soon see.'

"She lit a match, and I saw the shopwoman, the shopwoman I used to buy sugar or an egg from, everything a sick person needed. She lit the lamp on the table and said to me:

" 'Go back to bed or, God forbid, you'll catch cold. I saw through the window that your light was out, so I brought you a tinder. It's not good to be in the dark on such a terrible night.'

"When I heard this, I nearly lost my breath!

" 'You came for my sake on such a dreadful night?'

" 'I don't know, I was just walking. I know every stone here; there's no danger.'

"The shopwoman said good night and opened the door; the wind pulled her kerchief into two wings, and she was torn away into the whirlwind.

"The storm quieted down that night, but I couldn't sleep. What kind of a shopkeeper was she? To bring matches on such a night? I lay there and thought that my son wouldn't have done it for me; my husband in America, certainly not. What's so bad about being alone? Nothing. I'd just *told* myself that it was bad.

"I could barely wait for morning to go see the shopwoman to find out if the storm hadn't carried her off somewhere that night. Finding her there, standing with a broom and sweeping around her shop, lifted a weight from my heart.

" 'How did you manage to get home last night?'

" 'I managed . . . nothing happened to me.'

"Although she answered like that, I didn't leave. I wanted to find out how it had occurred to her to bring me a package of matches in such a snowstorm. I sat down on the bench under the tree next to her shop and waited.

" 'You need something?' the shopwoman asked.

"It had become uncomfortable to sit there; I bought something and left.

"For Sabbath, her shop would be closed with a little lock, and the shopwoman would lie under the tree, a pillow under her head, and sleep. One Sabbath as I walked by, she was lying under the tree, her eyes wide open.

" 'There's no sleeping,' she says, 'before a rain, it seems. I can never sleep just before a rain. It's suffocating. Sit down for a while, the shade is good here under my tree.'

"I sat myself down and right away I remembered the storm and the matches she had brought to me, and I said to her: 'I ask you, how did it occur to you to bring me matches on such a such a life-threatening night?'

"It seemed that she couldn't sleep; the air really was suffocating. Talking was difficult, but silence worse yet. The shopwoman responded, speaking very simply: 'It was a kind of remembrance for me.'

" 'What do you mean by a remembrance?'

" 'As good as nothing,' she said, 'but I'll tell you now. My father was a flour dealer. An honest Jew, but a hot head. One autumn, he was getting the flour ready, sack upon sack; he'd borrowed the money for it from Jews in town, and so people said there'd be a run on flour that winter. Winter came and there was no stampede. The sacks of flour stood there, but they may as well have been thrown out. My father lost several hundred rubles and went broke. Have you ever seen hungry wolves? That's the way the creditors looked when they came demanding their money. They came running with their wives and their children. My mother stayed in the bedroom, lay in bed and cried. We, the children, got up in the space above the oven [1] and sat as though there were, God forbid, a flood down below. Father remained for the wolves. He sat alone at the head of the table and talked to them, to the creditors: "As God will help me, I'll pay you back. But now, I have only my soul."

" 'The screaming in the house rose to the skies and to the apple orchard behind our courtyard where it was heard by King Solomon's Bride (that's what people called her), a woman who'd lived in the town for many years. She'd arrived when she was still young, with a small child and built a house with a glass-roofed addition. People said she came from the Brotskys. [2] Others said from the Rothschilds abroad, and because she'd had a bastard, the family banished her here to the ends of the earth for ever and ever. She spoke French, she and her child. The chambermaid, Avdotchke, who took care of the child and who worked for King Solomon's Bride, told the whole town that she walked around in her house wearing blue shoes with silver tassels. Once every year for Rosh Hashanah and Yom Kippur, she went back to her rich relatives, and she returned with a big green suitcase packed full of bank notes. She never visited anyone in town. When Bertchick the Coachman brought her registered packages from the train, she asked him for news about the whole town: who had given birth and what the baby was called, who had died, who was rich, and who helped the rabbi decide questions of Jewish law. After this, she gave Bertchick a glass of wine, and then Bertchick had enough stories to tell for weeks on end.

" 'When the creditors, those wolves, were on the rampage in our house, mother fainted in the bedroom. The neighbor women tried to revive her, and Avdotchke ran and brought smelling salts back from King Solomon's Bride. It seemed that she'd told the story over there, how the wolves were gnawing on father who was sitting at the table, whiter than his own flour, how Shayke the Peddler screamed: "What do I know! Except that seventy-

---

1. In Yiddish, *piakalek*, which refers to the space behind or above the large tiled ovens in Eastern European homes. The oven was used both for baking and heating.

2. The Brotskys were a very rich Jewish family, similar to the Rothschilds, in Russia and Ukraine. They made their fortune in sugar.

five rubles should be mine! What do I know!" . . . Suddenly it became quiet in the house, as if someone had covered over all the screaming with a cloth. King Solomon's Bride was up on the porch, in fact, wearing those blue shoes with the silver tassels. When she came into the house, all of the creditors poured into a corner, like sheep that have spotted a wolf. Father stood up and remained standing—mute, speechless.

" 'Tell the people they should come to me Wednesday morning, and my business manager will pay the debts,' was the way she stated it.

" 'Father was still standing there, mute, and King Solomon's Bride looked at the creditors and pronounced between clenched teeth: "But not any more than what is owed you. The bills will come directly into my own hands," and she rapped her finger on the table, which meant that no one could fool her.

" 'Mother revived from the fright. She ran from the bedroom, and started to wander about the dining room, and cried quietly with a melody: "From the fiery lime kiln Thou hast taken me, oh Lord our God." King Solomon's Bride didn't look at her. The people didn't leave. They were standing there, not like creditors, no, just the opposite. They were thanking God they hadn't been asked to leave.

" 'And you will give me a promissory note,' she said to father.

" 'Distractedly, Father began to search for a note in his drawer, found one at last, and with a trembling hand wanted to sign his name.

" 'King Solomon's Bride smiled. "What is your signature worth?" she said. "Let your children sign their names to me, they may have to pay."

" '"Children. Children, come here! Get down from the back of the oven!"

" 'The creditors started coming back to the table, to see how we children would sign the note.

" '"Write in your own language," King Solomon's Bride said.

" 'I was so afraid to sign my name that my teeth were chattering from terror.

" '"You will bring this note Wednesday morning when they come for their money," she said, pointing to the creditors.

" 'King Solomon's Bride wound her way through the house, looking in every room, even the bedroom. Mama followed after her and never stopped saying: "From the fiery lime kiln Thou hast taken me, oh Lord our God . . ."

" 'After she went, the people left without so much as a "good evening," and father went to the prayer house. In the middle of the week, Mama was still sitting, saying women's prayers.[3]

" 'Wednesday morning, father arrived with the promissory note in hand. The business manager never even looked at the note; he simply tore it up and threw it away like it was the smallest scrap of paper.

" 'Mama sent us, the children who had signed the note, to ask when we needed to pay the money.

" 'When we arrived, King Solomon's Bride came over to us. She took hold of me by the tip of my chin. I was the smallest, and she asked me: "Do you want to pay?"

" '"Yes . . ."

" 'She laughed, let go of my chin and said, "When the light goes out for someone, you must bring him a tinder. . ." And she left.

" 'We went home and told father and mother what she had said.

" '"Indeed, she's a jewel of a person, but she speaks somewhat oddly, like a 'may it never happen to you,' kind of person," so Mama said.

"The shopwoman sank into thought, and then she added, 'But I often think about King Solomon's Bride, and when I saw from the window that your light was out during that storm, I had an impulse: if it cost me my life, I had to bring you a tinder. The foolish things one remembers,' she said, and yawned, now truly sleepy.

"I left. After all, it was Sabbath, and the shopwoman was under the tree to sleep, not to tell stories. I hate to bother people," Tulia Shor added.

"And what happened to King Solomon's Bride? The shopwoman never told you?"

"Why do I need to know about King Solomon's Bride? I have plenty of my own stories, believe me. When you sit here in this little park on East Broadway and feed the doves, such unimportant things crop up. But I have

---

3. *Tkhines* are prayers that women said in Yiddish. Men prayed in Hebrew.

to go now, today's Thursday. My son will be coming soon." She shook her head and walked away.

It seems, that on Thursdays she wanders around, Tulia Shor, all over the city. It is easy to meet her on Thursdays. It's a good thing to remember.

The Captain

. . . .

I met Tulia Shor, as usual, at a bench in a little park. She stopped me because I didn't recognize her. She was no longer wearing her red and white checkered dress, but a long black coat from the old country. I could tell by its green baize lining.

"Good to see one another," she stopped me.

I was indeed delighted, just as if she were an old friend of mine, and the truth was—I already knew a lot about her life.

"You know who I met yesterday?" she said to me, and pointed, indicating that I should sit down next to her on the bench.

I sat down. Tulia Shor touched my hand and said: "Listen, maybe you have to go somewhere? Then go. Don't look at me. A person who's alone is always looking for an ear to listen to him. Who knows, maybe you're offended with me? In fact. . ."

"No," I assured her, and asked her to tell me who she had met yesterday.

She pursed her lips so that they were as round as a little wheel and said very quietly: "I met King Solomon's Bride, you hear?"

At that moment, I wondered if Tulia Shor was making up her stories. She was just a woman, an idler, who liked to tell absurdly strange stories, and I asked her: "I ask you, you never saw King Solomon's Bride yourself, how is it you could recognize her?"

Tulia Shor looked at me slyly, from the side, and said: "Oh, you don't believe me either? That's the way it is. If you were to begin telling all the stories about your life, not even your own father would believe you."

"No, God forbid, I believe you." I hid my suspicions quickly. "Really! Where did you meet King Solomon's Bride?"

Tulia Shor stretched out her hand and showed me a finger: "Here you have a witness," she said. "You see my cut finger? Yesterday I went to the pharmacist to get my finger bandaged. As I was standing there, in comes a gray-haired, regal-looking woman in a blue coat and blue shoes, as fine and thin as gloves, you hear? A young man is walking with her and they're speaking French. 'Maman,' he calls her, 'Maman!' It rang a bell for me! King Solomon's Bride. I walked over closer to her and said loud enough for her to hear (I pretended I was reading it from a piece of paper): 'When you see that the light has gone out for someone, you must bring him a tinder.'

"The woman trembled so much that her purse dropped out of her hand. The young man picked up the purse and said something to her in French.

" 'Who are you?' she asked me. Her face had turned completely red.

" 'You wouldn't know me,' I answered her, 'and my name, were I to tell you, wouldn't mean anything to you, but I know who you are. I saw you once, wearing blue slippers with silver tassels, come to the doorstep of the miller, the bankrupt, and you rescued him from the wolves, the creditors. You remember how quiet it became in the house?'

" 'Ah, yes. You do know me,' the woman said.

"There were little tables in the pharmacy. She sat down at one of them and said, 'Sit down next to me. It's a good thing to remember one's youth.'

"She was lost in thought. The redness in her face was gone, and she seemed pale. The young man brought us some sweets. He said something in French and left. I said to her, 'I want you to tell me—although it was many years ago—stories from the past. Even if they're about a person's very own life, they're easy to tell. They don't belong to anyone anymore. Tell me, I'm asking you, why did you rescue the miller then, the bankrupt?'

"King Solomon's Bride was quiet for a little while longer. She took out a white handkerchief, laid it down near her on the table, and then a cigarette holder, a thin one, silver. Slowly, she put a cigarette in the holder and held it, unsmoked, between her fingers. She made these preparations, as if she meant to sit there an entire day.

" 'I see,' she began, 'that you know many stories about me. Maybe even more than I do myself. There, in that place where I spent ten years of my life, when a calf was born, its owner would whisper in its ear right away: "You know, King Solomon's Bride lives here." You think I didn't know that people called me King Solomon's Bride? Bertchick, that no-good, when he was sober would bring me my packages from the train, but when he was drunk would come and tell me all the stories in town about King Solomon's Bride. And stories become mountains, but perhaps you know more about that than I do . . . people said that I was a grandchild of the Rothschilds. But that was just a big lie. My father was simply a rich enough Jew. He got rich because he was a partner in a shipping company on the Black Sea. He was friendly with the Gentiles, his partners, and the fear of his life was: "The Gentiles shouldn't be talking about it." Whatever happened in our house, didn't matter to him. The only thing that mattered was: "What would the Gentiles say?" I was supposed to marry the son of one of his partners, a Christian, whose wife was Jewish, an apostate. Once when he had too much to drink, he said to me, "Deary, except for you, every Jew has a scurfy head,[1] even your own daddy, too . . . and he's the richest of all the partners, the Jew." I didn't allow him to finish. He was drunk, but what he said made me see red. I gave him such a slap that he sobered up in one second. I left the wine-table and, walking away, I said to him: "Every apostate is scurfy, too. Just take a look at your own head." When I got home, they all fell on me—just as you called the creditors—like wolves. My father never ceased ranting: "What will the Gentiles say?" My mother puffed herself up like a turkey and wiped her eyes. She must have used ten handkerchiefs a day. And to make matters worse, I was pregnant. . . . They locked me in my room and told all acquaintances that no one could see me, that I was sick. I lay in bed and I thought about my father's ships, sailing on the Black Sea, and thought that a black misfortune stronger than they were was sailing after them.

A captain worked in the shipping office. That's what people called him, although he wasn't a captain. He was really a middleman. He spoke every language of all the ports on the Black Sea—Greek, Romanian, Turkish,

---

1. The original Yiddish term *parakh* signifies an unpleasant skin condition, probably seborrheic dermatitis, of the scalp and face that was common to people in shtetls and in Eastern Europe at the time. Here it's used as an insult, meaning a disgusting or loathsome person.

French. Was a playboy. For him, unloading a shipload of merchandise and selling it in Greece or Turkey was as easy as drinking a glass of wine. The shipping office considered him a treasure. He was as rich as any of the partners. People used to say that he had a wife in every port, but that he wasn't married to any of them. A bird on the wind.

" 'When I was lying there in bed, shut up in my room, he came in suddenly. He'd asked about me: "Where's Elie?"

" 'My mother had puffed herself up like a turkey again and had become nauseous. My father said that I was sick and no one could see me. The captain could see through that. He sensed a disaster and said, "I want to see Elie, I want to talk to her. . ."

" 'Then my mother dropped her handkerchief and fainted. The captain came into my room. He felt my forehead like a doctor and said, "People are foolish, Elie, just as foolish as your mother." Although he had insulted my mother, I didn't feel like giving him a slap. Just the opposite. His hand on my forehead was warm and good, and he added, "They're so foolish that they don't understand a simple fact—that when the light goes out for someone one must bring him a tinder. What's the matter with you, Elie?"

" 'I told him the story about the slap; I don't know why but I started to cry.

" '"That was good, Elie, good! A good slap!"

" 'He took my hand and kissed it twice. He paced the room, cursing in all the languages he knew, all the while repeating: "A good slap." Then he came over to me and said: "Elie, people talk about me and say that I have ten wives, but that's a lie. I have three all told, and not one of them has ever slapped me. You would be my fourth, but my true wife. Elie, you might give me a slap sometimes, too, but as I am a Jew, I'm worth it. Yes, I'm worth it sometimes. . . ," and he began to laugh loudly and happily—a true bird on the wind.

" 'I told him, "Captain, I have something else to tell you . . ."

" '"You don't have to tell me anything," he said, "I already know all the stories there are to know in the world. I am a Jew, and a Jew knows all the world's stories." He rang the bell and bid the maid serve wine.

" '"Natke, bring some wine for me and my bride!"

" 'He married me in the largest hall in the city, and all the partners came to the wedding, with so much respect that my father stopped ranting, "What will the Gentiles say?"

" 'My former bridegroom and his parents were ruined within four years by the captain. They dealt in hides and the captain couldn't sell their merchandise. The hides were dragged around to stations from city to city. Within four years, the partnership dissolved.

" 'I didn't want to travel with him on his trips. A favor, that kind of favor, a person should accept but then not flaunt. I asked him to build me a house in a remote town, somewhere among fields and rivers and poor Jewish people.'

"She lit her cigarette, smoked and was silent. Then she finished her story.

" 'When Avdotchke came running to get smelling salts for the miller's wife and told me that she was lying in the bedroom, too afraid to see the creditors, I remembered how I'd been lying shut up in my room, my family afraid to let anyone see me—and then I ran to save her.'

"The young man who spoke French returned. She gave me her hand and said,'Don't think too often about our old King Solomon and his bride,' and she left. I hadn't asked her her real name, and I still don't know it. The shopwoman never told me either. Still, in any case, the name suits her: she could have been King Solomon's Bride."

Tulia Shor finished her story. She was greatly moved and added: "I tell you, one small seed of goodness can sow a forest, and if a person didn't know this, didn't see it with his own eyes, didn't hear it with his own ears, he couldn't live through a single day."

Tulia Shor again remembered that her son would be coming soon; it was a Thursday, and, as always, she shook her head and left.

May 1943

Charter Members

· · · · · · · ·

M r. William Indelman and his wife, Blanche, were very unhappy with the meeting of the Grushkove Society. While they were eating, Mr. Indelman never stopped talking.

"Now he's what you call a thick blockhead, that Applebaum. Popnick, he mentions, but *me* he forgets to mention! What has Popnick ever done for our Society? I ask you. Nothing. He comes to a meeting and drinks a cup of coffee. Popnick is just smart enough to be first to clap bravo when Applebaum speaks. Puts his two thick little palms together and claps. And for this he deserves a medal? Have you ever heard anything like it, how he praises Popnick to the skies? 'Our very, very dear and beloved landsman, Reb Shimon Popnick!' That Popnick can barely sign his name with an X. How does he come to be called a Reb? I ask you, how does he come to be called a Reb?"

Blanche saw that red spots had popped out on her husband's forehead. She wanted to calm him down and said, "How's that your worry? Just because Applebaum calls him Reb Shimon Popnick, does that make him a Reb? Or his taxes will be lowered because of it? How's that your worry?"

The two families, the Indelmans and the Applebaums had been friends for as long as they could remember. Mr. Indelman and Mr. Applebaum were both born in Grushkove and had been neighbors in the old country. Mr. Indelman was the son of a cantor, and Mr. Applebaum the son of a butcher, but here in America, their family pedigrees evened out. For Purim, the Applebaums went to the Indelmans' to eat hamantashen because Blanche was

87

a specialist in hamantashen. For Hannukah, the Indelmans went to the Applebaums for latkes, because Mrs. Applebaum's latkes tasted like paradise. When Mr. Indelman was busy on Sundays with business matters, Mrs. Indelman went to the movies with the Applebaums; and just the opposite, when Mr. Applebaum was away traveling for several days, Mrs. Applebaum went to a restaurant with the Indelmans, and they never let her pay. Even their children, Abe and Morris, who were almost the same age, grew up like brothers. They went to summer camp together, played dominos together, and read the funnies together.

But the closer it got to Sukkos, a cool wind blew, not only outdoors, but also between the Indelmans and the Applebaums. The Grushkove Society elections were held in the week of Sukkos, and that week was not a time for friendship.

Even before Rosh Hashanah, people from the Grushkove Society began to spread stories: Indelman said that Applebaum wasted the Loan Fund's money and didn't even get any return on it. Applebaum told how Indelman had had the local hall painted four times and the walls were still spotted. So much for the painter he'd chosen. In half a day's time, they knew the stories at the Indelmans' and at the Applebaums'. The Rosh Hashanah exchange of good wishes between the two families came out rather cold. And they grew accustomed to being satisfied by sending each other a printed card with a dove on it and the standard greeting: *l'shona tovah tikoseyvu*. During election time, Indelman always remembered that Applebaum's father had been a butcher, and that he—Mr. Applebaum, even though he was very successful here—was still a butcher-boy, as his father had been, a couple of calf shanks.

The more Mr. Indelman talked about the meeting, the angrier he became. "You've ever heard of such coarseness from a butcher-boy—not to mention me? However, I am a charter member! I built the Society! Levin he mentions! Why? Levin brought in a new member—Feffer! That Feffer comes to a meeting once in a blue moon. He makes the Society any happier with Feffer? Fine, fine, fine, and then suddenly, the calf shanks creep out."

That night, Mr. Indelman couldn't sleep. He kept remembering how much work he'd put in scraping money together for the Loan Fund, in searching for the picture of the Grushkove synagogue that was now hang-

ing on the wall of the Local; how he had knocked the Society together out
of splinters, and now they'd forgotten to mention him.

Blanche woke up several times and said to him, sleepily, "Let him go to
hell! Lie down and go to sleep!" And soon her nose and mouth were swallowing the air in such sleepy pleasure that her husband envied her.

The next day, Mr. Applebaum and his wife, Ida, dropped in at the Indelmans unexpectedly. They missed Blanche's coffee, so they said, and had
stopped by.

Mr. Indelman was incensed when he heard the butcher's voice in the
hall. They sat with their coffee and were silent. Blanche served snacks and
sweets at the table and carried extra dishes back and forth. She kept as busy
as she could to save herself the torture of the silence. All the while, she kept
looking at her husband, warning him not give way to his fury. But it didn't
help. Mr. Indelman fixed a pair of fiery eyes on Applebaum, and out of a
clear sky, asked him: "Tell me, Borukh, what has Popnick done for our Society? List his accomplishments for me! Go ahead. Maybe I'm blind and can't
see. Maybe I'm deaf and can't hear! Maybe I'm lame and can't think . . .
maybe. . ."

Blanche stopped him. "So maybe it's enough already with listing your
virtues? A blind man, a deaf man, a lamebrain! Enough!"

Mr. Applebaum heaved himself up from his chair like a bear going to
break down a tree. "So I forgot to mention your name; should I be punished
for this? It was so noisy; this one pesters you and that one . . . a man is only
a man! I could have sworn that I *did* mention you! Ida said to me: 'How come
you forgot to mention Indelman?' Can you believe it? So, the world isn't
going to end because of this. Understand me, Velvel, I simply forgot. . ."

Blanche supported him: "Well, it's already been done! People love to be
mentioned . . . it shouldn't be that way, but never mind, everyone remembers it in his own way. . ."

Mr. Applebaum raised himself with difficulty, sat back down in his
chair, and began anew: "I could have sworn . . . Ida told me . . . and if you
want, ask Itzkhok-Noteh what I said about you at the meeting . . . just out
of curiosity, ask Itzkhok-Noteh . . . here's his telephone number—ask
him. . ."

Like a bear breaking the first twig on a tree, Mr. Applebaum wheezed,

pulled out a piece of paper and a pencil, and wrote Itzhok-Noteh's telephone number. (Before the elections, he had all the *landsleit* telephone numbers learned by heart.) "Just out of curiosity, ask Itzkhok-Noteh. . ."

They drank up their coffee, ate some nuts, and Mr. Applebaum shook
Mr. Indelman's hand good-naturedly: "Velvel, we're old friends, and we'll
remain friends . . . let's forget it. . ."

Mr. Indelman's hand was as cold as if he had just arrived from Siberia.

Walking back from the Indelmans', Mr. Applebaum said to his wife, "It's
good that he's in a huff! Remember the banquet for Rabinovitch that Indelman planned? There weren't enough seats for us at the head table! Remember how we had to sit over in a corner by the windows? We survived it. Let
him see how it feels to be on the other side of the door for once! I, too, had
to forget!. . ."

Ida encouraged him: "It's not such a bad thing! It'll be a good lesson for
him!"

When the guests were gone, Blanche took the note with Itzhok-Noteh's
number and laughed: "Here's a remedy for you! Go call Itzkhok-Noteh." But
a second later, she stopped laughing and called her husband. "Velvel . . .
here on the other side of this note . . . all the names that he mentioned."

Mr. Indelman went over to her and read the names: "Rabinovitch,
Levin, Popnick, Eshman; and Indelman is crossed out! You see? Crossed
out! Plain and simple. No Indelman, you understand! None."

For a while, Indelman looked at the note, as if it contained a secret mes-
sage. He even felt it with his finger. Then he said, "I'm going to send it back
to him. Let him chew on it."

He called his son. "Abe, take this note back to Mr. Applebaum and put
it into his hand yourself. Tell him . . . tell him . . . 'My father is sending this
back to you.' "

The blowup happened two days after Rosh Hashanah; on Yom Kippur,
they didn't even exchange wishes. Electioneering was in full swing.

At the annual meeting, held during the regular work days of Sukkos,
the Grushkover *landsleit* were in a fever. Mr. Indelman and Mr. Applebaum
who held the Society in their hands and who were guiding its future, were
both as strained as cannon barrels before a battle. Mr. Indelman spoke to

the *landsleit*: "Who are we now, the Grushkover *landsleit*? Alas. There's nothing more left of Grushkove. . ."

The Grushkovers' hearts trembled. All of them felt like orphans, even though they were Jews with businesses, with children and grandchildren.

Mr. Indelman said to them, "Indeed, we need to be among our own, be a little closer, more like family, brotherly."

The Grushkovers heard him and were grateful.

Mr. Indelman continued: "Our dear, dear landsman, Mr. Applebaum, has said golden words about Popnick—a very dear, worthy landsman, Reb Shimon Popnick, a modest man, a quiet man. He will be a good president, and he deserves it; indeed, he deserves it! I know that you'll agree with me. I am a charter member and I know that we're making a good match[1] for the Society with Popnick."

The Grushkovers' warmed hearts grew even warmer.

"Indeed, let Popnik be president—a quiet man, not a big shot." People, almost with tears in their eyes, clapped bravo.

When the meeting was over, and Popnik was elected president, Mr. Indelman walked over to Mr. Applebaum and said to him: "I think this is exactly the right thing to do. He's deserving of it! Why shouldn't he be president?"

Both men, Mr. Indelman and Mr. Applebaum, were red, blazing—Mr. Applebaum from chagrin and Mr. Indelman from the sweet feeling of quiet revenge: You wanted Popnik? So now you've got Popnick! The calf shanks have been cut down to size.

For Hannukah, the Indelmans went over to the Applebaums' for Ida's latkes. The two charter members chatted together about the president of their Society.

"Such a president we have—no feet, no hands, no brains. But, thank God, he still wears a hat.[2] It was your idea," Mr. Applebaum said to Mr. Indelman, with a dig.

---

1. Molodowsky used the word *shidekh*, which signifies a match made for a bride and groom but can also mean any match of like characters, personalities, and so forth.

2. "Still wears a hat" is a reference to the fact that Popnick is observant; he keeps his head covered, as an observant Jew does.

Mr. Indelman actually rose from his chair. "You were the one who praised him up one end and down the other! Since you praised him, maybe you knew something I didn't, so I nominated him for president."

Ida served the latkes. This time, they were even better than last year, crispy brown on both sides, a pleasure for the eyes and for the mouth—the taste of paradise.

March 6, 1955

Family Life

. . . .

As Paul Orens was driving his car, he was thinking about his wife, Julia, with whom he had just quarreled. He was so irritated that he couldn't keep still and talked quietly to himself, giving voice to all the insults that he had not said to his wife: "What is Julia? She's the yardstick of my earnings. When business is good, she smiles and calls me darling. But let it slow down a little, and she becomes a block of wood, a real block. Shuffles around in her bedroom slippers and won't talk. The nerve of that block of wood—to serve me cold coffee. What's this? Hot coffee's too expensive? No! It was meant as an insult . . . serving me cold coffee. And her answer is: 'Get a maid—she'll give you hot coffee.' "

In fact, the moment Julia had said to him: "Get a maid. She'll give you hot coffee," Paul was filled with an immense desire to serve his cup of coffee to her right on her slippers (these slippers were the focus of his resentment), but he had controlled himself. He had stood up and left the house without saying good-bye.

"She has plenty to eat," Paul Orens said to his steering wheel, "she can buy a dress any day [1] she wants. She's not short of anything. She has everything she needs here for the children. But the yardstick has already taken her measure: when it's a little slow, I get cold coffee."

Now it was hard for him to drive. The car, as if to spite him, banged

---

1. In the original Yiddish, "any day" was "Mondays and Thursdays." Traditionally, these were days Torah was read, but the phrase has come to mean "often," sometimes ironically.

several times, as though something had come unscrewed in the tires, and Paul blamed Julia for the car, too: "Drag myself across the towns in an old car to sell televisions, radios, broilers, troubles, headaches. Collect payments, carry the accounts, work like a horse, listen to the car clattering—and drink cold coffee."

He stopped at a gas station. A young man danced cheerfully around his car, washing the windshield, looking for all the world as if to say that this was giving him the greatest of pleasure, said "Yes sir" to Paul several times, looked at the engine and checked the air in the tires. Because of the young man's cheerfulness, Paul's anger dissolved, as though someone had washed it away along with the dust from his windshield.

As he was leaving the gas station, he realized he was hungry and remembered that along with the cold coffee, he had also left the roll. He'd had only one bite of it—and he stopped at a luncheonette to eat.

"Hot coffee!" he ordered from the waitress—and she seemed like an angel when she answered him with a smile: "Sure!"

Now there's a real person for you—he thought about the waitress—and what do I get? Cold coffee and bedroom slippers?!

Paul arrived at the small town of Sunnyhill, where he had several steady customers. He decided to make life easy for himself this time—he'd stop by the Shmidts first. There was never any haggling with them and they made their payments on time. Theirs was a house where he could always relax—and if a man had become a little unstrung, the most reasonable thing to do would be to go to the Shmidts. Mrs. Shmidt was a good-natured, polite person, and didn't greet him as a salesman but as a friend, served him refreshments, and never forgot, when he was leaving, to say: "Take care of yourself." Even her hair was always done up with pins as if she were ready to go to a wedding—adding overall comfort and cheer to the house.

The truth is that it's better to go to people like the Shmidts at the end of a day, when a person is already tired of dickering with the customers, and finish the work day humanely, without heartache. But today—today he would treat himself—and he turned his car to go to the Shmidts.

Paul rang the doorbell, but no one answered. Well, there you have it—he thought and remained standing as if insulted. When something doesn't go your way, nothing else does either.

He drove to the Shapiros. This was the only family in Sunnyhill where it was hard to sell anything, either by talking or bargaining; but they were prompt with their payments, along with their complaints. The last time he sold the Shapiros a television set, he'd given it away cheap, with only a small percentage for himself. Each time Mrs. Shapiro paid him the installments, she complained to him. Not about the television set (the television worked well), but about the programs.

"Oh! What do you get from a television? Last night, I watched and watched, but there was nothing to see."

Mrs. Wells, to whom Paul had sold a mirror, greeted him with a reproach: "You know, Mr. Orens, the mirror you sold us cracked."

Mrs. Wells wasn't lazy, and she led him into the children's room where the mirror was hanging, took it down from the wall, and showed him the left corner: here it is, this is a "damage," a real "damage." . . .

The complaints lay heavily on Paul this day with the "damages," with the difficult dunning for money. The heaviness depressed him, was excessive, and wore him out.

He decided to try the Shmidts one more time. He would go there and unwind. Incidentally, he was stubborn in this way—at least he could accomplish one thing on this unlucky day, at least one thing should turn out the way he wanted. And he drove over to the Shmidts.

Mrs. Shmidt opened the door for him, but he hardly recognized her. There wasn't a single hairpin in her hair. She had a bathrobe on and was actually wearing bedroom slippers. Paul noticed the slippers first thing.

"What's the matter, Mrs. Shmidt? Aren't you feeling well?" he asked her with sincere concern, and took her hand like she was an old friend.

Mrs. Shmidt was moved by his sympathy, and she said to him, "Worse than sick, Mr. Orens, worse than sick . . . a crazy day . . . there's nowhere to turn."

She took a handkerchief out of her pocket, a sign that she was ready to cry, but she didn't cry. Instead, she firmly wiped her mouth. She wasn't wearing any lipstick, which made her look even older and sadder.

"Yes, Mr. Orens . . . my Harry is the nicest man on the block—everyone says so. . ."

"You know, I think so, too," Paul murmured, "a very fine man. . ."

Mrs. Shmidt dragged herself slowly over to a chair and sat down, as though it were hard for her to stand.

"Yes," Mrs. Shmidt said, "a fine man, but this morning he was crazy. He slammed the door and ran out of the house like it was on fire. And why, you ask? Because of a silly thing. I'm ashamed to tell you. He's in a hurry in the mornings. A job is a job, and a person can't be late. Well, he's nervous. He slams the door and is gone. What is a wife? A tied-up dog! I can't slam the door. The children are coming back from school, the exterminator has to come today, and here you've arrived. A house is a house, but my husband slams the door. Suddenly, everything is too much for a person. Go wipe the dust from the mirrors, but my Harry is a fine man. Nevertheless, he doesn't understand this, he slams the door! It's so coarse, worse than if he'd hit me over the head with a stick, and he doesn't understand this. He's a fine man, but all day long that door slam has been ringing in my ears. And I can't do anything right. Clean the floors, and bake cookies, sort the wash for the laundry. . ."

It seemed that sorting the laundry was the most bitter reminder for Mrs. Shmidt. She took out her handkerchief and this time, she really began to cry.

"Excuse me, Mr. Orens, you've just arrived, but sometimes a person just can't help it."

Her tears fell rapidly and were little and sweet, just like her sweet little work in the house, that was now too much for her.

"And the whole quarrel happened because of a cup of coffee. Just imagine, Mr. Orens, because of a cup of coffee. Well, how can a person be so rude? Because of such a trifle? It's an insult!"

Paul Orens stood up. All his sympathy for Mrs. Shmidt disappeared. Maybe you're a yardstick too, just like my own wife, he thought, and said to her: "Cheer up, Mrs. Shmidt, and good-bye." He smiled and left.

Driving home, Paul stopped at the same luncheonette he had been to in the morning. He wanted to see the waitress, who was as good as an angel and had served coffee with a sweet, young smile and a happy "sure." But the waitress wasn't there. Instead of her, a man was working, a man with wild whiskers and a serious face, who looked as though the world were on the verge of being upended. He served the coffee without a "sure," without a word, as if he knew that serving was a thing one didn't do lightly.

"Where is the young lady who was working here this morning?" Paul asked the waiter.

"She worked her eight hours, and she left," the waiter answered matter-of-factly, and then added, a little resentfully, "Everyone asks about the young lady. A woman can be as dumb as a bottle of beer, but she can still wind everyone around her little finger. . ."

This was Paul's feeling exactly, and he replied: "Right as gold. You can say that again."

"That's the way it is," the waiter raised his eyebrows like someone who says: you can't fight the laws of nature.

Downhearted, Paul drove home. Making it up with Julia seemed like a mountain standing before him, what with her complaints and her slippers. It was a sad time for him. But as he drove by a flower shop, the thought occurred to him: I'll buy her some flowers! Yes. Yes, she deserves it, she's probably cried as much as Mrs. Shmidt . . .

He bought the best roses, a whole dozen.

When Paul got home, Julia was lying in bed, pretending to sleep. The children, Miriam and Judy, were walking around on tiptoe, in their pajamas, and said to their father: "Mama doesn't feel good."

"I know," he answered them tersely.

He went over to Julia, put his hand on her head, and said to her, just as he had to Mrs. Shmidt: "Cheer up, Julia!"

Julia raised her head, ready to start crying.

"This is for you," Paul said, and Julia saw the flowers in his hand. Her eyes opened wide in surprise, and she smiled.

"You're crazy!" she said, paying him a joyful compliment.

She danced around in her slippers and ran to put the flowers in a vase. Now they were different slippers. Even the pompoms were dancing, as though they thought the flowers were for them, too, and that they had missed flowers for a long time.

Paul told Julia everything that he'd heard from Mrs. Shmidt, except for those things that didn't suit him: because of a trifle, it wasn't worth the bother . . . it was unseemly for adults to behave that way.

Happily, Julia called the children: "Judy, Miriam! Come and see the flowers your father has brought!"

The girls, in their pajamas, came running, smelled the flowers, shrieked, pushed each other and overturned the vase, but no one got mad at them: the bold beautiful roses were a reminder that the world can still bloom here, withstand rains and storms, and bloom.

March 1955

In a Living Room
. . . .

I f Mr. Kasher could have gotten rid of just one word in the English language, he would have banished the word *funny.* He'd have paid a thousand dollars to do it, and it would have been money well spent. And it was
all because his wife with the three names, Hinde-Bayle-Helen, steered her
house with the word *funny,* like a captain at the helm of his ship.

Helen had taken the photographs of the beloved people, who looked
out of their frames with such Sabbath calm, down from the walls of their
house. His mother, her hands folded; his aunt Tillie, a bouquet of flowers on
her lap.

Helen said, "Funny," took the photographs down, and in their place
hung up something that would at least be more suitable! And that was simply a picture of a bird with a long tail of blue feathers, then a bird with flap-
ping yellow wings, and in fact a third bird with a little crown on its head.
She had read in a magazine that birds were in style and each house needed
at least three birds.

With the same word, *funny,* Hinde-Bayle-Helen carried off the case of
books, the inheritance that remained from her father-in-law, and put a small
credenza with glassware in its place.

Mr. Kasher considered the walls of his house and amiably, without any
anger, God forbid, began a conversation with his wife. "Tell me, Helen"—
in a pleasant conversation he called her Helen, and Hinde-Bayle when they
were having words—"tell me, Helen, how, in fact, is that bird with the blue
tail any more beautiful than my Aunt Tillie? Aunt Tillie had a truly regal

beauty. Her silk dress glistened down from the picture, and furthermore, she was saintly and wise. When she looked at me out of her picture with those wise eyes while I was drinking my morning coffee, there was meaning and good taste. Make it clear to me, Helen, how is that bird more important, and why does my Aunt Tillie have to give up her place to it?"

Mrs. Kasher shrugged her shoulders and said, "Funny," as if to say, how could one compare Aunt Tillie to a bird? "Aunt Tillie is Aunt Tillie and a bird is a bird. Once, it was the style to have photographs of people, and now it's the style to have birds. I'd like things to be as they should be for us. People don't have to be funny. You know?"

Aunt Tillie went to lie on a shelf in a closed cupboard. Next to her, squeezed in a corner, were standing the photographs of Uncle Sholem Itzkhok with his wife, Baylke, with their four daughters, who were, in fact, called Sarah, Rebecca, Rachel, and Leah, with their husbands, Berl, Yehudah Leyb, Alter, and Tsalie, and the grandchildren, eleven grandchildren, *keyn eyn hore.* The youngest, Leah's daughter, dressed up in little white socks, was lying on her grandmother Baylke's lap. A beautiful regal family, like a forest, with children like doves, was standing, dusty and displaced, next to the photograph of Aunt Tillie, which was lying sadly face down, the back of the picture up—while in Mr. Kasher's living room, the pictures of birds from Africa and India and who knows where else were arranged—a miracle no one had to buy birdseed for them.

Mr. Kasher wasn't the only one who missed the photographs. So did their four-year-old son, Semek, who was in fact named after Uncle Sholem Itzkhok. The four-year-old Semek already knew each person in the photographs by name, their relationship to him, how the photographs had come over on a ship, why they were hanging on the wall. Semek didn't like the birds; he missed the people and the stories about them.

The case of books, that was the inheritance from Mr. Kasher's father, wasn't any easier for Helen until she got them out of the living room.

On the eve of Passover when Mr. Kasher returned home from having had a shave and a haircut, in a joyful holiday mood and ready to sit down for the Seder, his wife, Helen, aglow, met him at the door and announced her news. "Go to the living room, you won't recognize it! It's so beautiful; it's a pleasure!

Even before he went in, Mr. Kasher's heart told him that the case of books was gone, and he said to Helen, "Of course, there's already been a pogrom in there. . ."

From his plain, hard words, a dark cloud rolled over the shining home that was readied for Passover. Mr. Kasher looked at the glass display case with the knick-knacks, little vases, little creamers, little pots, and little pitchers that were shimmering in various colors and glittering in the living room where the case of religious books had stood before. A longing took hold of him for the old brown case with its four-cornered glass panes that had stood there for so many years, and for the old religious books with the rubbed-off Yiddish letters on their spines, that stood there like old devoted watchmen, who stand and guard and ask for no payment.

Surprising even himself, he said to Helen, agitated, "I won't lead the Seder! I don't need glass idols in my house!"

"Funny," Helen murmured, but she didn't have the courage to say more.

"I won't lead the Seder!" Mr. Kasher repeated, and he felt that now, at last, he held the upper hand over his wife and over her word. Like a person who feels the sweetness of taking revenge, he said to Helen, "You think that it was for these glass rags that Moses our Teacher led the Jews out of Egypt? Parted the sea for them? You think too few people were drowned? It was in vain that he led them through thunder and lightning to Mt. Sinai? Forty days of not eating and not drinking, forty years of wandering in the desert, in the sands, with tiny children and with no bread and no nothing, in de-filed places, and wild animals and lions! You think he did that for the sake of glass idols?"

From his deepest innermost being, a spring of both yearning and re-sentment gushed out of Mr. Kasher, words he hadn't heard in years and had never thought about until now, when they poured out so easily from his mind and off his tongue.

"Wars were fought and people died and he caused water to gush out of a stone. And you think he did it for these glass trinkets?"

Helen stood there, frightened. For the first time in her life, she felt that Passover was a ruthless holiday. So awesome and holy a holiday, that even in her own living room, not so much as a hair could be moved. She felt guilty, deeply culpable, that she had disturbed the Passover holiday, and, as always when she felt guilty, she said to her husband, "You're right, Archie, you're right. Tomorrow, believe me, tomorrow morning, I'll bring back the books from the basement. But right now, please lead the Seder. Sylvia is coming with her husband and with Julke. Tomorrow morning, you'll see, tomorrow. . ."

Sylvia brought wine for the Seder, and Julke asked the four questions.

Helen didn't mention the new glass display case, and she winked at Sylvia not to ask. The case was standing there like evidence of idolatry; no one would look at it, but it would still be a shame to smash it up.

A couple of times, Mr. Kasher mentioned the books that needed to be brought up and put in their place. Helen was silent. She'd made no more promises, but once she sniffed: "Funny, everyone else has a glass case, why can't we?"

"Funny," Mr. Kasher repeated the word like a defeated man. The word was stronger than he was and he didn't know how to overcome it.

The birds on the wall were silent, like stern watchmen guarding their gains.

July 13, 1947

A Long Journey

. . . .

Ever since Yidl the Horsedealer built his house with its high, second-story across the street from Reb Shimon Bronshtein's house, Chava, Reb Shimon's wife, stopped sitting on her porch.

Reb Shimon Bronshtein's house, with its wide windows facing the street, with the two old oak trees on either side of the porch, commanded great respect for itself. And when Chava, Reb Shimon's wife, sat on her porch in the summer under the thick shade of the oak trees, the heat couldn't get at her. The Bronshteins were very rich and their family pride was even greater, and the thick shade of the oak trees that fell on half the street drew a border around their house and announced: don't mix with us, we are the Bronshteins.

Unexpectedly, Yidl the Horsedealer bought a small piece of land exactly opposite the Bronshtein's house, and on that small plot whistled up a two-story house that was in fact taller than the Bronshteins'. When that happened, the street and her porch were no longer places for Chava. She didn't sit there any more.

On summer evenings, a bright lamp could be seen in the second story of Yidl the Horsedealer's house, and the sound of a gramophone could be heard. Then Chava would carry a soft chair out the back door and sit in her garden. She called her daughter Goldele to come to her: "There's nothing to see at the horsedealer's."

One night, Arke, Yidl the Horsedealer's son, came galloping up on a gray horse, leaped down so lightly that he barely touched the ground, and

103

stood there. He patted the horse cheerfully on its neck, and the horse raised its head as if hearing music. Both Arke and his horse were hand-some—they could have been painted in a picture.

Chava saw Goldele standing at the window, not taking her eyes off Arke. Goldele had stretched her head out the window and her lips were moving as if she wanted to call to him. Chava was almost frightened. Gold-ele . . . she was pressed to the window as if she were stuck to it. Chava went over to her and said hastily: "What are you looking at there?"

"Nothing, I'm looking at the street. . ."

"Don't you dare look, you hear?"

Goldele left the window. She cast her eyes down, as if she were carry-ing resentment away.

Goldele was sent from Zahaike to Brisk to study.

"It won't hurt a girl of fifteen to study a little. I won't have her carrying on any 'romances' with the horsedealers," Reb Shimon Bronshtein said, and his wife, Chava, added, "Much better, better than, God forbid . . . we don't need Yidl the Horsedealer for an in-law. . ."

The moment his wife uttered the word "in-law," Reb Shimon was struck with a fever and hastily opened the window. Chava understood she had said a word too much, and there were no more conversations about the "horsedealers" at the Bronshteins' house.

For Passover, Goldele returned home wearing a brown dress with a black apron, the uniform of the school where she studied. As she drove into town, the first thing she saw was the second story of Arke's house. A pink early-morning spring light lay mysteriously and warmly on the high roof. Goldele felt that the pink warmth on Arke's second story could melt the snow.

During the holiday, Goldele went to see the water flowing in the river, the Zahaike. She was standing, leaning on the railings of the wooden bridge when Arke came up to her.

"I knew that you would be here, Goldele," he said to her.

She was silent. She knew that he would be here, too.

They both stood and looked at the Zahaike, wide and rushing, as wide and rushing as Goldele's happiness that Arke was standing next to her.

"You're leaving after Passover, Goldele?" he asked.

"They're sending me away to study," she said, and her eyes were so full of tears it seemed they could flow like the Zahaike, springlike and beautiful.

Arke never forgot Goldele's springlike eyes.

They crossed the bridge and left by way of a path beyond the town. A gentle Passover wind sang in their ears as if they themselves were singing. Arke took her hand and said, "Goldele . . . we will be married, remember what I'm saying to you!" His eyes were hot as the spring sun.

Goldele never forgot his sunny eyes.

In town, people said that Goldele Bronshtein and Arke the Horsedealer's son had gone for a walk behind the town and that they had agreed to run away.

On the last day of Passover, her mother came into Goldele's room and sat down on her bed.

"Daughter," she said to Goldele, pointing to the bright lamp that was burning in Yidl the Horsedealer's second-story window, "your father can't bear the shame. He's weak, and he can't bear it. You hear, daughter?"

She heard. Each word fell like a stone on her sixteen-year-old head, and she cried.

After Passover, when Goldele had to return to Brisk, and her suitcase was already packed, she went to her mother and said, "I don't want to go to Brisk. I don't want to learn when Napoleon died."

Chava trembled.

"Who died?"

"Napoleon died, a French king. . ."

Chava calmed down about Napoleon, but her trembling didn't cease. The second story with its bright lamp was standing across from her, like a lion ready to devour Goldele and the Bronshteins' house.

Reb Shimon Bronshtein wrote a long letter to his younger brother in America. He wrote that they needed nothing, God forbid, except luck. He would send a dowry with Goldele, several thousand rubles, and all that a bride needed. She had to be sent out of the country. She had met with a disaster. She had eyes only for the horsedealers.

Goldele was sent to Brisk to study and from there to America to see the family. When she was already on the train from Zahaike to Brisk, Arke came to the station and stepped up onto it. Like a thirsty person looking for a drink of water in the desert, he ran through all the train cars and stood across from Goldele.

"Arke!"

They sat next to each other. The wheels of the train rushed, singing like the roaring spring river Zahaike.

"When will you come back, Goldele?"

"They're sending me to America. My father—he's weak. . ." Goldele didn't finish. She said no more.

The Zahaike overflowed its banks and flooded the world.

At the Brisk station, they got off and said good-bye. Arke took Goldele in his arms and held her closely for a while. He kissed her and looked at her, devouring her with his eyes. His eyes were deep, dark, and serious.

In America, Goldele was married to her cousin, Irving Bronshtein. Her father, Reb Shimon Bronshtein and his brother, Benjamin Bronshtein, had come to an agreement about the dowry, and Irving opened a sweater factory. The factory was called Extra, and the business prospered. Irving was a cheerful man. He taught Goldele how to dance, he taught her English, and she loved him. But somewhere faraway, there remained a rushing river, and a spring sun shining above that river. This she did not know how to transfer to her husband, to Irving.

Goldele heard something about Arke, that he was in Belgium in the diamond business. Later, she heard, he was in America and owned garages in Los Angeles. He had been divorced twice. By chance, she would hear news of him, just as by chance a leaf from a tree comes in through an open window. A hint of greenery moves one's heart for a while and then passes into oblivion.

Goldele's father-in-law, Benjamin Bronshtein, went with his entire family to the Zahaike Society's twenty-fifth jubilee. With him came his "estate"—his three sons, his daughters-in-law, and his grandchildren. Benjamin Bronshtein had something to show off: one son had insurance offices, Bronshtein and Company; the second had a big business, Books and Pictures; and Irving, his Extra factory. Not such a bad business, either. The Bronshteins took up an entire table. They rushed and sang and enjoyed themselves with all the Zahaikers.

"It's lively at the Bronshteins'," the Zahaikers said, and went over to have a little drink. Sitting at the lively table, Goldele remembered the two shady oak trees whose heavy leaves rustled over their porch in Zahaike when there was the least little wind. And just as if out of the thick recesses of her memory, Arke emerged. He stood next to her with two full glasses in his hands and she heard his voice, as before: "Goldele . . . l'chaim. . ."

"Arke!"

Goldele felt his eyes, deep, dark and serious, the same as when he had said good-bye to her at the Brisk train station. Arke, as if he were listening to her memory, said to her, "You have the same eyes, Goldele."

They barely spoke. Just remembered the twenty-five years they hadn't seen each other. She introduced him to Irving and to her two daughters, Bobbie and Bessie, whose young faces, with their mother's eyes, were aglow.

Driving back, Irving wanted to know who the man was who had toasted her: "Goldele . . . l'chaim." Irving had heard how gently the stranger had uttered his wife's name, "Goldele."

She answered, "A neighbor . . . from Zahaike," but she felt that Irving didn't believe her.

Irving never wanted to go to any more Zahaike Society events.

The Bronshteins' lively table had been give the evil eye, or so old Benjamin Bronshtein said. One year later, Books and Pictures went bankrupt, and one son was impoverished. Irving, Goldele's husband, took sick. He went from hospital to hospital, and four years later he died of a bone disease. Goldele couldn't forget Irving's glance that last day in the hospital. He had had an almost childlike expression in his eyes, grieving, with a reproach, as though people owed him a debt he could never collect.

For many nights, she couldn't sleep. She kept seeing Irving's sad eyes and felt herself guilty before him.

Goldele married off her two daughters, Bobbie and Bessie, and she remained alone in an empty house with silk curtains and empty beds. In the evenings she would sometimes remember Zahaike, and the two oak trees over the porch, and their thick shade that had fallen so heavily over her life.

Alone, without her daughters, and wearing a simple gray dress, she once went to a Zahaiker event. A person should put lonely days aside somewhere, she thought, getting ready to go. She justified much to herself as if she were doing something wrong in going.

She left her coat in the cloak room, stood by the banister, and looked at the arriving crowd. Whom could she approach? She hadn't seen the *landsleit* for so long. Unless . . . unless . . . perhaps . . . she was ashamed to think about Arke.

"It's drafty in here, Goldele," she heard, and she knew that Arke had come up to her even before she had seen him.

"I knew that you would be here, Goldele."

She was silent. She, too, had known that he would be here.

"Remember, Goldele, how we stood on the wooden bridge over the river in Zahaike? And I said to you then . . ."

"Yes, I remember," she replied before he could finish speaking.

"I've traveled the whole world, on ships and trains, on horseback and on foot, and never met a woman who was like the one I saw through the window in the shade of the oak trees at the Bronshteins' house. I've been divorced twice, and they were fine women, but they weren't like her." He patted Goldele's half-gray, half-black hair. "You look a little bit like her."

She laughed and had to struggle to keep from crying in the eyes of all the Zahaikers.

Goldele married Arke. She traveled with him to his home in Los Angeles. On the train, he said to her, "You remember, how we traveled together on that train?"

"I remember," she answered, before he could finish.

The express train rolled quietly over the broad expanse of Utah. The train ran easily and quietly, as though its wheels had forgotten the noisy travel of trains past.

"It's a long journey," she said and nestled her head on Arke's shoulder.

"Yes, Goldele, a very, very long journey. . ."

He took her in his arms. His eyes were deep, dark and serious, just as they once had been at the Brisk train station.

March 13, 1955

Luck

. . . .

Regina was just an average seamstress in the shop. She arrived with all the others, left with all the others, and went down to eat with all the others, but she earned a little less than they did because she was a slow-poke. It was her good luck that the presser, Abe, liked her work and praised her manner: "She's a schlimazel—but she does good work." This upheld her position in the shop, and people excused her for being a slowpoke.

Regina was grateful to Abe, and when they happened to meet in the cafeteria to eat, she said to him: "Sit, Abe, I'll bring you what you want."

With time, this became a habit; he sat and Regina served him. The cafeteria grew to be a comfortable place for them. It was almost like being in their own home.

Once when they left the cafeteria together, Abe bought two roses from an old woman who was standing on the street with her pail of flowers, and he gave the roses to Regina. It was a hot, dusty New York evening, but the roses were fresh and fragrant, and it seemed to Regina that she was walking in a flower garden.

A half a year later, Abe married Regina. The owner of the shop, Jack Green, gave them a gift for the occasion—a check for fifty dollars. He called them both into his office, wished them mazel tov, and gave them the gift. Regina glowed with the special light that good luck gives a person— even sunshine can't be compared to it.

The owner of the shop, Jack, had been a tailor in the old country. He was a golden craftsman, and he knew at a glance a fine piece of work when he saw it. In quiet moments, he missed the old needle-work, when a pocket really performed and one delighted in the appearance of a collar. He noticed Regina's honeymoon dress, and his heart beat with a longing for the old-style tailoring. He said, "Hey, Regina! That dress isn't from our shop!"

Regina answered him, as if someone had caught her committing a crime: "I made it myself, Mr. Green, for the honeymoon. I made it . . . I wanted, I wanted something new."

Mr. Green, his eyes shining, examined Regina's dress and rapped his fingers on the little wall of the small room where the designer, Miss Alice, was working.

"Look, Alice, look at this dress!"

Miss Alice, who was dressed and groomed as precisely as if she had been outlined by a ruler, examined Regina more than her dress and said, "It's fine, but it's not the style these days."

Jack Green, as though he hadn't heard what Alice said, continued: "Look, look at the pockets! Look at the pleats, the fine pleats. We'll make this style with thin little pleats . . . hmm?"

Miss Alice hesitated, but she agreed with him.

It seemed that it was a lucky hour for Regina to be standing under the chuppah. "Her style," as Mr. Green called the dress, was a success. It was a "seller."

Each time an order for dresses in "her style" arrived, Jack Green rapped on the little wall for Alice and always said the same thing: "She's made a hit . . . her style is selling," and he pointed to the orders.

Afterward, because Regina had made a hit, Mr. Green called her into his office and showed her the new fashion magazines. Embarrassed, Regina looked at the dresses, but didn't say very much. From time to time she'd point at a dress and murmur: "It seems to me, it doesn't need that. It seems to me, the sleeves should be wider. . ."

Jack Green looked her right in the eye and, with a red pencil, marked on the sleeve where Regina said "narrower" and where she said "wider," and where she said "it doesn't need that."

Abe used to drop in on the seamstresses, and from the side, see if Regina was working at her machine, or if she was in the office with Jack.

Regina worked at her machine very little. Although Mr. Green had never employed her as a designer, so as not to insult Miss Alice, Regina was always busy with the magazines.

Her styles caught on. Jack Green was delighted with her work. Her styles reminded him of the old days and he almost wanted to sit down and sew them himself. He gave her styles a name: Style B, and Style B sold well. It was a cure for Jack's soul, and good health for his pocket.

It often happened that when Abe finished his work and was leaving the shop with the others, Regina would still be in the office "styling the next season." Abe went to the cafeteria alone and ate alone by himself, never forgetting for an instant that Regina was sitting in the office "styling the next season."

When Regina came home later, he couldn't restrain himself and said to her, "You've been a seamstress at Green's for twelve years, and now all of a sudden you're a designer? What is this? Maybe you'd like to move over to Wolf and Berg Company; then you'd be a real designer!"

It bothered Regina that Abe took no pleasure in her success at the shop. She answered, "Yes, it's a real shame I didn't become a designer before; they earn more, and the work is easier."

Abe didn't accept such an answer. He'd get upset and argue. "Are you better than Alice? What's he need you for when he has Alice?"

This annoyed Regina, and she couldn't keep quiet. "What do you mean? Is Alice a god? Alice can design a style and I can too. What's the wonder in that?"

What was good luck for Regina (that she had become a designer) was a misfortune for Abe. He grew haggard. All the self-confidence he'd had ("the best presser in the shop") dissolved, just as if Regina's sun had risen and melted his security and happiness away.

Regina never told Abe when she'd gotten a bonus or a raise in her pay. She avoided talking about the office. Her weekly salary grew larger than his, but neither she nor Abe mentioned it.

Once, Alice happened to meet Abe and said to him, "Regina's successful, you know? Jack really likes her work."

Abe came home, punctured by what she had said. He thought over Alice's words again and again: "Jack really likes her work," and a heavy suspicion wrapped itself around his heart. What is this? A designer, all of a sudden! That old fool, Jack, loves to sit with Regina and have a good time. They sit and they turn the pages of the magazines. They sit and they mark with pencils. I should worry? They're just having a good time. . . .

On a hot, dusty evening, after work, Regina came into the cafeteria with Abe. A usual, she went off to get him something to eat. Abe sat there, smoked a cigarette, and waited for her, exactly as he had two years ago before they'd gotten married. Abe tried with all his power to turn the wheel back: when she's busy, she stays in the office, he thought, but when she's free, she goes straight home with him. Alice is jealous of Regina and that's why she was jabbering. Why can't Regina be a designer? She was a seamstress; now she's a designer. After all, she didn't become a rabbi. That *would* be a wonder. And the cafeteria seemed to him like it once had been two years before. The spoons and the forks that Regina put down on the white paper napkins seemed peaceful and homelike.

When they left the cafeteria, Abe bought two roses for Regina from the same old woman who was still standing with the same pail of flowers, and who in the middle of the dusty street, brought the freshness and the scent of a flower garden—to those for whom flowers bring joy.

On the way home, Regina said to Abe, "They're getting ready to go to a fashion show in Los Angeles. It's going to be a big show. They're getting ready for the fall season."

She was afraid to tell him that Jack Green wanted her to go with him to the show. Abe understood what she hadn't said and answered: "Let them go. I'm not obliged to take care of Jack Green's business."

Regina said nothing. The two roses in her hand hindered her movement, and she gave them to Abe to hold. Her hand had gone to sleep and she rubbed her fingers. In the house, she busied herself sticking the flowers in a vase and never stopped thinking about how she could get out of going to the show, that for Abe was "Jack Green's business." She stuck the flowers in water as indifferently as a stepmother gives something to her stepchildren to eat. The two roses stood there sadly, as though they knew they wouldn't last long.

A few days later, Alice edged her way over to Abe's pressing machine, stopped next to him, and asked, "Well, Abe, are you going to Los Angeles with Regina?"

Abe felt that Alice had come to rub salt in his wounds, and he answered her in the same tone that she had spoken to him: "If you're going, I'll go too."

Astonished, Alice's eyes popped open. "I?" she repeated, "if I go?" She laughed nervously. "I go every year!"

She's jealous of Regina; Abe saw this now on her face and felt it in her nervous laughter. Nevertheless, it hurt him that Regina still hadn't told him she was intending to go to Los Angeles.

So that people wouldn't notice he was upset, Abe went to work every day smoothly shaven, wearing a fresh shirt, careful that his tie matched, and not even forgetting to attach his silver tie clip which was engraved with his monogram. But just as the sun, in her full beauty, cannot conceal her spots, so a person wearing the most beautiful clothes can't disguise the sadness he keeps in a hidden corner of his heart. Well-dressed and smiling, he just wasn't the same Abe, who had once walked around the shop like the cock of the walk—the best presser—and didn't care two cents for the world.

It was especially hard for Abe to overcome his bewilderment, when in the middle of a bright day, Regina would leave the shop with Jack and Alice—to look at the fashions. They'd even eat lunch together on the way. For all the long years that Abe had worked in the shop, he had never known when Jack was in the office and when he went out. Now each time was an ordeal for him. The girls in the shop watched Regina as she left with the boss. They were jealous of her. Abe didn't watch her leave. Without looking, he felt her leaving, and sometimes noticed her coat that passed like a shadow from the office door to the door that led to the elevator.

One day, out of the clear blue sky, he said to Regina, "I'm going to change my job."

"What?" she asked, "did you quarrel with the foreman?"

"To hell with Jack," he said bitterly.

This was a blunt reminder to Regina that she, too, should be thinking about new job. But where could she go? Who knew she was a designer? Regina was silent. Silence was her answer to everything. The two rooms, the apartment that they rented, were almost always charged with silence. A silence that gave no relief.

The tumult of the fall season began in Mr. Green's shop. Summer was still steaming, but it was the fall season in the shop. Samples of woolen fabrics were brought in. Mountains of thick materials and fur accessories for dresses rose on the tables. The girls in the shop already knew that Regina was going with Jack to the fashion show in Los Angeles, and the news traveled from mouth to mouth.

"The one the boss chooses is the one who becomes the expert. What's new about that? But did Regina finish at a designing school?"

Alice who had a diploma from school, Alice who for many long years had a position higher than theirs—Alice goes to Los Angeles. That's only natural. That's the way the world has been forever. They sit at their machines and Alice goes to Los Angeles. That's her job. But Regina? She had sat there at her machine, a slowpoke and suddenly she was going to Los Angeles! And not going, she was flying. Regina, the slowpoke, was flying. The change in her luck had taken place in the shop right in front of their eyes and the seamstresses didn't know how to pass it off. They joked with Abe: "You're lucky you caught Regina before she started flying. She wouldn't marry you now."

Regina flew to Los Angeles, and the whole shop flew with her. They talked and they gossiped and they envied her. They weren't happy, but they prophesied: "She will be a star in Hollywood yet." She had already achieved so much in the shop that they could believe anything about her.

Regina left early in the morning. Abe didn't see her off. He went to work in the shop. That was his job. They said good-bye to each other at the subway station. Abe said to her, "So, you're really going? Hmm?" as though he had just found out she was going. "You should write." They kissed, as though a handkerchief were between them, their lips barely touching.

Regina took a taxi to the airport. Abe ducked away as if to get out of the rain and went down the steps to the subway.

As the taxi carried Regina over the streets of the city, it seemed to her that she was flying even before she saw the airplane. But her departure from Abe and his question: "You're really going? Hmm?" stayed with her, a painful regret.

When she returned, it was Sunday. She called Abe from the airport and he waited at home for her arrival. The two rooms were dusty. The sacks and boxes that she had left before her trip were still lying untouched on the table and on the floor.

A ruin, she thought, when she opened the door.

Abe greeted her. "So, you've sorted out Jack's business already?"

Regina put her arms around him and answered, "I'm not busy with Jack's business any longer. You don't want it and there's no need for it."

"No longer a designer?" Abe exclaimed. "Back to the sewing machine?"

Regina shook her head slowly—no—and answered him very clearly like a person dictating a telegram: "I've taken a job with Wolf and Berg Company. They saw my Style B and they liked it."

Abe looked at her with such surprise that it was as if she had not said anything ordinary but had blown live birds out of her mouth instead. He was not delighted. She stood across from him, wearing a tight fitting dress with small, thin pleats, Style B, and a new velvet hat from Los Angeles. She looked like a movie star, as if she had seized for herself all the self-confidence and assuredness that Abe had had in the shop before he had married her. He sat down on the unmade bed and began to jiggle his feet as if he were going somewhere, and going with no end in sight.

Regina was silent. She changed her clothes, threw on a housedress and slowly began to clean up the apartment.

February 13, 1955

Sylvia

. . . .

Sylvia had distinguished herself in her work with retarded children. Such was her achievement that at the age of twenty-three, she was invited to present lectures to teachers in her field.

The invitation included a reception for her. Prominent representatives in the world of education came. People held talks, drank tea, and ate cake.

Sylvia's parents, who were wealthy hardware store owners, were sitting dressed head-to-toe in new clothes and were afraid to speak a word to anyone in their tradesman's English, lest they ruin their daughter's career. Only when they heard the experts' strong praises of Sylvia's work would they comment a little to each other: "You hear that?"

And the answer was: "Shh, don't talk so much."

This was an evening of pure pleasure for them from Sylvia.

It was already late when Samuel Glazer, whom Sylvia had not seen in four years, came into the hall.

His sudden arrival confused her. She exerted all her attention to hear what people were saying and to know what to reply.

She applied the same method to herself that she used for a retarded child when his attention was wandering. She showed him something new. She began to look at the flowers on the table that she had not noticed until now. Roses and gladioli. By way of the flowers, she could get back to what the speakers were saying. She recovered herself.

Sylvia's mother, Mrs. Gitterman, also noticed Samuel's arrival. She tugged on her husband's sleeve and said to him, quietly, "Samuel's here, isn't he?"

Her husband, not raising his head, screened the audience from under his lowered forehead, saw Samuel and said very quietly to his wife, "He's here. He's really here."

Now the parents no longer heard the speakers. Their attention was transferred to the spot where Samuel was sitting, although they didn't look at him.

Five years ago, Samuel had been like one of their own in their home. Sylvia and Samuel were always mentioned together. Sylvia and Samuel have gone to the theater. Sylvia and Samuel bought books. Sylvia and Samuel have gone to the ocean.

No one had any doubts that Sylvia and Samuel would be together forever. How could it be otherwise?

But exactly four years ago, during the winter vacation, Samuel left to go to his parents in a small town near Boston and from there wrote a letter to Sylvia, that he would "probably" transfer to the university in Boston and finish his studies in chemistry there.

He came back to get his things. Sylvia helped him select his books that had been mixed in with hers on the bookshelves. She accompanied him to the train and asked him only one question: "Why had he so suddenly decided to move to Boston?"

"There are more opportunities for work," he answered, "and I'll be closer to my home."

After his departure, when she went outside the train station to go home, it had turned cold. It seemed to her that the cold would never end.

At home, her parents met her like a person who was returning from a funeral. And when Sylvia was lying in bed that night, her mother asked her if she wouldn't like a hot water bottle.

"It's so cold outside," explaining herself to her daughter.

Sylvia shook her head, no, and with a trembling mouth, smiled.

After Samuel's departure, the black cat of anger ran between the two families, the Gittermans and the Glazers, who were relatives and had been close for a long time. They didn't write a single letter to each other and were no longer guests in each other's homes. But flowers from Samuel arrived each year for Sylvia's birthday.

Sylvia's mother tossed out the flowers and said to Sylvia, "Flowers, he sends! Let his mother, Hannah-Beyle, eat them for breakfast."

Sylvia didn't protest when her mother threw the flowers out, and she never spoke about Samuel.

In college, she won a scholarship. She attended conferences and seminars in education. She brought home books and studied them. Her name began to appear in the newspapers. She gave a lecture, and she participated in symposiums. Her parents extolled her virtues to the neighbors and acquaintances, but hanging over their home was a hidden grief: Sylvia was an old maid.

Sylvia entertained acquaintances, bought paintings, and went to exhibits, sometimes with a friend and sometimes alone. She lived her life with a plan: she was Sylvia, and no one dared to ask her about her future.

Nevertheless, at home the Gittermans knew everything Samuel was doing. Secretly, they followed accounts of his life in Boston.

Samuel got his doctorate, Samuel was going out with a divorced woman. Samuel didn't get married. Samuel was in Washington because of his work. As if along with their lives, another life far off in the shadows accompanied them; there was still a connection between them.

When Sylvia received flowers for her twenty-third birthday from Samuel, she wrote to him for the first time: "Why do you remember my birthdays, Samuel? What do they have to do with you?"

He didn't answer her letter, but he did appear unexpectedly at the reception given in her honor.

When the reception ceremonies were over, Samuel walked over to Sylvia. He congratulated her on her success and added, "You've become more beautiful, Sylvia."

She blushed and answered him, "Thank you, Samuel. All things seem more beautiful when they are seldom seen, and it's already been four years since we've seen each other."

Sylvia's parents didn't know how to behave with Samuel. Sylvia's mother said to her husband, "Don't hug him. Let him see that we need him like a hole in the head."

They were astonished when they saw Sylvia give Samuel her briefcase to carry and say to him, comfortably, "Pull up the zipper on my boots, Samuel," exactly as if she had never borne him any resentment and had just seen him last evening.

They went outside, and her parents followed behind them. Samuel held Sylvia by the arm, as he had four years earlier, when they were going out together.

"How long are you staying?" Sylvia asked, trying to keep her voice natural, the way one would ask an acquaintance an ordinary question.

"Forever," Samuel answered her, and added quietly, "I waited a long time for your letter."

Her parents went to get their car. Mrs. Gitterman said to her husband, "Such an unexpected thing, his coming. You think it really means something?"

Her husband answered, "No one pays something for nothing. But I'm going to make sure they're married according to the laws of Moses and of Israel, in a true kosher wedding. I don't want to have a shuttle train between New York and Boston."

They got into their car and caught up with Sylvia and Samuel.

New York, 1954

A Glimmer of Youth

· · · · · · · ·

Together with some ten other people from the German camps, Sarah, Yoel, and their three-year-old son, Avreml, arrived in America.

In her purse, Sarah was carrying the addresses of two relatives, her uncle Chaim Broyder and her great-aunt, Chaya-Itte, well hidden, as if they were lifesavers.

When the ship arrived in New York, Sarah's uncle, a man with a high forehead and a long face, who resembled her father, met them. He had been in America for thirty-five years, and people in her family had said he was a millionaire.

Their meeting was not warm. One kiss for each, without any family feeling. The uncle considered the three newcomers, Sarah, Yoel, and Avreml, for a while and said, "So, all right, we're off."

The uncle arranged to have their baggage sent separately; then he and his three passengers got into a large, luxurious car and he introduced them to America.

The uncle said very little. Driving, he asked: "How old is the child? And what is his name?" When he heard that his name was Avreml, the name of his brother, Sarah's father, who had been shot dead by the Germans, he shook his head a couple of times and drove faster, as though he wanted to escape from this calamity.

After this, his curiosity was completely exhausted. Only after they had gone a little farther did he say to them, "My wife is not well and she isn't able to see new people. I'm taking you to Chaya-Itte."

Sarah and Yoel sat tensely, as though they were being taken to an inter-rogation instead of to relatives. In order to break the silence, Yoel said, "A beautiful city, New York."

"What else? You think it's Golovinke?" the uncle replied, as though it were incomprehensible to him that New York should need any praise.

The uncle summoned Chaya-Itte from her house by honking his horn several times. She came running out, saw Sarah, Yoel, and Avreml, and said reproachfully, "They've come with a child?" Nevertheless, she kissed them all and wished: "May good fortune have come with you!"

The uncle didn't get out of his car. He looked at his watch, said he was busy, his wife wasn't well, his business couldn't do without him for one minute, and that he would return tomorrow. He said all this like a rattled-off prayer[1] and drove away.

"Some uncle you have," Yoel murmured to Sarah, exchanging glances with her.

Chaya-Itte led them through a long hat shop and through a narrow door to her apartment, two rooms with a kitchen. She gave them a cold lunch. Cold meat, smoked fish, cheese, butter, a bottle of cold milk, and with it an explanation: "Here we don't have time to cook; we eat cold food. That's America for you."

Over the door of Chaya-Itte's shop was a silver sign that said Jeanette's, and Chaya-Itte herself was dressed up as though she had just come from a wedding—in a silk dress, a necklace, bracelets on her arm, and topped off with a little diamond comb in her hair. She looked as though she were a liv-ing jewelry display, and she gave a lecture to Sarah: In order to sell a hat, even to a tailor's wife, you have to be dressed like a queen yourself. That's America for you.

For every ten words, Chaya-Itte added, "That's America for you."

A few days later when their baggage was delivered, Chaya-Itte took one look at the suitcases and issued her appraisal of their entire estate: "Considering what they look like from the outside, it's not worth unpacking them. Here, people don't keep rags. That's America for you."

---

1. The author used the term *shimenesre* here, signifying the rather lengthy Eighteen Blessings that are said thrice daily.

Chaya-Itte, in truth, wasn't just one person, but two: one in the shop in her business and a second at home in the two rooms behind her store.

In her business, Chaya-Itte was Jeanette. She spoke English, and she didn't speak very much. "The less you speak, the better you sell hats," she said, "and above all, a person needs the right appearance. That's America for you." When Chaya-Itte was fitting a hat on a customer, she would say, "excellent!" with such authority, it was as though she were approving the second term of a president.

But at home, in her apartment, Chaya-Itte was not Jeanette; she was a hundred percent Chaya-Itte. She spoke and spewed words out no matter where, shouted and scolded. Her anger wasn't meant to injure or insult, just the opposite, it warmed the heart. It was a familiar part of Golovinke. When Avreml cried at nights, Chaya-Itte would say to Sarah and Yoel the next morning, "I'll have to throw you and your young man out. I have a headache, and I can't get enough sleep at night. But where could I throw you, since it's so hard to find an apartment. Unless a real house could be built for you. That's America for you. There are a million houses, but you can't find any place to roost at night."

In honor of the new-comers, Chaya-Itte invited some people over on Sunday—relatives, friends, and *landsleit*. Shouting and complaining, she made the arrangements for her party: "As if I don't have enough to do God sends me guests and all the fuss that goes with them, well? On the other hand, how can I pretend that you aren't already here? And I have to introduce you to people, too! That's America for you." She didn't stint on the refreshments either—fruits, sweets, food—crying all the while: "That's America for you!"

The uncle couldn't come to the reception. Over the telephone, he went through his rattled-off prayers: his wife wasn't well, he had a lot of appointments, he was busy, he would come another Sunday. But he did send a gift, a little coat and hat for Avreml with Mr. Shevetz, a Golovinke landsman.

Chaya-Itte dismissed his excuses with her own verse: "That Uncle is always busy; he's preparing a gold tombstone for himself."

Mr. Shevetz told stories and everyone laughed. Then he went over to Sarah, drank a l'chaim with her, and said, "I'm so glad I came here today . . .

truly, it's just as though I'm back in Golovinke . . . I've been reminded of my youth . . . sincerely."

After the guests left, Yoel said to Sarah, "What did he want from you?"

"He told me stories about Golovinke."

"Forget Golovinke!" Yoel said, disgruntled, and Sarah could only wonder at the tension in his voice. She didn't reply.

Right from the very first day, Yoel made up his mind to conquer America with as much zeal as a soldier given the order to attack. In the first week, he had already run through the entire block, asking who needed plumbing, pipes, and electrical appliances to be repaired. He had golden hands, and soon well-earned dollars began to appear in his pockets. Chaya-Itte said, "He's arrived."

The Golovinke *landsleit* gave Yoel the address of a locksmith shop that belonged to a landsman. Yoel went there and showed what he could do. He stayed with the job. Every Friday, he returned home with a check and with a gift for Avreml: a whistle, a teddy-bear, a drum. Chaya-Itte sang his praises: "He's already an American, he earns good money and he spends it."

Yoel spoke less than usual, exactly as if he were gathering all his strength for settling into the new country. When he earned his first raise in the shop, Chaya-Itte predicted he would soon be a foreman. "A boss, not a foreman," he replied, smiling.

Through a worker at the locksmith shop, Yoel found an apartment in a quiet neighborhood in Brooklyn, and he bought furniture on installments. Chaya-Itte wanted to give him a table that she no longer needed, and a bed, but Yoel said: No. He wanted everything new. Each Friday, he brought something new to the household: a radio, an electric broiler, a device to squeeze orange juice, an iron, a mirror, a card table. He even acquired a washing machine and a vacuum cleaner. The new apartment was full of things—furniture, dishes, children's toys. Sarah was busy, washing and pressing, dusting, airing out, arranging and rearranging all the household things.

Friends of theirs from the German camps often came to their apartment. They brought news: Yankl Zaremba had already found work. He had a job with a butcher. Sabina was working in a restaurant. Berl the Pshitiker[2] had had a nervous breakdown and been taken to the hospital. Esther and Shloyme had left to work on a farm. But Esther had injured her hand and returned. And Tsilie had met with good luck—she married a cousin. And so they passed the news around from one to the other. Like a small ship laden with troubles, bad nerves, and with a few drops of happiness, the small group of immigrants struggled to set sail on the wide sea of America.

During the day, Sarah sat with Avreml in a small park, where there were several trees, a bit of grass, and some ten or so benches. She didn't feel comfortable with the other young wives, who also came there to watch their children, and who were dressed in slacks, wore long earrings, had long, painted fingernails, and spoke English with each other.

One Sunday, the uncle paid a visit. He looked at the apartment, saw that the rooms were full of furniture and things, smiled, and said, "All right," and before his departure, left them a gift, a check for a hundred dollars.

After her uncle left, Sarah was seized with loneliness. It seemed that New York consisted only of buildings, vacuum cleaners, and the words, "How long have you been in America?" and "All right," like her uncle said.

Once, when Sarah was sitting with her child in the small square, Mr. Shevetz walked over to her unexpectedly. His face lit up with delighted astonishment.

"What are you doing here?" he asked, and sat down next to her like an old acquaintance who had been waiting a long time for this meeting.

Mr. Shevetz told her about his childhood, about his past life on the hillside in Golovinke.

"You surely wouldn't have known our family. We weren't the Broyders; we lived on the hillside, with the paupers, you know, behind the little river."

From his quiet boast, that he had lived with paupers, Sarah understood that now he was probably rich, and the poverty of days gone by was pleasant for him to remember and was even the diamond in his crown.

Just as though Mr. Shevetz could read her thoughts, he added, "Now I have a drugstore over there across from the square."

---

2. In the original Yiddish, *Berl der Pshitiker;* in other words, the Berl who was from the town of Pshitik (Przytyk), ninety kilometers southwest of Warsaw.

Mr. Shevetz sat with Sarah for a long time. He looked at his watch frequently, but always remembered one more thing to tell and didn't leave. With great pleasure, he told her that his family had had a nickname, "the comedians," not because, God forbid, they were actors, but simply because they could sing. At Purim, his father and uncles were the leaders of the Purim shpielers. With the money they earned at Purim at the rich people's houses, they were able to pay for Passover, for matzos, wine, and sometimes even a new pair of shoes. The rest of the year, they were rag-collectors, and in that business, you couldn't make enough for Passover.

When Sarah was on the way back from the park, walking by the drugstore, Mr. Shevetz saw her through the open door and stopped her. He gave her a small bottle of cologne, and when Sarah didn't want to accept it, he said, somewhat angrily, "When you don't take a gift from a landsman, you insult all of Golovinke," and put the cologne into the child's carriage.

The small gift seemed to Sarah full of warmth and friendship. The door of the drugstore became familiar, and it broke down the wall of her loneliness.

In a high voice that came from an inner happiness, Sarah told Yoel about her meeting Mr. Shevetz, saying that he had given her a bottle of cologne.

"It's worth about a quarter," Yoel said coldly.

Sarah, her eyes downcast and resentful, answered him. "For you it's worth a quarter. For me, it's worth more."

In the morning, on his way to work, Yoel went into the drugstore. He wanted to see this Mr. Shevetz again, whose gift was worth more to Sarah. Mr. Shevetz greeted him comfortably and politely, and, leaving the drugstore, Yoel thought: I *would* have to find an apartment right next to a Golovinke drugstore. Even a sage wouldn't have known!

Frequently, at lunchtime, Mr. Shevetz walked over to Sarah who was sitting in the park with her child. He'd bring an ice cream or a lollipop for Avreml and tell jokes and stories about Golovinke and New York. He told Sarah how he and his wife had been divorced eight weeks after their wedding, and from then on he'd been single. "A man is not a chess piece you can move around on the board so easily," he told Sarah, and added that his family, "the comedians," had all been very stubborn.

Mr. Shevetz used to sit with Sarah for half an hour and sometimes more and then went back "to slave" in his drugstore, as he jokingly referred to his work.

After he left, the park seemed greener, more familiar, and even the chattering of the young mothers, dressed in their slacks, didn't sound so strange.

Yoel became Americanized with the speed of an express train. He brought home English language newspapers with funnies and magazines about movie stars and fashion for Sarah.

"Why do you bring home newspapers with funnies and magazines when we can't even read them?"

"Everyone buys them. We should, too, and the reading will come by itself. What's the hurry?"

He brought records of English songs and was overjoyed to hear what "everyone else was listening to." Sarah thought to herself that Yoel had swallowed up America in one gulp, that he knew exactly what one had to do, and what everyone did. He had so much to do that he often worked overtime; he earned a lot of money and he was always bringing packages home. Both tense and tired, he didn't talk very much.

Once, when Sarah and Avreml and Mr. Shevetz were in a relaxed mood, eating ice cream that Mr. Shevetz had brought for them to the park, he asked, "How long have you been married, Sarah?"

"Five years," she answered tersely.

"A pity that I didn't meet you five years earlier," he said.

She brushed away his words, just exactly as if the wind would carry them away, and let them remain hanging on the trees in the park, like a youthful dream, like the memory of Golovinke, that she and no one else could see.

When Avreml was four years old, Mr. Shevetz brought him a wooden horse for his birthday and taught him how to ride it.

Avreml was delighted. When Yoel came home from work, the child ran up to him and told him the news: "Uncle Shevetz brought me a horse."

Yoel was enraged.

"People don't give such gifts for free," he said through his teeth. "How does he just happen to bring that kind of gift here?"

"Well, maybe there are still people who give such gifts for free, and Shevetz is that kind of person. What are you going to do about it?" Sarah said, her face reddening. Her high forehead was pink, and her gray eyes were blazing with glimmering sparks.

Yoel stalked through the room a couple of times, and then, walking by the wooden horse, he kicked it over rashly with his foot. An ear broke off the horse. Avreml, frightened, threw himself on the floor and cried bitterly. Yoel went into the other room and, with a heavy heart, looked through the funnies. Her hands paralyzed, Sarah got dinner ready.

In order to get away from the Golovinke drugstore, Yoel looked for another apartment on the other side of New York. Hastily, he packed up their things, muttering, "Run away from the camps, run away from the drugstore, run away from my luck."

Sarah, moving like a shadow through the rooms, helped pack up their belongings. She felt that Yoel was driving away the last glimmer of light from her youth and that by leaving the familiar green trees in the square, she was moving into a world where people didn't receive gifts for free.

· · · · · · ·

But Yoel couldn't run away from his luck. Two years later, Sarah was wearing a white uniform and working in the drugstore. People called her Mrs. Shevetz. She had come back to the little trees in the small park where a dream of youth had once shone for her.

June 27, 1954

Eternal Summer

. . . .

Tini had gotten used to her nickname, "the Swallow." She was a little
smaller than the other children in her junior high class, her nose a little shorter, her tiny chin a bit too narrow, and the name Swallow stuck to
her.

Learning was beside the point for Tini. Her homework seemed to do itself, and she appeared to have no cares in the world at all. This gave the impression that she only came to school to say good morning to the teacher,
tell stories to the other kids, and sing songs between activities.

Even in the middle of winter Tini had freckles on her face—on her
short nose and on her cheeks. On a frosty day, when Tini, her face summery, entered the class, one would have thought that spring was right behind her. Harry, who had long legs, always greeted her quietly: "Take off
your sweater. It's too hot!"

When, with half an ear, the teacher caught his playful greeting, she
smiled and let his teasing pass. She also thought to herself that Tini really
had come from the spring, and in order to drive away the wintry gloom,
she would call on her to tell about the cold countries. For Tini, cold countries bloomed with freckles, and it seemed that she was not so much answering the teacher with her story, but was amusing herself and making the
others happy on a wintry day. And indeed, this was why she was called the
Swallow.

Tall Harry lived on the same street as Tini. House to house, they were
neighbors. He was a good, hard-working student. The Swallow's carefree

attitude—doing her homework as just something in passing—Harry took to heart. At every opportunity, he would touch her short little nose and say, "A longer nose wouldn't hurt you at all, I assure you."

And once in a spring rain, when all the students were waiting on the school bridge for the downpour to pass, Harry noticed that the Swallow who was right next to him stood exactly as high as his underarm. He picked her up in one hand, and in the middle of the torrential rain took her to the bus station.

"Come, Swallow, I'm putting you on the bus."

Tini didn't even have time to look around, so fast did he step with her over the puddles in the schoolyard. The children laughed loudly and joked among themselves: "What does the Swallow care? Her shoes are dry!"

The other girls, Tini's friends, were jealous nevertheless that tall Harry, the best student in class, would carry her in the rain, striding across the puddles. Passing them by, Harry said, "She only weighs five pounds, the Swallow."

They all burst out laughing and Tini quarreled with him: "Don't you dare do such a thing again, you hear? And you know very well that my name is Tini, not the Swallow."

Harry answered her in all seriousness: "You better be quiet, or I'll drop you in a puddle. With your short legs you'd sink right in."

For several days after that, Tini didn't answer Harry's hello, but he took her books from her anyway and carried them to school.

"You think you can carry such a heavy load with your small hands?" was his insulting remark.

Tini's freckles glowed with anger, and her face was no longer springlike, but as hot as a day in July.

Her anger was extinguished suddenly, when one evening Harry heard her calling him with a woeful cry: "Harry! Harry! Come out! Harry!"

Harry came out to the street. Tini, wearing a light spring dress, was standing there and said to him, half-angrily: "Have you ever seen such a thing? Just today, when the old people are at the movies, the electricity goes out! It's dark, I'm telling you—it's scary!"

By the time they got inside her house, all the lamps were back on. The anger between them was extinguished for good. In that very light, Harry took Tini in his arms and kissed her. But he didn't forget to needle her where it would hurt most: "You think it's easy to give you a kiss? A person has to bend way over!"

Tini threw him out of the bright house and, slamming the door, cried after him, "Nobody asked you to bend over! Go see Helen, the beanpole. Then you can stand up straight."

This was the first time that Tini was sorry she was small.

The other girls in class were growing up and beginning to wear lipstick. Tini grew a little more, too, but she continued to be the smallest, still the Swallow.

Just as in spring, when the park suddenly turns pure green and the leaves on the trees grow fresh, green, and sculpted, so the children in the class seemed almost grown up, young and mysterious. Helen was tall, with full lips, and had thick black hair that fell to her shoulders. She was as tall as Harry. When Tini saw them standing next to each other, she was bothered by Helen's height, although she thought: What does Helen matter to me? She's as silly as a goose and can't figure out how to add two and two.

The last year in high school, Tini competed with the best student in the class, Harry. He was good in math, and she in physics. He was good in chemistry, and she wrote the best compositions. As was his old custom, Harry told her off: "You'd better grow a little faster, Swallow!"

Now his barbed words bothered her, and she didn't quarrel with him. She wouldn't say anything, but in her old childish way quietly stuck out her tongue at him. She did not mention Helen.

Tini and Harry were the only two from the class to win scholarships, and, sitting on a school bench for the last time, they began to quarrel: "You mean, they're going to give you a scholarship? Because you're so small, the surprise is that much bigger! You know?"

She answered him with a not-childish smile: "Write them a petition, then. Let them send it back."

It happened that Tini overheard a conversation between her parents. Her father said: "I'd be happier if Tini were a little taller and didn't have a scholarship."

Her mother answered him unconcernedly: "Well, why worry, we'll have to reinforce her with a couple of thousand dollars anyway!"

Her mother's strange word, "reinforce," stayed with Tini. She went to her room and remained standing a while and thought to herself—why did they need to "reinforce" her? She even looked at herself in the mirror. The mirror lit up her gray eyes, that were smiling and stubborn: No, I will not let them "reinforce" me!

Harry went to work that summer in a children's camp. He said to Tini, "I have to earn a little money. The scholarship won't be enough."

Tini remembered her mother's expression, that she had to be reinforced with a couple of thousand dollars. But she answered Harry, lightly: "When are you going? I'll come to the train station to see you off."

"It's not worth it," he answered. "I'm going with a group of children, early in the morning. It's work. It's not for fun."

Tini thought about Helen, about her full lips and black hair that fell to her shoulders. Perhaps Helen was going to see him off and that was why it "wasn't worth it."

Very early in the morning, she went to the train station. She wanted to see if Helen would be there. Tini's mother exchanged glances with her husband and said to Tini: "Take some money, Tini, you might need it." But she pretended not to hear and left. Her mother, Mrs. Epstein, said to her husband: "A nice boy, Harry. I'm telling you, a nice boy."

"Oh," Mr. Epstein wrinkled his forehead, "his father is a bookkeeper, a poor man. They have to count their pennies . . . and the children take after their parents."

Mrs. Epstein laughed broadly. "Well, and wasn't your father a simple teacher? Does that make you backward, hmm? Have some pity for poor Mr. Epstein!"

"Well, I'm different," he answered her, in a huff.

Helen was not at the station. Tini gave Harry a little box of chocolate, and said to him, "Have a good time, Harry!"

She came back home with an easy heart, all of spring in her face. Her freckles were glowing with joy and happiness.

That summer Tini got ready for college. She worked in the library, and she read a lot of books. She went with her mother to department stores to buy clothes. Earnestly, like a person doing an important job, Mrs. Epstein considered each dress that Tini tried on and told her that she would buy them and wouldn't consider the cost. Tini thought: this must be "reinforc-ing," and her desire to buy the clothes vanished.

Tini left to go to a small college town, Cherrywood, in New Jersey, and Harry to a college in New England. She received several postcards from him, and from time to time, a letter. He wrote about his studies and men-tioned that books were expensive. People would have to "reinforce" him too, Tini thought, and her eyes smiled stubbornly, as if she could lash her-self with a whip.

Near the end of the school year, Tini received a letter from Harry, that was signed "with love" and had a playful addition: "Don't make a date with anyone else, Swallow!"

Tini came home with Harry's letter in her purse. At each station where the train stopped, she stepped down from the platform and walked around for a while. The ground beneath her feet was so good, so bountiful, so full of song that each step she took was a joy. Just stand there for a while. Smil-ing radiantly to strangers and receiving their smiles back, was just that easy. When the ground sings, people sing, too. Under each station's name was written "with love." Snow Hill—with love. Yellow Creek—with love. There are words that throw off sparks and glow with starlight, and those words are "with love."Tini glided into her house as though she had been ice skating, happy and refreshed. She was holding a basket of flowers that she had bought at one of the stations, "with love."

Her father and mother kissed her. "How are you feeling?"

"Well!"

"And how is college?"

"Very good!"

The house was full of joy and was "very good."

Soon after Tini got home, Helen dropped by to say hello.

This time, Tini didn't notice Helen's full lips and black hair that fell to her shoulders. Sparks of good luck shimmered around Tini, sparks that make a person both happy and blind.

"Do you know if Harry is here yet?" Helen asked her.

"I do know. He should be here already. I have a letter from him."

"I got a letter from him, too," Helen said. And adding with a smile: "He wrote to me not to date anyone else. Have you ever heard of such nerve! That I should wait for him!" Helen left.

Just as before, when Tini was a child, when the lights had gone out suddenly and she was in the dark, and she had been terrified, so now, too, Tini thought that the light of day had been extinguished and she would stay in the dark—terrified! And just as before, she ran out of her house and over to Harry's: "Harry! Harry! Come out! Harry!"

A very surprised Harry came running out to her. She was standing there in a light, spring dress, afraid and half angry.

"Why did you fool me?" she asked him, her eyes shooting out all the sparks she'd accumulated in the bright day.

Harry stood opposite her, bewildered, and when he recovered his wits, uttered: "Say hello to me, Tini."

"I don't want any carbon copies of any letters from you," she replied. Her gray eyes were bright and earnest. Then she said, quietly and softly, like someone pleading for her life: "A person shouldn't do that, Harry. I don't want that, Harry. Don't write to me." She murmured a few more words that Harry didn't hear and couldn't dare ask her again. He saw her face, her eyes, as though she were telling herself, and him, and the entire open world—she didn't want that . . .

Harry was upset. He felt he no longer recognized Main Street. The next morning, he left for work in the children's camp. That year, Tini didn't see him off to his work at the camp and didn't bring any chocolate to him at the train station. Let him go there with anyone he wants, when he wants . . . she thought.

That summer Tini worked in the library and went with her mother to the department stores to be "reinforced" with clothes. A letter for her from Harry at camp arrived. He was working. There was a counselor there—a pretty girl, Thelma. She wasn't stingy with her kisses. She helped him pass the boredom of summer.

Tini answered him with one sentence: "Thanks for your sincerity. Tini."

Harry looked at the one sentence of her letter and regretted what he had done. The Swallow has flown away; she wrote only one sentence.

Tini left for college two days before Harry returned from summer camp. She needed to be at college a few days earlier, she told her parents. Her mother suggested that she wait a couple of days until Harry got home, but she answered her shortly: "I don't care to wait, Mama."

"She needed to be at college a few days earlier," Tini's mother told Harry, using Tini's very words, when he called the Epsteins on his return from the camp.

The Swallow has flown away, he thought, and he remained standing awhile longer by the unfriendly telephone receiver, feeling that Main Street had become empty.

Helen called Harry up. Thelma called him. He had "a lot of work" and couldn't see them. He lay stretched out, his long legs on the wicker sofa, and thought about Tini: For her everything is beside the point, and "thanks for your sincerity." She's flown away. Thelma is a pretty butter roll and Helen is a beanpole. Now he remembered that Tini had called Helen a beanpole. That was six years ago. Tini had thrown him out of the house and said: "Go to the beanpole, to Helen. Then you won't have to bend down so far."

Harry returned to college. Before the winter vacation, he sent a postcard to Tini: "Little Swallow, I'm going to get off at Cherrywood, and we'll go home together, to Main Street."

Tini laughed: Get off at Cherrywood! Just as though Cherrywood were on his way home. She laughed for joy. She stretched out on the floor and laughed.

She met him at the train station in Cherrywood. Her freckles were blossoming; her too short little nose was utterly childlike. "A Swallow"— Harry thought, and embraced her. There was a heavy winter rain. A swollen stream of water was running by the sidewalk, as though all of Cherrywood were soaked by rivers. Harry, his face earnest, said to her: "Tini, I'm going to carry you over the streams of water." They both remembered their childhood pranks. They were happy, with the full happiness of youth.

· · · · · · ·

On Main Street, both the mothers, neighbors for twenty-five years, met in the middle of the block, the telegrams in their hands. Her face brick red, Tini's mother spoke. "The nerve of today's children! They don't say anything and they don't ask—not even their parents!" She was extremely happy that Tini had gotten married without being "reinforced."

Harry's mother complained: "Try to lead a son to the chuppah! They don't need you at all! A telegram and that's it!" She, too, was happy that Harry had struck oil, so to speak, and would have a golden wife, Tini. And she cried for joy.

The parents, the in-laws, ate dinner together, and scolded their children. Drank l'chaim—and scolded their children. They were happy and scolded: Today's children!

On Main Street, there wasn't a drop of rain. It was all sunshine.

Off the Track

· · · · · · · ·

During the three days that Zalman Wiener had been sitting shivah for his father, his wife Mollie had gone around enraged, saying, "It's unheard of for a man to sit out all seven days of shivah and keep the business closed! We can be ruined yet!"

To quiet her anger, Mollie sought out all the work that was possible to do in a house—she ironed the curtains, repolished the silver, and cleaned the rugs. The vacuum cleaner droned and rumbled noisily, as if all of Mrs. Weiner's fury were in command of its electrical soul.

Her husband, Zalman Wiener, was sitting on a low stool in the living room. Next to him on a little table, a candle, that he had lit after his father's death, was burning in a glass. The noise his wife was making with her work didn't reach him. There was a stillness around him, as if he were in another place.

Mrs. Wiener came in and turned on the radio. "Let's at least hear some news!" she said, and the room was invaded with a song, then static, and then a man's deep voice.

Zalman Wiener got up and carried the radio into the kitchen, where his wife was cleaning the shelves of a cupboard.

"You can listen to the news all you want to," he said, "I've had enough news."

"If you don't want to, don't," she answered, and hastily turned it off.

In the stillness of their home, her high heels could be heard, banging like angry hammers on the floor of the kitchen as she walked back and forth.

When they were sitting, eating dinner, Mrs. Wiener spelled it out for her husband. "You have two people in the shop who haven't worked for three days, and they're being paid. There's rent to be paid, taxes to be paid, and when there aren't any sales, well, if everyone closed their business when something happened, half of the businesses in New York would close their doors!"

Mrs. Wiener stretched her hands out to her husband: "I don't care about the losses. But it irks me about the men. They're not working, and they're getting paid. All of a sudden they should have a vacation? It's the first time in my life I've ever heard of such a thing!"

Zalman Wiener didn't answer his wife. He chewed without appetite on a piece of bread and listened to her indifferently, as if no one were talking to him, but from somewhere outside a voice had come in and that conversation didn't concern him.

Mrs. Wiener was quiet for awhile. She was boiling with anger that her husband didn't answer. She moved over a little closer to him and continued. "Do you really think that people will wait for you? Those people who need buttons, or thread, or ribbons, or lining, or lace, or gold stitchery, or hooks and eyes, or elastic, or pendants, or beads?" Because of the energy that burned inside her, the words came rolling out, one after the other, like hail, as she accounted for each article they had in their store. "They can find it somewhere else, from someone who isn't as pious as you are! It'll be a loss of at least seven hundred dollars for us!"

Her face was blazing, and her round, plump hands were moving with such life and eagerness, it was as though the death of her father-in-law had no connection to her, and sitting shivah was an unexpected nuisance.

Zalman looked at his wife and uttered only one word: "Shhh!"—as though even this one word was hard for him to say. His "shhh!" interrupted Mrs. Wiener. She got up from the table and began to rinse the dishes again. The plates and spoons and forks knocked and struck one against the other as if they were fighting, and each strike was a skirmish on a battlefield.

When Mrs. Wiener finished her war with the plates, she changed clothes and got ready to leave the house. She smoothed her gloves over her fingers and said to her husband, "When Ellen brings Maxy, you should give him a glass of milk before he takes his nap. I'm going for a little walk. I've got a headache from all this luck."

Zalman Wiener smiled when he heard his wife say "luck" and sat back down in his place next to the lighted candle.

Mrs. Wiener left the house, but she came back to remind her husband again, not to forget to give Maxy his milk before his nap.

"So you're worried about your kaddish, too," he said to her, not lifting his head.

Mrs. Wiener looked at him sharply, as if to assure herself that he was in his right senses. "I want that child to drink his milk. What does that have to do with a kaddish-shmaddish?" she said angrily to her husband.

She walked down the stairs with a heavy feeling. How could her husband think up such a false accusation, that she, too, would die sometime? In fact, what was this all of a sudden, a story about a kaddish?

Mrs. Wiener went over to her sister, Helen, who lived on the same block. She always went over to her sister when she wanted to get the grievances against her husband off her chest.

"He's going to sit out the entire seven days. Have you heard of such a thing in America? And he won't allow the store to be open so the men can work. No, he wants to show respect for his father! Have you heard of such things in America? What's more—this respect is going to cost us several hundred! And the men—they're not working, but still taking in a few cents, and it's the height of the season, a time when we actually make money— and just now his father goes and dies on him!"

Her sister put down the sweater that she was knitting, straightening the corners of a knitted sleeve several times, and shrugged her shoulders. "Is this news to you, that your Zalman sometimes overdoes things? When Schwartz's mother died—well, did he close his store? When Greenstein's wife passed away, may it never happen to anyone—well, didn't his people keep working in his luncheonette? But what can you do? Your Zalman is like Yudl with the honest buckets. Remember Yudl the Water Carrier? They paid him for three pairs of buckets, and he let the water overflow from the barrel. He did it his way and really poured six buckets worth! That was overdoing it a little, going off the track a little."

The sisters fueled each other's fire, and Mrs. Weiner went home loaded with hard feelings.

When she got home, Maxy was already asleep. Zalman was lying down on the sofa, dozing. But the slam of the door, and the metal taps of Mollie's high-heels on the floor woke him up. Mrs. Weiner began to speak, as though to herself.

"When a person overdoes things, it just won't do! When Schwartz's mother died, well, did he close up his business? And at the Greenstein's, when his wife, may it never happen to anyone, passed away, his employees still worked. Why do your employees deserve a vacation? No, it's a little off the track—Yudl with the honest buckets!"

Zalman Weiner adjusted the wick of the candle in the glass and said to his wife, "Mollie, I promise you, I only have one father to bury."

Early the next morning, Mrs. Weiner went to the drugstore, and from there she called Jack on the telephone, the older employee in her husband's business. She didn't want to call from her home, lest her husband hear her conversation.

"Jack, you're surely coming over to see my husband. I know, this is costing money. Maybe he'll listen to you. And you'll be part of the minyan. You pray, pray, what else? You pray, Jack. You can let Dick know and you can come together."

Mrs. Weiner hung up the receiver and said to herself, "That's it. No more free vacations. At least they can come to pray!"

Jack and Dick came over in the evening. On the way, the younger employee, Dick, said to Jack, "According to the union, we work for him at the shop; that's what we get paid for! We don't have to go to his house to pray! That's not our job! I'm a union man. I'm not any praying man. What won't a woman think of!"

Zalman Weiner thanked his employees for their visit. He told them about his father. This was the first time he had ever spoken to them about things other than the business. Both of them listened and said nothing. Dick excused himself, saying that his mother wasn't well, and left. Jack stayed for the minyan. He kept up with the others' praying in the same businesslike manner he had at the store. Out of habit, he even stole a glance at his watch to see what time it was. Mrs. Weiner looked several times at Jack to see how he stood and prayed, and it gave her pleasure. "That's it. At least it's something!"

Several weeks later, after Zalman had finished sitting shivah, Mrs. Weiner heard her husband shout at four-year-old Maxy, "A boy as big as you still smears peach all over his face? I pay so much tuition for you and you act like a little bum! You think I'll pay money for you for nothing? I'm going to tell the rabbi."

Astonished, Mrs. Weiner's eyes opened wide. What was he talking about? What tuition? she thought, and her heart was filled with anxiety. What was the matter with Zalman? On tip-toe she walked over to the door of the living room, and as carefully as one walks up to a sick person, she went over to her husband. "Zalman, who are you talking to?" she asked him.

Her husband answered her very simply, "To Maxy."

Mrs. Weiner blinked her eyes, dumbfounded.

"What do you mean," she said, "what do you mean, to Maxy?"

"I've enrolled him in a yeshiva."

"Who?" Mrs. Weiner repeated.

"Maxy. . ."

For a long time it was quiet. Then Mrs. Weiner began to stammer: "He's just a baby. What does this mean?"

Her husband was as silent as when he had been sitting shivah and she'd told him he should open the store. She took it as an insult and almost shrieked, "But still you could have asked me! It's true I don't think much of that, but still. . ."

Her husband interrupted her with a severity he seldom used: "No 'but still,' Mollie. Since no one is sitting shivah anymore, there's no 'but still'. I've done it."

"You want to throw money to the wind? He's just a baby . . . that, that's unheard of! Giving everyone a vacation."

Mrs. Weiner felt sorry for herself, sorry that her lot was different from that of all the neighbors in the building and all her acquaintances. Tears began rolling. She grabbed her coat and ran over to her sister Helen's to pour out her heart.

"It doesn't bother me that he throws money to the wind," Mrs. Weiner said to her sister, "but why does it have to be different for me? Different from the Rubensteins, different from the Adelmans, different from the Singers. . ." Mrs. Weiner went through the names of all her acquaintances, and the longer the list grew, the more bitterness she felt for her husband.

Her sister added fuel to her fire. "Really, Maxy's just a child, a baby. It's still years until he starts learning . . . to pay for him . . . to put down real money for something so crazy!"

When her sister mentioned "real money," Mrs. Weiner could no longer contain herself. She tore herself out of her place and said, "No, I'm going to tell him. He can't play the goat that runs away from the herd for me! I don't want to be different from the others!"

She ran back through the street in a rush, the way one runs to put out a fire.

New York, 1946

Eliahu Zalkind's Bookkeeping

· · · · · · · ·

For all the years that Eliahu Zalkind lived in America, he always spoke rapturously about his ship-brother, Mr. Karpl.

"This Mr. Karpl was a Jew, both a wise person and a doer of good deeds, and . . . I don't know what all! But the main thing was—he knew America!"

So Eliahu Zalkind said in a quiet moment, when he remembered how he had come from a shtetl in Lithuania forty years ago and had fallen right into the huge metropolis of New York.

In his shtetl, Eliahu Zalkind was the "writer" for the Loan Fund, which functioned as a sort of bank where Jews could take out a loan when they were pressed for money. Eliahu Zalkind was the bookkeeper, the collector of debts, the keeper of the keys to the Loan Fund. Twice a week, Mondays and Thursdays,[1] using a brush tied to a long stick, he swept the room that housed the Loan Fund. All the housewives in the shtetl swept with twig brooms, but he, Eliahu Zalkind, swept his office with a brush. Because of this, the work was not a humiliation for him. To sweep with a broom—that was one thing; to sweep with a brush—that was for the Loan Fund.

Eliahu Zalkind kept the books of the Loan Fund accurately and lovingly. The books in fact were bookkeeping entries, but they were also a record of the shtetl. The Loan Fund was especially busy just before holidays, before a fair, before an army draft, before winter, before a wedding—generally speaking, on all the "befores" of an important day. Then, Eliahu

1. See note 1 for "Family Life," page 93.

Zalkind would write in his books: Twentieth day, month of Tammuz.[2] A loan without interest in the amount of twenty-five rubles to Reb Avram Kornfein, in honor of the wedding of his youngest daughter, the maiden Chaya Gitl, may she have good luck.

A couple of months later, Eliahu Zalkind wrote on the opposite side in his bookkeeping ledger: Receipt in the amount of five rubles to the account of Reb Avram Kornfein for the loan without interest in honor of the wedding of his youngest daughter, Chaya Gitl, who with luck was married on the thirteenth day, month of Av.

Tuesday, fifteenth day, month of Elul. A loan without interest in the sum of thirty rubles to Reb Shimon the Graindealer for the great fair before Sukkos, God grant him success. He is a needy man. And across from this was written: Thursday, twenty-seventh day, month of Shvat. Reb Shimon, the Ryedealer, with God's help, repaid the entire thirty rubles. He had, praised be God, a good fair.

The salary that Eliahu Zalkind received for his work was precisely calculated by the elders of the town: he had to make a weekly living, to make the Sabbath, and in about fifteen or sixteen years, have enough for a dowry set aside for his daughter. He lived, literally, like royalty, and in fact they said in the shtetl, "Oh, such a job! But how many Loan Funds are there?"

However, it seems that working with money makes a man proud; Eliahu Zalkind, when he himself was once pressed for money and didn't know how he would pay for new Passover clothes, said right after the holiday: I'm going to America! A person can make some capital there, not have to sit year after year at a Loan Fund and sweep the floor with a brush twice a week, Mondays and Thursdays. And, in fact, he left right away with the entire family, his wife and small daughter, for whom a dowry had to be set aside in fifteen or sixteen years.

Sailing on the ship with them was a Mr. Karpl, a Jew who had already been in America, returned home, and was going back to America again, and

---

2. Mr. Zalkind makes his entries in a mixture of Hebrew and Yiddish. The days are recorded in Yiddish and the months in Hebrew. Tammuz corresponds roughly to June/July; Av, to July/August; Elul, to August/September; and Shvat, to January/February.

who wore a checkered scarf around his neck on which was imprinted with dye: "All wool." This Mr. Karpl was more like a professor than a passenger on the ship. All the emigrants stuck to him like glue, wanting to know what it was like there in America. Where did her power come from, and what was the reason that everyone was drawn to her?

Mr. Karpl told them that first of all in America each person was called "Mister," which meant something like a landowner. Whether a shoemaker, a tailor, a street sweeper, a porter, a peddler, each person had the title Mister. And no questions asked. He was a Mister. Take himself, for example. He was a button maker. No one would dare to call him simply Karpl. He was in fact, Mr. Karpl. And that was exactly what all the emigrants on board called him: "Mr. Karpl."

Eliahu Zalkind attached himself firmly to Mr. Karpl. One night, the ship was barely splashing, like a lazy duck on the water. The ocean was almost asleep, the stars were arranged in the sky, as if in their father's vineyard: here a branch of stars, there a cluster of stars, here a huge constellation of stars shooting brightly in the middle of the heavens, in short, the true beauty of the night! The moon reflected, and multiplied herself by two: one in the heavens, the other scattered in moonbeams on the waves. On that very night, Eliahu Zalkind sat down next to Mr. Karpl, and Mr. Karpl explained the secret of America to him.

"Dear man," he said, "you should know that Columbus found America, and in this land, as soon as you have a dollar, it's just as soon gone. One day you have him—the next day he's rolled away. It's a constant chase. You understand? Because one day you have him, and the next day, he's not there. The whole trick is this: to chase hard enough to have him always in hand and still be an honest man."

Just to be sure, Eliahu Zalkind asked again: "What? What do I have to have in my hand?"

Mr. Karpl straightened the checkered scarf around his neck, looked for a while into the ocean, then at his companion, and then answered with a calm and irrefutable authority: "As they say—dollars. You understand? Columbus found such a land. And it has its own ways. You don't understand them, and you can't change them. You roll with the wheel, dear man, with the wheel. . ."

The ship splashed through the sea like a lazy duck on the water, the sea slept, the stars in the heavens were arranged as if by a father in his vineyard, and the moon multiplied herself: one moon in the heavens, and a multitude of moonbeams sparkling on the waves. And Eliahu Zalkind understood the secret of America.

In New York, Eliahu Zalkind realized that what Mr. Karpl had said was indeed the truth. He didn't have to look twice for people to call him Mr. Zalkind. With dollars, it was exactly as Mr. Karpl had told him. One day you had them, the next day you didn't, and it was such a chase that you could barely remember you were still a person.

Eliahu Zalkind wanted to become a bookkeeper, just as he had been for the Loan Fund. But it became evident to him that bookkeeping for the Loan Fund and bookkeeping in America were as far apart as the shtetl was from New York. Even the numbers were different. They seemed to be the same, yet they were different. At home, for example, a two was a two, a number. It stood up. It had a little head and twisted foot. It was a substantial two. But here, you made it in a hurry with no head, no foot; a fly's little leg was a two in America. The same thing with the five and the seven; with everything and everyone. It was a chase.

Since nothing came of the bookkeeping, Eliahu Zalkind remembered his brush. He knew all about brushes from the time at the Loan Fund. He knew what kind of a brush sweeps and what kind of a brush does not. He began to deal in brushes and to learn more about them; that brushes in America were important, very important. For each thing, there was a brush: a brush for the floors, a brush for the dishes, a brush for the windows, a brush for the rugs, a brush for the bath, and even a brush for the fingernails. For the glassware, another brush. His brush for the Loan Fund office couldn't begin to compare to brushes in America. And these brushes were lucky for him. He slowly began to build a brush business that eventually grew so wide and so long, it took up half a block. Out of habit, Eliahu Zalkind himself, with his own hand, still swept out his place of business, twice a week, on Mondays and Thursdays, just as he had done for the Loan Fund.

But an enormous longing for bookkeeping remained with him. There was a bookkeeper in his brush business who did the books in a manner Eliahu Zalkind could never understand, except for the yearly summary. The bookkeeping records in his business were completely foreign to him. They had something to do with Columbus, who had found America. It was Columbus's country, his bookkeeper and his bookkeeping; perhaps it really wasn't bookkeeping.

Eliahu Zalkind took counsel with himself: why couldn't a person have two sets of bookkeeping? One would belong to Columbus, and one would in fact be his own. And so Eliahu Zalkind established a Loan Fund for his landsmen's society. There, he himself, provided the first fine few dollars, but in return, he was the treasurer. He watched over the books, he collected the money, and he did the bookkeeping.

He bought a ledger that was identical, like two drops of water, to his old book for the Loan Fund, and in it, he wrote in his old style: fine numbers that looked respectable. A two was a two and not a fly's leg. A five was a five, a seven was seven. Eliahu Zalkind entered the accounts in his old style: "To Mr. Reb Morris Hirshman, for a dangerous operation, a loan without interest of two hundred dollars. God help him to come through safely."

A couple of months later, Eliahu Zalkind noted down the opposite side of his ledger: "From Mr. Reb Morris Hirshman, who is, thank God, now healthy after his dangerous operation, received a payment of fifty dollars toward his account."

He kept the books for his Loan Fund in a small bookcase in the brush business store. Every Sunday, when the Sambatyon [3] of New York rested, the factories rested, the shops, the banks, the workers and the employees—then Eliahu Zalkind worked at his Loan Fund. He took out his books, laid them on a small table, and did the sums, adding up the paid debts. He did the book-keeping, so that it had sense and order.

What had Mr. Karpl, his ship-brother, said? That Columbus's land has its own way. The Jews of the *landsleit* gave donations to the Loan Fund, and it grew rich; it was almost a bank. People praised him, Eliahu Zalkind, to the skies, thanking him, acknowledging him, even making him the presi-

3. The Sambatyon (in Yiddish, *Sambatyen*) is the legendary impassable river of rocks be-hind which the Ten Lost Tribes of Israel were supposed to dwell. Here it is probably refer-ring to the East River or the Hudson River in New York.

dent of the Loan Fund, but they appointed someone else to do the books—
an accountant. Eliahu Zalkind never noticed, between all the praises, the
compliments, the blessings, and the appreciations, that they had taken the
bookkeeping out of his hands.

Now an accountant did the books for the Loan Fund. Instead of cor-
rectly made numbers, flitting flies' legs stood in remarkably straight lines. A
bookkeeping without sense or understanding, no record of where the money
went, for what reason, who it had helped, or what it had accomplished. The
bookkeeping for the Loan Fund became unintelligible and strange to Eliahu
Zalkind, just like the bookkeeping was at his brush business.

He often thought about his ship-brother, Mr. Karpl, who had told him
the secret of America: Columbus discovered a land that had its own ways.
You had to roll with the wheel, dear man, with the wheel . . .

And the best example was the bookkeeping for his Loan Fund.

Eliahu Zalkind remembered the conversation very well. He even remembered Mr. Karpl's checkered scarf, on that quiet night when the ship
had splashed like a lazy duck in water, when the sea had slept, and the stars
had been arranged as if by a father in his vineyard, and the moon had multiplied—one moon in the heavens, and the other scattered in a multitude of
moonbeams on the waves.

A wise man, Mr. Karpl, a wise man!

New York, 1947

Married Off

· · · · · · · ·

During the four weeks preceding the Carmelia Club's Third Seder, Elka Nussbaum worked around the clock. She called people on the telephone, she wrote letters, she visited friends and relatives, she met people in lobbies of hotels, she was busy up to her ears. She had a habit of talking for a good ten or fifteen minutes, her hand on the doorknob, after saying good-bye. She was hoarse from talking, and her feet hurt.

A day before the celebration, she lay in bed and rested. She said to her husband, Shloyme, "I haven't felt tired all this time, it's only today that I feel it in my bones."

"Nothing comes easy, Elka," Shloyme answered. That his wife was such an active woman in the Carmelia Club was a great pleasure for him, and he happily tousled her hair.

Lying in bed, her hair disheveled, and resting against a pillow, Elka said, "People are saying that several members of the Young Carmelia have signed up to go to Erets Isroel. Have you heard anything about it?"

"Let them go," Shloyme answered easily. "What do we care? Our Alec still has two more years of chemistry, then a year of physics, and then has to write his thesis . . . what do we care?"

Elka didn't say anything. She looked at a green butterfly, its wings struggling against the ceiling. "He wants to go right through the ceiling," she said, and laughed, pointing out the butterfly to her husband.

Adorned with a new permanent wave, Elka came to the Third Seder. Sitting up high at the head table, at the dais, she screened all the tables, to see which of her tickets had come. She was so busy checking that she didn't hear Mrs. Enshel, the chairwoman, give her speech and welcome the audience.

Elka considered each of her tickets with a loving look and waved her hand at them. And she held a quiet grudge against those who hadn't come: my vegetable lady, a calamity of a woman, hasn't come! Gives me a couple of dollars to get off the hook and stays home. I need her dollars like a hole in the head. She doesn't come herself, just sits and watches television. What a log! As if that's more important than the Carmelia Club . . .

And therefore, her pleasure was even greater when her butcher with his wife and daughter arrived, dressed up for Passover, and sat at the third table. Elka blew them a kiss. Then she went over to them and said, "I hope you will join the Carmelia Club. It's never a bad thing for a Jew to do."

Elka was not only the pestle to the mortar of the Carmelia Club, she was its cornerstone as well. Since she and her husband had founded the Club thirty years before, she had been elected president four times. And now that she was out of office, no longer the president, she did all the hardest work. She sold tickets, collected things for the bazaar. She was Elka. And whatever needed doing for the Carmelia Club, she did it.

The six hundred people who had come to the Third Seder warmed her heart. There they all sat, like one family, dressed for the holiday, singing together, rejoicing together, building Erets Isroel together.

The best speaker couldn't make a better appeal than Elka could, and she barely spoke, but would fire out individual words that had nothing to do with each other. Suddenly, she would forget what she wanted to say, stop herself, try to recall, and then add right away: "I forgot to tell you." The crowd laughed at her awkwardness, but several of her fired-out words stayed with them and even touched their hearts.

At the Third Seder, because she was so moved, almost overjoyed with the huge attendance, her speech became utterly entangled and she said to the audience, as though they were all her close cousins: "I prepared, believe me, a very beautiful speech, only I've completely forgotten it. Just let me look at you all a little." The audience laughed warmly. Elka's blue eyes, clear and almost pensive, looked out over the tables, and she said: "Let each one of us read what is in his heart; I couldn't say anything to you more beautiful than what you have in your hearts anyway. . ."

Her appeal was successful. The mood was dignified. The chairwoman thanked the gathered audience, praised Elka, and joked a little. Everyone was happy.

At that moment, Mrs. Shapiro, wearing a white hat with three tall, green feathers, glided into the auditorium. She was the leader of the youth club, Young Carmelia. Her light spring dress floated between the tables as she came up to the dais. In a loud voice, in portentous words, she announced that she was bringing a gift to the Club: eight young men and women had signed up to go to Erets Isroel. The audience greeted her news with applause. Mrs. Shapiro pointed out the chairwoman, Mrs. Enshel, and said: "I will use this occasion to tell you that, Rose, our chairwoman's daughter, is the leader of the group. The apple doesn't fall far from the tree."

There was an ovation for Mrs. Enshel. She smiled, but her face was pale and her painted lips tightly clamped.

Elka thought about her son, Alec. He was a hot-head. Who knows, maybe he had signed up, too. And sitting there at the head table, she forgot about the huge audience in the hall. Her heart was pounding about her Alec, and she would have given anything to know where he was at this moment and what he was doing.

On the way home, Elka was uneasy and anxious. One of her friends, sitting next to her on the bus, said simply: "Our chairwoman, Mrs. Enshel, didn't look so happy that her Rose had signed up. I'm telling you the truth, I wouldn't want to suffer that myself either. We raise our children and want them to stay at home. How can you send a child off? Like they're packages?"

As she spoke, her full face expressed a healthy motherliness, a deep attachment to her family.

Elka answered, almost not hearing her own words: "I know. I understand what you're saying . . . I know."

At home, Elka found her husband and son, Alec, in the middle of a quarrel. Shloyme was standing, one hand spread out on the table, his other hand waving in the air as if he wanted to grab onto something. Alec was sitting in the middle of the room, riding on a chair, his stubborn, young chin resting on the back of it.

"Mazel tov, Elka!" her husband greeted her. "Your son doesn't need a father or a mother, doesn't need advice or accounting. He's his own free man and does whatever he wants. He's set loose on the world. He doesn't need anyone's advice."

Suddenly, he shouted at his son: "And don't sit in that chair like you're riding a horse when you're talking to me! This is something . . . something . . . you already have plenty of nerve! Why are you a Zionist, he asks me! I should answer him at the snap of a finger? He sits there, riding a chair and I should spell it out for him, right now, why I am a Zionist!"

Elka had never seen her husband so furious. She had never heard such a heated rush of words spew out of him before.

Their son sat on the chair and looked at his father with a kind of wondering curiosity, as if he were seeing the sun fall out of the sky into a basket, and he didn't understand what the heavens were coming to.

Elka understood that Alec was among the eight who were intending to leave. She remained standing between her son and husband and thought: What should she do, where should she begin, and what should she say?

Very slowly, she took off her hat and coat. Alec turned to look at his mother and said to her, "I've signed up to go to Erets Isroel."

This wasn't news to Elka. She went over to her son and put her hand on his shoulder with affectionate friendliness, just as if he had bought a ticket to one of her undertakings, and said, "I am very pleased you have such a desire, Alec. Ten thousands of young men your age don't even think they're Jewish. Why shouldn't I be pleased with you?"

His mother's words calmed Alec. Indeed, he felt that he was one in ten thousand and he was very pleased. His mother's good hand was after all on his shoulder, as though she were continuing to admire him.

Shloyme, overwrought, couldn't stand this unexpected loving declaration between his wife and son, and said, "So kiss each other! Let's bring this to an end; kiss each other!"

Later, he was angry with his wife: "What a idea! Alec decides and registers himself! What's he's going to become in Erets Isroel? A stonecutter? You live your life so your son can be a stonecutter? That was okay thirty years ago. Then, everyone was a stonecutter. But it's no good now. He's a fool,

Alec! And you, too! What do you mean by patting him like that? I don't like such underhanded ways. You either say yes or no! Patting all of a sudden. . ."

"I know how to talk to Alec better than you do," Elka answered him, and she moved in the chair so heavily it seemed she could have weighed four hundred pounds.

Shloyme yanked himself away and left the room.

Elka took a step after her husband, but then stopped herself. It wouldn't do any good to quarrel with him either, she thought. Quarreling with Shloyme was the same as quarreling with Alec. It would solve nothing.

With half closed eyes, like a blind person testing the way with his feet, Elka went over to the telephone and called up her cousin, Sophie. She was astonished that her voice was cheerful and even happy.

"Sophie-doll, why weren't you at the Third Seder today? I sent you two letters. It was a wonderful Seder. There were six hundred people."

Sophie had lots of excuses: her two daughters, Mildie and Evelyn, had taken it into their heads to go to the ocean. Evelyn was crazy about swimming and water sports, but especially swimming . . .

Elka raised her head and thought for a while. She said to Sophie, "Sophie-doll, the thought just occurred to me. Let's all of us go to the ocean together this summer. Evelyn, Mildie, my Alec. We could really have a good time. Yes, I need a rest, a person needs to rest, Sophie-doll. . ."

We need to forget about this brouhaha with Alec for a while—she thought leaving the telephone—it'll be good for Shloyme and for Alec, too . . . for Alec . . . to get this idea out of his head a little.

Lying in bed, Elka mentioned to her husband: "I was just saying to Sophie that we should to go to the ocean together this summer."

"What's this, all of a sudden?"

"We need to forget about this brouhaha with Alec for a while. It's better than quarreling with him. Let him swim a little. Mildie will be there, and Evelyn. The girls will be a wedge to drive this idea out of his head and drive in another. When you're twenty years old, swimming is better than quarreling."

"Female tricks!" Shloyme answered, disgruntled, "hotsy-totsy-shmotsy . . . swimming, of all things!"

Sophie came over with both daughters, Evelyn and Mildie, to talk about the trip to the ocean. Evelyn, wearing a full crinoline skirt and a tight sleeveless blouse, fluttered around Alec's room, examined the pictures of Erets Isroel on the wall, and said to him, "Alec, bring the pictures with you to the beach and you can tell me about them. Alec, your room looks just like it's in Israel. . ."

Evelyn looked at Alec with youthful, delighted joy. Alec followed after her fluttering full skirt, intoxicated with her delight.

"See, Evelyn, see how they plow the fields. See, Evelyn, see how they catch fish."

Evelyn smiled, with the small eyes of a Japanese dancer, and melted from joy.

· · · · · · ·

They really enjoyed that summer by the ocean. Alec was busy with Evelyn: Evelyn came, Evelyn went, Evelyn wants, Evelyn doesn't want. Alec went to the Young Carmelia meetings with Evelyn.

Evelyn loved to swim early in the morning. She would dive into the water, swim out on another side of the beach, hug Alec with a wet, tanned hand and murmur to him: "Come with me to the depths of the sea, there where paradise is to be found!" They laughed a lot—young, sunny laughter.

Evelyn told Alec that he shouldn't interrupt his college studies. And she had iron proof for him that he had to finish: "Our choreography professor told us that if a person quits his studies, he never amounts to anything. And our professor is an Irishman, a smart man. He has a moustache a half mile long."

"Evelyn, you're leading me astray. I want to go to Erets Isroel."

Evelyn stood, her head down and her foot up, and answered Alec. "I want to go there, too! But a person has to finish college first. The Irishman told us."

Alec obeyed Evelyn and the Irishman.

Sitting on the beach at the seashore, Elka pushed hot sand onto her feet and said to her husband, "It was a lucky thing that we came to the ocean. Alec has gotten this idea of going to Erets Isroel out of his head a little. In the meantime, he's going to finish college. Later, let Evelyn take charge of him. He'll obey her faster than he will you or me. Sophie told me that she wants Alec to marry Evelyn. I'm very happy. Evelyn . . . why ever not?"

Shloyme looked at the waves, as if he didn't hear Elka talking to him. His gaze slowly followed their rush, back and forth, as if they were forever regretting something, wanting it back. Very quietly, the way people say the most ordinary thing, he responded, "You know, Alec won't look at me. He won't look me in the eye. He likes Evelyn, but, but . . . he thinks we're liars, Elka. And so he won't look at me."

Elka hastily brushed the sand off her feet and stood up. "What's the matter with you? I've never told a lie in my life, and you tell me such a story—that he thinks we're liars? Go for a swim! That'll knock the heat out of your head! It's the best thing for you, Shloyme!"

In the fall, Elka had plenty of work for their fundraiser, the Raffle. Sitting up high at the head table, she screened all the other tables, noting how many of her tickets had come. She considered each of her tickets with a loving glance and waved her hand to the people.

Her vegetable lady had also come to the raffle evening. She and her husband. Elka went over to them, put her hand on her shoulder and said to her warmly, "I hope you'll become Carmelia people. It's never a bad thing for a Jew to do. Believe me."

About Hannukah time, Elka celebrated the wedding of her son Alec to Evelyn. After the chuppah, when the young couple was dancing, Elka said to her husband, very happily, "So, Shloyme, who has to quarrel with a child? You see what can be done with kindness!?"

Shloyme shook his head and said nothing.

Home for Passover

. . . .

M rs. Miller didn't believe that the earth rotated. She had spent thirty-four years in her women's dress shop on Center Street. In summer, when it was the slack season and she had enough time to sit outside and see what was going on, she knew—the earth stood fast.

Her two daughters, Sarah and Bessie, who had both finished high school and Bessie was going to college, had once been chattering about how the earth rotated. Then Mrs. Miller felt herself lost: her daughters did not want to be businesswomen at all, and she said to them: "I have never yet seen it move an inch. I've been in this place on Center Street for thirty-four years and not even one brick has moved from a wall—except that Schwartz had to rebuild his house after the fire and they moved the post office. And that's no small thing! We'd all be scattered and not even one little bone of ours would be left, if the earth rotated! For six years I've had a sticker hanging in the shop—a dress I can't sell to anyone. It's still hanging there, just the way I hung it up. It's never moved. It would be no small matter if the earth were to rotate!"

Her older daughter, Bessie, who was dark-complexioned and had a narrow, smiling little nose, loved her mother very much and tried to calm her down: "Mom, people aren't absolutely certain about that . . . There's nothing people know for certain. . ."

A slight smile was hanging on her thin little nose. But Mrs. Miller had already calmed herself down.

"What's this? *They* know? People learn plenty of things in colleges, but even with all their wisdom, they still don't know how to sell a dress."

During the thirty-four years in her dress shop on Center Street, Mrs. Miller had grown rich. For her there wasn't a Sabbath or a Sunday, a holiday or a rest. Just Rosh Hashanah and Yom Kippur. The neighbors estimated that she was worth about a quarter of a million dollars.

When people asked her for a donation, Mrs. Miller would count out several dollars anxiously, and the neighbors would say to her, sometimes jokingly and sometimes seriously, "Mrs. Miller, they say you have, *keyn eyn bore*, a pretty penny." But she would shake her head and answer them: "Our people, if we didn't watch our money, we'd have to go begging from house to house."

At one time in her life, Mrs. Miller knew what it felt like to need a dollar; she needed, but she didn't have. That was twenty-two years ago, when her husband had died. The girls were still small. The bills came pouring in, but she didn't have the wherewithal to pay them. Her husband's brother, just then had no money, or so he said. Her own sister wasn't in a hurry to open her purse either . . . you may as well throw yourself in the fire. The green-grocer lady, Mrs. Jaffe, had had pity on her then and loaned her a hundred dollars. She seemed an angel in Mrs. Miller's eyes. The rest of the money she knocked together by pawning her pearls, and she rescued herself.

Each year for the Seder, Mrs. Miller took a bottle of wine, kosher for Passover, to the greengrocer lady, Mrs. Jaffe. Every year, for twenty years, the same thing. She never, not even once, failed to bring a bottle of wine to the Mrs. Jaffe's Seder.

Sometimes, Mrs. Miller did an accounting for herself: twenty-two bottles of wine was no less than thirty-six dollars, which was too great a percentage on the hundred dollars she had kept for one year's time. But what did it matter? She enjoyed it.

Each year she thanked Mrs. Jaffe, and both women even shed a tear. During the twenty-two years' time, Mrs. Jaffe had gotten fat, aged greatly, and was not any richer than she once had been. Mrs. Miller, on the other hand became rich and thin, wearing her pearls around her neck to hide the wrinkles that age had bestowed upon her. Both women wished each other a happy holiday and wept for the twenty-two years gone by, and for the fact that life passes so quickly.

When the season wasn't going well, Mrs. Miller would go outside on the sidewalk to bring in customers. She knew exactly what to say to convince them to come into her shop. The neighboring store owners couldn't understand how she was able to pull them in, but people came into her shop. The store owners gossiped about her: "She doesn't have enough, poor thing, for Sabbath! A poor widow!"

Mrs. Miller couldn't live if she didn't take in money each day. It wasn't so much that she needed to earn money, as she needed to be in motion. If things weren't moving in her dress shop, Mrs. Miller became upset, exactly as though all the dresses on hangers were screaming at her: "Sell us. Sell us at any price! We need to get out of here!"

She could stand for long hours in the street and talk to the passersby. In the evening, her legs were stiff, but that made her happy: the store wasn't resting.

The dresses on their hangers were the liveliest things in the world for Mrs. Miller. She knew each dress and how old it was—two weeks, two months, a year. There were dresses that she couldn't sell, the stickers, and she hated them the way people hate an old maid who can't be married off. Pity that turns into hostility. Such was the feeling she had for her stickers, which hung there and hung there, unwanted.

When her daughters, Bessie and Sarah, were growing up, they didn't attach much importance to their mother's shop. Bessie, with the narrow, smiling little nose, would take a dress off a hanger the way a person brushes a crumb off the table. It meant nothing to her to put on a dress two or three times and leave it lying there, take a new one, and leave that lying there too.

Sarah was worse yet. She never wore dresses from her mother's shop. She bought them for herself in a department store.

Mrs. Miller used to say to her daughters, "For you, one dress or another is nothing. For you, the earth is rotating . . . what value does a dress have for you? The fact that each dress carries its own bill doesn't matter to you."

It pained Mrs. Miller that her daughters didn't respect her accomplishments in her business. And therefore she got skinnier. The pearls around her neck could no longer hide the deepening wrinkles. Mrs. Miller ordered a blouse with a high collar and wore the pearls over that. People shouldn't see how her daughter's luxuries were eating her up alive. You couldn't be a good saleslady with a skinny neck. You look needy, and you can't sell. You look needy, and people are put off.

Bessie, with the narrow little nose, finished college. She got married to a young engineer, Irving, who hardly ever spoke, but always whistled a little tune. Bessie's college and her wedding made a big dent in Mrs. Miller's fortune. "Such a wedding can make you go begging from house to house," she would say.

One day, Bessie and Irving went to her mother and told her that they were building a ranch house.

Mrs. Miller didn't know what "ranch house" meant. It was the first time she'd ever heard the word. But she felt her pocket shudder, and she asked, "What is this ranch house? Is it some kind of brick?"

Bessie's narrow little nose smiled as she reassured her mother. "No, it's not another kind of brick, it's a kind of architecture."

Mrs. Miller was used to hearing words she didn't understand from her daughter and son-in-law, but she knew that those words cost her money. In all simplicity, she asked, glancing sideways at her daughter and son-in-law: "A ranch house at least has a roof?"

Bessie kissed her mother and laughed happily. Irving laughed and whistled a little tune.

Because of the ranch house, Mrs. Miller went to Miami for the first time in her life, in order to give these thoughts a rest. The house construction was eating up money the way a cow eats grass. In a half year, Mrs. Miller had laid out sixty-seven hundred dollars, and three hundred for something called a barbecue oven.

When it came to the barbecue oven, Mrs. Miller felt she was sick. She didn't even go outside and try to bring in customers.

The children, Bessie and Irving, Sarah and her boyfriend, all of them kept after her—she should go with Irving's mother, Mrs. Pearl, to Miami for a rest. Mrs. Miller let herself be talked into it. The cost was the same as a barbecue oven, she supposed.

Mrs. Miller put on her blouse with the high collar, the pearls on top of it, put several gold bracelets that jangled noisily against the other on her wrist, and she was all set to go to Miami.

For a long time she stood outside the locked door of her shop and read the sign: "Closed for a month for winter vacation." Mrs. Miller didn't recognize the door of her shop. Even the street seemed different to her. The whole area had changed.

Traveling with Mrs. Pearl on the train, Mrs. Miller was amazed that her in-law went into the dining car as if she were going into her own kitchen. Mrs. Pearl was not a rich woman. She was a beautician and had never had an extra dollar. Mrs. Miller took her to be a poor woman. Mrs. Pearl ordered one dish and then another. The waiter, a friendly man with a double chin, served them plates decorated with sprigs of greenery, just like a Gentile bride. In the dining car, a couple of dollars burst like soap bubbles. Only Mrs. Pearl and the friendly waiter enjoyed themselves. Mrs. Miller and the journey did not agree with each other. Every turn of the wheels seemed to cost money.

Mrs. Miller sat out four days in Miami and got sick. She figured that each hour's sleep in the hotel cost her three dollars. The sea roared and hissed and grew angry. Mrs. Miller lay there and thought and wondered how the poor woman, her in-law, could sleep, knowing that for each hour's sleep she was out three dollars. Sleeping—something that God gave us entirely for free, just like air and water—sleeping here in Miami cost money. That kind of sleeping, and we'll have to go begging from house to house, Mrs. Miller thought. Then she remembered how her educated daughters had once chattered about the earth's rotation. Maybe they were right. If the earth were to stand fast, soundly and firmly, there wouldn't be such things . . . and the sea, how it's crying! Maybe the earth really is rotating; it's just at home that no one notices it.

She began to suffer from headaches. She told Mrs. Pearl that she couldn't stand the climate in Miami. She couldn't suffer the summer in the winter. Winter should be winter. The Miami summer wasn't good for her health.

Fearfully, Bessie met her mother at the train station when she returned from Miami. She took her to the ranch house.

In the ranch house, the doors opened with a single movement. The windows moved both right and left. The shelves in the cupboards could rotate either way. With great pleasure, Irving showed his mother-in-law everything, whistling a little tune all the while.

Bessie, with a slight smile on her narrow little nose, saw that her mother was completely bewildered by all the tricks: the windows, the little tables on wheels, the shelves that rotated in the cupboards. She tried to calm her. "It's nothing, Mom, a little screw turns it."

Sickened by Miami and by the ranch house, Mrs. Miller returned to her own home for Passover.

With a special feeling of affection for Mrs. Jaffe, she brought a bottle of wine, kosher for Passover, to the Seder.

At Mrs. Jaffe's, everything smelled like fresh apples and conserves and carried the scent of green pepper—just as in an autumn garden, ripening and withering mingled in the air.

Mrs. Jaffe thanked Mrs. Miller for the wine, and, just as in years past, tears came to her eyes. Both women shed a tear for the twenty-three years already gone by, and for life that passes so quickly.

Mrs. Miller almost cried with happiness. Now, here in Mrs. Jaffe's grocery store, she recovered herself. Everything was as it had been last year, for the last two years, for the last twenty-three years. Here was a drop of stability, that came from kindness. Here the earth didn't rotate. Center Street and Mrs. Miller were standing fast.

New York, 1956

Elaine

· · · · · · · ·

Elaine was especially delighted when her professor told her that she could stay on and work with him in the laboratory for the coming year. She blushed and lowered her head in embarrassment.

"Thank you," she murmured, making an effort not to seem too excited.

She called Marvin, the young man she had been seeing for about two years, and told him the good news. Marvin answered her, almost disgruntled: "Well, what are you so happy about? How can a person work for such a buffalo?" Marvin didn't like Professor Shapiro. He called him, for no good reason, "the buffalo."

The professor, Adam Shapiro, an old bachelor who often talked to himself, hardly ever looked at the young women, his students. He didn't believe they had the desire to learn, and when one of them worked carelessly, he would reproach all of them with the same words: "Girls, if you've come here to catch a boyfriend, hurry up, catch him and get married. That has nothing to do with chemistry."

After his little talk, the professor smiled benignly and knowingly to himself, which meant: I know you very well, you can't fool me.

The students smiled along with him and were not insulted. They responded to his words the way people react to a solar eclipse—it gets dark, indeed, but no one gets angry because of it.

Elaine was proud that Professor Shapiro had chosen her to help him in the laboratory and had even arranged a small salary for her. She started wearing low-heeled shoes after the professor had said once to her at work,

"I cannot comprehend how a person can stand on such tall cedar trees," pointing at the high heels of her shoes.

The very next morning Elaine came to work in low-heeled shoes, silently indicating that she was one to obey.

Professor Shapiro was famous for two things. First, he was fastidious. Each thing had to be in its own place, even a pencil. He would hand homework back to the students without even having looked at it if there was a blotch on the notebook or a crossed-out sentence. But about his person, he wasn't so particular. The hem of his jacket sagged somewhat, and his tie looked lopsided. This only meant that clothes had nothing to do with work.

Although he was a bit uncouth, the students really liked him. They would accompany him to the bus, bring coffee to his table in the laboratory where he worked, and sometimes it happened that they would bring him a new shirt and a necktie when his clothes were too wrinkled.

Professor Shapiro took the gifts. He never thanked the person who had given them to him, but offered his thanks to a second student. Each one acted as though she had given him the present, and then told all her friends that she had already received a thank-you from Professor Shapiro. Even Elaine, who worked closely with him, and whom he knew well, had received several thank-yous for someone else. No one wondered about this. It was just Professor Shapiro.

When Elaine told her parents that she would be working with Professor Shapiro for the coming year, her mother, Mrs. Finkel, turned the side table lamp on to light up the room, just like she did when guests came. And her father, Mr. Finkel, went out himself and brought back ice cream. Her mother asked, "Have you told Marvin already?"

"Yes!" Elaine answered briefly, a smile poised on the tip of her finely shaped upper lip. She remembered how Marvin had called Professor Shapiro a "buffalo."

A short couple of weeks later, Marvin told Elaine that he was going to leave his studies at the university. He would begin working with his brother in his chemical factory where they made dyes for textiles. It would give him a better start, he said. He wanted to get married and become a man with a position.

Marvin spoke in a businesslike manner. He told Elaine this easily, as if he were talking about a trifle: "You won't have time to work in the laboratory . . . I think you'll have to tell your professor."

For several nights after this, Elaine couldn't sleep. She didn't want to stop working for Professor Shapiro. And day after day, she postponed telling him that she wouldn't be working for him in the coming year.

One day he found her, wearing her coat in the laboratory, standing and looking through the window as though she were trying to decide something. Her face was strained.

Professor Shapiro went over to her, put his hand on her shoulder, and said, "Elaine. What's the matter, Elaine?"

To his immense surprise, she burst into tears. She spread both hands on the windowsill and sobbed quietly.

Shapiro remained standing there, chewed his lip, and didn't know what to say to her. He muttered, "You shouldn't cry."

He stood next to her, looked at her young shoulders that were trembling, and felt a great tenderness for her.

"Elaine," he said to her, wiping the glass of his wristwatch—which was what he usually did when he was trying to explain a difficult formula to those thickheads—"Elaine, you shouldn't undertake any business while crying."

Thus, he finished and as if nothing had happened, he slowly put on his coat, took Elaine by the arm, and left the laboratory with her.

As had happened before, Elaine accompanied him to his bus, said good-bye to him, and went back to the laboratory.

Marvin became more insistent. The first question he asked Elaine each time he saw her was: "What's going on? Have you spoken to Professor Shapiro?"

Once Elaine answered him, upset: "What's the hurry? I still have time . . . he'll find an assistant for the lab."

Marvin looked angrily at Elaine and didn't say anything. This was their first quarrel, a quarrel without words, without a reproach, but still—a breach.

Professor Shapiro never reminded Elaine about her tears. He acted as though he had entirely forgotten it, as though it had never taken place.

Elaine felt that leaving the laboratory would be hard for her. She was used to her little table, to Professor Shapiro, who paced the floor and talked to himself, to the quiet sound of the glassware and pipes and tubes on her table, and to the picture of Newton on the wall. Without all of this, she'd be lonely. Once she said to Marvin, "Why do I have to quit working, Marvin? It isn't necessary."

Marvin answered her forcefully. "I won't even discuss it. A person has to establish a home . . . he has to . . ."

Elaine walked next to him and looked at his face which had clouded up. An almost unfamiliar face. She had never seen Marvin this way. Walking along, she put her hand around his neck and said, "Smile, a little, Marvin. Don't be so upset."

"All right," he answered, but his "all right" was said with such determination, it was as if he were saying to her, it's either this or that.

Elaine pulled her collar around her neck; she seemed to have gotten colder. She buttoned up her coat and reached her hand out to Marvin's coat to button his collar. But he turned his head and pushed her hand away.

Tears came into Elaine's eyes. Without a word, she turned and left. Marvin didn't call her back. He walked straight ahead stubbornly, as though he were walking on railroad tracks.

One day, when she came into the laboratory, Professor Shapiro handed her a letter. He gave her the letter, not looking at her. She recognized Marvin's handwriting and her heart skipped a beat. What did Marvin have to write to Professor Shapiro? She read the letter over. Marvin had written that Professor Shapiro should look for another assistant for his laboratory, that Elaine was getting married and had to give up working. She had to devote herself to her home.

From the stiff way Elaine stood there, Professor Shapiro knew that Marvin had written the letter without her knowledge. He didn't say anything, and when she went over to her table and sat down to begin working, he turned and began talking to himself as usual.

When she was putting on her coat to leave, she said, "Are you going home, Professor? I'll accompany you."

Silently, he put on his coat, took Elaine by the chin and asked her, pointing to Marvin's letter lying on the table, "Well?"

Elaine gazed at him for a considerable time, as though what she was preparing to say to him was very important to her.

"I don't intend to get married, Professor. Not just yet."

After she said this, a weight lifted from her heart. Professor Shapiro muttered something to himself, as they were walking down the stairs.

There was a real to-do in the college when Elaine invited her friends to a reception at her home to celebrate her wedding to Professor Shapiro. He came to the reception in his usual suit, but with a flower in his lapel. Elaine behaved in her usual manner when she met her friends. They drank, wished her well, chatted, and left. The next morning, Elaine went to work at the laboratory, like every other day. She came in and felt herself to be at home—it was a good home, devoted, and quiet, and where Professor Shapiro walked around, talking to himself, and the portrait of Newton hung on the wall.

January 1956

Brothers

· · · · · · ·

I srael Pressman drove to the Titkove *landsleit* meeting in a good mood. He
was bringing a bottle of whiskey to drink a l'chaim with the brothers on
the Board and with the other Titkovers who would be coming to the meeting early. It's a democracy, you drink with everyone—he thought—and it
won't hurt the election either.

He had been the president of the Titkove Society for seven years, and
he was just as much the boss there as he was in his own home. His sister's
daughter, Florence, handled the Titkover's Aid and Loan Fund, and all the
Titkovers called her "our Florence." The Titkovers' chorus was led by his
wife's brother, Ben. The Titkovers' banquet was held in Shimkovitch's
restaurant, Shimkovitch being "our Florence's father-in-law." Israel Pressman was the august king of the small kingdom called the Titkove Society.
He had no doubts whatsoever that anyone could ever wrest the gavel from
his hand.

Driving to the meeting, he thought about Wolf Solomon who, in the
last two years, had gotten rich. For years Solomon had been a certified poor
man. The half-director of a half-bankrupt antique store. But with God's
help, he had tried his hand in real estate and within two years sprung out a
rich man. He started making contributions to the society, and when he
came to a meeting, he offered his hand to everyone. The Titkovers grew to
respect him. Once Pincus Moses even stood up and gave his own place to
Solomon to sit down. Just like that, to show him respect. For no special reason. But because of this, Wolf Solomon drove him home afterward, all the

way up to the Bronx. Lucky that Wolf Solomon never opened his mouth, and therefore no one would elect him president. When his son became bar mitzvah and the Titkove *landsleit* had a celebration for the Solomons, it was his wife, Sonia, who made the speech. Wolf Solomon sat there, played with his gold pen, and smiled.

Nevertheless, Israel Pressman decided that they should push him up to be vice president. Money talks even without a tongue. And the signature "Wolf Solomon" would look good on paper, too.

Israel Pressman was completely absorbed in his thoughts. Mrs. Pressman had to remind him a couple of times, "Stop! There are still red lights!"

To this her husband replied, "We have to make him vice president."

Mrs. Pressman understood immediately what her husband was talking about, and she answered him tersely, "Solomon? Yes."

Mrs. Pressman helped her husband run the Titkove Society with all her strength. She telephoned the landsladies everyday. She knew who had to go to a doctor, whose children were taking exams, where one could look for a summer cottage, and who had just had a grandchild. She sent telegrams of congratulations, she visited the sick at the hospital, she sent flowers to new mothers. Her work was especially intense before the society's elections. One could say that she ran a first lady's office for the Titkovers.

Israel Pressman valued his wife's abilities, and on solemn occasions he referred to her as "Mrs. Pressman."

"Mrs. Pressman will be at the banquet, and she, the first lady of the Titkovers, will greet you."

For the seven years that her husband had been president, Mrs. Pressman was sincerely attached to her *landsleit*. When she sat with him in the place of honor at the head table, wearing a hat with velvet flowers, she looked around at the audience with true love. She felt a deep gratitude that they were all Titkovers, and that she was their president's wife.

When the Pressmans arrived at the meeting, several couples were already there. The new member, Philip Abrams, who had recently moved from Lakewood to New York, was seated at a side table. He was talking heatedly with Wolf Solomon, who was sitting there, playing with his gold pen and smiling. With them at the same table were Pincus Moses and the tall Tsvi Rattner with his tiny wife, Belle.

For quite a few years, Tsvi Rattner had packed a stone of resentment in his pocket against the president, Israel Pressman. Three years ago, when the Titkovers published their souvenir magazine, and all the members of the Board were pictured with large photographs and big inscriptions, his own picture was the size of a penny and stuck in on the side. After that, Tsvi Rattner couldn't sleep a single night because of the heartache, and the resentment against Pressman remained like a stone on his heart. Each time, Rattner met him, he stood up straighter, as though his anger had stretched him up even higher.

Israel Pressman walked over to their table. Just like putting a lid on a steaming pot, the heated conversation fermented. Tsvi Rattner stood up and called Wolf Solomon over to the side, and, standing with him, waving his long arms about, whispered, "Pressman won't do!"

Mrs. Pressman went over to her husband and said to him abruptly, "Something's cooking about the election here."

She straightened her husband's tie and swam strategically over to Mrs. Solomon.

The new member, Philip Abrams, who had moved from Lakewood, was being received at the meeting. Abrams thanked the Titkovers, praising each one of them to the skies. Just as his father Simeon Heschel Pressman had embellished Titkove, Abrams said, now his son, the president Israel Pressman, was embellishing the Titkover Society in New York. He remembered how Tsvi Rattner's tiny wife's great uncle had had an inn where poor Jews could stay the night free of charge. Tears of rapture stood in tiny Belle's eyes. He remembered Pincus Moses' two-story brick house in Titkove, where his grandfather had had his own study house. Thus Abrams called to mind Titkove, with its beautiful families, with good Jews, with pious Jews, their inns, their shops, and everyone's *yikhes*. The Titkovers melted from pleasure and didn't feel the time passing.

Israel Pressman looked at his watch.

"We still have to have the election," he said.

Now Tsvi Rattner lifted the stone from his heart and threw it. "The elections aren't a goat; they won't run away. Let people sit for a while and enjoy themselves."

His tiny wife supported him: "Yes indeed, let's have some pleasure for once."

"Let's enjoy ourselves a little," Mrs. Solomon chimed in, and her word carried weight. Last year, the Solomons had been the largest contributors to all the society's undertakings.

Two little smiling flames like two small devils now sprang into Tsvi Rattner's eyes. It set his heart at ease to see that no one obeyed the president.

Israel Pressman now felt his heart contract. He no longer heard Abrams praising the Titkovers to the clouds with their *yikhes* of yesteryears. All he could think of was Joseph, whose brothers had sold him to the Ishmaelites. He looked at those around him at his *landsleit* brothers, and they seemed to be so strange, so remote, that even those he had known from his childhood now had different faces. They were not the same. He couldn't recognize them.

Wolf Solomon sent out for Cola-cola. The bottles clinked, the people drank, and they laughed. From their laughter, it seemed to Israel Pressman, that underneath him, from somewhere deep underground, an earthquake was taking place, shaking him out of his quiet seat.

The elections did not take place.

He returned home from the meeting, furious. Red flecks were visible on his cheeks, as if someone had just slapped him. He wandered around in his own home as if he were lost, the way someone stands at a crossroad and doesn't know which way to turn.

His wife, Mrs. Pressman, slowly took off her hat with the flowers, that now seemed withered. She took off her earrings that were pinching her ears. She sat down on a chair and brushed her knees with her hand a couple of times. And then she regained herself. She started toward the telephone. Her husband tried to stop her: "Where are you going? Who are you going to call? Ignoramuses, gluttons! Give them Coca-cola? Liars! Moses' grandfather never had any study place in his brick house! Fakers, boasters . . ." and more and more insulting words against his brothers, the Titkover *landsleit*, shot out of Israel Pressman's mouth, until Mrs. Pressman stopped him: "Ta, ta, ta, ta! Would we be happy without the Titkover Jews? So enough already, enough! Because a man tells one lie, does that make him a liar? What do you know about it! Because person exaggerates a little, he's already a braggart? A faker? What do you know! If you take out all the wormy peas, you won't have enough left over to cook. You don't like the Titkovers? What do you know!"

Mrs. Pressman stood for a while, her eyes closed, and then she started to the telephone, like a thirsty person who hears water splashing in a spring.

Israel Pressman didn't stop her. He was curious to see what she was going to do. He positively glowed when he heard his wife say, "Florence, tomorrow, first thing in the morning, prepare a letter. We're going to have a surprise party for Tsvi Rattner. Write a fine letter. The reason? How do I know? He's been in the society for ten years. He's turned fifty? Well, good. He's just turned fifty, he's a respected member, an activist. Florence, tell Mrs. Rattner very quietly, tell her, trust her with a secret, Florence, tell her that I'm working on this. You understand? Yes, yes!"

The tiny Belle Rattner melted like chocolate in summer when Florence entrusted her with the secret about the surprise party. The telephone receiver had not yet cooled before she called up her husband, Tsvi Rattner, at his business and revealed Florence's secret.

"And do you know who's working on it? Mrs. Pressman."

Tsvi Rattner's heart grew warm. The next time he met Israel Pressman, a smile blossomed on his face. He reminded him that they had once gone to the same cheder, and that together, before Tishebov, they had torn up thistles to throw at the girls' braids.

When Mrs. Pressman was putting on her hat to go to the Rattners' surprise party, she said to her husband, "People should have only good friends. What do we need enemies for? When a shirt gets wrinkled you have to smooth it out with an iron, and when a person gets wrinkled, you have to smooth him out with a surprise party. It's not so terrible! We can get along with our Titkover brothers."

Tsvi Rattner supported Israel Pressman for president with all his heart. He called Wolf Solomon over to a side, waved his long arms around and whispered to him, "Let it be Pressman! We don't have anyone better than him."

Wolf Solomon, from his experience in the antique business, knew that antiques could be real, false, or forged, or altered. He looked at Rattner, who was waving his arms just as he had when he had railed against Pressman earlier, and thought: He's the kind of antique that can be altered. He played with his gold pen and smiled.

Israel Pressman was duly elected to his eighth term as president of the Titkove Society. Mrs. Pressman was sitting next to him in the place of honor at the head table. The velvet flowers on her new little hat looked so fresh you could almost smell them. She looked at those around her with sincere love. She felt a deep gratitude to them, that they were all Titkovers and that she was their Mrs. President.

Next to her, sat the vice president, Wolf Solomon, who played with his gold pen and smiled. His wife, Sonia, in honor of her husband's being elected vice president, gave such a heartfelt speech that tiny Belle Rattner had tears in her eyes.

It was a touching meeting.

August 1954

On the Eve of the Journey

· · · · · · · ·

W ell, what do you have to say about your son?" William Chaimson
said to his wife suddenly, turning to her while eating breakfast.

Mary didn't answer her husband, didn't ask him to repeat his question,
and didn't even raise her eyes to express her distaste.

She was embarrassed to discuss this matter any more, about which they
had quarreled until late last night and today had avoided mentioning early
in the morning.

Although Mary didn't answer her husband, he went on talking to her
just as though she had said something to the contrary. "I'm the one who's
against his leaving? Not at all. I'm glad he has such wishes, but a person
shouldn't be such a hothead! You know? Ben's exactly like you that way. You
flare up immediately, just like a match! That's what he's inherited from his
mother. Both of you flare up just like a couple of matches! No accounting
and no logic."

Mary shook her head, as if to say: "Have it your way." She served her husband cereal and milk, but in such a way that it seemed she had put the plate
down sideways just to irritate him. Is this the way to serve a plate, sideways?
Is this the way a wife argues, without words? And he said to her, "We brought
him up that way, of course!" gesturing to the pictures of Dr. Herzl and C. N.
Bialik hanging on the wall, "That's the way we brought him up and I don't
have a single regret! He's a real man, our Ben, a man and a Jew—there aren't a
lot of fellows like him in all of America! But doesn't a person have to finish college? A person just lets four years float away to the devil? The money—and

above all, the time. Above all—the years! He'll become a good-for-nothing, a person without a profession, if he drops out of college now!"

Mary looked at her husband. She thought that he wasn't saying what he was really thinking. She was filled with a pain that made her hands feel heavy and her eyes start to burn. She took a breath carefully, so that it wouldn't be obvious she was sighing.

William Chaimson swallowed his cereal as hastily as if there, in this little bowl, were all the stubbornness of his son, Ben, and the silence of his wife, Mary. Chomp, chomp—he swallowed, and spoke angrily to his wife. "The worst is when people take things literally. Of course, people have to go to Israel, but that doesn't mean rush and leave! Rushing won't do!"

He took a slice of bread but set it down quickly, exactly as if he wanted to demonstrate that rushing wouldn't do.

"Such things have to be thought out very carefully. You have to look out for your children's future. But someone who doesn't even know how to provide for himself certainly can't be of any help to his people!"

He spoke with grief, with anger, just as if someone were teasing him, as if someone across from him were uttering bitter reproaches that he could not overcome. He almost shouted. "The worst thing is when a person has no sense! And there's no cure for that! To be an idealist and a fool—it's just as useless as . . ."

He stopped himself. He lacked a comparison and was astonished at himself.

William Chaimson was a good speaker. He was never at a loss for a proverb, an example, or a joke. He could crush his opponents, inside and out, with a phrase, or a verse, until nothing remained but a flustered body with a divided soul. And here, suddenly, in his own home, at his own table, where there was one and only one person to hear him, his own wife, here William Chaimson had run out of breath to bring his thought to a conclusion.

Mary looked at her husband, saw that he was in a fury, that his forehead was blotchy red, and she didn't want to provoke him further. She was silent. What could she say to him? she thought. The boy wants to go to Israel, the boy says that college is nothing compared to a settlement in the Negev, and she didn't want her husband to have to answer for that.

She asked, "Do you want some compote, Willie?"

William jumped as if this was the worst thing she could have asked him. He got up from the table and spoke quietly and with irony: "I understand that you're the good mother. He's sure of you already! You're the big Mrs. Zionist, and I am the villain, the opportunist, the, the . . ."

Again he was at a loss for words to finish the phrase, and he remained standing in the middle of the room, thoughtful. Why was he blaming Mary?

His wife, just as though she could hear him thinking, said to him, "Who are you complaining to? What it amounts to is that you're making *me* out to be a Zionist!"

She laughed. His agitation died down, and he began smiling: "You recall a story that happened thirty-five years ago?"

Smiling, Mary said, "For six weeks on end you taught me 'The Jewish State'[1]—remember? For six weeks on end! I really don't know how I stood it!"

They both laughed, as though their youth had suddenly returned, demanding happiness and laughter.

Smiling, William Chaimson pointed to Dr. Herzl's portrait and said, "He didn't go to Israel either. Jewish colonists were already there, the Biluim,[2] who plowed the earth with their noses. Herzl didn't go. He founded the Jewish state in Basel. . ."

Mary was frightened by her husband's heresies, and she cried out, "Hush! Hush!"

They were both silent. Ben walked in. He sensed that their conversation had been about him, smiled, said one word, "hungry," and sat down at the table to eat.

The father joked a little with his son. "So, when are you leaving?"

Ben spread butter on his bread calmly, looking at his father from time to time, and replied, "Pa, I wouldn't want to think that you are in favor of only

1. *The State of Israel* is the pamphlet by Theodore Herzl that argued for a homeland for Jews in what was then Palestine.

2. The Biluim was a student agricultural movement in Palestine that arose after the 1881 pogroms in Russia. It was the first *aliyah*, and it failed.

other people sending their children to Israel. I don't think that way about you, Pa."

It was so quiet in the house that if anyone had so much as uttered a word, they would all have been astonished. It was a stillness that could only be broken with a lie, because the ultimate truth had already been spoken. They all felt it and were silent. On the wall, hung the pictures of Dr. Herzl and Bialik, as if they especially wanted to participate in the silence.

July 25, 1948

The Shared Sukkah

. . . .

The back door of Osher Friedman's house was exactly opposite the back door of Reb Shmuel the Trustee's[1] house. A low fence, made of boards that reached half as high as the two doors, stood between the two houses. Osher Friedman was a dry-goods dealer and had a large store in the market. In his house, they lived comfortably: there was chicken for Sabbath, and fish, too.

Reb Shmuel the Trustee eked out his existence running the community's Loan Fund. He did the accounts, wrote out the receipts for the loans and collected the payment on the debts. In his house, they lived frugally; he was almost a poor man. His children drank tea in the morning, but with only half a piece of sugar, enough for a child. No need to drink up a whole box of sugar at one time.

And just as the houses stood with their back doors to each other, so too the families stood with their backs to each other. From a distance, it was "Gut shabbes" and "Gut yom tov"; they didn't really mix with each other. The fence stood between them.

Osher Friedman's beard was in fact broader than Reb Shmuel the Trustee's, and his pockets were broader too, but in spite of all his wealth, he didn't know how to get people in town to call him Reb Osher. And Reb

---

1. The Hebrew word, *nemen*, means "trustee," and connotes a person who has the reputation of being entirely trustworthy with money and who manages the finances of the congregation or organization.

Shmuel the Trustee was just naturally called Reb Shmuel. He was a learned man, a very honest Jew; indeed because of this, he was made trustee of the Loan Fund. People called him Reb Shmuel, nothing else but Reb Shmuel. And when a town insists on a habit, no one can tell them otherwise. Go argue with a town.

Every year just before Sukkos, Osher Friedman and Reb Shmuel the Trustee built their sukkahs next to each other at the fence. Osher Friedman would toss several boards up against the fence, so that it made a wall for both their sukkahs, and would call to Reb Shmuel the Trustee through the back door: "Reb Shmuel, you can build your sukkah onto the fence; it'll save you several boards."

Reb Shmuel the Trustee answered him the same way every year: "Well, well. A good idea, certainly. May we live to see another year."

That was about the extent of the yearly contact between the neighbors—a bit of friendliness and a small favor from the richer man to the poorer.

Every year the two families celebrated the holiday in their sukkahs with the shared wall that belonged to Osher Friedman.

No one got more pleasure from the wall than Reb Shmuel the Trustee's daughter, Khinke, and Osher Friedman's son, Borukhl.

After the meal, when the grownups would leave the sukkah, the children, Khinke and Borukhl, would stand with their little noses pressed up to the space between the thin boards. "What did your family eat today?" Borukhl asked, pressing his nose to a crack in the board very nearly opposite Khinke's little nose, and Khinke listed all the good holiday food—the fish with the meat, the tsimmes, adding a little boastfully, "And what did you eat today?"

Borukhl listed all his holiday food—the fish, the meat with the tsimmes—and added his own little boast: "We ate grapes and dried dates, too."

Khinke would pull her nose away from the fence and say, "I don't like grapes or dried dates at all."

And each year Khinke left the wall aggrieved, not because of the grapes or dried dates, which they didn't have, but because Borukhl was above her, above her with his grapes and dried dates.

Each time she promised herself that she would not ask Borukhl what they had eaten, but she could never restrain herself. Something pulled her to talk with him from behind the shared wall. This was the beauty of Sukkos.

Reb Shmuel the Trustee, through his brother-in-law, a lumber dealer, moved up to a partnership in a forest holding. First he got a small percentage for his attention to the accounting, and later he got a small share in the business itself. The forest belonged to several Jews who were forever quarreling about the accounts. Reb Shmuel the Trustee did his calculations precisely down to the very last kopek, and they took him into the business; he became a partner.

Things went well with the forest, and in town people began to talk: Reb Shmuel the Trustee would be a rich man.

In spring, when Osher Friedman's wife, Zisl, was planting flowers under her window, she called through her back door to Hannah-Libe, Reb Shmuel the Trustee's wife: "Hannah-Libe, I still have some seedlings left, would you like to plant them under your windows?"

Then Hannah-Libe felt that she had indeed become a rich woman: Zisl wants me, Hannah-Libe, to grow the same flowers under my windows.

"Yes, why not?" she answered Zisl, "I'll pay you for them, of course. It will be very good to have flowers under the window."

And Hannah-Libe planted the flowers under her window. In summer, the flowers grew taller than the fence. The fence between the houses seemed to grow lower; the same flowers at Osher Friedman's and at Reb Shmuel the Trustee's were like a sign of friendship between the two families.

Just before Sukkos, Reb Shmuel the Trustee, was standing next to the window with the flowers and thought that it was time to build the sukkah with his own boards, without Osher Friedman's wall. But how could a person say such a thing to a neighbor? They had lived next to each other all these years and built their sukkahs on Osher's wall. It was Osher's privilege. Thus thinking, he noticed Osher Friedman standing at his window, too, and he called out to him for no good reason, neither here nor there, "Reb Osher, it's already time to think about a sukkah."

Osher Friedman smiled to himself in his broad beard and answered, "Well, well, by all means. After all, you have a forest now."

Reb Shmuel the Trustee answered him just the same as always: "Well, well. A good idea, certainly. May we live to see another year."

In Reb Shmuel the Trustee's courtyard, it was apparent that he had indeed become a lumber merchant. For his sukkah, men brought a big stack of planks. New and planed, they brightened up the courtyard.

Osher Friedman was very busy on the eve of the holiday. The days were beautiful and sunny, and his dry goods store was filled with customers, Gentiles from the villages and landowners from their estates. They were in a hurry to come to town to buy things before the rains began.

Osher Friedman enjoyed a good business and was in high spirits, and with a broad smile, early one morning, he called out to Reb Shmuel the Trustee over the fence. "Reb Shmuel, build the sukkah a little bigger. I see you have plenty of boards—let us be with you in the sukkah. I am too busy in the shop, just now, *keyn eyn hore.*

"It would be my honor, Reb Osher, it would be my honor."

Being called "Reb" Osher was worth more than money to Osher Friedman. Because he was rich, people called him Pani Friedman. But Reb Osher—that, he seldom heard. And it was a happy man who said to Reb Shmuel the Trustee, "It's a deal?"

"A deal. May we live to see another year."

Zisl was a little out of sorts and said to her husband, "How can we eat in someone else's sukkah? We'll hire someone to build our own."

"Oh, well, oh well," Osher Friedman smiled, "let him enjoy it. If you could have seen how he brightened up when he said: 'It would be my honor, Reb Osher, it would be my honor.' That was the way he said it. He was a poor man for so long. Let him enjoy his money a little. That's a greater mitzvah than building our own sukkah, greater than building our own.

"Well, I don't know," Zisl said, "to eat in a strange sukkah . . ."

"A sukkah is a sukkah. It's not a house. Jews eat together in a sukkah. It's a sukkah, after all."

Reb Shmuel the Trustee had the sukkah erected quickly with the new boards—a palace! A carpenter came to make two doors for it. He took three planks down from the fence so that Zisl could have her door directly across from her back door; the second door of the sukkah was built directly across from Hannah-Libe's back door. When everything was finished, Zisl and

Hannah-Libe each stood next to their doors and marked out the places for their tables to be placed.

"We can put the tables here, as we would for a wedding," Zisl said and thought the same as her husband: Let her enjoy it. All her life she's suffered, let her enjoy the holiday preparations now.

"It won't be, God forbid, too crowded," Hannah-Libe said, enjoying the taste of being a rich woman.

Both women left, happy with the shared sukkah.

The neighbors began talking.

"Rich people speak the same language."

"Osher Friedman's been a rich man all these years, and now Reb Shmuel the Trustee has caught up to him."

"One rich man loves another."

"What else is new? Should a person have to sit with a poor man? And look at the cheap fish in his plate? Now they can show off their carp's heads[2] to each other."

Khinke was bewildered with happiness. From the top of the sukkah, the fresh, thick, green fir branches bowed down over the walls. Two tables were standing in the sukkah: the table Zisl had placed, and the other, Hannah-Libe's.

To Khinke, the sukkah seemed like a world of joy. She felt the greatness of the holiday. When kiddush was said in the evening, Boruchl would see her new dress with its mother-of-pearl buttons.

Khinke flew around like a butterfly in the sukkah all day, as if she were afraid it might disappear. Every few minutes she ran to her mother with the news: "Zisl has put in a bench already. Zisl has hung up a lamp."

Khinke spread a white tablecloth on their table in the sukkah. It seemed to her that the whole world had been spread with a white light and with the fresh green of the branches over the roof.

In the evening, Khinke sat at the table across from the burning candles.

---

2. The author used the term *platke*, which is "a cheap freshwater fish"; carp is much more expensive, and indicative of the prestige of the person who can eat it. The fish's head is served to the most important person, hence the Yiddish term that translates as "carp's head" or in English, "big shot."

She didn't look at the second table where Borukhl was sitting, but through her lowered eyes she saw that he was looking at her. The mother-of-pearl buttons were shining as if they, too, wanted to please Borukhl. The candles, the challahs, the spoons and the forks—all shone with the kind of joy that no holiday had ever had yet.

After the meal, when everyone had left the sukkah, Borukhl went over to Khinke. "Khinke, ask your father not to take the sukkah apart, so we can always sit together in the same one," Borukhl said.

"Yes, I'll tell him," Khinke answered.

She wasn't looking at Borukhl, but at her mother-of-pearl buttons, that seemed to be blooming.

"And your father will do it?" he asked.

"He will do it. I'll ask him."

"It's a beautiful sukkah," Borukhl said, and his eyes were shining with a smile of good fortune.

"It's a beautiful sukkah," Khinke repeated after him quietly, and looked at him. Her eyes were also shining with the light of good fortune.

The shorn fir branches with their final greenness, seemed even greener above the first awakening of young joy.

The Rashkovitcher Wedding

· · · · · · ·

D ad, it'll be too far for you to walk from here to the synagogue. It's
about ten blocks, and that's a long way to go, I'm telling you, a long
way. How can you drag yourself so far everyday? Even for me that distance
is hard. It's fine when the weather is nice, but what happens when it rains?
Or snows? And the wind in New York! It can lift a person right up!"

So Mrs. Vafelnik was talking to her old father, talking with a smile on
her face, a face that was completely round and blond: her eyebrows, the
down on her upper lip, and the curls on her forehead. Everything about her
was very round and very blond, just like an angel.

Mrs. Vafelnik loved homemade wine. Not just for the wine itself, simply because a home should have it. It was good to sip, it was good to honor
their guests with; it made for a complete house—when there was a little
homemade wine.

She stood over a wide pot full of fresh grapes, and, while talking to her
father, worked eagerly with her rolling pin, crushing the grapes. The tight,
crackling skins of the big black grapes were popping with quiet explosions.
Mrs. Vafelnik's full round arms were a little like her short round rolling pin,
and it seemed that all three were permeated with the cheerful hard work
that flowed out into the quiet humming melody of the grapes.

"Listen, Nokhum," Mrs. Vafelnik said to her husband, "where *do* such
strong winds in New York come from?"

"Wind! Who knows where it comes from?!" her husband answered, and
he went into another room. It was hard for him to listen to his wife trying to

convince her father that he shouldn't move in into their new apartment with them.

"It's because of the ocean, I'm sure of it, because of the ocean," was Mrs. Vafelnik's geographical theory. "In the old country, there never were such winds, such bothers."

Mrs. Vafelnik didn't stop talking, as though a moment of silence would make clear to everyone that she didn't want her father to move in with them.

Her father, Mr. Rabinovitch, his beard short and neatly trimmed, smoked a cigarette, didn't look at his daughter, and was embarrassed for his son-in-law, although he agreed with what she said: "Yes, of course it's a long way from a synagogue."

"Yes, the wind in New York is dreadful."

"The rain is dangerous."

He didn't want to get angry with his daughter—above all, he didn't want to endure the humiliation of a quarrel and have it known that his daughter had blocked his way into her house.

"Sarah's house is closer to the synagogue," Mrs. Vafelnik said. "From her house it's only two steps to the synagogue. It's a much more Jewish neighborhood there. The neighbors are people you'll feel comfortable talking to right away," Mrs. Vafelnik said, coaxing her father to go live with his other daughter Sarah.

"You have to walk uphill to Sarah's, Sarah says. Sarah told me I'd get tired. Sarah said it's hard even for her to go uphill," he countered.

Mrs. Vafelnik was quiet for a while and then murmured, "Going uphill isn't good for sure, and it certainly isn't good to be so far from the synagogue either."

Mr. Vafelnik came back from another room with David, their son, a three-year-old child, who quickly took hold of his grandfather's beard and touched both his cheeks, delighted they were there for him to take hold of.

His grandfather hugged the small boy and patted his back, but had no words for him. The humming sounds of the bursting grapes under the rolling pin in his daughter's two hands filled his ears, but it seemed to him he was still hearing about the New York wind, and because of that and the distance to the synagogue, it was impossible for him to find a corner in his younger daughter's home.

Mrs. Vafelnik suddenly got angry with her child: "He doesn't let you get out a word! Such a pest of a child!"

She wanted to put the small boy to bed, but he didn't want to go. He ran around the table and hid under his grandfather's legs, filling the room with screeches and laughter that weren't agreeable either to his angry mother or his quiet, silent grandfather.

"I'm going to go get the vacuum cleaner!" Mrs. Vafelnik said, scaring her son.

The little boy's face crumpled and he began to cry. He was afraid of the vacuum cleaner. He had seen the vacuum cleaner swallow up little pieces of paper, a match, the dust, a piece of wood, and his mother had told him that when the vacuum cleaner got angry, it could swallow a child up, too, and David didn't want to be in the vacuum cleaner bag.

The grandfather carried his crying grandchild away to sleep in his little bed. The child was sobbing. His grandfather gently stroked his back, calming him down: "There, there, the vacuum cleaner isn't going to swallow you up."

He lay the crying child down and thought: for the child, it's the vacuum cleaner, and for an old father, it's the wind, the rain, and the distance to the synagogue. He said to his grandson, "The vacuum cleaner, the wind . . . it's all nonsense. Sleep, go to sleep . . . it's all nonsense."

His voice was halting, soft, and convincing. The child sensed another wronged person, touched his grandfather's beard, laughed a little, and agreed to go to sleep.

The old man was intending to leave, but Mrs. Vafelnik wouldn't allow it. She had already finished her work with the grapes. The wide pot was in the kitchen, and from there Mrs. Vafelnik said to her father, "Dad, what are you thinking of? Leave here without eating?"

She listed all the dishes she had made for him, how she had made them, and how they were cooked. She never stopped talking. "It's the taste of paradise," she coaxed her father. "What do you mean by leaving without eating?"

He didn't think it would do to refuse. Just now, today after the talk about "the wind," it was better to eat the "taste of paradise" at his daughter's. The less anger, the better. A person could stand a few hard feelings, but not humiliation and not melancholy; he did not want to bring that upon himself, and anger was humiliating.

He ate every dish that she had prepared, agreeing that they tasted of paradise. And when his daughter asked him again about the plums—"But the plums? How did you like the way those plums were cooked?"—he simply could not remember that he had eaten plums.

Later, when he was out on the street, it was raining. The rain hummed, just like the grapes under the rolling pin. The humming overtook him with loneliness. He didn't want to go to his house where he had lived alone for two years after the death of his wife and he'd been left with two daughters. Yes, even with two daughters one can be alone, he thought. At the subway he remembered there was a meeting of the Rashkovitch Society, his *landsleit*, tonight.

A person should go see his own people, he thought. He wished he could push back the time, when his house was a home, when the shtetl was a home, and everyone around him old friends.

I'll go see my own people, Rashkovitchers. In Rashkovitch, the synagogue wasn't so close either; but it was a very easy walk. They had wind there, too, but it wasn't dreadful. You just buttoned up your collar—it was a familiar wind. Yes, yes, I'll go see my own people there, Rashkovitchers.

The oblong room, where the meeting was held, was completely lit up, just as though all the people of Rashkovitch had brought their own lamps and lit them. At the door, he met Mr. Ribak, an old acquaintance.

"Mr. Rabinovitch! I was hoping you'd be coming today! My grandson will be bar mitzvah, and the first of all, I need a tallis, and a Rashkovitcher wouldn't go anywhere else but to you to buy a tallis. And second, will you teach the boy a few prayers, the ones a bar mitzvah boy should know . . . a blessing . . . you know? What a person should know in Hebrew . . . you already know what."

The old man revived. A home, that's what the Rashkovitchers were, a little bit of home.

"Well, well," he answered in his familiar Yiddish, "well, I'm here."

He straightened up, his sixty-four years seeming to be younger than an hour ago at his daughter's house.

Mr. Ribak presented Mrs. Wolf, a guest from Chicago, to the audience.

She was indeed a Rashkovitcher, Chaya-Eydl, from the "brick house." (They had had the only brick house in the town, and everyone called them the people from the "brick house." Berl, "from the brick house," Chaya-Eydl, "from the brick house," and Shimchek, "from the brick house.")

Chaya-Eydl had to thank them for the introduction. She stood up and, a little embarrassed, laughed; two gleams of fire shone in her eyes, and in a womanly way, she straightened her full shoulders that were rounded by age.

"What can I say? I'm not much of a speech maker . . . I wanted to see the *landsleit*, the Rashkovitchers. I'm all alone, lonely enough. My children are married, thank God, so I came to the Rashkovitchers. And let us all be healthy."

Here, Chaya-Eydl stumbled, not knowing how to pull out another word, and she sat down.

The Rashkovitchers were touched. They had heard their own language, simple words from their old home, the old Rashkovitch melody, words that had gotten stuck in Chaya-Eydl's throat and couldn't be rescued if her life depended on it. They gave Chaya-Eydl the kind of ovation they wouldn't have given to the best speaker in the world.

Old Mr. Rabinovitch looked at Chaya-Eydl and longed for a home.

A fine woman—he thought—a good woman, a refined woman, as quiet as a dove.

He said that he was going in the same direction, and that he would accompany Chaya-Eydl home. On the way, they talked about Rashkovitch, about being alone, about loneliness. He reminded her that people had once spoken about a match between them in Rashkovitch, but she had left and gone to America, and nothing had come of it.

"My father was ashamed to say that he had no dowry for me. The brick house was in fact brick, but you can't eat bricks, and I was sent to America."

Mr. Rabinovitch thought about his daughter, about the wide pot of grapes that burst under the cheerful rolling pin, and about the New York winds. He was afraid that when he left the subway, a lonely rain, a sky that seemed to need a roof for itself, and a wind would meet him outside.

He felt at home here with Chaya-Eydl in the subway. A person could say a word or two, see a smile, and the white handkerchief she took out of her purse and wiped her lips with recalled a familiar restfulness and comfort.

He leaned over to her and said quite unexpectedly, "If you want, Chaya-Eydl, we can get married. I won't ask for your dowry now. I have, thank God, what it takes to live. I sell tallisim, and some seforim . . ."

Chaya-Eydl laughed, a little embarrassed.

"What can I say?" she lifted her round shoulders, "perhaps it was meant to be that I came to New York."

Chaya-Eydl wanted to say something more on such a serious occasion, but she couldn't rescue any more words to save her soul. She took out her white handkerchief, wiped her mouth, and smiled.

Mr. Rabinovitch saw a home for himself, a home with a golden roof where no wind and no rain would never reach.

To Hear the Megillah on Purim

· · · · · · ·

Each year on the eve of Purim, Osher Grebnik closes up his glass business and drives from Brooklyn to the Bronx to the small synagogue
A'havas Akhim [1] to hear the reading of the megillah. He drives there with
his wife and their two daughters. A distance of an hour's drive by car. Hears
the reading of the megillah, makes a considerable donation to the synagogue, and disappears until Purim the next year. Osher Grebnik tells the
same story to the worshippers at A'havas Akhim year in and year out, as to
why he comes to hear the megillah read there, and that if someone were to
give him a million dollars, he still wouldn't go anywhere else to hear it. The
old worshippers at A'havas Akhim already know Osher Grebnik's story
word for word. Nevertheless, they stand around him and pay attention,
taking pleasure in their synagogue, A'havas Akhim. Osher Grebnik always
begins with the same words: "Rosh Hashanah and Yom Kippur are for
God—a person can pray in any synagogue, but Purim is for people. I come
to A'havas Akhim because I met a man here, a real mensch, as they say—the
kind of person a man should be."

When Osher Grebnik gets to these words, the shamesh joins in: "Reb
Isroel Jaffe! No small thing, Reb Isroel Jaffe." He says this very quietly so as
not to interrupt Osher Grebnik's story.

"I came to America, to a great uncle, a man who was loaded with money
and a dread of old age. He would sit down and count out all the troubles a

---

1. The name of the synagogue, A'havas Akhim, means "brotherly love."

person has when he grows old. All sorts of illnesses—paralysis, loneliness, isolation—the list of troubles was a big one, indeed. My great uncle saw all the details in front of his own eyes: here you are lying, God forbid, with no one to bring you a glass of water; here you're standing and you cannot get across the street by yourself; here you're sitting and you can't catch your breath. Because of this dread, my uncle grew stingy; he needed every penny for his old age. He didn't want to loan me the few dollars I needed to bring my family over. It was enough for him, he complained, that he'd sent a ship-ticket for me. He shouldn't have done that either. As for my family, I should worry about them myself and figure out how to bring them over. Anyhow, what was the hurry? The family could be brought over in a few years.

"At that time, I still used my real name, Novogrebnikovsky. My uncle, who was stingy with money, was stingy with time, too. He told me that a long name wouldn't do; who had time to pronounce it? So I obeyed and split my name in three parts. The first part, I threw away, the last part, I threw away, and only the middle part remained—Grebnik. To this day, I regret that I split my name apart. But you can't put to it back together again.

"My uncle's advice, and my shortened name, didn't help me, and I didn't have any way to bring my family to America.

"I'm a person who is quick to have regrets. I already regretted that I had come to America. But you can't go back. It was the fast day[2] before Purim, and I went to a synagogue, A'havas Akhim, for the afternoon prayers and to hear the megillah. But my heart wasn't in a holiday mood. I probably was sitting with my head hanging down. A man came up to me and asked, 'A greenhorn, are you?'

" 'A greenhorn,' I answered him, although I wasn't too happy that he could spot me and my new American pedigree so fast.

"We started talking, and when I told him the whole story about my great uncle here and my family on the other side, he looked at me and said, 'That's no problem. I'll bring your family over. Be here tomorrow morning in the same place, and we'll arrange it.'

"After he left, the truth must be told, I thought that maybe he'd been making fun of me. People had told me that here in America there were all

---

2. The Yiddish phrase *Ester tones* signifies the day of fasting before Purim.

kinds—fakers, as they call them, and that a true *lamed vavnik*[3] was very hard to meet. I was already regretting I had told him the whole story, lest I drag myself into a mess. But what's done is done, and you can't put it back together again.

"The next morning, when I came into the synagogue, I thought no one would be there. But in fact he came, and he brought me a check. 'Here is the deposit for the boat fare,' he said.

"This was the first check that I'd seen in America, and, to put it plainly, I was afraid. Greatly confused, I asked him, 'What does this mean? Is it so easy to give people money? And is it so easy to take money here? You don't know me and I don't know you. Let's go to the rabbi and have him write this down. Let there be a witness.'

"But the man looked at me and answered me just as he had the evening before, 'It's nothing. You'll give it back to me.'

"When I went home with the check in my pocket I was afraid to look at it. I was not very experienced with checks, and I was really afraid of what might come of it. But it was too late, and you can't put things back together again.

"And, as a matter of fact, with this same check a few short months later, I brought over my family to America.

"Returning the money to the man wasn't so easy, even though I already had enough, thank God, to pay him back. If it was before Passover, or before Sukkos, he always said, 'It's nothing. Keep it for awhile, maybe you can use it for the holiday.'

"Until one day I decided that once and for all I would go and pay back debt I owed him. But in the meantime, he had moved to another neighborhood. He no longer came to the same synagogue.

"So I went to his house, laid the money on the table, and wished him well, all that needed saying. He received me grudgingly, was in a rush to be off, and didn't even want to hear the story. He was an entirely different person, and it really irritated me. I couldn't restrain myself and asked him, 'How have I sinned? I needed money, and you loaned it to me. You did me a

3. The *Lamed Vavnik* signifies one of the anonymous thirty-six holy men whose existence, according to legend, allows the world to continue.

real favor. Just a favor? No, a huge favor! Now, when I've brought back what I owe you, you are like an entirely different person and even seem angry, God forbid! How have I sinned?'

"He smiled, indeed, as only a Jew can—a little sad, a little funny—and said to me, 'You know, Mr. Grebnik, that a Jew in America is very busy. He has no time to look for good deeds to do. And therefore, if he is worthy and he has the means for doing a mitzvah, well, then he's happy. And when a person is happy, he loves to chat. But now, you'll have to excuse me; that you've just come—what's it to me? Not a thing. Go and be well.'

"That's what he said to me, and his name was Reb Isroel Jaffe, and I met him right here in A'havas Akhim. For me, this was the greatest miracle of Purim. And there's no better place to come to hear the megillah, than here in A'havas Akhim."

August 14, 1946

Malkele Eshman

· · · · · · ·

The family gathering of the Eshmans was noisy. The family conisited of more than forty souls: the four Eshman brothers, their wives, sons and daughters, sons-in-law, and grandchildren, and their old mother, Malkele Eshman, whom all the children called "Mamale" to her face, and "she" behind her back.

Even though they used the endearing name, Mamele, for her, they were afraid of her. She was the boss of Eshman and Sons, furniture stores in different parts of the city.

Malkele Eshman used endearing names for all of her sons, daughters-in-law, and grandchildren—Dovidke, Borukhl, Semkele, Julkele—and her two round eyes, shining like little cherries, glowed at each one of them. But she paid her sons' salaries as if they were strangers. She was the boss of the business.

The family gathering was usually held in winter, on the first day of Hannukah. Here they did the yearly accounting and decided on how much money to give to the various charitable organizations the Eshmans gave to annually, and then they all ate supper together.

After this, they named the eldest son, David, president of Eshman and Sons.

"The king loves his crown more than his kingdom," Malkele said to her other three sons, her round cherry eyes lighting up (alluding to the fact that David loved his title—president), and she congratulated the "president" of Eshman and Sons, to whom she paid a salary as though he were a stranger.

The program at the family gathering concluded every year with the gifts that Malkele gave to the grandchildren. If, among them, a boy was about to become bar mitzvah, Malkele gave him a silk tallis and said, "If you can't be the president of the United States, at least you can be, with God's help, a president of Eshman and Sons."

David had been president of Eshman and Sons for fourteen successive years after the death of Malkele's husband, Osher Eshman. Malkele treated him respectfully because of this. He signed all the checks (under the sum of two hundred dollars), he signed all the contracts with the customers, and he straightened things out with the debtors.

The brothers muttered that he ran the company with old-fashioned ways, and they were not happy about it, but he would pretend not to hear.

His office door was always ringing with people coming to see him. When he went away for a few days' rest, the office girl collected all the papers and put them on his desk under a paperweight—a brass cat.

His wife, Bessie, round as an apple and red as an apple, wore a stiff corset that pushed little cushions of fat up under her arms, but that in no way made any difference in her appearance—she was as round as ever.

Often, she dropped by her husband's office, rested her round girth near him at his desk, and asked: "How much longer can you work for the Eshmans? I don't mean that you should quit, but how about going away for a few days?"

Among themselves, the daughters-in-law talked about their mother-in-law. "She's stronger than brick," they said.

Once, Malkele heard Bessie and the younger daughter-in-law wrangling about whose husband worked harder. Bessie had said, "You think being president of Eshman and Sons is easy? Just listening to the office bell ringing all day long swells the nerves."

Then Malkele's shining cherry eyes lit up.

"When we started our carpentry shop in a goat shed (in fact we shared our office with the goats; we were on one side of the wall and the goats on the other), Osher, may he rest in peace, didn't have the title of president, and his nerves were never swollen."

Both daughters-in-law, the president's wife and the younger daughter-in-law, straightaway got themselves out of the room; even a second was too long for them. Malkele watched them go, shook her head, and muttered: "A lot they contribute, the ladies from Eshman and Sons! Their nerves are swollen!"

But she didn't like being angry with her daughters-in-law. She had them come back from the other room. "Ladies"—she called her daughters-in-law "ladies" when she wanted to straighten out a rough patch with them—"don't think that I begrudge the firm Eshman and Sons, *keyn eyn bore*. The past is the past, and now, thank God, things are going well. Nerves are just like clocks. However you wind them up, that's the way they go."

After their mother-in-law's sermon, the "ladies" didn't know if they should leave or not. Malkele said, "If we were to drink a glass of tea, it would be very good, very good." Her little cherry eyes looked merry and crafty at the same time, and both daughters-in-law left to make tea, just managing to slip out.

The evening meal, after the family gathering, was merry. The profits were good that year. The youngest daughter-in-law, Julkele, carried stuffed chickens—baked and roasted, Hannukah latkes—baked and fried, and various kugels and vegetables, to the table.

After the meal, when it came time to name the president of Eshman and Sons, Malkele saw that the younger sons were whispering to each other. William and Sem went into another room. And then Borukh and Sem, and then William and Borukh.

Malkele opened the door and remained standing at the threshold. "What's going on?" she asked.

William tugged at a button on his vest and said angrily, "Fourteen years being president is enough! We have to have what they call modern advertisements! The business is suffering! He thinks it's still a goat shed!"

Malkele took a step closer. Her shining little cherry eyes had grown large and black and fierce. "No disrespect," she said. "You hear! No disrespect!"

Her sons were silent; William muttered again, "The business is suffering . . . first of all, business is . . ."

Malkele winked at her son: "Williamke, it doesn't matter what people say before an election. Dovidl is the president! And about the 'modern advertisement' " (Malkele could in no way pronounce *modern* but pronounced the word exactly as it was in Yiddish— "matern"),[1] "you can take care of them and Semke can quarrel with the customers! But, no disrespect!—I said! Dovidl is president, he signs the papers."

Later, when she congratulated David, the president, he pressed her hand limply and didn't say anything.

Not one thing had changed in the office of David Eshman, the president of Eshman and Sons. The same solid desk stood there, brass cat on the top. The same office girl behind the glass wall tapped on her typewriter, but the bell on the door stopped ringing, and the telephone next to him seemed like a person who had fainted, only coming to in fits and starts.

A longing to hear the bell on his door awoke in David Eshman. He read the newspaper and listened, wrote a letter and listened. He heard the door to William's office slam every time. He heard it, exactly as if his heart were beating in William's office, but in his own office, it had already died. Just the king in a deck of cards, he thought to himself.

He held the newspaper in front of his eyes, as if it were shielding his face so that he wouldn't have to meet anyone else's glance. From behind the newspaper, he saw how his brother dashed in through the second door to the office girl and said something to her as if whispering a secret. The girl shook her head, her permed hair shaking as if in agreement. She was a bit of a yea-sayer when William was there.

What two-faced dollies, they are, the office dollies—David Eshman thought and looked at the girl's back with repugnance, as though she were a bitter enemy of his. He took to leaving his office for several hours.

David Eshman would come home, tired as though he had worked the whole day at a smelting factory. He'd say to his wife, "Open the windows! The devil only knows what kind of a reek there is here in the house."

One time, William came into David's office with a new customer right

---

1. Malkele mispronounces the English word *modern*. However, the Yiddish verb, *matern*, meaning "to be tormented or harried," expresses her reaction to the new kind of advertisements.

after concluding a contract with him. He introduced the customer to his brother: "Our president, Mr. David Eshman. He has to sign the papers."

David's heart skipped a beat; his brother had concluded a contract without him. He's going to dance to my tune for this, he thought, and said to the customer: "I'll look over the contract, and we'll send it to you in the mail."

William looked blankly into his brother's eyes and, utterly unaware of what he was doing, tore off a button from his vest. He noticed that he was holding a button in his hand, but couldn't figure out where it had come from. It was a button from his vest, nevertheless.

When the bewildered customer left, David bellowed in a voice he didn't recognize as his own: "Get out of here, if you don't want me to break your head!" and he put his hand on the brass cat that was sitting next to him on the desk.

The office girl on the other side of the glass wall disappeared as if a devil had carried her away.

Malkele appeared at the door. With her round cherry eyes, she looked first at her younger son and then at the elder, and both sons sat themselves down in their places.

"My heirs," she said, "fighting already! Meanwhile, you're all still dancing to my tune! Some businessmen! Modern advertisements! Some presidents!"

Once again, her round cherry eyes took measure of her sons, first the younger, then the elder, and both of them shifted on their chairs, as though someone had pushed them.

"Even when Osher, may he rest in peace, and I didn't have enough to eat, we still took all our customers to the theater without any of your quarreling or modern advertisements. I had a little angel painted over a child's cradle on a card and sent it to all our customers, and what that angel could do! How many cradles it sold for us! And without modern advertisement. I myself baked twenty-seven cakes and sent them as Purim presents to our loyal customers, and all this without modern advertisement. My daughters-in-law don't do that!"

When she recalled the cakes, her cherry eyes smiled with cheerfulness and love for the old days. She looked at her sons and added, "You need enthusiasm, not envy. Meanwhile, you're not such great businessmen or presidents! And modern advertisement! And let's have it quiet around here! You hear? Velvel, you hear?"

William looked at the button he was still holding in his hand and answered discontentedly, "I hear," and he waited for his mother to say something to David, but she didn't say anything more. She was silent for a while; her eyes half-closed, she considered her sons irritably. Malkele got up and, with an angry little laugh, went over to David's desk and picked up the brass cat.

"I'd like it better if we didn't have this cat," she said, and left the room.

The brothers remained sitting and didn't look at each other.

"She's a great advertising lady," William murmured admiringly, a "first-class advertising lady." David shook his head several times. He picked up the contract, gave it a cursory look, and signed.

"Send it by mail," he said, almost like issuing a command. William took the contract and silently left the room. Order had been restored at Eshman and Sons.

July 18, 1948

The Lost Sabbath

. . . .

At least twice a day, Mrs. Haines goes over to visit to Sarah Shapiro, her neighbor. She does this out of kindness. She is teaching Sarah Shapiro—who has been in this country a total of two years, having dragged herself through Siberia, through Japan, and finally making it to New York—how to keep house in America, and how to think about vitamins. Wearing a red ribbon in her hair that she never, ever takes out, Mrs. Haines sticks her head in through the door and, before you know it, is talking about vitamins. She speaks eagerly, with feeling, as if this way she'll keep her neighbor, Sarah Shapiro, alive.

The red ribbon in Mrs. Haines hair looks as if it were alive, as if it had swallowed the vitamins all at once and become tinder bright.

Teresa Filipina, Mrs. Haines six-year-old daughter, comes in along with her. When her mother is busy with her theories about vitamins, Teresa Filipina turns around and goes into the kitchen to try out the faucets—to see if water comes out of them when she turns the handle. Mrs. Haines is constantly calling to her daughter. "Teresa Filipina! Schlimazel!" she says when she sees that the child is wet.

"Why call such a small child by such a long name, Mrs. Haines?"

"What can I do? My mother's name was Toibe Faigl, and you aren't allowed to give half a name; the dead person would be very disappointed.

Sarah Shapiro calls the child by her Yiddish name, Toibe Faigele, and gives her a prune to eat and teaches her a rhyme: "Toibe Faigele, / a girl like a baigele."

The child repeats the rhyme, nibbles on a prune, and laughs.

Teresa Filipina's grandfather also calls her Toibe Faigele. He comes over to them every Friday night and brings her a lollipop, and Teresa Filipina understands that both her grandfather and the neighbor, Sarah Shapiro, are somehow connected to Friday evenings and to her Yiddish name, Toibe Faigele.

At times, the small child visits Mrs. Shapiro by herself, without her mother. She taps on the door and, before anyone can ask who is there, she says her Yiddish name: "Toibe Faigele."

Mrs. Shapiro gives her a piece of bread and butter and speaks to her in Yiddish, like her grandfather: "Eat, Toibe Faigele! Eat! It's amazing, always feeding her with vitamins."

Teresa Filipina sits on a chair and eats with purpose and with great pleasure. Furthermore, the piece of bread and butter she eats at Mrs. Shapiro's is somehow connected to her Yiddish name, to her grandfather and to Friday night, when her grandfather brings her a lollipop. Teresa Filipina fulfills her duty to eat—obediently and earnestly, with a child's enthusiasm.

Whenever the little girl disappears, her mother looks around for her and calls out through open windows so all the street can hear her: "Teresa Filipinele! Come here! Where are you, schlimazel?" in half English, half Yiddish.

When Teresa Filipina hears the word *schlimazel,* she knows her mother is angry. With a sly smile, she puts the piece of bread and butter on the table; she is no longer Toibe Faigele, and she begins to speak English right away: "I'm here, Ma" . . . and her small little steps ring out quickly in the stone corridor.

Mrs. Haines asks Sarah Shapiro with friendly reproach: "Please don't give Teresa Filipina bread and butter. What good does that do her? A little starch?—*krokhmel?*" she repeats the word in Yiddish. The child needs protein.

But Teresa Filipina doesn't know what she needs. As soon as her mother leaves her neighbor's house, the little girl comes back in, and in a second becomes Toibe Faigele once again and finishes eating the piece of bread and butter she has left on the table. She eats obediently and earnestly, until the last crumb is gone, like a person finishing a prayer.

On Friday evenings, Teresa Filipina's mother lights four candles. She puts on velvet slacks, sticks a red handkerchief in the pocket of her white blouse, and the red ribbon in her hair shines in the light across from the yellow flames. Teresa Filipina stands, looking at her mother's fingers as she lights the candles. Soon her grandfather will be coming, and he'll give her a lollipop, and he will call her Toibe Faigele—and that is Sabbath.

One Friday night, after her mother had put on her velvet slacks and lit the candles, she told Teresa Filipina that her grandfather would not be coming. He was sick and was in the hospital. Teresa Filipina was sad: without her grandfather, without her grandfather's lollipop, and without her Yiddish name, Toibe Faigele, she was left with half a Sabbath. Then she remembered the neighbor, Mrs. Shapiro. She went over and knocked on her door, looking for the other half of Sabbath.

"Toibe Faigele," she announced before anyone could ask who was knocking.

At Mrs. Shapiro's there were no candles on the table. She was wearing an ordinary housedress, not velvet slacks; it was like every other day.

"Oh, Toibe Faigele! Come in, Toibe Faigele!"

Teresa Filipina stood in the middle of the room and looked around. She went slowly into the kitchen, looked at the table, returned, and, saddened, went to the door.

"What are you looking for, Toibe Faigele?" the neighbor asked, following her.

"Nothing," Teresa Filipina answers in English.

"Why did you come, then?"

The child didn't answer and moved slowly to the door.

From the second apartment, the sound of Mrs. Haines's voice could be heard in the summer evening air: "Teresa Filipina! Where are you?" And already the word, schlimazel, is added in anger.

Everything had become very ordinary.

This time, Teresa Filipina didn't run to her mother. Her little steps, tapped slowly on the stone floor of the corridor. She went down one floor, sat on the stone step, and cried.

New York, 1948

Rosele

· · · · · · ·

Twice a week Rosele goes to clean the two rooms and kitchen of Shimon Weinstock. Because Mr. Weinstock's door isn't locked (he has lived in the same building for twenty years, and the neighbors are just like his own family), Rosele doesn't knock on the door; she simply remains standing at the doorstep. Mr. Weinstock, who even to this day loves to use Russian expressions, although he's been in America for forty years, says of Rosele in a mixture of Yiddish and Russian: *"Zi poyavet zikh,"*[1] she appears. She remains standing a while at the doorstep, as if she is deciding what to say, but in the end says nothing. She puts a few rolls, a little butter wrapped in wax paper, and cheese on the table, and then a short conversation between her and Weinstock takes place.

"How much did you pay for it, Rosele?"

Rosele smiles and very quietly tells how much she has paid. Weinstock puts the small change on the table, Rosele picks it up, and then carries everything she's brought into the kitchen and begins putting it away where it belongs. A little later, while she's still in the kitchen, Weinstock says to her from the second room, "Thank you, Rosele."

He gets no answer. Even though Rosele nods her head, Weinstock is in the other room and can't see her. Rosele moves around so quietly, that one can hardly tell someone else is here in the house. But Weinstock's heart trembles if he hears a glass clink or water rushing noisily from the faucet.

1. In this phrase, *zi poyavet zikh,* the pronouns are in Yiddish and the verb in Russian but with a Yiddish pronunciation.

No more Golde, he thinks, and is grateful to Rosele that she comes in and brings life to the house, since his wife Golde died two years ago.

Shimon Weinstock is used to Rosele's silence. After Rosele's husband died, she rented a room from the Weinstocks and has lived there for eight years. During those eight years, no one has ever heard her speak in a loud voice; she disappears into her work and "*poyavet*," appears, after her work. People call her Rosele, although that endearing name doesn't really suit her. She is short and round and has extremely thick hair. However much she combs it, it sticks out like a wires through a sieve on her head. As a matter of fact, this is the only aggressive thing about Rosele: her hair. It cannot be kept down; even when she shampoos it and it dries quickly, it's already standing straight up like a sieve on her head.

When Rosele finishes cleaning the rooms, she remains standing in the doorway between the kitchen and the next room. Stands and is silent. Silence is customary for Rosele. What's there to talk about? A person does his day's work; that says it all. Help someone get through a hard time; that says it all. What's the need for talking?

Getting ready to leave, Rosele asks, "Perhaps you need something? I'll bring it."

Weinstock knows that this means Rosele is intending to leave. And for him, it's a shame; after all, when someone's in the house, he doesn't feel the loneliness of Golde's death as strongly.

Twice a week, Tuesday and Saturday evenings, Rubenstein and Arele come over to Weinstock's to play cards. Both of them bring Yiddish newspapers. Before they sit down to play cards, Arele and Rubenstein quarrel with each other, exactly as their newspapers quarrel. Once in a while it even goes so far as Rubenstein saying to Arele, "You're a reactionary!"

Arele doesn't keep quiet. But he has a different way of quarreling. He tells his opponent straight out, "You don't have any sense," thus ending all debate.

Rubenstein usually winds up talking the whole time. When Golde was alive, she'd to listen to their quarreling until the coffee was ready in the kitchen. Then she'd serve the coffee and sit down to listen to more of their quarreling. She enjoyed it.

"Quarrel, quarrel," she would say, "anyhow, it's not going to change the world."

Golde died so suddenly that Arele didn't attend her funeral. He doesn't have a telephone. A boy came to announce the bad news, to come to the funeral, but Arele wasn't at home just then, and he missed paying respects[2] to a woman, a friend, whose home he had come to punctually for twenty years twice a week—Tuesday and Saturday evenings.

Now that Golde is no more, not much has changed at the Tuesday and Saturday gatherings. Arele makes the coffee. He always finds the clean coffee pot, and the coffee already measured out, covered with a plate. Rosele prepares it.

Arele makes the coffee in the kitchen, listens to Rubenstein stating the claims of his newspaper, and answers him from time to time with a word or two. When Rubenstein gets good and angry, he dubs Arele: "a reactionary," and once in a while, he adds, "you're a damn reactionary." Then Arele leaves off his coffee making, goes into the room, and gives him back what for: "You don't have any sense. A reactionary is someone who is in fact a reactionary! But me? W-h-a-t? How so?" He smiles contemptuously and goes back in the kitchen.

Then all three feel that Golde is no more, and because of this Arele has to stay in the kitchen and make coffee, and can't even properly defend his newspaper. Weinstock feels it especially, and he walks around the room, with such loneliness, that in order to drive it away, he asks suddenly, "Maybe I should go out and bring in a little cake?"

Rubenstein suddenly remembers. "My wife sent something with me! I completely forgot it!" and he pulls out of his coat pocket a small bag of cookies that his wife sends over every Saturday evening since Golde is gone. At that, Rubenstein always makes a joke: "It's a shame for such good cookies to be eaten by a reactionary."

Then Arele runs in from the kitchen and says to him, "You're *treyf*, but your wife's cookies are kosher."

---

2. In her original, the author wrote *khesed shel emes*, which signifies the mitzvah of accompanying the deceased to the interment.

It doesn't bother him one iota that his answer has no semblance of logic. He has said his piece and is happy.

Weinstock, who's worked for twenty-five years in a furniture factory with Rubenstein and Arele, and who remembers them both when they were young men, now grown old on the job, isn't bothered by their quarreling. He's forever had his own claim: "You can't steer the world. She steers it by herself; that's how it seems anyway."

After Golde died, he doesn't even say this. He listens to them, to the bickering, and is happy, because at least something in his house hasn't changed—there's quarreling here every Tuesday and Saturday evening. He wanders around in his house, and feels that all the corners are empty.

Once in summer, when Rosele had finished cleaning the two rooms and the kitchen, Weinstock went downstairs with her. Together, they went for a walk in a park.

"Come, Rosele, we'll go for a little walk," Weinstock said, "it's hot in the house."

Rosele walked next to him, not saying anything. In the park, they sat down together on a bench. Weinstock wanted to tell her how very grateful he was to her, that she didn't allow his house to go to ruin, but just then he remembered how he had met his wife, Golde, the first time. This swam up so clearly in his memory that he remembered every single detail, and he began to tell Rosele about it.

"That was when the Williamsburg Bridge hadn't been built yet, and to get from Brooklyn to Manhattan, you had to take the Grand Street ferry. Quite a while ago by now. I was all of seventeen years old then. Took the ferry on Saturday after *havdolah*. The ferry couldn't budge from its spot. It was snowing, ice was floating in the river, and the ferry made slow time until five in morning. When I got off the ferry, I was so frozen I couldn't move my hands or feet. I barely made it to my aunt's house. And there I met Golde . . ."

The details of that trip were so dear and so important to Weinstock just then, that he completely forgot what he wanted to say to Rosele. She sat there, the thick hair on her head darkening like a smudge in the clear summer evening. Weinstock spoke, and the distance of the past disappeared; it was like yesterday, it had almost become like today, like now.

Weinstock gave a start. He noticed that he was sitting by himself on the bench. Rosele was walking down the way to the park's exit. Walking very slowly. Her head with its thick hair, like a smudge in the clear summer evening, was hanging down. Weinstock said to himself: "you donkey," and he ran after her. At the exit of the park, he caught up with her and saw that she was crying. He didn't approach her, but returned to the bench.

For two weeks, Rosele didn't come to clean the two rooms and kitchen at Weinstock's. Only then, did he feel that his house was a complete ruin. In fact, an absolute ruin. On the third week, Rosele was again standing on his doorstep; she "*poyavet*, appears." She put several fresh rolls, a little butter wrapped in paper, and cheese on the table; and without a word, went to clean the kitchen and get the coffee ready.

Weinstock walked around his house, and for the first time he felt that the corners weren't empty. There was a person here in the house. A person close to him, doing his work, the quiet Rosele, who had cried in the park while walking to the exit gate.

This time he didn't say to her, as usual, "Thank you, Rosele," but went to her in the kitchen. "You'll stay here, Rosele, what's the point of being alone?"

He didn't have time to say more. It was Tuesday—the lucky day. Rubenstein and Arele arrived. They had no doubt been quarreling about their newspapers on the way over, because Rubenstein crossed the doorstep with the words, "You're a damn reactionary! As I am a Jew, you're a reactionary!"

The coffee was boiling. Arele and Rubinstein were quarreling. Weinstock walked around the room and thought that his house was not a ruin. And Rosele sat at the table listening and, with deep joy, was silent.

New York, 1947

In a Jewish Home
· · · · · · ·

Although it was an ordinary Wednesday at the Flexners' house, it seemed like the day before Passover. Mrs. Flexner, a kerchief on her head and wearing a big apron, was wiping the dust out of the corners and polishing all the brass locks on the doors until they gleamed like gold. She had washed the windows. All the chairs were standing upside down, their legs in the air, and Mrs. Flexner was inspecting each one to see if they were clean—in short, like the day before Passover.

Mr. Flexner sat, reading a newspaper, as though this whole business was no concern of his, but when his wife began to dust the walls around him with a feather duster, he said to her, still reading his newspaper, and for no apparent reason, "You should have a department store deliver new parents to your daughter. Believe me, Yetta, it wouldn't hurt."

Mrs. Flexner was exasperated. In such circumstances, she always used the same expression: "Someone else in your place," and so in fact did she begin: "Someone else in your place would not be sitting there with a newspaper in his hands, trying to set the world straight, deciding whether Churchill or Weitzman is right. Someone else in your place would care if the curtains are hanging straight. Just look here, one side is longer than the other, and when a person is trying to get a daughter married, he has to forget about Weitzman and Churchill, and should . . ."

She stopped because she didn't know precisely what a person "should" do. She set to waving the feather duster more energetically and muttered, "Fanny is already eighteen years old, and before you know it, she'll be nine-

206

teen, and while you're sitting there reading your newspaper, she'll soon be twenty, also. Some business to sit there and read Weitzman's speeches! He's probably married off all his children already—let him do what he wants; and Churchill, of course, I am not obliged to worry about. He has a government job, so let him worry about his own problems.

Mr. Flexner laid the newspaper down to the side, to make clear to his wife that she was completely muddled about Churchill. She had him mixed up with Bevin. Bevin was involved with Weitzman, not Churchill. Churchill was already a played-out fiddle, hanging on the wall.

Her husband's answer made Mrs. Flexner so angry that she stopped waving her feather duster on the wall and began speaking to him kindly, explaining, "Shimon, Fanny is coming today with a young man, who is worth thinking about. If there's dust in the house, he'll think that we are, God forbid, poor people, and that won't do. It just won't do for the curtains to be crooked, do you understand? It just won't do. So go ahead and stand on the chair and straighten them out. He is a young man who doesn't just happen along every day. Works in a drugstore. And that's no small thing. A significant person, an important man with a college education, a boy with some status. You don't want your daughter to marry just anybody, but a somebody who knows how to get on in the world."

Still speaking, Mrs. Flexner moved the bench over to the window, and Mr. Flexner stood up on it to straighten out the curtains, and finishing his work, said, "So now even a prince can come here, the Prince of Wales can come here, not just a drugstore boy."

Mrs. Flexner shook her head sadly. She really didn't like it when her husband mentioned names from his newspaper that her ancestors hadn't heard of. When he mentions these names, she feels that he isn't a devoted father, that Fanny (who is eighteen years old already, and soon enough, before you know it, will be nineteen, and then twenty) doesn't matter very much to him.

What will happen after Fanny's twentieth birthday, Mrs. Flexner is afraid to think. Terrified that Fanny should not overtake her twentieth year, they bought her a thin Astrakhan fur coat that cost several hundred dollars. When she wore it, Fanny looked like a rich lady who had gotten lost in a poor neighborhood. They bought her a matte velvet hat with a wing, which made Fanny look as though she would soon be appearing on a big stage, where hundreds of people would gaze in wonder at the beauty of her hat. They bought her a genuine snakeskin purse; you could say that Fanny was wearing half the Flexner's entire fortune.

Mrs. Flexner claims, "When a girl's beautifully dressed, the world looks at her differently."

Mr. Flexner answers his wife, as usual, reading his newspaper, "The world isn't impressed with a fur coat, Yetta, the world has other things than Fanny's coat to think about."

Mrs. Flexner flares up. "Which world are you talking about?"

"And which world are you talking about?"

"I didn't mention the world. The world doesn't have to marry Fanny off for me! Someone else in your place . . ."

And Mrs. Flexner stands there, stuck, because at that moment she cannot for the life of her think what someone else in his place would do, and she mutters to herself, "Fanny is already eighteen years old, and before you know it, she'll be nineteen . . ."

When all the chairs were properly arranged and the curtains straightened, Mrs. Flexner took off her kerchief and apron. Fanny arrived wearing her Astrakhan coat, her hat with the velvet wing, and her snake skin purse, and with her young man, who worked in a drugstore and who was worth thinking about.

Mrs. Flexner put on the face of a pious woman who is standing for the entire Eighteen Blessings. Her face prayerful, she observed her daughter and the guest. She winked at her husband to leave the room—he shouldn't bother Fanny or say too much.

Mr. Flexner sat in the kitchen and read his newspaper.

Mrs. Flexner carried food out on small trays (brand new little trays) for her daughter and her young man from the drugstore: fruit, and sweets, and nuts, and all sorts of tasty things. When the procession of sweets was completed, Mrs. Flexner tried to hear what Fanny was saying to her friend.

"Put down your newspaper, Shimon, put it down. How can you read it now? He called her 'darling' if I'm not mistaken. It seems to me, I'm sure I heard, 'darling.' How can you read a newspaper? If that's the way it stands already, something may really come of it," Mrs. Flexner said dreamily, more to herself than her husband. "If it's already come to 'darling,' then it's obviously going well."

A pleasant warmth spread itself over Mrs. Flexner's face, just as if here now in the middle of winter it had become summer, and a honey-like sweetness spread itself over the world. Then, all of a sudden, she grabbed her head. "I forgot! There's no soda water! What will happen if they want something to drink? How can a house hold its head up if there isn't a bottle of soda? It won't do, it just won't do.

"Shimon, do me a favor and have pity on your child. Go out and bring back a bottle of soda. You can read your newspaper later," and scornfully she took hold of his newspaper as though she wanted to take it out of her husband's hands.

Mr. Flexner flared up, answering his wife in a manner so out of keeping with the situation that she stood there astonished, not understanding at first what he was saying.

"My whole family was murdered, you know that, Yetta . . . and you act as though a bottle of soda were a matter of life or death! Tea will be fine, coffee will be fine, milk will be fine, water will be fine, everything will be fine."

Mr. Flexner, his nose turned white, sat back down to read his newspaper. Mrs. Flexner put on her coat and went out to bring back a bottle of soda.

At the door, she turned around to her husband and said to him, "Shimon, if Fanny needs anything, you should give it to her. Such an opportunity doesn't happen every day."

April 1947

A Wedding

. . . .

T he guests and relatives who had come to Willie Fishman's wedding, were flabbergasted when they were introduced to the bride, Frances. In the corners of the broad hall and next to the pillars that held up the ceiling, small groups of people whispered to each other, talking more with their hands and eyes than actually speaking, and every now and then, one could overhear a word.

"Replace the bride! Have you ever seen such a thing?"

Willie's mother, Etel, her eyes smiling and wearing a taffeta dress that indeed rustled like that of a happy mother-in-law, walked around among the guests, carrying a tray of food, and implored them, "Take something."

She indicated various cakes and cookies and said as she walked by, "I baked these myself . . . take some."

By walking around with her tray and praising her homebaked desserts, she could busy herself the whole time and avoid getting into a long conversation with any of her friends, relatives, or acquaintances.

Etel's older sister, who in the family was still called Sora Rivka, her old-country name, had come to the wedding from a small town in New Jersey where she lived. On the way, her car had wheezed and snorted and stopped; and Sora Rivka got to the wedding very late, in fact, after the ceremony.

When she came into the hall and caught sight of the bride (although several days earlier she had received a letter from Etel saying that "things have changed for Willie, something has happened, and I'll tell you the rest when I see you"), she turned her head several times as if she had suddenly lost her eyesight. She remained standing stiffly in her place like Lot's wife who had been turned into a pillar of salt. She saw her sister, grabbed Etel by the arm and pulled her over, but couldn't get any words out, only exhaling her hot breath: "E-t-e-l . . ."

Etel shrugged her shoulders and answered with a stiff mouth, "You can see . . . so, be quiet . . ."

Etel never stopped smiling; it looked as if her smile had been painted on her face along with the powder and the makeup on her cheeks and forehead. Etel led her sister up to the bride and walking with her, whispered in her ear, "Sora Rivka, go and kiss her . . ."

Sora Rivka, whose face like Lot's wife was still stony, broke out a smile over her two venerable double chins and very slowly moved over to the bride, as though she were afraid of being prickled by something. She kissed her nephew, Willie, gave him a mazel tov, and when she saw his face with its open, happy smile, she warmed up and kissed the bride twice, even with sincerity.

The bride, Frances, young and tall, held Sora Rivka's full brown—freckled fingers in her thin warm hands, with many bracelets on her wrists. For some time Frances held her hand, and Sora Rivka felt like an aunt, a real aunt. Nevertheless, she was dazed and forgot all the things one is supposed to say to the bride and began looking in her little silk purse for her handkerchief. The bride, Frances, who was perfectly at ease, did not forget to ask Sora Rivka why she was so late in coming to the wedding and had missed the ceremony.

"Have you seen Berish?" Etel asked her sister. Relieved, Sora Rivka turned away from the bride and went to say mazel tov to her brother-in-law, Etel's husband.

Berish, an ironmonger with work-hardened hands and a dark face, just as if it had gotten rusty from working around all that iron, laid a hand on his sister's-in-law shoulder and said to her with a private smile, "So, Sora Rivka, how d'you like the bride? It's a different world we live in—hmm?" and not waiting for an answer, he gave her a glass of wine. "So, let's drink a l'chaim!" he said simply, businesslike and tough, as though he were standing on the stone floor of his store and not on the soft plush carpet that swayed and gave way under his feet.

Sora Rivka drew in her breath deeply and, after drinking the wine, asked her brother-in-law, "And where is Sarah?"

Her mouth remained open; pure astonishment at an incomprehensible event lay on her mouth and made her seem almost childish.

Berish laughed deeply from his chest, raised his shoulders, and said, "Where should she be? In New York! Don't ask, Sora Rivka. Once upon a time a knife used to get rusty. These days knives don't rust, and a person is stainless, too. No matter what he does, he doesn't rust, he sparkles. Nothing bothers him."

Berish went over to the musicians to request a tune, and Sora Rivka remained standing, her mouth open, as if she were waiting for someone to answer her question about Sarah—whom she had met many times at her sister's house and whom she loved, regarding her as a niece, and once had even given her a bathing suit as a present.

Tall, thin Frances, the bride, was wearing a crown of flowers on her head with a short white veil that only came down to the middle of her forehead, really just a hint of a bride's veil. Her eyes—gray, sparkling, and shrewd—smiled warmly at the guests. Not far from her sat her father, the lawyer Jacob Shteinheker, who had exactly the same eyes as his daughter, and Mrs. Shteinheker, the bride's mother, who had light blonde hair.

Frances went up to Etel (she was a head taller than her mother-in-law) and bent her sparkling eyes closer, practically in Etel's face, and said, "Ma, don't work so hard, you'll get tired. They can help themselves, let them take what they want," almost as if she had said, "Don't let them make you feel guilty. It's a wedding like all other weddings."

Etel shook her head in agreement: "You're right," but didn't stop walking around with the tray, as though she needed something to prop her up. The tray of food was her support.

Willie never left his bride's side. Several times he straightened the little white veil on her forehead. He said something into her ear, and Frances smiled, her eyes sparkling, the many bracelets on her arm quietly jingling, and laughed, too.

Berish requested a happy tune from the musicians, an old melody that he remembered from his own wedding. (The fiddler said to him, "Ha! Ha! That's from before Columbus's time!") The guests were drawn to the tune and went off to form a circle dance. While the guests were enjoying them-selves in the dance, and Frances and Willie were spinning around in the middle of the circle, young, lighthearted, and joyful, Sora Rivka took the tray away from her sister's hand and they went into a little side room where a table stood, covered with yet unopened bottles of wine and beer and yet uncut cakes.

Sora Rivka blinked her eyes a good deal and, holding Etel's hands tightly in her own, asked her, "Etel, what's happened here? Is it so passion-ate a love? Is it some kind of . . . kind of thing . . . is this a kind of *lyubov?*"[1]

Etel's took off her smile, the way someone takes off a warm coat on a hot day. She even wiped her eyes, that were tired from absorbing all the strange and curious looks, and she said to her sister, barely moving her tongue, "You think *I* know? He says he's in love . . . you think I can stop him? He's his own man now. He's already a partner in a drugstore. That's fine, that's fine, but—well, what's a mother for? I begged him to put off the wedding for at least half a year, at least not the same week that had been arranged with Sarah . . ."

Sora Rivka grabbed her cheeks with both hands and pinched them hard. Her two venerable double chins trembled.

"Well," she answered.

"Well! But he wouldn't . . . it has to be now, he said, because he had a vacation. It's summer, and people aren't sick as much. He had the time now, he said, to go on a 'honeymoon.' "

"This is what comes of a honeymoon," Sora Rivka said and groaned, "a person should be protected from such extortion . . ."

Her eyes closed, she leaned her elbows on the table, crushing one of the cakes.

"See what you did?" Etel said hastily to her sister and set herself con-tentedly to perform the small job of cutting around the damaged cake and saving the pieces that were still whole, so they wouldn't be wasted. Cutting the cake, Etel had her earlier smile on again already, as she had had for the

---

1. To express her dismay, Sora Rivka uses the Russian word for "love," *lyobov,* rather than the Yiddish word, *libe,* emphasizing the non-Jewishness of this wedding.

entire evening of the wedding, and she carried this smile, together with the cut pieces of the cake around to the guests.

Sarah, Willie's first fiancée, whom he had jilted six weeks before the wedding, had for the past two years been in his parents' home like one of their own. She'd often bring presents from her father's antique shop to the Fishmans. A picture, a silver cigar case for her future father-in-law, for Berish; a brooch for Etel, a tray. A happy young woman, with unruly curls at her ears, she endeared herself to Berish, to Etel, and even to Sora Rivka when she came to her sister's house. Sarah loved everyone who was related to Willie—his father, his mother, his aunts. Willie called her "my butterfly," and her movements really were somewhat like those of a butterfly. No one was surprised when Sarah, out of the blue, stopped by to call for Willie to accompany her to her father's lawyer, or to go with her to buy a Mother's Day present for her mother, or something for her father's birthday. Willie was always ready when Sarah called for him to go somewhere. "Sarah is asking me," or "Sarah wants," were the words they were used to hearing from Willie at home.

And it was, in fact, at her father's lawyer's office that she, together with Willie who had accompanied her there, saw Frances for the first time. The first things Sarah noticed were Frances's thin hands and all her bracelets. She couldn't see her face. Frances was standing, leaning with both hands on the windowsill, looking out at the street.

Frances's father, Jacob Shteinheker, called his daughter: "Frances, come meet my young clients."

"Ah!" Frances spoke up cheerfully. She turned around and greeted them. She put her hand to her forehead, as if she were trying to remember something, and said to Willie with a smile of someone who is asking a riddle, "It seems to me that you took a pencil away from me once and wouldn't give it back."

Frances's father turned around on his roller chair and, with sparking eyes, looked curiously at his daughter.

It appeared that Willie and Frances had once been students together in public school. They both remembered their childhood games and laughed when Frances mentioned the name of one of their teachers: "She used to come to class in her slippers. You remember?" Frances said, "we were always afraid for her."

Sarah saw that Willie was standing, his whole body leaning over to Frances. He even touched her bracelets. Sarah saw Frances's face, long, almost thin, and darkly tanned, as if painted with copper. Sarah felt a nagging pain and regretted that she had asked Willie to go with her to the lawyer.

When Sarah and Willie left Jacob Shteinheker's office, they were both silent, like a couple who has just left the rabbi's house after a divorce. Sarah gathered her strength and said to Willie, "She's not that beautiful, your old school friend."

Willie made a motion with his hand as if he were pushing her words away and didn't answer. He looked straight ahead and smiled, but Sarah felt his smile was not for her.

Two weeks after Sarah and Willie had gone to Jacob Shteinheker's office, Etel asked her son, "Willie, why don't we see Sarah?"

Willie was standing, knotting his necktie in front of a mirror, and answered his mother, not looking at her, "I don't know . . ."

"You aren't seeing her anymore?"

Willie didn't answer Etel's question. He said coldly, "If you need her, call her up."

Etel didn't ask any more questions, but had a heavy feeling of guilt regarding Sarah and resentment for Willie, who so calmly knotted his tie and didn't even answer her questions.

Sarah came over to the Fishmans' twice to see Willie, but she didn't find him there.

"I'll wait for him," she said to Etel and sat down and leafed through a book, just turning the pages, not even pretending to be reading.

Etel went over to her, stood quietly for a while, the way a person stands next to a mourner, not knowing what to say, and then she murmured the first word: "Sarah . . ."

Sarah closed the book and remained sitting, not moving.

Etel said, "Sarah, I don't know what's going on with Willie . . . I don't know anything . . . I can't tell you anything . . ."

Sarah got up and walked through the room to leave. She would have closed the door, but Etel held it and went outside after her, walking down from the second floor. They didn't say a word to each other, only followed one step after the other, one step after the other, the way a person follows another down into a cave. At the exit door to the street, Etel said, barely lifting her eyes to look at the young woman, "Sarah, you know how much I love you, and Berish does too, you know that . . ."

Sarah left quietly, not even saying good night, but her lips seemed to be moving. It was a spring evening. At the door of the building, a street musician was standing, playing a fiddle. He was a cripple with a wooden leg. Sarah walked over to him, gave him a coin, and consoled herself that there were people more unfortunate than she.

The guests ate the wedding supper with gusto. Their curiosity had been satisfied with the whisperings they had heard and told each other about Willie's new bride and about Sarah. They had already gotten used to Frances with her short wedding veil and her thin figure. Besides, a few of them had already downed quite a few l'chaims, and the alcohol had made them broad-minded and forgiving.

The bride and groom left for their honeymoon right after the dinner. Sora Rivka asked her sister, "What's the hurry? Will the honeymoon will run away?"

"It's the style, they say," Etel answered unwillingly.

"So, maybe all of this is a style," Sora Rivka said. And it seemed to her that the entire hall with all the wedding guests had found themselves on an unknown, immense, turbulent river, and no one knew where the current was carrying them.

Later, near dawn, when it was already getting light, Etel and Berish and Sora Rivka returned home. Berish walked over to the wall, took down the picture that Sarah had brought from her father's antique store, and thought for a while about where to put it. Then he took it to the closet where they kept old things.

"It shouldn't be hanging there in front of our eyes," he said, "a heartache . . ."

A pale spot with a dusty, dark border surrounding it remained on the wall. Etel tried to wash it away but couldn't get rid of it. In its place, they hung the photograph of Willie and Frances in their wedding finery.

Herschel Eisengold

. . . .

T his was a family trait of every Eisengold: when they took on a job,
they did it with their whole heart.

Herschel Eisengold, a traveling jewelry salesman with Excellent, the
large firm, was absorbed in his work with even more than his whole heart,
because of something that had happened to him. When he had started
working at Excellent, one of the vice presidents of the firm had said to him:
"Mr. Eisengold, you really know how to talk to a customer." And the vice
president had smiled and winked his left eye.

Herschel Eisengold never, in his entire life, forgot this event.

His home, one could say, was a university. His wife, their two daughters, and even the neighbors, all were forever hearing from him that selling
jewelry takes a special know-how, and if you don't have it, nothing will
help.

"Each business," Herschel Eisengold said, "requires not just a mastery of
the trade, but a distinct mood, a feeling, one that a person should never
allow to fall away. And selling jewelry calls for a refined conversation, and
then only about the very happiest of things: weddings, a bris, bar mitzvahs.
Such a conversation usually brings to mind the gifts people need to buy for
all these occasions—watches, pins, rings, earrings. You understand? Now
this is the point! The principle is that you cannot allow, ever allow, the conversation to descend to unpleasant things . . . you never mention wars,
massacres, anti-Semitism, holdups, and other such things, because what is
jewelry? Jewelry is delight, jewelry is a good feeling, and the selling of a lit-

tle piece of jewelry can evaporate like a small cloud. Here he is, and there he disappears. So it is with jewelry—here you need it, and there you can live without it.

His habit of engaging customers in only refined conversations about the happiest of events, Herschel Eisengold transferred to his home, also. But here he spoke to the listeners in his university. And in telling them about his business, he was exhilarated, just as if he were seeing the customer in front of his eyes again.

"Now today, for example, I sold a widow a pair of earrings. A woman, loaded with money, with property, and with plenty of pounds, too. How could you conquer such a fortress? When she speaks slowly, and moves slowly, and listens slowly, and then suddenly she moves her mouth, wanting to say something, but says nothing—not yes, not no. How can you conquer such a fortress? But you do conquer her. Now *this* is the point!"

And here, the story about the vice president, who fifteen years ago had told him that he really knew how to talk to a customer, usually comes up.

The neighbors, when they hear the story about the vice president, think up a reasonable excuse, smile for a while, move backward to the door, and leave.

The daughters, after hearing a little lesson from their father's jewelry university, quickly tie on light head scarves, and run out into the street, where they don't learn business know-how, but where a world rushes by— makes a racket, bangs, sings, and chases.

When Herschel Eisengold is alone with his wife, he tells her about other things that happen to him in his trade.

"Sometimes you actually come into a house where there aren't any children. A family without children means—no needs, no joy, no gifts—a naked house. What can you do in such a case? How can you make customers out of such people?"

This is the academic question Herschel Eisengold poses for his wife, and he looks at her with such a mysterious gaze, it's as though he's holding a magic ring in his hand that he, and he alone, knows how to move.

"What can you do in such a case? Tell me."

His wife, Esther, doesn't answer, because her husband clearly doesn't need her answer. It's enough for him to have one mute listener in his business university. It doesn't bother him if the listener dozes off or yawns. Herschel Eisengold sees for himself a customer to whom he must sell his merchandise and, with exceptional wisdom, converses with him, leading him into a "refined conversation."

"A person needs to have friends. So our wise men say. Good friends. A good friend is the dearest thing you can wish for. And you should take care of a friend. Take care of him like the eye in your head. You need to jot down his birthday and give him a present, too. You need to know when it's his silver or golden wedding anniversary, you shouldn't forget when his son or grandchild becomes bar mitzvah. With a little gift, that costs only a couple of dollars, you buy a friend for your entire life. Yes! You need to know how to carry on a refined conversation, and then they buy! Now *this* is the point!"

His wife, her eyes tired, listens to him. It seems to her that she has been hearing for a long time, a very long time, from childhood on it, how one sells watches, pins, earrings, rings.

Sometimes she tries to interrupt her husband: "Our Irene, she's not even fifteen years old yet, she's already going out with boys. What do you have to say about that?"

Herschel Eisengold raises a finger to clean the corners of his eyes, both corners of his right eye, then both corners of his left eye . . . and then, searching mightily for another pursuit, finds his ears and works them over with two fingers, saying to his wife, "So? She's going out, hmm? She's going out?"

After he cleans his ears out thoroughly, Herschel Eisengold smokes a cigarette, smiles, and says to his wife, "Esther, you'll be interested to hear how I sold a ring today to a widower, an ordinary widower. He didn't even have it in mind to buy anything, although it's true, he was thinking about remarrying. The main thing, I'm telling you, is in fact that you need to have a refined conversation. One should tell a widower, an ordinary widower, that he doesn't have too much time to think. If he should meet an appropriate person, at an appropriate occasion, at an appropriate time—it's good he should have a ring ready in hand . . . and he bought it! You understand? Now *this here* is the point!"

Esther sits on a chair, rocking herself slowly back and forth, as if the wind were swinging her. From time to time, she puts her hand to her throat, is quiet for a while, and then rocks herself again, and asks her husband, "And how do people live who don't sell jewelry at all?"

Herschel Eisengold answers her, smiling. "There you have the point exactly: you have to know how to talk to a customer."

She touches her throat and is silent.

One time, the president of the Excellent firm, passing by, put a hand on Herschel Eisengold's shoulder and said a few words to him. A day later, Herschel Eisengold talked with the president in his reception room for about an hour. The president ended the conversation by saying, "Remember, it's thirty percent of your earnings, whenever you use the Excellent firm."

A couple of months later, Herschel Eisengold came home with a photograph of a building. High up on the roof was a sign: "Eisengold Excellent, Affiliated."

After that, the business university at the Eisengold's house became a large institute, with separate departments. Employees from Eisengold Excellent Affiliated began to arrive at their home. They were all men with precisely ironed pants, precisely tied neckties, precisely shined shoes, and with precise conversations about the different kinds of jewelry, the main topic being Herschel Eisengold and his special method of selling.

Now came the time when Herschel Eisengold spoke very little about himself. His employees spoke, telling about the special cases and how Eisengold's method worked.

From time to time, Herschel Eisengold threw in a word where the speaker had left out an important point. Food was served to the employees by Sulamit, a young mulatto, who knew exactly on which side to serve a plate, where it should be placed, how many and which words to say to the guests and the boss, which ones to call "sir" and which ones were "Mr." followed by their two names.

Esther always sat at the same place at the table, rocking back and forth on her chair, as though the wind were swinging her. Now a mountain of jewelry with various names rose up around her. The stories about her husband's methods doubled and multiplied in the various mouths, shot through with thinly veiled flatteries and sparse laughter. In a word, it was a refined conversation about the happiest of things, to which was added only one new expression: "Eisengold Excellent Affiliated."

The daughters went away to colleges in strange towns and from there punctually sent Mother's Day and Father's Day presents.

Every once in a while, a conversation from another world slipped into the Eisengolds' house. This happened when a man came seeking a donation for a hospital, a school, an old folk's home, an orphanage, for the troubles in Europe, or for the building of the state of Israel.

Then Esther would serve tea and sweets herself. She listened carefully and asked questions. Like a person who has tuberculosis for whom the garden windows have been opened, she breathed deeply, taking in sickly pleasure from this new, unexpected speech.

Herschel Eisengold wiped the corners of his eyes. First both corners of his right eye, then both corners of his left eye, and then searched mightily for another pursuit and found his ears. Zealously, he worked them over with two fingers and said absently to the man, "You mean they actually eat in the old folk's home? Hmm? They do?" Or, "You mean they're actually building the state of Israel? Hmm? Actually building?" Or, "You mean they actually pray in the synagogue? Hmm? Actually pray?"

The man is happy that Herschel Eisengold, that is to say, Eisengold Excellent Affiliated, has lent an ear to his subject, to his presence.

Herschel Eisengold's eyes gleam. Like a cat waiting for the moment the bird dozes in a tree, he is looking for an excuse to turn the conversation to his jewelry business. Beaming with satisfaction, he tells about his clients, the special character of various kinds of jewelry buyers, and the refined conversation one has to have with each and every one of them . . . he tells about rich and poor buyers, lucky parents, childless couples (may it never happen to you), widowers, divorcees, boasters, and solid customers.

The man listens and smiles uncomfortably. Esther rocks on her chair.

The man carefully pulls on the reins to return to his own subject, but in vain. Herschel Eisengold sees in front of him a stubborn person, a fortress who must be conquered. After a couple of hours of refined conversation, Herschel Eisengold allows the skinny little man to go with a skinny little check and with this advice: "The most important thing is to know how to carry on a conversation! Now *this* is the point!"

The man slips out to the street with a feeling of resentment. Later, he turns in a report to his organization: "Even if you cut off my membership, I will never go back to the Eisengolds' house again. He can give you a heart attack."

Herschel Eisengold began bringing home newspapers that ran big advertisements for Eisengold Excellent Affiliated. Esther glances at the large letters of the ads, shakes her head, and is silent. Herschel Eisengold's eyes smile, smile at each letter individually. He compares the advertisements in different newspapers, reading them through slowly, with great pleasure. Then he looks at them for quite a while, and for no apparent reason, closes one smiling eye, while the second begins to smile, even happier.

On one of the advertisements he added in pencil: "Not all that glitters is gold, Eisengold is the best gold!"

"Now that's it! That needs to be the slogan of Eisengold Excellent Affiliated! Hmm? What do you say? Hmm?"

His wife looks at him with tired eyes and shakes her head. He doesn't look at her and says enthusiastically, "Now that's it! Hmm! What do you say? Hmm?"

For the first time, Herschel Eisengold sat down on a chair and wanted to hear what his wife had to say. This was after Sulamit told him that Mrs. Eisengold was lying in bed with a blanket over her head and wouldn't answer whether she wanted to drink her coffee in bed or come to the dining room.

Esther lay there, all curled up, the blankets like a sack, wrapped around her legs and up to her head. The only words that he heard from her after an hour of asking and talking to her were, "I don't want to get up."

Esther lay there a whole day, not moving when the light was turned on in the evening, not even touching the food Sulamit brought to her (perfectly prepared on a tray) for breakfast, lunch, and dinner. The food stood on a glass table next to the bed until it grew cold, and Sulamit deftly carried it away.

The doctor, because of his huge glasses, looked like a person in disguise, shrugged his shoulders when Herschel Eisengold told him in another room, "We're not lacking even the finest thing in our home. The children are successful. There's no reason for her to be sick."

The doctor stared through his glasses and concluded in a purely scientific manner, "All the symptoms of depression."

Exactly twice a week, Herschel Eisengold went to visit his wife in the private hospital for patients with nervous disorders. He always had a large bundle of newspapers, with advertisements for Eisengold Excellent Affiliated with him. On the way to the hospital, sitting in his car, he looked over the ads, smiled at each letter individually, and wrote remarks on them with a pencil.

The doctor, with the huge glasses on his face, always greeted him with the same words: "Your wife is improving, she's improving significantly." And escorting him out, the doctor had the same words: "Patience, Mr. Eisengold. It's a slow process, Mr. Eisengold."

Herschel Eisengold looked at the doctor and smiled, asserting to himself with pleasure: "He knows how to talk with a customer. He knows, it's obvious."

New York, 1947

The Divorce

. . . .

For seven years now Nakhum Romnik, or Romi, as they call him in the shop, has been buying a Yiddish newspaper each day and reads all the stories about runaway wives and divorces. He began doing this after his wife, Pearl, divorced him and even today, he can't understand how it happened. His wife was quiet, didn't demand too much from him, was loyal, wasn't a runabout, wasn't a spendthrift—one could say she almost wasn't there at all. After every meal, she'd ask her husband, "Nakhum, are you full?"

"After you eat, you're full."

Finished eating, Nakhum went out to the street to get a glass of soda water and each time called to his wife: "Pearl, are you coming?" and, not waiting for her answer, closed the door behind him.

"Already? He's gone already?" Pearl called after him, and with her customary silence, she cleaned the lids of the pots and washed the oven racks.

It was always quiet in the Romniks' house—perhaps it was the quietest house in the city—and was as clean as Passover eve.

In short, she was a good wife, her only fault being that once a week she went to her sister's and always returned from there a different person, walking around as if someone had bewitched her. Indeed, she cooked and indeed she cleaned, but she did it all without saying a single word—just plain angry.

Her sister, who had a small store where she baked and sold knishes, had a habit of saying to her: "Why are you sitting there with him, Pearl? Come to me, you can help me sell knishes, I'll give you ten dollars a week, and you'll be a queen."

Her sister was a cheerful person and would sing to her then: "The little Hasid liked her a lot, / And brought her a coral bibelot."

Once when his wife returned from her sister's in a sulk, Romi had said to her, meaning no harm, "When you come back from your sister's, you're angry with me. Make up you mind, if you like it so much at your sister's, go stay with her."

Pearl didn't answer, just as though she were not hearing what was being said to her. She lay down on the bed and closed her eyes. Romi took this to mean: she goes to lie down for a while—so, she's sleeping. But he regretted his few words as soon as he had said them. A man may be permitted a slip of the tongue once in a while, but he felt bad and wanted to talk it over with someone so he'd feel better. He picked up a chair, carried it outside of the first floor of his building, and put it down next to the landlord who was also the superintendent. The landlord knew all the neighbors, what each one was suffering from, and what all their troubles were.

"My wife," Romi began, "always comes back from her sister's in a sulk."

The landlord, who wore a sleeveless vest as if it were his uniform, was smoking a pipe and asked, without the least curiosity, "Is that so?"

Romi told him his troubles: "Now today when she came back, I said a few things that maybe I shouldn't have said."

The landlord crossed one leg over the other and asked again, for no reason, just for something to say: "Is that so?"

In the morning, Romi's wife packed up the few dresses she had (she didn't have very many) together with a little linen (she didn't have much of that either) and left for her sister's. Before she left, because she was an honest person, she straightened the whole place up, cleaned everything, even fixed all the things that needed fixing, and left, and didn't want to come back. Romi went to talk to her several times. She was quiet, had not a word of complaint, and with her head bent down, she said, "It's just not worth it."

Then came the divorce. Romi didn't seem to realize that he was left without a wife.

This was when he began reading the stories about divorces; but they were all different, not like what had happened to him.

"Everywhere, when people get divorced there's a reason, you can understand it. But with me . . . just like that, she goes to her sister."

Romi didn't read the newspapers at home. After his wife left, he didn't like to be at home too much, and he would go to a lunchroom, right on the same street, have something to eat, and read about the divorces. The lunchroom closed at nine o'clock at night. Romi would leave with the boss, even wait for him to close and lock the door; Romi would try the door once in a while to see if it was really locked.

It's seven years now that he's been sitting at the same table in the lunchroom. People are used to him, to him, to his newspaper, and to the stories about the divorces that he retells if the boss, or the boss's wife, have time to listen to him.

Every once in a while, Romi finds a story in the newspaper about an especially interesting divorce. With good cheer and gusto, he tells all about it like a specialist who comes across a bizarre case in his field.

"Now I can understand *that* divorce! The wife runs away with another man, but before she runs away, she robs her husband! Now I can understand that! You can grasp it! But just like that . . . and for no reason!"

Romi doesn't say any more. The lunchroom boss and his wife nod to each other, which means—they've agreed from the start. They look at the clock, because when Romi finishes reading his newspaper, it's time to close up.

Walking back home, newspaper in hand, Romi stops to talk to his landlord some more. The landlord, wearing his sleeveless vest as if it were his uniform, smokes his pipe, crosses one leg over the other, and asks without the least curiosity, "A divorce? Is that so?"

Romi tells him about the divorce in the newspaper. He tells it word by word, almost as if he knows it by heart. He concludes, almost enviously, "I can understand that one! There's something you can grasp there . . ."

The landlord shakes his head.

Romi goes to his room. He cuts the story of the divorce out of the newspaper and puts it in a small box, where he collects all the clippings about divorces, and talks to himself with the expertise of a specialist who knows his field inside and out. Only one case is incomprehensible: "But a story like mine—well, there just aren't any like it."

Friendship

. . . .

Of the three children that Shloyme Yalowitz had, not one remained at home. All three, Sarah, Ben, and Bernie, as soon as they earned a few dollars on their own, left as though they were checking out of a hotel. They took the best things with them; the worst were left strewn about on the floor, not even piled up together in a corner. The daughter, Sarah, rented a room close to the office where she worked, and later her parents learned that she had married an Italian, the bookkeeper in the same office. Her father didn't want to see his daughter any more. Her mother, Trynah Yalowitz, was once a guest at her daughter's summer home by the ocean. There she saw how her daughter wore shiny combs in her hair like an Italian shikse and cooked vegetables with cream, which didn't taste at all like Jewish food. The son-in-law had a short trimmed mustache and called his mother-in-law, "Mrs. Yalowitz." The daughter never came home, she wasn't exactly invited either—they didn't want the neighbors to find out about her goyish match.

The sons, Ben and Bernie, were each busy with their own affairs, Ben in his used furniture store and Bernie in a strange enough business—talking on street corners to a passing crowd before the elections of congressmen, a president, a mayor, or a governor.

Trynah Yalowitz was able to bring her children together only for her funeral. She died from an utterly trivial illness, one that at its onset doesn't normally lead to death: her hand began to hurt, and she died almost by chance, as though everything in her life had just been by chance, too, including her son-in-law, the Italian, and her son, the one who spoke on street corners on the eve of elections.

Shloyme Yalowitz was left alone. Thank God, his hands still served him well. He knew how to stitch seams on a machine and didn't have to depend on anyone. But he resented all four members of his vanished family, not for any definite offence any one of them had committed, but just because he was left alone.

Ben, from his furniture store, was the only one who dropped in once in a while to see his father. He came very early, before his father left for work, stood by the door several minutes, lit a cigarette, and just as the cigarette was finished, he left and threw the butt into the street. Shloyme Yalowitz lived in a room owned by his *landsleit*, paid for it promptly, and received from them exactly what they had agreed upon. He was completely at home there, except for one thing: on no account, did the *landsleit* want to hear complaints about his children.

"Your children are like all children in America," the landlady cuts him off, meaning that she doesn't, on any account, want to listen to stories about the special resentment Shloyme Yalowitz carries around in his heart against his two sons and daughter.

The only person who would listen to Shloyme Yalowitz's resentment against his children and his wife who had died so unexpectedly was old "Grandpa," as everyone on the block called him, because he was the oldest person in the neighborhood. He spoke a language that no one knew; it could have been Greek, Armenian, or Turkish. If one could believe him, he had lived there for fifty years. The two old men were well able to communicate with each other, although Grandpa, in spite of his fifty years in America, barely spoke a few words of English; and Shloyme Yalowitz, who for thirty years had only heard his machine pecking out seams of women's dresses, didn't know any more English either.

They usually talked about the children, "the young people." Shloyme Yalowitz told about his resentment, frequently throwing in a Yiddish word or two, sometimes even a biblical verse. And Grandpa if he didn't exactly understand, shook his head even more vigorously, which meant that he was in complete agreement. He knew the names of Shloyme Yalowitz's children, Sarah, Ben and Bernie, just as Shloyme Yalowitz knew the names of Grandpa's children: Jack, Janet, and Joe. Grandpa told all about them, throwing in plenty of incomprehensible words and folk sayings, and Shloyme Yalowitz shook his head sympathetically.

One could say, almost with certainty, that except for the names of their children, the old men knew little else about each other. But this meant nothing; it hid their deeply held conviction that youth is always unjust to lonely elders, and they listened to each other with greater appreciation.

In order to finish a long chat as they were getting ready to leave, they'd say to each other with real feeling and significance: "Yes, the young people."

Their friendship sustains itself, one can say, especially in summers. Then, they both sit on the bench that stands next to the only tree on the block. The moon shines toward them between two streetlamps and reminds both of them of times past—one of his shtetl in Volin, and the other of a quiet village in his homeland. It seems like a bygone dream, but the moon, the same one from the past, is a witness that the dream had once really existed.

Winters separate them. In winter, they say only good evening, or good morning; they mention "the young people" only in order that the thread not be broken until spring, and each one carries his old, half-frozen body back to his warm room and his bed.

On the first spring evening when the birds sing to each other in the lone tree, exactly as they did in Volin and in Greece, Shloyme Yalowitz and Grandpa sit on the bench, awaken just like the birds, and chat: "Yes, the young people."

New York, 1946

A Letter

. . . .

People are usually very honest with a doctor. Not only with the doctor himself, but as soon as they step into the doctor's waiting room, they know—in here, a person has to tell the truth. There's nothing to hide: people are sick, are broken, agitated, offended, sometimes wronged; all of which finds expression in the various illnesses they need cured. This is clear when people come to a doctor and no one is ashamed of it.

The three patients had already met several times in the doctor's waiting room. Seeing each other once, and then again, they got acquainted and chatted among themselves. It's natural at first, for a person to talk about what's bothering him, and one of the patients began talking about his illness.

He had stopped sleeping, not because of troubles, and not, God forbid, because of pain, but simply because he had lost the habit of sleeping. It had all started because of a silver anniversary invitation and, moreover, because of his name, Yenkl.

His fellow conversationalists, the other two patients, exchanged glances: they clearly thought he was a little mixed up. How can it hurt a person if his name is Yenkl?

The patient, the storyteller, caught their glances and continued his story.

The silver anniversary party was for an old friend of his, a fellow from the same town, who was also called Yenkl. They had both gone to the same cheder and then studied together in school—they were fellow townsmen.

When he and his friend Yenkl were still small boys, he had caught a

230

scolding and a slap from the rabbi, both unexpected and unwarranted, because of his friend, the second Yenkl. One of the boys had put out the fire in the stove. Had just poured in some water, and the wood sputtered feebly, its soul struggling to stay alive, and the fire was completely extinguished. That Yenkl had done it, but by mistake, when the rabbi heard—Yenkl—he slapped *him*. Later, just as oil will float on water, it came out that that Yenkl had really done it, but by then it was too late, and in any case, you can't take back a slap. And it happened frequently, that when one Yenkl did something wrong, the other caught the slap. One other time, the rabbi took a pinch of tobacco and muttered, "They're both brats," and that was the end of it.

He and his friend Yenkl had in fact both come to America at the same time, had both taken the same courses to learn bookkeeping, and again had sat on the same bench. He was in fact the better bookkeeper (good with accounts, with logical combinations), in short, a specialist. And that one, his friend Yenkl, a mishmash, a windmill; he couldn't balance the accounts. By all rights, he, the better accountant, should have become the cock of the walk, but things don't always add up the same way, and that Yenkl became the bigger achiever. Got himself connected to the right places and became a director in a bank. He was a doer, a comer, in short—Jacob Pulver.[1]

It's been four years now, the patient continued, that he's been working in a bank, where Jacob Pulver—Yenkl—is the director. He doesn't envy him. He has his own job, and that one is what he is—the director, so let him be the director. Sometimes Yenkl doesn't notice him. Walks right by him as if they were strangers. Sometimes he doesn't recognize him at all, just as if he's never seen him before. If he just happens to be in a friendly mood, he'll remind him how he had loaned him the rabbi's slap. But, if he has to go to see him in the main office, he has to make an appointment. Sometimes it happens that the girl, the front office secretary by the door (he has a secretary inside his office, too), tells him to come back later because "Mr. Pulver" is busy.

With God's help, Mr. Pulver will celebrate his silver anniversary—and not just anywhere but in a huge hotel. He doesn't want to go. All the direc-

1. The word *pulver* means "powder," usually gunpowder.

tors, all the big shots, will be there; and a person can't enjoy himself at such a gathering. He'd thought it over—he would send flowers and write a letter. It doesn't take a scholar to write a letter to Yankl? But it's a real problem when Yenkl is his director, and go try to guess what kind of a mood he'll be in when he gets the letter.

And so the letter took away more of his health and strength than a whole year's work at the bank did. The hardest part of such a letter is the greeting, the very greeting.

He wrote one letter, beginning in a familiar manner: "Dear Yenkl," and wished him all good things—and, really, what *did* he have against him? But as he read the letter over, he felt that it just wouldn't do. It was a lie: when he has to see him he has to clear it with the front office secretary, and sometimes she sends him on his way; he can come back later. So why should he humiliate himself and write "Dear Yenkl"?

He'd already torn up that letter up and written a new one: "Distinguished Mr. Jacob Pulver," but this seemed like a mockery. They had gone to cheder together, he had collected a slap from the rabbi because of him, they arrived in America together (one could say they had lived their lives side by side) and out of the blue, "Distinguished Mr. Jacob Pulver"—it just didn't add up.

For seven consecutive evenings, one after the other, he wrote a letter, and after each letter, he couldn't sleep. In the morning, what he had written looked foolish; so he tore it up, and in the evening, wrote another. The result was that he lost the habit of sleeping. From that "silver wedding" invitation on, he began having sleepless nights. Pills didn't help, and bottles of tonic didn't help either. He didn't feel any pain; it was just that he couldn't get back in the habit of sleeping, no matter what he did.

One of the two patients, the listeners, asked him, "And how, in fact, did you begin the letter: 'Dear Yenkl,' or 'Distinguished Mr. Jacob Pulver'?"

The patient didn't answer. It was his turn. The white uniformed assistant called him in: "The doctor is waiting for you."

December 22, 1946

The Amsterdams

· · · · · · ·

E very couple of months, Mrs. Amsterdam visits the doctor's office, always to complain about the same problem (something is gnawing in the pit of her stomach), always to get the same medicine, and in several months, the same thing again.

Whom she tells about how she'd come by her illness is all the same to her. She feels comfortable right away with the other patients in the waiting room, speaks quietly in a half voice, and it seems to be very important to her that people should understand and know what she's talking about. And then, she smiles, as if she were tasting a drop of honey on her lips, only the honey is bitter.

"When people suffer from bad children, they get used to it. That's the way of the world, and that hurts a lot less than when you suffer heartaches from too good children, too successful children."

So Mrs. Amsterdam says, and she looks around at her accidental listeners to see if they understand her, and then tells about her successful son.

"From childhood on, he did everything with his whole heart. Read a book so doggedly that he accompanied each little sentence with his finger: read with his eyes and accompanied it with his finger. So, he really knows, and knows everything too well. This characteristic comes from my husband's family, from the Amsterdams. They're real thinkers, inquisitive minds, pedants, and my son is a hundred percent Amsterdam. Above all, he can't stand it when someone makes a mistake."

Mrs. Amsterdam touches the third button of her blouse, the spot where it's gnawing in the pit of her stomach, all because of the Amsterdam family trait. She looks a while at her accidental listeners, to see if they understand her, and goes on about her son.

"When he was studying in middle school, everyone knew that he would get a scholarship. He earned it, but he never got it because he is an Amsterdam. There was the incident the time the teacher talked to the students about the word *apparatus*. As a teacher should do—he wrote the word on the blackboard, pronounced it, told where the word came from, in short, he did what he was supposed to do. My son, the Amsterdam, lost no time, wrote down the word on a piece of paper, carried it up to the teacher, and told him that according to the rules of the English language and to the derivation of the word, it should be pronounced 'appareytus.' Or maybe just the opposite: the teacher had said 'appareytus,' and he had said, 'apparatus.' Who can remember who said what? In short, he showed off all his knowledge. And when my son says something, he knows what he's talking about.

"When he came home and told us the story, I said to him, 'Borukh, you can say good-bye to your scholarship. You will see it like the moon at the end of the month. What's the difference to you, if he says "apparatus" or "appareytus"? The Empire State Building won't fall down because of it. Let it be the way the teacher wants it.'

"But both the Amsterdams, my husband and my son, decreed, 'No, a mistake has to be corrected, even if the teacher makes it.'

"In short, soon after this, there was another incident, and the scholarship was no longer. Burned up like a matzo.

"The tragedy is that he knows it all. Which king was when and what he did—my son knows it. If you mention a fly, he already knows how many legs she has. And he never makes a mistake. If anyone disagrees with him, he goes, brings back a book, opens it to the exact page, and shows that he's right. And in fact, he is right. And that just isn't good.

"When the scholarship was no more, my son started to work with a partner in an antique business. He started reading all the books about antiques, again running his finger under each sentence. When he applies himself to something, he can really do it. The partner didn't exactly understand antiques, but he knew how to run a business, and we were happy. So let him be in antiques. And then Queen Elizabeth the First interfered."

The listeners, the patients, heard "Queen Elizabeth the First" and pricked up their ears.

"What does Queen Elizabeth have to do with this?"

Mrs. Amsterdam touched the third button of her blouse and said, "In the antique business, it's very important. A customer came in who loved old things, antiques, and bought a vase in my son's store—a beautiful vase, with flowers painted on it, water lilies, it was really something to look at. I saw the vase. You'd get a pretty penny for such a vase. You could live for a year on what it cost. The partner sold the vase, not my son, and the partner told the customer that the vase came from the time of Queen Elizabeth the First. The customer was on fire about that vase, and it was already a done deal. But as bad luck would have it, my son took a look at the vase, drew his finger over the bottom, and said, stressing his words to correct the partner's mistake: 'It's from Queen Victoria's time. Water lilies belong to the time of Queen Victoria.'

"He said his piece and left. The partner stood there, confused. The customer was also a little ashamed. That is to say, he really didn't know that much about antiques, and you could tell him something was from Queen Elizabeth's time when it really was from Queen Victoria's. He postponed the sale, and then left.

"And so a dispute started between my son and his partner.

"The partner claimed that it was all the same to him—Queen Elizabeth or Victoria. Both were good, as long as you could make a couple of dollars from them, but my son, the Amsterdam, said that in his antique business, things have to be exactly right, just like in a university. He wanted professors to come to the Amsterdam antique business and learn exactly what belonged to Queen Elizabeth and what belonged to the time of Queen Victoria, because for him mistakes are not allowed to happen. Naturally, I maintained, that the partner was right, but my husband and son, the Amsterdams, both claimed, 'No, a mistake has to be corrected, even if your own partner makes it.'

"In short, that was the end of the partner and the end of the antique business.

"You understand," she said in her half voice, "the world keeps on turning, with no limit of mistakes or inaccuracies. There are even a few lies, too.

The world keeps on moving and both sides work it out with each other. You don't have to follow every sentence with a finger. A word isn't gold. It rusts a little, it doesn't matter; but the Amsterdams don't want to understand that. Now we have another heartache with my son's engagement. It's a wonderful match. The bride is dying for him, but my son is arguing with his in-laws about King Solomon."

"What happened with King Solomon?" one of the patients asked.

Mrs. Amsterdam didn't have time to answer. A white-clad assistant came into the waiting room.

"Mrs. Amsterdam, the doctor is waiting for you."

Mrs. Amsterdam smiled, as if she tasted a drop of honey on her lips, only the honey was bitter, and she went into the doctor's examining room.

December 1946

Unhappy Celebrations

. . . .

"When a person is a little less than a person—it doesn't hurt as much. He just blends in with the crowd. He lives his life. But it's worse when a person is more than a person, because it's that little 'more' that really hurts. That little 'more' hurts more than the little 'less.' Then people compare him to the stalk of a cabbage, in fact to even bigger things than that, but they also avoid him."

Such was the preface one of the patients made when he was nearly the last person in the doctor's waiting room and was chatting with his neighbor on the next chair.

It was hard for him to clarify this thought. He repeated himself several times, took off his glasses, wiped them, and then finally got around to the crux of his medical problem. The toes on one of his feet had grown numb, almost stiff, and sometimes this feeling lasted for a couple of hours. It scared him. What did it mean for a part of a living man to grow numb? The doctor said it was caused by aggravation, and, in fact, it had started when his third daughter had gotten married.

His listener asked, "The match wasn't successful, you mean?"

"No, it's a very good marriage." Three of his daughters had married well; nevertheless it was their weddings that gave him the greatest grief.

Then he smiled, as if to say, "Each trouble has its own color," and smiled even more broadly. "The problem is that the matchmaker just isn't good."

"What do you care about the matchmaker?" the second patient asked.

He didn't answer this question, said nothing for a while, and then began talking about his oldest daughter.

"How can she even be compared to her sisters, the married ones? It's like night and day! She's an entirely different person, intelligent and understanding. When she smiles with her long, gray eyes, she more than speaks. Everything has already been said, and no answer is necessary.

"When we were traveling on the ship with the four girls, still just little girls, the three younger ones ran around, getting into mischief; we had to keep an eye on them so that, God forbid, they wouldn't fall overboard. But she, the eldest, Miriam is her name, she was only interested in figuring out how many languages people spoke on the ship. She listened, counted them up, and wrote down their names in a little book.

"And that's not all. She wrote down which languages people spoke loudly and which ones they spoke softly. And the list sounded like a song: 'The priest speaks Czech and speaks softly. / The woman in the blue dress speaks French loudly.'

"And so her entire list went, noting each one's clothing, their language and their manner of speaking. Our sides ached from laughing, when we read the list.

"When we arrived in America, we never had a moment's trouble with our eldest daughter, with Miriam. She did very well in school and won scholarships. They even paid her to go to college. She studied such an odd thing, a thing I had never heard of before in my entire life—archeology. How people once lived and what kind of clothing they wore and what their houses looked like—she was interested in all of it. Her room looked like a museum. On her walls—pictures of all kinds of buildings, illustrations with lions, birds, churches, and, let it not be said together,[1] the Temple of Jerusalem.

"The younger daughters were something else again—girls, like all the others in America. One was a department store. She bought and bought— clothes, odds and ends, pins and needles—everything had to be paid for. The second was a beauty parlor. One day her hair was this way, in the morning her nails were some other color, and eyebrows—shorter, longer—

1. See note 1 for "The Daughter-in-Law," page 32.

she made up her face this way or that way, so I didn't even know who she was some days. The third one had her own craziness: hikes. Walking, riding, running—sports.

"Several men started to call on Miriam; they all had the same interests. A Mr. Rubin began coming to see her. He had taken up archeology, too. They made drawings together, talking about everything, he brought several books over to the house—all about archeology. Each book was like an entire holiday. They read all of them. The books were in different languages. Mr. Rubin became like one of the family, comfortable with everyone. Once we asked him to have dinner with us. He asked a lot of questions about Hanke. My wife asked me later, 'What's all the concern with Hanke, the "beauty parlor"?'

"Miriam didn't even raise an eyebrow when she heard this. And a few weeks later, she left on a trip with her professor to a museum in Ohio. We had no suspicion that she had done this on purpose. Mr. Rubin didn't stop coming over to the house. A couple of times, he took all the daughters to the theater, and once he took Hanke. When they left, the youngest daughter, Eileen, of the hikes, said, 'Hanke is going to get married to Mr. Rubin.'

"When Miriam got back home, her match was already off. Miriam bought presents for Hanke and Rubin. At the wedding, she looked like a princess. Not a sign of resentment could you see, not a shadow on her face. Even for us at home, we couldn't see if she was hurt or not.

"In the middle of the war, a young man, an Erets Isroelnik, came to us— Amkuni, also one of those people, the archeologists. Miriam had met him through her work at the Institute. Together they had to restore the appearance of some kind of old wall in Egypt. For hours at a time, they worked together at the institute, and even in our own home they spent a lot of time poring over photographs and drawings. According to them, the world really couldn't exist unless one knew precisely how that wall appeared, a wall that had been ruined maybe two thousand years ago.

"This Amkuni, in the middle of his work, had a habit of leaping suddenly to his feet and singing Hebrew songs. The girls learned all the songs from him. Miriam understood what she was singing; Eileen and Prodl didn't understand a word, but sang anyway. Once Amkuni said jokingly that he wanted to take an American wife back with him—he could save on the cost of his documents. Eileen, who was quick on the spot, answered him right away: she would go. she'd love to hike in Erets Isroel. When it came to talking about hikes, Eileen knew all the details: which mountains you could hike, which ones needed ropes or chains; and Amkuni decided then and there that she would get along well in Erets Isroel.

"Then, for the first time, we noticed that Miriam was upset. She wanted to say something, her mouth trembled, but she said nothing. She went into her room and sat down to work. It seemed that she liked Amkuni. Eileen left the house and came back later when Amkuni was working with Miriam, but he didn't sing any more songs that evening.

"He spent a couple of months in New York. Before he left, Eileen went shopping with him and bought, it seemed, what she needed for herself, also. And Eileen left with him.

"The project with the ruined Egyptian wall was finished. On the way to the ship, Miriam talked about it with Amkuni. Eileen was loaded round with gift packages and baggage. She replied to questions that no one had asked and said things that shouldn't have been said. She was utterly happy, not taking any care about what she said.

"When we got back from the ship, my wife cried. 'We don't have happy weddings from our children,' she said, crying.

"I went to Miriam's room, to see what she was doing. I didn't want her to be alone. She was standing, bent over the table, drawing. She knew why I had come in, looked at me, and smiled. 'Don't worry, Pa,' she said, and went back to her drawings.

"But I noticed that her mouth was trembling, and that broke my heart even more than if I had seen her crying."

The narrator took off his glasses, wiped them, and put them on again.

"So you can understand what an unhappy celebration means, I'll be brief. My third daughter also got married through Miriam's matchmaking. Exactly as before, God forbid, as though there were a curse on our house— that we should not be allowed any happiness even when it comes on a joyous occasion. Now I have three sons-in-law, educated people, fine people, Miriam's equals—but it gives me no pleasure. My toes have grown numb, and I know it's because of that, the grief from the marriages."

"And what's happening with your Miriam now?" the listener, the last remaining patient, asked.

The white-clad assistant came into the waiting room, and the storyteller had only enough time to say, " '*Yosif da'at yosif makhov.*[2] The more one knows, the more one suffers.' That's a very fine saying when you read it in Ecclesiastes, but when it comes to your own door—it's not so nice."

"The doctor is waiting for you," the assistant said, and the patient with the numb toes went into the examining room.

December 1946

2. "For in much wisdom is much vexation; / And he that increaseth knowledge increaseth sorrow" (Ecclesiastes 1:18).

"The Kretchma"

. . . .

The boss of New York is of course the mayor, but the boss of Brownsville[1] is Nyoma Khurgin. A considerable number of all the garment operators[2] in New York live in Brownsville; Nyoma Khurgin has lived there forty years now. Coming from Zaritshe, he settled in Brownsville and has never moved anywhere else.

"I remember Brownsville, when it was as big and beautiful as Zaritshe. There were several wooden houses and large flocks of goats. Apartments were very cheap, and the garment workers got a move on and made Brownsville their own town. And now, wherever there's a door, you can be sure a garment worker's living behind it," so Nyoma says.

In Nyoma Khurgin's kitchen, there's a large table, as big as a tailor would have in his house, and this table is needed because of Friday nights. Friday nights the operators play cards at Nyoma Khurgin's, but their real business is to talk over what's going on in the world.

1. For a description of Brownsville, once the populous center of Jewish garment workers, see Alter F. Landesman's *Brownsville: The Birth, Development and Passing of a Jewish Community in New York* (New York: Block, 1969), particularly chapter 4.

2. In this context, *operator* signifies a garment worker who sewed not by hand, but on a machine. For a description of the garment industry and the hierarchy of workers, see Irving Howe's *World of Our Fathers: The Journey of the East European Jews to America and the Life They Found and Made* (New York: Schocken Books, 1976, 1989), 156–59.

"That 'may his name be blotted out'[3] made another speech, and he's barking against the Jews."

An operator, Shorty Harry, says this. The truth is that Harry is as tall as anyone else, but he's called "Shorty" because he says he's always "short in the pocket."

Even if someone were to give Nyoma Khurgin a free ticket to the theater on a Friday evening, he'd still rather stay home. It's simple: Friday evenings he doesn't belong to himself, he belongs to his community. People sit on all sides of the big table with him, and if there isn't room for everyone, they just pull up a bench for a second row.

Nyoma Khurgin belongs to six organizations. He helped build the first folkshul in Brownsville and also helped build the synagogue, Anshey Zaritshe.[4]

The board of the folkshul got angry with him. "You're building a synagogue? Who are you—a rabbi or an operator?"

But Nyoma Khurgin always answers them calmly: "Am I building it for *you*? No, I'm building it for other Jews . . ."

People in the folkshul were angry with him for so long that several people signed up as members in the Zaritshe congregation.

But then the Anshey Zaritshe members also complained to him. "A folkshul, of all things? Brownsville will be overrun with heretics."

But Nyoma Khurgin gave them exactly the same answer: "Am I building it for *you*? No, I'm building it for other Jews . . ."

They quarreled with him for so long that several people from Anshey Zaritshe started to support the folkshul.

When the hullabaloo with Erets Isroel began, Nyoma Khurgin took to helping the trade union campaign.

"Am I asking so much from you? I'm asking only for one dime." And Nyoma Khurgin would pull in a couple of hundred such dimes as easily as

---

3. The curse "May his name be blotted out" refers to a person so horrible that one doesn't utter his name. Here, of course, it is referring to Adolf Hitler.

4. The name of their synagogue, Anshey Zaritshe, means "People of Zaritshe."

you can take a hair out of milk. One of the operators used to get angry with Khurgin. "What do you need Israel for? Are you going there?"

But Nyoma Khurgin has his own style—just wait it out. If someone gets mad at him, sooner or later, he'll just have to quit—"to stop," as they say in America. You just have to be patient. Speaking of this, Nyoma Khurgin carries a small box of tobacco, and he rolls his own cigarettes. By the time he finishes rolling his cigarette, and one for the sorehead, that guy has already cooled off, and then Nyoma Khurgin seals the cigarette with one lick of his tongue, and answers in his own good time, "Am I sending you to Erets Isroel? No. You have a job on 38th Street. I'm not sending you there. But when someone in Zaritshe doesn't have a job on 38th Street, you think he shouldn't be allowed to go to Israel? A dime is all he's worth to you? What d'you mean?"

Nyoma Khurgin says "What d'you mean?" for no real reason; he's not waiting for an answer, because he knows, in fact, that the guy can't answer him. Nyoma Khurgin knows exactly which shtetl each man comes from, and he always brings this up as part of his argument. He gets at Shorty Harry through Seltz, because Shorty Harry is a Seltzer.

"You think Seltz is paradise? If someone would give them a visa, they'd come straight to America. But when getting a visa is so hard—how can they come up with twenty thousand dollars?" Nyoma Khurgin rolls a cigarette, taking long enough for Shorty to get it through his head, and then finishes with one blow: "So, give me your quarter and be quiet!" thus upping the ante from a dime to a quarter.

Rukhl, Nyoma Khurgin's wife, even calls her house "the kretchma."

Fridays, she bakes cookies for "the kretchma"; Hannukah, she makes latkes for "the kretchma"; the First of May,[5] they have schnapps in "the kretchma."

Nyoma Khurgin loves to tell how he and Rukhl got married.

"Exactly like Isaac and Rebecca, not a hair's difference,"[6] he says.

---

5. May Day (on May 1st) is the international Communist/Socialist day of celebration.

6. In fact, the story has many differences. Rebeccah drew water for Abraham's servant, who was commissioned to find a bride for Isaac. See Genesis 24.

"When I came from Zaritshe to Brownsville, I rented a roomke[7] as big as a baked potato. Round walls and a round ceiling and black, just like a baked potato, just a little bit burned. Evenings, I would sit there and read the paper. One time, someone knocks on my door, and a girl walks in. Dark and tall and thin and she laughs, so you could see all her teeth.

" 'Maybe you have something for my goats?' she asks.

"That was what she said—for the goats. It turns out that her mother raised goats.

" 'How many goats d'you have?'

" 'Plenty goats . . . '

"I gave her all the old pieces of bread I had, and she left. In the morning, there she is again. 'Maybe you have something for my goats?' standing there laughing, showing all her teeth.

" 'I'm an operator, not a baker' . . . but I really liked her. The most important thing for me is that she laughs. And even today, there isn't much special about my Rukhl, but just like then, she doesn't puff herself up. She laughs."

And Rukhl, who is standing nearby, in fact, laughs.

When people talk about the goats, she comes alive: "A goat has to eat . . . I was just looking for something . . ."

Nyoma Khurgin supports her: "Saul went looking for donkeys and found a country;[8] you were looking for some food for your goats and found an operator."

The operators love "the kretchma" and wouldn't trade it for any society in the world, and they also love to hear the story about the goats, even though they already know it by heart.

And that's how it is in "the kretchma."

7. Nyoma Khurgin (Nyoma is a short form of Benjamin) uses many Yiddishized English words. Here the Russian/Yiddish diminutive -ke is added to the English word room to mean "a tiny room."

8. For the story of Saul and the donkeys, see 1 Samuel 9.

Do-All

. . . .

J ekuthiel Goldblatt would under no circumstances get rid of his
mustache.[1]

"The only thing that remains for Jekuthiel Goldblatt, he who once
ruled a kingdom in Bialystok[2] on Surazhsky Street, is his mustache. For me,
it's a memory, a reminder," he says of himself, touching it to make sure it's
still there.

Shorty Harry loves to tease him about his mustache: "I'd like to know what
else he had there on Surazhsky Street in Bialystok, beside his mustache?"

That's all it takes. As soon as Shorty Harry asks this question, Do-All
goes to pieces. Begins waving his arms around and talking, talking without
end.

"What a question! Who *didn't* know Jekuthiel Goldblatt in Bialystok?
Unless maybe you were dead. If someone wanted decent shoes, he went to
Goldblatt on Surazhsky Street. And when Goldblatt said they were good,
they were good. When Goldblatt said they were cheap, they were cheap.
When Goldblatt felt like fooling a rich man, a real pig, he fooled him. And
a favor once in a while for a loyal customer, he could do that, too. And
when Jekuthiel Goldblatt walked out on the street, it was one 'Good morn-

1. In the original Yiddish, this story is entitled *Mak-en*. No one seems to have heard of a
store with this name in Brownsville in the 1930s, but from the description, with its clublike
membership and large building with many checkers and watchers, it sounds like a prototype
discount chain store.

2. Bialystok is a city in Poland near Brest in Belarus.

ing' after another 'Good morning,' and one 'Gut shabbes' after another 'Gut shabbes.' But what's here on Pitkin Avenue?[3] Nothing. Jekuthiel Goldblatt is just another cog in a Do-All chain store. And what's a buyer there? Also, nothing, just a customer—legs with a number. He shells out his few dollars, takes his thank-you, closes the door behind him, and is gone. You don't know who he is, and he doesn't know who you are, he's just a stray in from the street."

If you didn't stop Goldblatt in the middle, he could talk away a whole night about his kingdom on Surazhsky Street. But Nyoma Khurgin usually stops him with just one question, and since Goldblatt never has an answer, he stops talking.

"So, you miss the Bialystok pogrom, too?" is the question.

Goldblatt usually comes to the kretchma on Thursdays because on Thursdays his wife, Dolmatsia, goes to a meeting, and he "hops right over to the kretchma to keep his soul alive."

Dolmatsia, who used to be called Dvozhke, draws up nourishment from America like a mushroom on a stump, and draws up and up and up as if there is no end.

Dolmatsia is in love with America because of two things: the moving pictures and the sales. Three times a week she goes to sales. And then, a load of stuff is brought home. Lamps, little tables, tablecloths, and especially, dresses. A green dress, a red one, a black one, checkered or with stripes, with circles, with buttons and zippers.

Dolmatsia says that if she lived in Bialystok on Surazhsky Street for a hundred years, she could never buy the kind of dresses she can buy here in a month.

"An evil spirit has hopped into my Dolmatsia's closet and teases and teases her that she doesn't have nearly enough clothes," so Goldblatt says. And as he's talking you can see how it's eating him up. If he's talking about Dolmatsia's clothes now, he'll be on to telling about her visiting cards next.

"She had cards printed up. 'Dolmatsia Goldblatt' in little letters, and 'Do-All Store' in enormous letters, that completely overshadow 'Goldblatt.'

3. Pitkin Avenue was the Fifth Avenue of Brownsville, full of the more successful shops, theaters, and other businesses.

'So how come you need with your own hands to bury the name Goldblatt? Who is "Do-All" to you? What's "Do-All" to you that you have to make it stick right out on the front of your visiting card?' "

So Jekuthiel Goldblatt complains to her, and people in the kretchma call him Do-All.

Dolmatsia has her reasons: When people see "Do-All Store," they come running up to her as if she were a queen. And what is Goldblatt? Nothing. "What difference does the name make anyway, as long as people come running?" Dolmatsia says to him, chewing on her chewing gum.

On the days that she doesn't go to sales, Dolmatsia sits by the telephone and makes her connections.

"A job has to be followed through with connections," so she says, and she's forever going to all the Do-Alls in New York, to their card parties, their birthdays, and all of their celebrations.

"You just don't know America," she says. "You can't survive one day here without connections."

When Goldblatt dropped by the kretchma today, he was pale and worried. The only semblance of pride about Jekuthiel Goldblatt was his mustache.

"My Dolmatsia has gone to Long Island. She left a note that she would be late. Some kind of a Do-All party."

Goldblatt played pinochle. But it wasn't his night for cards, and he looked at his watch continually to see how late it was. He was the last one to leave the kretchma. It was already twelve o'clock when he finally got up.

"My Dolmatsia has probably not gotten back from her connections. You know, America didn't just take Jekuthiel Goldblatt from me, it took my Dvozhke, too, but at least she gets pleasure from it."

He looked at his watch again and said, "I have to go. In about nine hours, the store on Pitkin Avenue has to be open."

Sholem Moishe

· · · · · · ·

Sholem Moishe owns three things, and he loves all three very much. He has a three story house on Saratoga Avenue,[1] in fact the same house where Nyoma Khurgin lives. He has a wife, Gina, and he has a silver cigar holder with a wolf's head on the end. He's had his cigar holder for twenty-five years, exactly as long as he's nursed a grudge against Semek Filitzer, or Phony Semek, as Sholem Moishe calls him, ever since the time they found themselves seated next to each other in a Yiddish Theater.

Although the story took place many years ago, Sholem Moishe remembers every detail, as though it had happened yesterday. He even remembers how Semek Filitzer had exchanged glances with his wife, when he found Sholem Moishe sitting in the same row and in an adjoining seat. Then Sem Filitzer had rubbed his hands and called over the fellow in the buttons, who was standing by the door, to change the seats. (Sholem Moishe says that at that moment he felt like his heart had been torn out.) There was no other place in the same row, but Semekl Filitzer wasn't lazy, and he went up to the ticket office to change the tickets, came back, and took his bald head and his wife to a place two rows up. He couldn't stand it, that Sholem Moishe, an operator in his shop, should sit next to him in the theater.

---

1. Saratoga Avenue was not quite as famous as Pitkin Avenue, but still one of the more important streets in Brownsville.

When Sholem Moishe tells the story he never forgets to add, "One thing he forgot, Phony Semekl. He forgot that this is America . . ."

It was then that Sholem Moishe decided he would open up his own shop. The very next morning he went out and bought himself the silver cigar holder with the wolf's head, exactly like the one Sem Filitzer had, and came into the shop, the cigar holder in his mouth. In about two weeks, he found himself a business partner with some money and thumbed his nose at Semek Filitzer.

"Nothing in the world was ever sweeter than to thumb my nose at Phony Semekl then."

Sholem Moishe's wife calls him Mr. Okin at home, but for himself, being the boss, Sholem Moishe is good enough, without the Mr. and without the Okin. And even though Mrs. Okin calls her husband, in public and in private, Mr. Okin, it doesn't help. People keep their own habits, and they call him Sholem Moishe.

Today's a good day for Sholem Moishe. Yesterday, people voted for him to be president of Anshey Ahavet Isroel.[2] Now he's sitting on the green bench outside his house, telling his neighbors about how he became the president of the Fourth Society.

"When I wanted to get the 'top hat,' Phony Semek, off his bench, all I did was . . . but do I need so much time to tell it? For their 'anniversary' I handed over a little 'check with two zeroes' . . . and he, Phony Semek, turned white. He knew his term was coming to an end. You think Phony Semek would hand them such a check? No. It would squeeze his soul. He's as stingy as a dog, but he gobbles up prestige like a turkey. So, they picked me for president—it cost me a hundred."

Sholem Moishe looks into the open mouth of the wolf's head on his cigar holder, exactly as if he could pull his stories out of it, and it contained stories to no end.

Mrs. Okin hates it when her husband tells his tales to the neighbors. And when no one is nearby, she scolds him: "Sholem, you haven't been an operator for fifty years, what do you have to tell them these tales for? You

2. The name of their synagogue, Anshey Ahavat Isroel, means "People Who Love Israel."

have a son, a doctor, it isn't fitting for him when you do that . . . Sholem Moishe!"

Now Mrs. Okin is calling her husband for the second time to come inside: she wants him to get off the bench.

"Mr. Okin, an important telephone call . . ."

"Answer it yourself," he calls back to her, and doesn't budge an inch. He launches into a new story, how the Phony Semek wanted to support the refugees and become a chairman of the Refugee Fund.

"Phony Semek has a tongue that belongs to God above, a pocket that belongs to the devil, and a soul that belongs to his wife, Virginia. When he wanted to be a chairman, he stood up to deliver a speech: 'Our hearts must open for our unfortunate brothers, let us open our pockets for them . . . '

"And how much do you think he gave, Phony Semek? Five bucks he gave . . . and wanted to be elected chairman. So I bought up the birthright,[3] and when the crowd began handing over their fifty cent pieces, I led the way with twenty-five bucks. Phony Semek began to stammer right away, and the crowd voted for me."

Mrs. Okin tells him again through the open window that his coffee is waiting for him on the table.

"Mr. Okin, your coffee will get cold . . ."

"All right," Sholem Moishe answers, still sitting there.

When Nyoma Khurgin and Rukhl walked over to the guys on the bench, Sholem Moishe left and brought back a chair from the cellar. Carrying the bench was easy for him. When Sholem Moishe lifts a bench, you'd think it was made out of paper. He turned it so that it was right next to the green bench. For the new listeners, Nyoma Khurgin and Rukhl, Sholem Moishe begins to tell a new story with fresh vigor. Sholem Moishe tells his stories without arrogance: just the opposite, with something like a little mockery and a little spite.

"It's a trick to be the president? The trick is in not letting 'someone' get what he wants."

And when Sholem Moishe says "someone" he means Sem Filitzer.

---

3. "Bought up the birthright" is a reference to Esau, who sold his birthright to his brother Jacob for a pot of lentils; see Genesis 27.

"Phony Semekl almost fainted when the new addition was built on to Rodfey Sholem.[4] Well, as usual, there has to be a celebration. And who's going to lead the celebration? The 'top hat' goes around, puffs himself up, calls everyone on the telephone, things are cooking . . . I nominated the butcher, our Anshel. He is a rich guy. He has four stands in East New York and in Brownsville, so I say to him, 'Mr. Segal, it's time for you to be a mensch,' and he flares up like a match in straw.

" 'What do I need? What? Am I any worse than the others?'

" 'Here's how people baste the roof of Rodfi Sholem. Why shouldn't you be chairman? Didn't you put enough into it, too?

"Mr. Segal turned red from pleasure then.

" 'Well, why not? Will people vote for me?'

" 'When you grease the wheels, they roll, and if you serve a meat banquet[5] . . . they'll vote . . . '

"Mr. Segal tapped his head and began speaking in English: 'What are you talking about? That's still a hundred dollars . . . '

" 'Fifty-fifty, Mr. Segal,' and I donated the other half. It's not every day you go to a covering[6] at Rodey Sholem . . .

"So who would refuse to be chairman? Anshel didn't refuse either. After this story, Phony Semekl lost maybe fifteen pounds . . ."

Mrs. Okin again tries to get her husband off his bench. She sticks her head out the window and scolds him in English: "Mr. Okin, what's the matter with you?" and when calling him this time doesn't help, Mrs. Okin has to come outside herself.

Mrs. Okin doesn't like to sit with the tenants. She gives them a pretty hello, grants them a refined smile, and she collects the rent from them. More than that, she won't do. Now she's come down from the first floor and has walked over to the two benches; she still won't sit down. She

4. Rodey Sholem, meaning "Pursuers of Peace," is the name of their synagogue.

5. Meat being more expensive than milk, a kosher dinner featuring meat is more impressive.

6. *Covering* (*badekn* in Yiddish) refers to the veiling of a bride before the wedding ceremony. The speaker is referring to the opening ceremonies for the new roof of the synagogue.

stands a while, lifts up the skirt of her dress as if she were wearing glass underwear, and then sits herself down on the steps of the stoop, a little distance away, that is, and says to her husband: "Mr. Okin, please, maybe it's enough already . . ."

But her Mr. Okin is a long way from obeying her. He has looked deep into the opening of the wolf's head of his cigar holder to see if there's another story in there, and as a matter of fact, he begins another one.

"When his son and mine were together in high school, mine had the better head."

But here Sholem Moishe is stopped short, as if someone has sliced his words with a knife. Mrs. Okin had got up and called out, "The doctor!"

Their son, Robert the doctor, is getting out of a huge car, long-nosed and shiny. Now Sholem Moishe finally stands up from the green bench. He apologizes with his eyes and hands to his listeners. He takes the briefcase from his son's hand, and all three go upstairs. But Sholem Moishe, briefcase in hand, comes back to say with a wink of his eye, "I'll tell you one thing, in a nutshell: as long as I live, Phony Semekl will never be president in Brownsville . . ."

The Brothers

· · · · · · ·

W hen a person gets rich suddenly, it's not so much apparent in any one thing so much as it is in his eyes and his lapels. His eyes stiffen up and so do his lapels. For Sem, the elder of The Brothers, it was apparent in one thing only: he wore a ring with a huge green stone, as big as a matzo, on the little finger of his right hand.

The Brothers had gotten rich in some three or four years. And from what? From horseradish. They were expected to come today for latkes in the kretchma. Rukhl said the latkes wouldn't be just plain, but would be with "something." And in fact, today, Shorty Harry brought the latest news about The Brothers, that they were no longer Eisner Brothers, but Eisner Brothers and Company. They have now, it seems, risen very high . . . and Nyoma Khurgin recalled how they borrowed the first twenty-five dollars to rent the little horseradish store.

"I gave them five dollars, Shorty Harry gave five, Seinfeld gave them five, and the two other fives I don't remember, but seems to me that guy, or . . ."

Before Nyoma Khurgin can remember who it was who had loaned them ten dollars, in come The Brothers themselves, Sender and Shaulke— Sem and Semek, as they're called here.

The brothers, when they were still operators, used to sit with Nyoma Khurgin in the kretchma all evening long, especially in slack season when there wasn't much work, and now when they walk in, they feel completely at home and sit right down.

Sem set his eyes on Rukhl and then turned them to Nyoma Khurgin and asked, "So, how are you?"

This job over, Sem began cleaning his pipe, then filled it with tobacco (he keeps his tobacco in a little silver box with two handles), started lighting it and with the pipe in his mouth, asked one and all and anyone, "So, where are the latkes?"

Nyoma Khurgin, it seemed, intended to answer both questions together, as was his habit. He slowly rolled a cigarette. But just then two bottles of Lord Calvert whiskey showed up on the table. Semek, the younger of The Brothers, had put them there, and he said, "Brother operators, let's drink a l'chaim!"

Shorty Harry looked at the bottles.

"You're drinking only Lord Calvert these days?"

"When you drink, drink with a Lord. You should only drink with operators" Semek replied, and with this he lifted his eyebrows artfully, so that his hat began to dance on his forehead. Semek pointed his eyebrows at one operator and then another, and his hat seemed almost alive; the hat worked while Semek opened the bottles of whiskey, and the crowd laughed: "Bravo, Shaulke, bravo, Semek!"

His older brother, Sem, it seems, hadn't known about the two bottles of Lord Calvert that his brother had brought with him. He also hadn't expected that Semek would be doing his old trick with the hat for the kretchma, the one he used to do in the old days. Semek blew several thick smoke rings out of his pipe, one after the other; his face seemed to be covered by a curtain.

After the first l'chaim, Sem left, before the latkes were served. He had to go to the Astor Hotel[1] right now was his excuse. He had to meet someone there.

Nyoma Khurgin waved his hand, the same hand that's holding his cigarette, sending the smoke over to Sem: "An ordinary person can still be a president of the United States. What's your hurry to leave the kretchma?"

"A lady's waiting," Sem ventured to joke, and left.

---

1. Sylvia Schildt suggests that this was probably the Astor Hotel in Manhattan, where latkes definitely would not have been served.

After Sem left, the kretchma breathed more easily. The crowd began remembering the different stories about the horseradish. Shorty Harry reminded Semek how he had gone with him to rent the little horseradish store.

"You remember, Semek, the whole store on Amboy Street didn't look any bigger than a 'paper box,' so narrow and small . . ."

Semek jumped right in: "Do I remember? I still remember how at dawn I bought the first sack of horseradish in the market. Carried the first sack of horseradish myself on my shoulders, grated it myself and cried—as I am an operator!"

"You were never a real operator; it was a miracle you got into horseradish," Nyoma Khurgin said.

Now, for the first time, Semek gets a little heated. "What horseradish? We'd still be paupers with the horseradish, too. We'd have to go and ask Levinchik to take us back into his shop. The miracle was something else. And I'll tell you about it. When I saw how we grated the horseradish and the jars just stood in the window, I knew things were bad. But I fell on an idea—I went over to a printer and had him print up some blue labels, 'Imported,' and pasted the labels on the jars. And it was just as if magic had come into the store. The bottles began moving and were out the door . . ."

Semek told how they packed the bottles in little green paper sacks and fastened them with rubber bands. Amboy Street, and Hertzl Street, and Strauss and Hopkins Avenues began to eat "imported" horseradish, and The Brothers then moved up from Amboy Street to Saratoga Avenue, until they arrived on Pitkin, with the huge show windows, with flowers and display stands of all varieties of horseradish—"Domestic" and "Imported." That, in fact, was when Sem bought his ring with a stone the size of a green matzo.

The crowd at the kretchma was flushed with excitement and paid close attention to how The Brothers became Eisner Brothers and Company, and Rukhl asked comfortably, "Who samples your horseradish now? Remember, you used to come over with a little jar for me to taste?"

"Now we have a 'system,' and with a 'system' there's no need to taste."

"It tastes itself already," Shorty Harry jokingly assists.

Semek loves to tell stories about his "factory" to his brother operators. He flicks a finger, pushes his hat up on his forehead, and says: "Listen, here's another story. When we had already moved to Pitkin Avenue, one time someone came to us to collect taxes for the 'imported' horseradish. 'Where do you import it from? How much horseradish?'

"Sender didn't know what he should do, but I knew a way: the best recipe for good health is to be honest. So I say to the agent, 'You know, sir, what we have imported? Grandma's horseradish grater from Derhitshn.'[2] Now the agent was a fellow Jew, and he had to sit down to laugh; he's probably still laughing. After he'd had a good laugh, he said to us sternly: 'But aren't you deceiving honest people when you write "Imported"?'

" 'Sir,' I said to him, 'do we state on the label "Imported horseradish"? No. It simply says: "Imported." ' If the ladies had the sense to ask: "What's imported?" would I then tell them a lie? Could I save them by telling them about the grater? But since they don't ask, it's probably better for them that way. The womenfolk—excuse me, the ladies—with the green feathers buy from us now . . . you hear, brother? (Semek is really heated up.) The ladies with green feathers are a different type of lady. They speak politely and at the same time, complain. 'Will you please give me,' they begin, and point with a gloved finger to a jar of horseradish. The taller the feather on the hat, the smaller the finger she sticks out. And how do all these ladies happen to be on Pitkin Avenue? I'm telling you, one time I'm standing there, thinking: You ought to be ashamed. Your old man is sweating somewhere in a shop, or is doing a sale, and you're out here in the green feathers, clucking 'please' . . . oh, well, let's drink another l'chaim."

Just then the latkes with "something" arrive. Rukhl means to sell them, a nickel a latke.

"What is this 'something'? Rukhl wants to become rich, too?" Semek haggles.

Nyoma Khurgin reproaches him: "Just because you're on Pitkin Avenue, you've completely forgotten what's going on in the world? No war? No refugees?"

Semek is really enjoying himself: "A nickel apiece! A bargain! You can't get such latkes in that Astor restaurant . . ."

But when it came time to pay, Rukhl ordered Semek to put out a dollar a latke. Semek bargained, not with words, but with his hat. The hat danced

2. Deretchin was a shtetl about twenty-six kilometers northwest of Slonim in Belarus.

and answered Rukhl's claim that for Eisner Brothers and Company it costs more.

"So, one of The Brothers is still with us: the other, your Sem, has already gone over to the green feathers . . ."

So Nyoma Khurgin teases Semek.

Semek is delighted with the compliment. He comes back, sits down again, and later, standing by the door, he says, "I'd give up five dinners, anytime, at that little Astor restaurant for one schnapps at the kretchma. You hear, anytime . . ."

When Semek is gone, Shorty Harry says, "We'll see how long he keeps his word . . ."

Nyoma Khurgin is silent. And slowly, as is his custom, he rolls another cigarette.

The Crow

. . . .

S horty Harry suddenly began wearing beautiful neckties that cost a dollar or more, and Bella Montshinke, the young woman who worked in
the drugstore on the street corner, began coming to the kretchma.

Bella had once met Rukhl near the house and helped her carry in some
packages.

"Here, let me help you," Bella had offered.

A few days later, she brought Rukhl a tablecloth she had bought at a
sale, "practically for free."

Rukhl spread the cloth on the table where it looked like it had belonged forever, and the whole room lit up. Rukhl couldn't pry her eyes off
the tablecloth, and she kept it.

From then on, Bella began to drop by the kretchma. She used to come
over, wearing three strings of pearls around her neck, and sit at the table
across from Shorty Harry. Bella wasn't a beauty—she had wide, heavily
painted lips, and her hair was parted so perfectly straight in the middle of
her head that you would have thought she had spent the entire night combing it; in the morning it would be perfect. And she used to wear shoes that
cost no less than ten dollars.

Bella had an odd name on Saratoga Avenue. First of all, people said that
she didn't want to get married. Because her first fiancé had brought her, a
sixteen-year-old girl, to America and left her about four years later, she had
given her word she would never marry. And secondly, people said that in

every house where she rented a furnished room the landlord had fallen in love with her. The wives didn't want them to rent any room to her, and she had to live somewhere far away, as far as Eastside Parkway. They called Bella "the Crow." It was best not to let the Crow into their houses. Bella either didn't know what people said about her on Saratoga Avenue, or she pretended not to. The three strings of pearls on her neck, the straight part in the middle of her hair, her wide, brightly painted lips were always exactly the same, as if they had been painted once and for all for a picture.

One evening, as Shorty Harry was walking to the kretchma, he heard a long, drawn-out call: "Yoo o hoo . . ."

The voice was cheerful and summery, and Shorty Harry at that very moment remembered it was in fact summer; it was evening, it was warm, and the breeze was ruffling his hair. Harry remembered of all of this and saw that it was Bella calling him.

"I'm going up to the kretchma, too," she said. "Come, we'll walk up together."

The kretchma was on the first floor. Nevertheless, Harry thought that it was worth it for them to go up together.

After that, when Harry would go to the kretchma, he'd wait for the cheerful voice calling him: "Yoo o hoo . . ."

In fact, it was after that that Shorty Harry began to wear his beautiful dollar-plus neckties.

And, in fact, it was the same evening, when Bella had called to Harry—Yoo o hoo—that she also told him he was pouring too much sugar into his tea. Just one spoonful was enough, she said, too much sugar was not good for the kidneys. Bella spoke quietly. Her bright red lips were burning, but her white hands with the long fingers of a drugstore girl flowed with coolness, with summery coolness.

What does she want from me? Shorty Harry wondered, as he walked home from the kretchma. He remembered that the women called her the Crow, and it bothered him; she had such a cheerful voice and such white hands. Funny what people can say.

When the crowd at the kretchma would sit and play cards, Bella would lean her head on her elbows and remain silent. It was easy for her to be silent, and for hours. To be silent and chew gum. To be silent and smoke a cigarette. To be silent and consider her tinder red fingernails. It seemed as if she were greatly occupied with her silence.

One Friday night, when they all had been playing cards until late, Harry went down the stairs with Bella. He walked with her to Eastern Parkway. They walked and were silent. It seemed to Harry that the gentle, warm evening had nested itself in the wide sleeves of Bella's white coat.

When Bella opened the door to the entrance of her building, she said, "Come in. We'll drink some coffee."

Harry followed her in.

There, in Bella's room, Harry understood why her part was always so perfectly combed. Her room gleamed with cleanliness and order. An ashtray was placed on a blue plate, the lamp on a white, ironed doily. The wide sofa was spread with cushions: four small ones and a bigger round one in the middle. Several books were standing on a shelf, and next to them was lying a bone-handled paper knife to cut the pages. A red geranium was blooming at the window.

Harry remembered that on Saratoga Avenue, people called Bella the Crow, but wondered to himself: this didn't look like a crow's nest.

When Bella put two cups of coffee on the table, Harry asked her, "Tell me, Bella, is it true what people say about you . . ."

Bella didn't wait for him to finish the question, and answered him, "Yes, it's true, Harry, it's true. What the women say . . . and would you like to marry me?"

Harry saw her wide, brightly painted lips and the red blooming geranium at the window. And again, he felt like he had that other night, that it was summer, and that New York seemed to him like a city in bloom.

"I would . . . yes," he answered without a qualm.

In the morning, Sabbath, Shorty Harry told the kretchma that he was getting married to Bella.

Everyone, even Nyoma Khurgin, who had his own philosophy and was seldom surprised about anything, took notice this time, and said, "With Bella?"

"Yes, this coming Sunday."

When Shorty Harry left, Rukhl shook her head. "When Jewish enemies no longer exist, that's how long she'll live with him, the Crow."

Nyoma Khurgin slowly rolled a cigarette and set forth a bit of his philosophy of life: "Nothing's impossible in the world. Even heaven and earth can meet . . ."

Two years have already passed since that Sabbath. The Crow often comes to the kretchma. And when everyone is playing cards, she sits, her head supported on her elbows, and is silent. And Shorty Harry still wears his beautiful, dollar-plus neckties, and waits for the Sunday when they will be married.

New York, 1946

Avrom Leyb the Shoemaker

. . . .

Avrom Leyb the Shoemaker was heartsick when, on the eve of Sukkos, he had received two rubles from Borukh the Wholesaler: even in the middle of praying, grief struck him to the heart. To have handed over so many mitzvahs to him for two rubles. He reminded himself how Borukh the Wholesaler had said to him, as was his style, sniffling through his nose a little: "Reb Avrom Leyb, you'll go to the Talmud Torah and you'll take the children's shoes and you'll repair them, and however much is owing you, we'll figure it out, sniff, sniff, sniff"—so he had sniffled away, and thereby hadn't made such a bad deal for himself.

Avrom Leyb the Shoemaker had worked his heart out so that the shoes of the Talmud Torah boys would be repaired the way they should be. He had redone the soles with the best leather, sewed on new toes, blackened the tongues, repolished the fronts. He had reinforced the heels with a piece of cowhide. Would *he* cheat the Talmud Torah children? A few more little nails pounded in and more cobbler's thread sewn in—would *he* cut corners on the children from the Talmud Torah? And when it came time to pay him, Borukh the Wholesaler handed over two rubles for all of the work and packed up all the mitzvahs into his own pockets! On the very eve of Rosh Hashanah, Yom Kippur, and Sukkos, when people should pray for a good year, Borukh the Wholesaler, seized all the credit for the Talmud Torah for himself . . . that's what it means when you're a wholesaler!

When Avrom Leyb the Shoemaker remembered this, he regretted it to his very bones. Never mind that a person had to toil to make a living, but to work for Borukh the Wholesaler's mitzvahs? There is no justice in that.

Avrom Leyb the Shoemaker didn't realize that summer was already rolling away. Summer flies by quickly. The garden grows—here are carrots, here are green onions, and here cucumbers are springing up. The house is full, *keyn eyn hore*, and when life is easy, the days roll by as if on wheels.

One evening, after Tishebov, Avrom Leyb the Shoemaker went out to the street, carrying a pair of gaiters over to Sarah the Beer Dealer. Having collected his money, he walked slowly home. It was warm and mild, just like in paradise. In the sky, there was no sign of a cloud, as if there were no worries in the world at all. Then suddenly, Avrom Leyb thought he heard someone saying a "hello" to him and, right after that, "sniff, sniff, sniff," and he recognized the voice of Borukh the Wholesaler.

"Reb Avrom Leyb, maybe you have a little time? I'd like something . . . yes, something . . . come in . . ."

"Yes, I'll come in," Avrom Leyb the Shoemaker answered briefly, and kept on going.

Just then, an autumn wind hit him right in the nose, even though it was warm outside, and he thought: It's getting close to Rosh Hashanah and Reb Borukh the Wholesaler is already eager, it seems, for his wholesale mitzvahs again! No, he's too clever. He manages to collect a basket of mitzvahs for himself every year.

Thinking this, Avrom Leyb warmed up and began taking quicker steps. His feet carried him straight to the Talmud Torah. As he walked through the narrow little street and strode through the empty square, he noticed the children in the courtyard. With a practiced eye, Avrom Leyb the Shoemaker measured the feet of the children and saw how many shoes had already been worn out. Here stitching ripped out, there a toe sticking out.

Walking along, he thought: Two rubles! Two rubles was money. An entire Sukkos could be provided paid for with that. But he didn't stop and didn't turn to go home.

He argued with himself: Well, couldn't a person provide for Sukkos without the two rubles? How was it the two years before that, before Borukh the Wholesaler ordered the repairs? And the three years before that? And every year before that? And, the garden, thank God, was doing well this summer.

He went over to the supervisor¹ of the Talmud Torah.

The supervisor, Reb Myer, quickly realized why Avrom Leyb had come and asked him to sit down.

The supervisor, Reb Myer, had a habit, when he needed to speak to someone, of saying first, for no apparent reason: "Well, let's see now . . ." and only after this did he arrive at the matter at hand. Even when Eli the Watercarrier, came to collect his six groschen for pouring water at the hand pump, Reb Myer would ask him: "Well, Reb Eli, let's see now . . ." and only after this ask how many buckets of water Eli had brought, although the cost was the same from week to week.

Now, Reb Myer said to Avrom Leyb the Shoemaker, "Well, let's see . . . that is to say, you've come here for something . . . that is to say . . . you already have a person who takes care of the children's shoes, indeed, the same Reb Borukh the Wholesaler?"

Avrom Leyb didn't answer yes or no. He began indirectly: "You understand, Reb Myer, it's better to take them to be repaired a little earlier . . . just before a holiday, it's busy. Now, it's a little slow . . . in about two days, I'll come to you and I'll take the shoes. A sack can be made ready."

With great diligence and with a warm heart, Avrom Leyb the Shoemaker pounded the little nails into the children's shoes. He patched the soles from the best leather and licked the cobbler's thread with such gusto it might have been made of sugar. And all the while he murmured to himself: This way, I'm at least working for myself, and not for Borukh the Wholesaler!

When Avrom Leyb carried the repaired shoes for the children back to the Talmud Torah, he felt very very dignified: Thank God, I'm a somebody in town, I took care of the Talmud Torah children; and also provided for the holiday without the two rubles. And he walked across the empty square and across the narrow little street, the way a man walks through a fragrant vine-

---

1. Molodowsky's original Hebrew word, *mazhgiekh*, means "a supervisor, or custodian; an overseer, especially of the dietary laws in a community kitchen."

yard. It was the eve of the holiday. The work had been done for himself, and for the Talmud Torah. . . .

His wife, Mayte, had even said to him, "Now, see here, what is this? The Talmud Torah shoes . . ."

But Avrom Leyb interrupted her and wouldn't let her in on his accounting.

"The Talmud Torah shoes? They're just shoes—so long as they're repaired. Don't you worry about the shoes. They're my concern."

Mayte shrugged her shoulders and left him alone to do his own accounts.

The supervisor, Reb Myer, looked at the repaired shoes that shot out of the sack, saw the new heels, the shining newly reblackened toes, and said, as was his habit, "Well, let's see now. . . . Well, let's see." He was surprised that Avrom Leyb had not said a single word about Reb Borukh the Wholesaler. He'd come, brought the sack, and left.

Reb Myer distributed the shoes to the children. All the while, he said, "Well, let's see now!" and cried after the children: "Don't you go dancing around in the puddles . . . you won't drown, God forbid, if you walk in a dry place."

He spoke to the children, thinking about Avrom Leyb the Shoemaker, who had put down the sack, left, and never said a word about who had ordered the repair work.

The supervisor happened to meet Reb Borukh the Wholesaler, and said to him, "Avrom Leyb has already brought the shoes, Avrom Leyb has."

Borukh the Wholesaler's hands fell apart, and he said, "I didn't tell him to take the shoes . . . but if . . . well, it's all to the good." And once again, his hands fell apart, as if he couldn't understand what had happened. Reb Myer, out of courtesy, wished him a happy holiday and a good year, and left. "Well, let's see now," he said out of habit, and walked over to Avrom Leyb the Shoemaker's, to find out what was going on. Perhaps it was a secret donation.

"I have already distributed the shoes. Let me tell you, there was dancing, and if those soles didn't fall apart right away, they must have been made of iron."

Avrom Leyb's face lit up. He shook his head with great satisfaction, and his eyes were shining. The supervisor had come over to him, indeed, the supervisor, himself.

The supervisor was not in a hurry to leave.

"Well, let's see . . . how late is it now? Ay, you've done a fine piece of work for the 'brats.' It's utterly, as they say . . . a caprice!"

Avrom Leyb felt the true pleasure of a holiday eve, the kind of pleasure that not even the best tsimmes imaginable could come close to. He laughed, the way one says: The work grabbed my by the hand and I couldn't resist. And he said: "You think *I* would cut corners with the Talmud Torah children? If it's to be done, let it be done well! When does any of us have the chance to earn such a mitzvah?

It wasn't so much the words Avrom Leyb the Shoemaker said, but his entire appearance, his happiness, the holiday joy that poured out on his face, that touched the old supervisor to his heart, and a special flavor of the words came back to him: How goodly are thy tents, O Jacob, thy dwellings, O Israel.

He wished Avrom Leyb the Shoemaker a good year and left.

At Rosh Hashanah for the Torah reading, Reb Myer put a word into the ear of the Reader:[2]

"Give an aliyah to Avrom Leyb."

The Reader looked at him, astonished. Had he heard the name right?

"Avrom Leyb? Avrom Leyb, you said?!"

"Avrom Leyb the Shoemaker, yes!"

In the women's section, all the benches were shaking when Avrom Leyb's name was called to the Rosh Hashanah aliyah. Mayte, Avrom Leyb's wife, turned bright red and tears came into her eyes. She blinked her eyes rapidly to recover, not to let anyone see her confusion.

At Avrom Leyb's house, there was a true holiday. The kiddush and the blessings had an utterly different melody.

Avrom Leyb had not let the Talmud Torah children fall away from his hands. Every year before Sukkos, he would argue with himself: God be

---

2. Here *Reader* (*Bal ko'yre* in Hebrew) means "the man who is trained to read the Torah." Avrom Leyb will accompany his silently and recite a blessing.

thanked, one could provide for the sukkah without the two rubles. Ay, I repaired the soles of their shoes for them—merriment! Ay, I resewed the toes of their shoes—playthings! Let them just learn, the brats, just learn!

And Avrom Leyb felt, that he was indeed a person of worth in town. Carrying his sack of repaired shoes, he walked over the narrow little street and the empty square the way a person walks in a fragrant vineyard.

New York, 1955

Alter Iteleh's and His Daughters

· · · · · · ·

That's exactly what people in town called him: Alter Iteleh's[1] and his daughters. And, he had five of them: Eydl and Brayndl, the two older ones; Shayndl, the middle; and Etel and Hendl, the younger ones.

In childhood, they were like all other children: they played, they ran around, and once in a while caught a slap from their mother or a sharp look from their father when they behaved too childishly. Such children should belong to a respectable house. But as soon as they reached ten or twelve, they developed their father's eyes, quiet and thoughtful, as if they, like their father, knew the *Gemore* by heart.

Alter Iteleh's house was a home like all respectable homes, but nevertheless it was something of an institution in the town. People wouldn't say, "go in" to Alter Iteleh's house but "slip in"—and "slip in" to Alter Iteleh's meant: there you will understand; there you will have counsel.

When two partners couldn't reach an agreement, and didn't want the town to know about it, and were ashamed to cause an uproar by going to the rabbi, they would quietly slip in to Alter Iteleh's house on an evening for a chat. Alter Iteleh's told them a few instructional tales, so indirectly that they seemed to have nothing to do with the partners; and as naturally as a story is told in conversation. Alter Iteleh's didn't pretend to be an arbitrator,

---

1. Alter Itele's is the name he is known by. Here, Itele, a woman's name, probably refers to his mother, and she was impressive, because his name has him belonging to her and not to his wife, Libe Tsirl.

but by the time the two men left, there was peace between them. Between one story and another, they had reached an agreement.

When Alter Iteleh's was telling his stories in such a situation, his daughters slipped into the room. They didn't crowd in, God forbid, but came in one at a time, slipped into the room, with their quiet, thoughtful *Gemore* eyes, listened attentively for a while, and then left.

They knew since childhood, not to carry tales out of their house; their father had taught them this when they were tiny children. From the ear to the mouth is a short distance for a fool, so he said to them. For a wise man, it's a longer distance. A person doesn't need to repeat everything he hears.

If it happened that a businessman was a little slipshod with his accounts—a hundred was concealed somewhere in his business and could not be found: it seemed the accounts tallied—that was good—but a hundred was still missing from the total. In such a case, Alter Iteleh's called his oldest daughter Eydl. She was the expert in accounting. When Eydl did an account, a pencil in her thin bony fingers—a number was a number. When she wrote it—it was iron. The calculation was correct. Her thoughtful *Gemore* eyes saw nothing else then, but the numbers. The town had no need of a better bookkeeper than Eydl, and this was sufficient for the control of all the shtetl's businesses.

When it came to languages, the most accomplished was Brayndl. If someone needed a request written to the powers that be, or to have a paper read to him and explained, Brayndl knew the subject in detail. First, her handwriting was small and beautiful: it was perfection. Each letter had a separate grace. And her thinking was just as clear. Apart from this, her father, Alter Iteleh's, did give her some advice about what is necessary to write, and what is better not to mention. The documents combined Alter Iteleh's wisdom with her ideas and penmanship, and they were a success.

The middle daughter, Shayndl, as soon as she grew out of her childhood braids, turned into a real rebbetzin. She knew geography and history and maps, everything that is learned in a classroom. She had close ties to all the town's children. Every Monday and Thursday she prepared for a test.[2] She and a multitude of children always filled the house. They studied ge-

---

2. See note 1 for "Family Life."

ography lessons so intently that pages shot out of books and wherever they landed, became here, a Gibraltar, and there, the high Mount Everest; the American river, the Mississippi, the twentieth page, flowed under the table, and all of this was happening in a shtetl near Bialystok.

Shayndl didn't like keeping her knowledge to herself; she wanted to share it with her entire gang of friends, and the noise in the house rose to the rafters. Her father, Alter Iteleh's, would smile and say, "Shayndl, open a school and be done with it."

Thus did everyone, young and old, each for different reasons, slip in to Alter Iteleh's house. Nowhere was this more evident than on the floor. On a rainy day, the floor was well-trodden with footprints, and its gloss worn dull in times of the summer drought. The maidservant scrubbed the floors every couple of days, as clean as egg yolks, but just as quickly new marks made paths and tracks that gave the house its special familiarity, the obvious sign that this was Alter Iteleh's home.

Thus, Alter Iteleh's daughters grew up, and his leather business grew up also.

His wife, Libe Tsirl, began to travel abroad at every headache. Aching bones? A foreign spa. A little too stout? A foreign spa. Melancholia? The good foreign air. In short, to be abroad became an ordinary thing, and his wife began bringing back new ideas from her trips.

After her first trip, Tsirl learned that a balcony would be very good for the health, and they built a second story with a balcony. After the second trip, Iteleh's Alter's wife brought back from abroad the considered opinion of all her doctors that big rooms were better for the health than small ones, because in big rooms, people could breath; and small ones made breathing a torment. They started rebuilding the house. The small rooms were turned into large breathing-salons. Alter Iteleh's indulged all his wife's foreign ideas, as if these things were no concern of his. A bigger room, a smaller room—just as long as a person was still a person.

A small dispute, nevertheless, arose between husband and wife when it came to putting in the floors. The wife pronounced the words "parquet" floor, that is, a floor made out of little pieces of wood, all lacquered and shining like a mirror.

In the shtetl, people began to whisper: A rich person is rich after all.

Parquet floors! Who can slip in to Alter Iteleh's house now? Everyone will be afraid to step on the little mirrors of the floor!

But it never came to that. When Libe Tsirl wanted to order the parquet floor, she listed for her husband all the reasons they should have them. First, a parquet floor was beautiful. Alter Iteleh's sat and listened and was silent. Second, a parquet floor looked rich. Now, Alter Iteleh's squinted his eye, as if a fly were biting him, but he continued to listen and was silent.

Third, with a parquet floor the maid wouldn't have so much to wash; she'd give it a whisk with a brush and be done. At his wife's mitzvah theme, Alter Iteleh's rubbed his nose a little, as if he were getting a cold, and was silent.

As usual, during a conversation, the *Gemore*-eyed daughters slipped quietly into the room. Didn't crowd in, God forbid, but came one at a time, listened, stood for a while, and left.

After Libe Tsirl's long talk and Alter Iteleh's silence, his wife, now a little angry that he had no desire for foreign things said, "Oh, and by the way, people have a little more respect for a parquet floor; they won't be tramping on it so much with their boots. A home isn't a train station, after all."

After she said this, the house was very quiet for a while. Because of the silence, the daughters had come into the room, and seeing both their father and mother silent, they sat down at the table and were silent, too.

Then Alter Iteleh's told one of his instructional tales and finished by saying that if people had too much respect for the floor they would have less respect for him and for her, for Libe Tsirl. And that, he didn't want. In a town, Alter Iteleh's let his wife understand: "There are people with galoshes and those without galoshes. When the floor is made of boards, anybody can come in, because boards can be washed. But if a Jew wears a pair of ordinary boots, should the door be closed to him?" Alter Iteleh's asked and answered himself: "No." And it was this "no" that settled the question once and for all.

The daughters with the *Gemore* eyes, although they had said nothing (they didn't mix into their parent's discussions), could be seen to agree with their father's "no." Shayndl, of the geography books and the classes, said simply, "Mama, it's too easy to slip and fall down on a parquet floor."

Her mother frowned at her, but Shayndl, for whom the Mississippi flowed under the table, smiled with her *Gemore* eyes, and left the room.

In the shtetl, people found out that there would be no parquet floors at Alter Iteleh's. "How could it be otherwise?" people in the town chatted, "Alter Iteleh's is still Alter Iteleh's with His Daughters."

The town carpenters carried wide, heavy boards into the newly rebuilt house. Libe Tsirl hung expensive curtains in the windows and had a new table carried in, but the floor remained as it always had been. Every couple of days, the maidservant washed the floors, just as clean as egg yolks, and very quickly, people marked and scuffed new paths, paths that gave the home its special familiarity, the obvious sign that this was Alter Iteleh's house, where the entire shtetl could slip in.

December 1, 1948

Slander

· · · · · · ·

M unia the Miller became a rich man, because he was a "taker." Be
there even a scrap of business, he took it all for himself. Were there
a wedding in town, he sent over a sack of flour—and didn't come after any
payment: he wasn't going to go bankrupt.

When they built the rail line from Vilna to Kovalnik, Munia the Miller
was ready for it. He already had a contract to deliver flour to all the bakeries
along the line. In Kovalnik, this caused an earthquake: Should *one* man take
all the business for himself? What could possibly be enough for one town
miller? But Munia had the contract, and a contract is cast in iron.

Delivering flour along the railway line in fact made Munia rich. His
house was already a different house. A soft sofa, adorned with plush and
tassels, was brought from Brisk. On the stoop next to the door, they put an
alderwood mat down so that people could wipe their shoes before entering
the house, because the floors were polished.

The town envied Munia. They couldn't stand to hear the name of
Munia the Miller, and people called him nothing less than the "taker."

Munia's son, Avreml, traveled around to the bakeries in a britzka and
paid close attention to the business. The coachmen in town, that he hired
to deliver the flour, called him Pani Avreml.

Avreml became a real dandy. Summers, he wore a light colored suit, like
a landowner. Munie's wife, Pearl, traveled to country villas—half the summer in a forest and half the summer to a vineyard in Leshnitseh, as far away
as perhaps the fifth province.

In Kovalnik, people slowly got used to the fact that Munia the Miller was a rich man, that Pearl was a rich woman, and that Avreml was Pani Avreml, a real lord. No one even talked about it very much when a huge wall mirror was delivered to Munia's house, and the doors of his house were remade—instead of iron latches, they installed brass locks, so polished and shiny you could see them for a mile.

Pearl didn't travel alone to the country villa and the vineyard; Avreml, her son, went with her. This was the only thing that people in Kovalnik couldn't swallow, and they muttered: "Pearl has become so delicate that she can't travel by herself, she needs someone to accompany her."

In Leshnitse, at the vineyard, Avreml met Sterra, a young girl, from Libave: in Kovalnik the news arrived that this Sterra was a beauty, the likes of which had never been seen before.

For Avreml's wedding, people traveled to Libave. For the wedding, Pearl ordered a new dress of full-length black satin, with a fur-trimmed, green velvet evening coat. In Kovalnik, people said that the satin was imported, and that the green velvet coat cost as much as they could earn in a year.

The wedding took place right after Shavuos. Pearl and her young daughter-in-law, Sterra, didn't return to Kovalnik, but traveled to the country villa and to the vineyard. In Kovalnik, people waited, wanting to see what this Sterra was like, so special that they had to go search in Libaveh, as if in Kovalnik, and even in Brisk, there were no such maidens for Avreml.

Sterra arrived in Kovalnik at the end of summer. She traveled with Avreml in his britzka and held an open, light-colored parasol over her head to prevent the sun's rays. The neighbors peered through their windows to see what Avreml's Sterra looked like.

"Summer's no longer scorching hot, but she needs a light-colored parasol!"—the neighbors promptly denounced the newcomer to their town.

Chaya-Gitl the Storekeeper came out of her store to take a look at Sterra. Sterra got down from the britzka, wearing a pair of fine brown shoes with green high heels. Chaya-Gitl noticed the shoes with the green high heels, scowled, and went back inside her store. Chaya-Gitl was not a gossiper. Her only words were, "I should worry? They're not in *my* store." But Stereh's fine brown shoes with the green high heels had smacked her right between the eyes. There was something not "suitable" about them for a respectable daughter-in-law. And she repeated this to the women who came to her store: "Her shoes are so scandalous that my enemies should wear them! But it's not my worry. It's as they say: 'not in my store.' "

The women spread Chaya-Gitl's words around Kovalnik: "Her shoes are so scandalous that our enemies should wear them." Adding, on their own, that although the sun was no longer scorching, she carried an open, light-colored parasol . . .

People brought the story in to Kovalnik, that Sterra wasn't much of a "bargain" after all. In her town, in Libave, they said she had already gone around with a Gentile. In fact, it was because of this, that her parents had sent her to the vineyard in Leshnitse, where Avreml had caught hold of her.

The millers in Kovalnik set their hearts to rest and warmed the story up with glee: "Now there you have it! All those those riches, and still to have snatched up the kind of daughter-in-law that our enemies should have!"

When Pearl took her daughter-in-law, Sterra, to the synagogue for the first time, they received a cold "Gut Shabbes." Sterra came back from the synagogue as if she'd been soaked in the rain. No one had even looked at her dress, which was the most beautiful in the synagogue; it was as if there were a wall between her and all the other women, and no one had looked over to see what the person on the other side did.

Avreml had two rooms built on to his father's house, with a separate entrance and porch facing the street. The two porches, right next to each other, stood there, provokingly, almost arrogantly proclaiming the newly rich man.

Sterra spread fine carpets in her two rooms, and on her table she placed a lamp with a blue cut-glass globe. Sterra lived in the two rooms as if in another world. The neighbors were very distant with her—only a "Good morning" or a "Good year." Her house seemed like a little piece of Libave that had been imported to Kovalnik and couldn't fit in.

At the beginning of every month, Chaya-Gitl the Storekeeper went to everyone in town to collect money for the Orphan Bride Fund. This was her mitzvah. People knew that when Chaya-Gitl came around, it was a new month. She always collected the same amount of money from each house.

This was invariable, a constant like the moon. At the beginning of the month, the new moon arrived, and at the beginning of the month, Chaya-Gitl arrived. Passing by Munia the Miller's house, Chaya-Gitl thought: Why do I need to go to the daughter-in-law and wipe my shoes on her porch? God will provide the other two groschen.

A few days after the beginning of the month, Pearl said for no obvious reason, "Chaya-Gitl hasn't come for her two groschen!"

There was an uneasiness in her words, as if by uttering them the moon might disappear from the heavens.

Sterra turned her head. Her mother-in-law's uneasiness had an effect on her, and each time she noticed Chaya-Gitl passing by, she remembered with a heavy feeling the words of her mother-in-law: "Chaya-Gitl hasn't come for her two groschen!" And for Sterra, this became the sharp-cornered fence the shtetl put up around her.

People continued to talk about Sterra, that she didn't eat any cholent—Pearl didn't want anyone cooking on Sabbath—so the daugher-in-law ate dry food. The entire Sabbath she lived on dry food.

The "Good Morning" for Sterra became even colder. It rang out almost like *"Dzhen Dobrie,"* which is Polish for "Good day," the way people say to a Gentile. Take your Dzhen Dobrie and good-bye. That's all I have to do with you.

People said that when Avreml drove out in his britzka to the bakeries, Sterra sat alone by herself and played cards. "Not any Gentiles here, so she sits and plays cards," they gossiped.

Her mother-in-law, Pearl, felt that the town was turning its back to their house. From time to time, she would let fall a word or two: "People are envious!"

Sterra's uneasy eyes took measure of her mother-in-law, and she went around as if she were on an island, whose bridge to the world had been taken away.

Reb Aaron the Dayen's wife, Mirl, had gone to Chaya-Gitl's store, and, returning home, she confided to her husband, "She sits and plays cards . . . she doesn't have anyone over, so she sits and plays cards . . ."

Reb Aaron the Dayen was a man who said very little. He studied in the synagogue and in his home. While he was studying, if he came across a problem that he couldn't solve right away, he would leave the book open, get up and pace the floor. He would walk right up to the wall, as if the house were too narrow for him. At the rabbinical court, Reb Aaron the Dayen hardly said anything either: if someone brought a false claim, he'd motion with his hand as though he wanted to push those words away silently.

Reb Aaron raised his head from the book he was studying, as though he were coming out of another world, and asked his wife, "Which she? What she?"

Mirl answered, "She. Sterra, Munia the Miller's daughter-in-law. She sits by herself and plays cards. She has no one to keep her company, so she sits . . ."

Reb Aaron motioned with his hand, as though he were throwing off a false claim in the rabbinical court.

His wife wanted to defend herself and said, "Chaya-Gitl didn't go over to her even for a donation."

Reb Aaron closed the book he'd been studying, as if he didn't want it to be involved in such a conversation. Irritated, he said to his wife, "This is slander . . . listen to me. Chaya-Gitl didn't go to her for a donation. Why didn't she go for a donation, in fact?"

Reb Aaron stood up from his place and began pacing the room, back and forth.

Mirl wiped her lips and defended herself. "I know . . . they're talking . . ."

Reb Aaron just shook his head. His wife slipped out of the room.

The big fire in Lishke had just happened that week, and Reb Aaron the Dayen was collecting money for the burned-out people.

A tall man with long bushy eyebrows, Reb Aaron the Dayen took a walking stick in his hand and left the house to go over to Munia the Miller's. He didn't go to Munia's, but went up on to Sterra's porch. Sterra didn't know all the people in the town, but she recognized Reb Aaron the Dayen. People had pointed him out to her just as soon as she had arrived in Kovalnik: that man is Reb Aaron the Dayen.

When he came in, Sterra stood up.

"Good morning, Sterra," he said. "I am coming to collect donations for the burned-out people in Lishke."

He called her by her name, as if she were a respected married woman in Kovalnik. This was as clear in his voice, as if he were giving a verdict in the rabbinical court. For a moment, Sterra looked at Reb Aaron, and then her eyes lit up as if they reflected all the fearful glow of the fire in Lishke. Her mouth moved, but she was silent. She brought a chair for him. Reb Aaron moved the chair to the table and leaned on it with an elbow. Sterra went into a second room and brought back a donation.

When she came back, her eyes were damp and exhausted as if a tear had extinguished the fire in them. Her hand was small and narrow, and the two silver rubles took up the entire length of it.

Reb Aaron took the donation. "May you be ever able to give, Sterra. I only wish Jews didn't need it," he said, and left.

Before Reb Aaron had collected the money for the burned-out people in Lishkeh, everyone in Kovalnik knew that Reb Aaron had gotten the first donation from Sterra, Munia the Miller's daughter-in-law, and that Sterra had given two silver rubles. In Chaya-Gitl's store, it was as noisy as a railway station. Chaya-Gitl turned her wagons around and said, "And why not? She has, so she gives. Why shouldn't he collect from her? Isn't she a Jewish daughter?"

When Pearl and her daughter-in-law arrived at the synagogue on Sabbath, people greeted them with a pious "Gut Shabbes." Sterra answered them, "Gut Shabbes," and through the glass panes of the women's section, she saw with her own eyes the tall form of Reb Aaron the Dayen who had caused her to become a respected married woman in Kovalnik.

And when the new month arrived, Chaya-Gitl collected the first two groschen from Sterra, Munia the Miller's daughter-in-law.

New York, 1954

Brayndl

. . . .

Brayndl Akhse's never put on airs that she was Reb Chaim Itche the
Stargazer and Akhse's daughter. She mingled with everyone in the
whole town, and all the young men were after her.

In her wide dress with its many starched ruffles, Brayndl seemed as if
she were ready to go dancing. When she floated out to the street in the
early evening, there was a gathering around her immediately. Brayndl felt it
was entirely proper for her to be seen with Pinye, the klezmer's son, although he was only a "musicmaker."

Pinye sang like a bird. When he sang a melody in his tremolo, people
hearing it melted from joy. He was the best violinist in his father's band.
Once at a wedding, it occurred to Pinye to sing, as he played his violin. The
band stopped playing. The crowd listened, holding their breath. It seemed
an entire forest of birds had come to sing at the wedding.

Because of Brayndl, Pinye stopped going around with Rukhl the Dress-
maker, a pretty girl who earned good money. He began hanging around the
main road, waiting to meet Brayndl. She was usually accompanied by her
friend, Perele the watchmaker's daughter, but Pinye sang straight into
Brayndl's ear, as if this song were only for her. Brayndl smiled, with her
white, widely spaced little teeth, and all the ruffles on her dress danced to
each turn of the melody.

Brayndl's mother, Akhse, was furious that her daughter went around
with Pinye, and she reproached her: "How do you come to be going around
with Pinye, the musicmaker? You think he's your equal? You're not a child

anymore! You're almost eighteen years old! And still going around with Pinye!"

The ruffles on her dress fluttered, and she said, "Why not? I love to hear him sing." She said her piece and went on her way. She floated away from the porch, as though the outdoors were calling her: "Come! It's summer, there's sunshine and song."

Akhse considered her daughter: "She's like a wind, a soaring bird, a thoughtless being. How did I get such a daughter?"

Akhse had the only wine store in town. It's true that people could get wine from Berl the Vintner and from the cellar of Sholem Moishe's house, but it wasn't as good as Ahkse's wine. At Akhse's there was real Tokay, real wine from the Caucasus, and even real wine from Erets Isroel. Akhse conducted herself in her shop as if she were in a pharmacy. When people came to her for a bottle of wine, she asked them about the occasion they needed it for: a wedding, a bris, an engagement party, a gift to be sent, a guest to be entertained, and then would Akhse go out and bring back a bottle of wine.

"This is for you. This is what you need."

And people could count on what Akhse said: this was the correct wine to serve.

Akhse's husband, Reb Chaim Itche, was seldom in the store. He was an absent-minded man and had written a book. In town, people said he that he was writing another book about the stars in the sky. Because of this, they called him Reb Chaim Itche the Stargazer with the additional name, "Akhse's husband." And indeed he had a long name: "Reb Chaim Itche the Stargazer Akhse's husband." If it happened that Reb Chaim Itche had been left to mind the wine store by himself and a customer came in, he never took it upon himself to select a wine. He cried out to Akhse, who was in another room, "The party for Shprintze's daughter's fiancé. What kind of wine should I give them?"

And Akhse answered him very precisely, "Give them a Tokay from the third shelf on the left-hand side, the bottle with the gold label." And Shprintze's daughter's fiancé drank the Tokay from the bottle with the gold label, and it made for a better match.

At Akhse's house, it was even more orderly than at her wine store. Her house sparkled and glowed with linens and vases. There was even a statue on the table in the parlor, a bust of Dr. Herzl, the only statue in town. This gave such importance to her home, that it was a privilege to visit her.

On a hot summer day, Brayndl stopped Ziml, a young man who was managing his father's sawmill with four cutting machines, and called to him through the window, "Ziml, hitch up your wagon, let's go to the river to bathe. It's so hot, a person could melt!"

Akhse heard this and said to Brayndl, "So all of a sudden, in the middle of the day, he should go hitch up the wagon for you? The sawmill can just wait for you? How can such ideas fly out of a person's head?"

Brayndl smiled with her white, widely spaced little teeth and answered, "If he doesn't hitch up the wagon, I won't go. We shall see."

But not more than half an hour later, Ziml was standing with the hitched-up wagon next to Akhse's house. Brayndl danced down from the porch to him and cried, "Ziml! I'll bathe on one side of the bridge, and you on the other. It's so hot, a person could melt."

Akhse watched the wagon drive off, clattering merrily along to the river, and considered her daughter: The fancies that fly out of her head! She does whatever she wants.

Driving back from the river, Ziml said to Brayndl, "Brayndl, is it true what they say, that you like Pinye, the klezmer's son?"

Brayndl moved a little closer to Ziml on the coachbox and smiled with her white, widely spaced little teeth. "What are you talking about, Ziml? He sings like a bird; how can anyone not like him?"

Brayndl's smile was so pure and full of joy that it seemed to contain the whole of summer, with all its greenness and sweetness. Ziml didn't reply. He thought that to have a voice like a bird was perhaps even better than having a sawmill with four cutting machines.

A guest came to Brayndl's friend Perele: her cousin, Shakhne, a young man who had his own watermill near Slavute. Perele was wearing a blue dress with a white collar and white cuffs. With her fine-featured face and delicate skin, it seemed she had just bathed in dew. Her parents, Gedaliah the Watchmaker and his wife Eshke, were hoping for a match. They said to each other that Shakhne was coming probably with Perele in mind. He stayed with them as a guest for several days. At their Sabbath afternoon table, Eshke served the very best of things: cake and raspberry jam. Shakhne was on the verge of signing the engagement contract with Perele.

It was already getting dark when Brayndl came over to see Perele. The starched ruffles of her dress fluttered around in the house with a saucy freshness. She asked the guest, "So how do you like our main road?"

Her white, widely spaced little teeth were shining as if she had just bitten into a fresh apple, and her face glowed cheerfully in the half-darkened house.

"It's worth it to go for a walk," she said, drawn to the window.

Shakhne moved his head as if he were hearing music. He didn't take his eyes from Brayndl and watched her every movement. He smiled, not knowing why.

They went outside for a walk. Brayndl fluttered down from the staircase first and stood there looking up.

"Look at the sky!" she said. "It makes me want to fly right up there."

Shakhne walked not next to Perele, but next to Brayndl. He touched her elbow, and in a while, held her arm. Perele's heart sank. Her white cuffs now seemed to her clumsy and overly fancy. She felt herself lost. Her smile did not hide the sorrow on her lips.

For several Sabbaths in a row, Shakhne came to his uncle Gedaliah as a guest. He didn't mention getting engaged to Perele. Perele didn't wear her blue dress with the white cuffs for him any more. She knew that Shakhne was coming because of Brayndl. Dark blue circles fell under her eyes, like those on a person who doesn't sleep nights.

Once they went on a walk to a young forest where the wild pears were ripening. Perele, Shakhne, and Brayndl were accompanied by Ziml from the sawmill. Passing by, Brayndl called to Pinye, who was coming toward them: "Pinye, come, you can sing something."

In the young forest, Shakhne called Brayndl aside and asked her, "Brayndl, would you like to see my watermill?"

Brayndl's white, widely spaced little teeth sparkled. One would have thought that the watermill was the one thing in the world she wanted to see.

"Oh, yes, yes, I want to see your watermill! When Perele goes to see it, I'll come with her."

Shakhne shook a twig of wild pears and said, "Brayndl, would you like to marry me?"

Brayndl's face was both merry and astonished, as if getting married were the wildest idea in the world and Shakhne had just thought it up.

"Why in the world would we get married?" she said, and the ruffles on her dress danced together all at once.

Shakhne stopped visiting Perele. In town, people muttered that Brayndl had spoiled Perele's match. Perele's mother almost stopped speaking to Akhse, barely saying from a distance, "Gut Shabbes," with a lowered head. Akhse was sickened: Why should she have unnecessary enemies? She reprimanded Brayndl. "What were you going to Perele's for when her cousin was there?"

"What's the matter? Am I not permitted to look at a person?" Brayndl answered.

Ahkse got angry.

"That wasn't just 'a person,' that was a fiancé, do you understand?"

"Well, people should hide him under a glass!" Brayndl retorted and left.

Perele began to suffer from head aches. They sent her to the forest near Slavute to rest. Eshke the Watchmaker's wife stopped greeting Akhse with her cold "Gut Shabbes." Akhse spoke to her husband, Reb Chaim Itche: "Chaim Itche, what is to be done about Brayndl?"

Chaim Itche came down to earth, out of his stars. "What's the matter with Brayndl?" He didn't understand what his wife was bothering him about.

Now Ahkse really got mad.

"Don't you know anything? People are saying that she spoiled Perele's match. You're a father, maybe you should give her a slap."

Chaim Itche hid his hands in his pants pockets. This was the first sign that he didn't intend to slap Brayndl. He calmed his wife down and gave her an example of the stars: "Each one moves in its own way, and you can't change it. What can we do?" he said. "Brayndl . . . attracts."

Reb Chaim Itche was embarrassed to say right out that "she attracts young men," and he got stuck several times. "She attracts . . . she attracts," and stopped. "She attracts people. What can we do?"

"Well, we'll have to marry her off then!" Akhse answered him, short and to the point, and went into her wine store. But Akhse resented her husband's calm, his example of the stars. She returned and rebuked him. "If your Brayndl spoils matches, people will throw stones at our windows! You hear?"

Reb Chaim Itche hands dropped apart, like someone who is helpless. And then, just as if heaven-sent, the matchmaker from Slavute came to propose a match between Brayndl and Osherl Kimmelman.

Osherl was the youngest son of Reb Josef Kimmelman. The family had a fabric store in Slavute, and they traveled to markets in the surrounding towns to sell remnants. The Kimmelmans were well known throughout the entire province. "They're busy everywhere," people said.

Osherl and his mother had come to the largest market in Slivovke, where Brayndl lived. All the Kimmelmans' wealth and enterprise could be seen on Osherl's person. He had sold all the odds and ends to a broker.

"So we'll have a hundred less," he said to his mother. "It's a hot day."

His mother left it to Osherl.

When he was standing, handing the merchandise over to the broker, Brayndl walked by. She liked one of the remnants and put her hand on it.

"We don't sell single pieces," Osherl's mother said to her. Brayndl took her hand off the remnant, but she remained standing there, looking at it. Osherl walked over to her.

"It's a pity," Brayndl said to him. "I like this one," and her white, widely spaced little teeth smiled covetously.

Osherl looked at Brayndl and said, "Take it. It's a gift from me."

The ruffles on Brayndl's dress danced, and she laughed. "That's all I need! My mother would throw me out of the house."

"We'd take you with us to Slavute," Osherl answered.

He looked at Brayndl like a man considering a unique picture and repeated once more: "I really mean it, I'll take you to Slavute."

Brayndl rocked her head from side to side twice, as if she were deciding: was worth it to go to Slavute with him, or not. She remained standing a little while longer, and then said, "How far is Slavute?"

"Very close," Osherl answered.

"Well, you can still come here then . . ."

She turned around and fluttered away.

About two weeks later, Osherl Kimmelman sent the matchmaker to Akhse to propose a match with Brayndl.

Akhse asked her daughter sternly, "Brayndl, do you know someone in Slavute?"

"What about Slavute?" she answered, blushing, and stood there, astonished.

"A matchmaker has come. Osherl Kimmelman sent him."

"Yes. . . . yes . . . I wanted to buy a remnant from him."

Osherl came with his mother so that she could have a look at the bride. On an ordinary Wednesday afternoon, Mrs. Kimmelman was wearing a heavy taffeta dress that rustled and announced from a mile away: "We're rich people." Ahkse was also wearing a heavy rustling dress that answered: "And we're not paupers either." From both their noisy dresses came a rustle that sounded like constant whispering.

Osherl came with the remnant in hand. Brayndl began laughing. Her white, widely spaced little teeth lit up with joy. They greeted each other like old acquaintances who have wanted to see each other for a long time.

Akhse served real Tokay wine from a bottle with a gold label. The wedding was to take place in about eight weeks. Osherl smiled thinly, joking, "With this kind of bride, we can't delay the wedding, she might stray into another market."

Perele didn't come to Brayndl's wedding. She had left town. Pinye didn't come to play with the band. He said he was no longer going to be a musician. Ziml didn't come to the wedding either; his sawmill was broken. The wedding was merry, with Akhse's wine, as befits a wedding. But a dark cloud of gloom was hanging over several roofs in town; Brayndl didn't notice. She wondered why her best friends hadn't come to her wedding. She wondered, and her merry, widely spaced little teeth smiled with sincere regret.

November 1954

The Rafalovitches

· · · · · · ·

I t was one of those blessedly beautiful afternoons at Brighton Beach, when the sky is so distinctly clear, it was as if it had been washed with a heavenly blue, and the sea looked exactly as if a choirmaster had given the waves their tempo, so that they ebbed and flowed in a harmonious murmur. In short, it was a very beautiful afternoon.

I was sitting on a bench with an old acquaintance, watching the boats pass by, boats that seemed, in their peaceful movements, to be on holiday, but we were not speaking about holiday matters at all, as sometimes happens, even at the seashore.

A middle-aged woman strolled by us, leading a small dog on a leash. She made no particular impression on me, but my acquaintance, watching the woman, gave a sudden start and blurted: "The doctor!"

She remained sitting so deep in thought that I almost decided not to ask her what had so surprised her about the woman.

After shaking her head and making incomprehensible grimaces at me for a while, my acquaintance recovered herself. She looked at me sideways, as if for a moment it was not clear to her who I was, and then said, "Sometimes life turns back its pages and gives rise to strange memories of things that have entirely disappeared, it seems, from one's memory. That woman is one of the Rafalovitches."

So my acquaintance said, and she laughed freely, with youth and joy, as if her laughter came from long, long ago, from happier times.

"Who are the Rafalovitches?"

"That's a story from years ago," she began telling. "I was a student then, studying in Odessa, struggling without money, making money from whatever work happened to come along: for a while, a children's governess, and for a while, an invalid's nurse—but those were good times, and happy, because when you're young, the world is full of hope, and the future seems like a paradise. By the way, Odessa was then a beautiful, lively city, with a big Jewish population, and it seemed like a paradise, too.

"Renting a room by myself was beyond the means of the kind of merry pauper I was. I made an agreement with a friend, who was a student in the same classes, and we both went out into the city of Odessa to look for a room the two of us could share. To look for a room was for us young friends a special pleasure. We would come running, see all sorts of people, and then finally drop off our few books and our weekday and Sabbath clothes, and we were set for the time being. And for more than the time being—people didn't want much more than that.

"Walking around, looking for a room, we arrived at the Rafalovitches'. The door was opened by a woman who seemed like a fine lady when you looked at her face and her carefully coiffed hair. But when you saw her shoes, or more accurately, her carpet slippers, then she seemed more like an old servant, and when you heard her voice, you had the impression that it had taken her a long time to learn to speak, and that she held each word very dear now.

"First of all, she considered us very carefully, a long time in fact, to see if it were even worth speaking to such characters, and then when she decided it was, she said, 'You understand, this isn't just an ordinary apartment. You will be at the Rafalovitches.'

"Then she demanded several conditions from us: We shouldn't invite company over because she liked it quiet in the house. We shouldn't eat any herring, not even in our own room, because she couldn't stand the smell. We shouldn't play any musical instruments, for example, a mandolin or a balalaika, because she liked only fine music. If we came back when it was raining, we should take off our galoshes on the other side of the door and carry them in by hand because the carpet that she pointed to, just inside the door, was washed once a year and was always clean.

"These were the four main conditions; then there were several other secondary rules.

"When we had agreed to all the things we shouldn't do, it would still cost us a little more, because, after all, we would be 'at the Rafalovitches.'

"She, the woman of the house, Sheva of the Rafalovitches, never was without her carpet slippers, so that it would be quiet in the house; the sound of steps shouldn't be heard. It seemed that even the cat that had the run of the house, walked on special soft, padded paws, and was quieter than all other cats in the whole world. The furniture was soft, and the sun shone dimly through the curtains, and Madam Rafalovitch's hair was so perfectly combed that if only one hair had dared to cross from one side of her part to the other, there would nearly have been a revolution. But such a thing could never happen to Sheva of the Rafalovitches.

"She called her daughter, a student at the medical school, who had one more year before finishing, 'the doctor'.

"The doctor had her own room—pink walls, a pink bedspread, pink curtains at the windows, and a pink rug on the floor. But she herself was very pale. She never had any company either. At the home of the Rafalovitches, such a thing was not accepted.

"Returning from the University, the doctor ate the evening meal with her mother so quietly that a fork didn't dare make a noise. Below us, three stories down, Odessa was alive. Odessa laughed and played mandolins. Groups of friends walked down the streets to the seashore. But all of this had nothing to do with the Rafalovitches. They referred to all this with the general name 'the plebeians.' The plebeians made too much noise. The plebeians didn't allow the Rafalovitches to sleep.

"After the quiet evening meal, the doctor went to her pink room to read a weighty book about diseases of the nerves, and her mother, wearing her carpet slippers, put the silverware back in the dining room cupboard, where it was recounted every day.

"The father, with a gray, neatly shorn beard, was like a guest in the house. He had betrayed the Rafalovitches once and for all by being a little man on the stock exchange in Odessa. Compared to the pedigree of his house, he was a man of small stature. This gave his wife so much grief, that walking around quietly in her carpet slippers, she once said, 'Only Sheva of the Rafalovitches can bear it.'

"One time, around January, Madame Rafalovitch's carpet slippers, surprisingly, were heard walking back and forth from the pink room to the large dining room to the kitchen. A guest was to call on the doctor. Madame Rafalovitch asked us not to sing or slam the door when the guest was there. (This was an additional provision to all the conditions for being 'at the Rafalovitches.')

"That evening the guest came, a tall young man in his thirties. He went straight from the hall to the pink room. The doctor was wearing a black dress with a red rose on her bosom. The red rose smelled of spring, and the doctor also had a pink countenance—having lost entirely her usual pallor. We, just two young goats, didn't sing that evening, but fooled around, speaking in sign language and half words, 'We're wearing a rose today, are we?' 'Yes, a rose.'

"The evening meal was noisy. The forks and the knives clattered. There was company. The doctor laughed, and even her father, with his gray neatly shorn beard, was eating along with everyone right at the table, eating and chatting. That evening, no one went around in carpet slippers.

"The doctor, the rose on her bosom, went off to the theater with the tall young man. He led her down the stairs, holding her by the hand.

"About twelve o'clock the doctor, the rose still on her bosom, returned from the theater. She went into her pink room, and from there we heard a muffled crying. We, two young goats, didn't dare imitate such crying. It was the first time we'd heard a woman, who had returned from the theater with a red rose on her bosom, crying.

"The next day we were allowed to sing again. No guests came. The doctor's face resumed its pallor. Sheva of the Rafalovitches walked around in her carpet slippers, and after the evening meal, she counted the silverware again in the dining room. She told us that the guest was the doctor's divorced husband. Every year, for her birthday, he came to take her to the theater.

"He still loved her, Madame Rafalovitch told us. He would always love her. Their parting happened because of an unrefined girl who sold soda water at the seashore, and who had worn a blue sun hat. In short, one of the plebeians."

My acquaintance interrupted her story. The middle-aged woman who was leading the small dog on a leash walked by us. My acquaintance went over to her and asked her if she was from the Rafalovitches. The woman turned her pale face, and she shook her head—no. She tugged on the dog's leash and left.

"A striking resemblance to the doctor," my acquaintance smiled. "Who knows? Some people don't want to return to their past. And maybe . . . in the end . . . the sea sounds the same here in Brighton, just as it did in Odessa. Maybe there are people here too, who are exactly like the Rafalovitches there."

July 6, 1947

In the Palace
·······

Peple in town called the house of the Mandelshtams the "palace." Avram Mandelshtam owned a blanket factory in Bialystok, but they lived in Podvolke, a nearby shtetl. His old mother, Hinde, didn't want to move anywhere else; she had been born Podvolke and she wanted to die in Podvolke. So she said, and her son gave in to her.

Although the palace stood in the middle of the main street, it had almost nothing to do with the town.

For vacations in summer, when the children, the Mandelshtams' two sons and two daughters, came back from the gymnasiums and universities where they were studying, the palace came alive. Accompanying the daughters was their governess, a dressed-up lady who wore a hat. In the shtetl, people calculated that the governess alone brought seven suitcases, as well as cases for hats, cardboard boxes, and other containers—altogether thirteen pieces of baggage.

Guests, male and female friends and relatives, visited the sons and daughters all summer long. Two maids cooked and baked and fried, served and removed the dishes. The palace rang and clattered and hummed with conversation and laughter.

In the mornings, they played croquet in the large courtyard behind the house. Frumke the Poultrywoman, who plucked chickens and geese at the palace, told everyone that when the governess played croquet, she wore pants just like a man.

The shtetl said, "What else is new? Money makes you crazy!"

In the evening, the palace was softly lit up, and sounds of piano playing and songs from the gramophone floated out from the windows. The palace was a special place of good fortune that found itself here because of old Hinde.

Each morning, the older Mandelshtam son, Ezra, walked to the post office at the end of town to collect the newspapers, journals, and books he subscribed to. It was almost a wonder to see such a quiet man come out of that noisy house, a man with brown, thoughtful eyes, who walked as tranquilly as if coming back from the synagogue. Walking back from the post office, his gait was even more calm. While walking, he read his newspaper. People got out of the way for him—first, because he was a Mandelshtam, and second, because he was so deep in thought.

One summer, all of Podvolke was rocked by unbelievable news. In the palace, they had arranged for a concert with new records for the gramophone, and they had invited Tilye, the daughter of Alter the Devout.

Tilye was the one and only daughter of Reb Alter Jaffe. Because of his strict devotion, people called him Alter the Devout. Alter prayed much and spoke little. And his wife, Tsipe, ran the dry-goods store quietly, without trickery and without bargaining. Their home was established, well-to-do, and honest.

Their only daughter, Tilye, stayed at home and read books. It was almost an event when she walked down the street, her hair in two long, chestnut-colored braids. And when she appeared, people would say, "Tilye is coming."

Once, when "Tilye was walking" she encountered Ezra, who was walking tranquilly, reading his newspaper. She got out of the way for him and laughed quietly. Ezra stopped and they both smiled.

"I am eager to see the newspapers," he excused himself. Tilye shook her head. They remained standing a while. A calmness surrounded Tilye. She, with her long braids, with her smile (all that remained of her concealed laughter) was a part of Alter the Devout's home—well-established and honest. Ezra was pleased to stand with her, just to stand.

"How do you have the patience to plait such long braids?" he asked, true wonder in his eyes.

Tilye smiled and didn't answer him. She just pulled on her braids, as if to make sure they were indeed that long. It was so natural for Ezra to turn around and accompany her home to Alter the Devout's house, that he didn't realize he had left with her.

"Come to our concert," he said to her, when he was saying good-bye. And on the evening of the concert, he went to call for her himself. He carried her light summer coat over his arm, and in this way led her into the palace.

When the gramophone was playing the recordings of new songs, Ezra went outside with Tilye to show her the lilac trees, that had been planted all around the palace. They walked and were silent. Between them was a quiet understanding of love that needed no explanation whatever.

Each morning, walking to collect his newspapers, Ezra would stop at Tilye's, and when he walked back, she came out and they strolled off together.

In the autumn, when the young people of the palace started to get ready to return to the gymnasiums and universities, Ezra said to Tilye, "You will go with me, Tilye."

Early the next morning, Tilye asked her mother to plait her braids. Tsipe felt that her daughter had something to tell to her. Her mother combed her hair. Tilye turned her head to her mother and said, "Mama, Ezra wants me to go with him."

Tsipe quietly finished combing her daughter's long, soft hair, her hand as gentle as if she were caressing Tilye's head.

"Well, may God bless you—let Ezra be truly meant for you!" she replied as devoutly as if she were saying a blessing.

The wedding was celebrated in Bialystok. Only the closest people came to the wedding—Tilye's parents and the family from the palace. Old Hinde traveled with them. She had ordered a silk hairband made of green and pink ribbons from the wigmaker, as befitted a grandmother at her grandson's wedding.

Tilye's good fortune was so great, that the town didn't envy her. Such a match occurs just once in a life time, what else is there to say?

In town, people said that Tilye was studying to be a midwife. That Ezra was studying engineering was understandable—he would direct his father's factory. But why did Tilye need to learn to be a midwife? Are they short of money to prepare for Sabbath, God forbid, at the Mandelshtams? And then they dismissed it, saying, what else is new? Money makes people crazy.

Tilye now came to the palace with the summer residents. She and Ezra arrived late in the middle of summer. Each morning, they walked together to the post office to collect the newspapers and journals. Their parcel was all the bigger now, because of the books that were coming for Tilye.

When Tilye walked with Ezra, he bent his head to her and spoke quietly, as if he were entrusting her with many secrets. There was so much joy and youth in their gait, it seemed they had just stepped out from under the chuppah.

Since Tilye entered the Mandelshtam family, the palace moved closer to Podvolke. Tilye's girl friends visited, and Alter the Devout and Tsipe came every Saturday evening, at the end of Sabbath, to drink tea with their daughter at the palace.

The second year after Ezra's marriage, summer was quiet in the palace. Death had cast a shadow over their roof and carried away the happiness and the noise of the Mandelshtams' voices: Ezra had traveled to see his father and, on the way, had perished in a train wreck. In his pocket, people found a letter to Tilye that he had written on the train: I have just parted from you, Tilye, and I forgot to tell you good-bye.[1] Good-bye, Tilye. It's a joy for me to write and repeat your name—Tilye, Tilye, Tilye. Ezra.

They gave her this note after Ezra's funeral. She held it and read it for a long time, as if it were a large book—the book of her love.

Two months later, she gave birth to a child. When they told her it was a boy, her eyes filled with tears, and she said: "Ezra."

Tilye remained in the city, in the apartment where she had lived with Ezra. His books, his pictures, the work that he had been writing, and the recordings of songs that he had loved to hear, all were there, and there Tilye wanted to raise their son, the little Ezra.

For summer vacations, she returned home to Podvolke with the little Ezra and his governess. And once again, people in the large rooms of the

---

1. The author used the Yiddish term zai gezunt, which has two meanings: "be healthy," and "good-bye."

palace could hear the name Ezra. Ezra is walking, Ezra is playing, Ezra is calling Tilye.

One summer, when the child was a little older, Tsipe suggested to her daughter that she was still young and that it was hard to live alone. Tilye didn't allow her mother to get into a long conversation. She interrupted, answering briefly: "There could never be another Ezra."

Her mother never spoke of it to her again.

When Ezra was thirteen years old, Tilye returned with him to Podvolke. They would have his bar mitzvah here. Old Hinde now walked leaning on a cane. It took her all of an hour to walk to the wigmaker's. She ordered a new silk hairband with quiet blue ribbons, befitting a great-grandmother going to the synagogue for a great-grandson's bar mitzvah.

Ezra was a boy with brown, thoughtful eyes. He was almost as tall as his mother and looked exactly like his father.

When Tilye saw her son standing, his face earnest and thoughtful, saying the blessings, it seemed to her that her husband was standing there. Ezra is standing there. Her face turned white. She covered her eyes with her hands.

When they came out of the synagogue, Ezra was waiting for his mother near the steps of the women's section. Tilye kissed him. Ezra took his mother's light summer coat and carried it over his arm, and he walked home with her into the palace.

New York, 1954

An Old-Country Erev Pesakh

. . . .

There were two wells from which we and all the neighbors around us drew our water. One well was in the courtyard of Chaim Moishe, whose main occupation was screaming: screaming at neighbors, screaming at cowherds who were leading their cows to pasture; screaming at children who were making a racket under his windows. He even screamed at his own chickens and geese in the courtyard, but he never once raised his voice to those people who came to draw water from his well. On the contrary, he was extremely pleased with them, and he demonstrated his pleasure as well as a screaming Jew could: he never, absolutely never screamed at them, and once in a while he even offered a tribute to the water in his well: "It's considerably better than Freida Leah's water."

The second well, in fact, belonged to Freida Leah the Rich Woman. And, just as rich people have all the luck, the water from her well was sweet and soft, and everyone knew that Freida Leah's water was the best there could be. We, and the neighbors, went to Freida Leah's to get our water for Sabbath, even though it was farther away. Consequently, on week days, it was lively at the courtyard of the screaming Jew. The bucket on the winch creaked from early morning on. Neighbors, men and women, met each other there with buckets, empty and full, and the owner of the well was delighted, even though he received no income from it, and from time to time offered the tribute to his water: "It's considerably better than Freida Leah's water."

And so it was the entire week, until Friday. On Fridays, the screaming

297

Jew went around in a fury, and screamed all the more at anyone who happened to be there. He resented it in the extreme, that on Fridays everyone went with their buckets not to him and his courtyard, but to Freida Leah the Rich Woman for their Sabbath water.

And just as he was proud of his well (a whole week it gave him pleasure and on Fridays pained him that it stood almost deserted), so Freida Leah didn't make much ado about her well. If people come for water, let them come. If they don't come for water, they don't come. She had absolute confidence in her sweet water and knew very well that just before Sabbath, people came to her; and we're not even talking about the other holidays, especially before Passover, when everyone wanted to have sweet water, and they went to her.

For Passover, the "season" began at Freida Leah's well several days earlier, before the holiday itself arrived. Polkeh, the Gentile woman who, in honor of the holiday, helped by washing floors, and scrubbing and cleaning in all the neighbors' houses, Polkeh was the first one to begin the "season" at Freida Leah's. She propped open the small, ornate door to Freida Leah's courtyard with a stone so that the crowd didn't have to open it each time, a door which closed by itself, and could, God forbid, slam on a person's leg. As soon as this door to the courtyard was open, the crowd was already walking back and forth with their buckets, carrying the sweet Passover water, praising Polkeh for having gotten the idea to prop open the door with a stone, although Polkeh's invention for the good of the public was repeated year in and year out.

Polkeh, who spoke Yiddish almost like a Jewish child, but with a Gentile accent, accepted their compliments with great pleasure: "Well, why not? You want people to have to find a little door on the eve of Passover?"

Freida Leah the Rich Woman, although she maintained her courtyard in good order all year long, with paths between the grass and with stones around the well, always kept this small door to the courtyard closed. But on the eve of Passover, her courtyard was open to all. Even if someone wanted to kosher their pots and pans in her courtyard, Freida Leah made it possible by keeping stones and pieces of iron burning in her oven. Over the specially cleaned courtyard of the rich woman, steam rose to the sky when people dropped the boiling hot stones into the kettles of her water. In short, it was the "season" at her well, and she provided all that was required of her.[1]

When the house was ready for Passover (the boxes of matzo covered with a white cloth, the pail of pickled beets in a worthy place in the kitchen covered with clean sackcloth)—when everything was just about ready for the search for *chomets*[2] to begin, that was the moment Khveder the Water-carrier showed up with two brand new buckets hanging from his water-carrier's yoke.

In keeping with the appearance of his new buckets, Khveder, too, was wearing a new cloth coat, and the first thing he did was to take a look at the size of the new barrel he needed to fill up. It was time for Khveder to do the last job people did for Passover—to get the water ready, naturally, from Freida Leah's well, so that no one had to carry their own buckets through the streets as they did on ordinary days.

Khveder was in especially high spirits during the Passover preparations because he had new buckets and could therefore collect more money. People even whispered that he had probably gotten them for a few days from the cooper who sold buckets and barrels, and that Khveder paid him for it with a few drinks of whiskey. However it was, people paid him more for carrying the water. This was his moment, the best time in the water carrying business.

The new, full barrel, was also covered with a white linen cloth, and the children were watched and warned not to track in any *chomets* where it wasn't allowed: they shouldn't be underfoot where they weren't supposed to be, and they should never forget, even for a second, that *chomets* was contaminating.

One time, just before the search for *chomets* began, when the Passover barrel was already full of water and covered with white linen, Andreike

---

1. This paragraph describes the traditional method of koshering pots and pans for Passover. A large kettle is filled with water into which red-hot stones and pieces of iron are dropped to make the water boil. Then dishes and pots and pans are added.

2. The Yiddish term *bdike-chomets* signifies the ceremonial search for *chomets* (leavened bread) that might have been missed in the process of koshering the house for Passover.

came to chop wood for Passover, so that no one would have to spend time during the holiday chopping wood.

Andreike was not just a simple woodchopper. He was a stout, well-off peasant, and before Passover, he came as a good friend to chop wood, and also in fact to earn a few kopeks and collect a few matzos as a gift. Andreike had gone on an errand to buy something in a store, and had left his horse in our courtyard to graze.

The horse was little, skinny and short, and it was plucking the meager grass in the courtyard. Precisely at that moment, the neighbor's son, Noteh the cheder boy, came into our courtyard. On the day before Passover, he had been let out of school and sent out of his house lest he drag in any *chomets* or tread on the newly washed floors with his shoes.

Noteh had a strange desire to ride. He had been caught riding a goat once, and then he had really gotten what he had coming to him—from the rabbi, from his father, from his mother, and also from the screaming Jew who had the "everyday well." In addition to this, people gave him a nickname, "Noteh the Rider."

For any other boy, this would have been sufficient punishment to keep him from riding. But Noteh, it seemed, never took to heart the lesson for which people had reproached him, for which he had received many blows, and for which they had dubbed him "the Rider."

Anyhow, when he saw Andreike's horse grazing in our courtyard near the fence, Noteh's old passion for riding returned, and he climbed up on the fence, and from the fence onto the back of Andreike's horse, and probably was very happy, because he didn't even notice that he and the horse had wandered into our entryway and walked right up to the Passover barrel full of water.

When Noteh the Rider realized that the horse wanted to drink the Passover water in a Jewish entryway, just before the search for *chomets* was to begin, he understood what an enormous misfortune had befallen him. And with the true devotion of a Jewish cheder boy, and even though he knew what punishment awaited him, he began to shriek: "The Passover water! The Passover water!"

We all came running into the entryway, and saw Noteh the Rider on Andreike's horse right there next to the water barrel. At that moment, we children all understood why Passover water needed to be covered: it shouldn't easily be gotten into.

Of course, everyone, big and small, screamed at Noteh the Rider. But he escaped a severe punishment because he had shrieked: "The Passover water!" In fact, there was no harm done, and in honor of the holiday, he was pardoned for his mischief and no one told his father.

Before searching for *chomets*, when everyone was in such a fine holiday mood, who would have thought of wanting, God forbid, to spoil Erev Pesakh for Noteh the Rider?

April 10, 1947

Godl the Shoemaker of Rehovot
· · · · · · ·

he sign that let people know a shoemaker lived here was inscribed:
"Sandler, Shoemaker to Women, Men, and Children."

The sign was the only new thing that Godl the Shoemaker had brought
to his shop since he had arrived in Erets Isroel. Everything else—the workshop, a low, small table (a strip of molding around it so that the shoemaker
nails wouldn't fall off), a small three-legged stool nearby, a container of wax
on the table for smoothing the cobbler's thread, the small board to protect
his knees when he cut off a piece for a sole, the apron whose color was impossible to tell, and the heap of old shoes for repair in the corner, and the
shoemaker's wife, Hannah Golde, a quiet woman, who was embarrassed to
talk to strangers—all of this was exactly the same as it had been in Pshitik.[1]

In Rehovot, Godl the Shoemaker acquired a goat, a source of great
pleasure for him because she gave milk, and he was even happier with her
now because a goat didn't need a permit here: she was a goat for free, a
daughter of freedom. He called her "Miriam the Prophetess," and in this
name, his wife saw an insult both to Miriam the Prophetess and to herself,
and she was angry.

In Pshitik, Godl knew that he belonged to the shoemaker's class. Here,
everything was topsy-turvy: his son Nokhumke became an officer in the
army, a veritable general, and always traveled home in a car, and when he
came into the house, the car waited outside for him as if he were a king.

---

1. See "A Glimmer of Youth," note 2, page 124.

Now, Godl doesn't know what position he has: he is a shoemaker, and his son, an officer. Godl is extremely proud of his country, Israel, proud of Rehovot, where the Israeli President lives, and proud of his son, Nokhumke.

"*Gad g'dud ye'gudenu; Meshiakhs tsaytn,*"[2] he says. Everything is ours, the President is one of ours, the army is ours, and the land is ours."

His daughter, Batye, is a teacher on a kibbutz. She has also confused him about his standing. His son is an officer, and his daughter a teacher—so, what kind of a shoemaker does that make him? What is his position?

Godl is pleased with the kibbutz: his daughter comes home suntanned, nicely dressed, wearing good shoes, and is always talking about a "party." The shoemaker sees good times for her, too: she doesn't have to worry about earning a living, she doesn't need a dowry, and she's always in a hurry to go back to the kibbutz because there's a "party." In fact, it seems to him that the Messiah will come to one of these parties at some point, and Batye doesn't want to miss him—if not, why else would she be in such a hurry? It's not like the Eighteen Blessings at the Synagogue, where one can be a little late.

Batye is a puzzle for him and for his wife. She is so occupied with the kibbutz, it's almost as if it were her own property.

Once she brought an egg cookie from the kibbutz and said they had baked it in an electric oven, that they'd installed there not long ago. She ate that cookie with such gusto, it was as if they had given her the Ox in the Messiah's time[3] to taste. Hannah Golde, her mother, doesn't think much of the kibbutz. A person could live there a hundred and twenty years with an electric oven and still not collect enough money for a dowry; she'll be left an old maid, and the kibbutz won't be worrying.

---

2. Godl (Yiddish pronunciation of the name Gad) repeats these two phrases like a refrain. The first, a tongue-twister in Hebrew, is the first part of verse 19, Genesis, Ch. 49—*Etz Hayim: Torah and Commentary* (New York: Jewish Publication Society, 2001) and is Jacob's blessing, as he is dying, for his sons—this one for Gad. "Legions of enemies will attack Gad; but Gad will go forth to them and they will surrender to him." The second phrase is in Yiddish and means "[These are] the Messiah's times"; in other words, "It will be, or already is, the best of times." When the Messiah comes; the millenium.

3. The Hebrew word *shorabo'r* refers to the ox or bull that will be eaten by the righteous when the Messiah comes, according to legend.

As she sees it, the kibbutz has taken away her daughter, but taken her in such a way that she can't worry, can't even prepare the dowry sheets—nothing. A daughter and the Messiah.

She feels this way especially when their daughter comes to Rehovot standing in a "tender," a truck full of young men and women who are singing songs exactly as if they were going to a wedding.

She says to her husband, "That's the kibbutz for you."

He replies, *"Gad g'dud ye'gudenu; Meshiakhs tsaytn,"* and feels an enormous tremor in his shoemaker's position.

On the wall, Godl has hung two pictures: Weitzman and Dr. Herzl. Weitzman, because he is the president and lives in Rehovot; Dr. Herzl because he has something to do with the Messiah.

Dr. Herzl's picture hangs right over the little table in the workshop and confirms with his large burning eyes: "Here, you need only understand—these are the Messiah's times."

It was a hard day for Godl the Shoemaker, when Nokhumke, his son the officer, came home on foot and told them that he had been discharged from the army, and that he was going to Batye's kibbutz.

Nokhumke was sitting there in his little khaki shorts, smoking a cigarette at ease and in comfort, as if he didn't have a care in the world.

The first thing Godl the Shoemaker thought about was the car. How had he gotten here? And Nokhumke had come home as though nothing had happened.

His father couldn't help himself and asked, "Where is the car?"

Nokhumke peered at his father and then caught on to what he was saying. He stretched his bare, suntanned legs, and said, "Who knows?"

Now for the first time, Godl the Shoemaker noticed that his son had large burning eyes, just like those in the picture of Dr. Herzl in his workshop. He went over to Nokhumke and gave him his hand. "May you have good fortune, Nokhumke. *Gad g'dud ye'gudenu; Meshiakhs tsaytn."*

On Sabbath, the work place was covered with a white tablecloth; in the house there was Sabbath calm.

Godl sat at the table and looked in a book of pictures of the people who had built Rehovot.

"Look at them, look at them," he said to his wife. *"Vashnye parshoynen!!*[4] It's just as they say. Aha! Remarkable people!"

His wife came over to him, stood a while, and without a word, went back.

Dr. Herzl looked down from the wall with his large burning eyes, reminding one that these are the times of the Messiah. And President Weitzman smiled comfortably and benignly, as if he were a guest in the neighborhood.

In Rehovot, there was Sabbath peace and quiet.

Tel Aviv, August 1950

---

4. The phrase *Vashnye parshoynen* is half Russian and half Yiddish.

Zorekh the Community's

. . . .

Z orekh the Community's [1]—that's what people called him—belonged to God and to the entire shtetl of Grudi.

One winter, about the time of Hannukah, he arrived in Grudi on a wagon that was packed with crates of merchandise. He helped the coachman throw the crates down into a storehouse, and when the man handed him two groschen for his work, Zorekh refused it and said, "Give it to the Community Guest Fund.[2]

The coachman remained standing there bewildered, the two coins in his hand, and didn't know what to do with them.

That was the story about Zorekh's arrival in Grudi.

He went into the town, right to the synagogue. There, he polished the Hannukah lamp, puttied a pane of cracked glass, and chopped away at the ice near the steps to the women's section of the synagogue. He took a broom from the entryway and swept the snow from the street by the synagogue, and then from several well-to-do houses nearby. He never asked anyone if he should do the work, and he never asked for any pay. In a few short weeks, people in the shtetl got used to this, that Zorekh did "what he wanted to," and they gave him the name: Zorekh the Community's.

1. In the original text, Molodowsky uses *kalsher,* a term deriving from the Hebrew word *kool,* meaning "community." A *kalsher* is a person active in community affairs.

2. In Yiddish, the Hebrew words, *Hakhnoses-orkhim,* signify the community or organization that provided for guests, especially poor people who needed a place to stay for Sabbath.

Zorekh the Community's was never without something to do. For the Passover preparations, he whitewashed the walls of the Talmud Torah, repaired the door of the bath house that was hanging by a thread, letting in drafts. He hammered planks around the well in Itzkhok Aaron's courtyard, where people came for matzo water even though Itzkhok Aaron had not ordered the repair. Itzkhok Aaron's wife fretted—what kind of a man repairs a well without asking the owner? But Itzkhok Aaron shook his head. "Zorekh the Community's does. Let him do it."

The entire town found ways to pay him. On Fridays, Zorekh the Community's walked through the streets carrying an alms box, and whoever wanted to could toss in a few coins. He never knocked on any doors, and he never went in to any house. But the housewives themselves sent out their children, saying: "Run, throw a groschen into Zorekh's alms box." It became almost a custom in Grudi, and to let a week go by without throwing a few coins into Zorekh's alms box was about the same as not paying a debt one owed him.

Sabbaths, Zorekh the Community's ate at Rakhmiel the Dyer's house. Just as he swept away the snow without asking permission, and without asking for pay, so one Friday evening after prayers, he went over to Rakhmiel the Dyer's house, said "Gut Shabbes," and said right out to him, "Reb Rakhmiel, keep me at your house for Sabbath."

This filled Rakhmiel the Dyer with pride. There were householders in town richer than he, where a person could get a better meal, but Zorekh the Community's had come directly to him, to his crowded little house with a meager kugel—to keep the Sabbath.

"By all means, Reb Zorekh, you will be our welcome guest,"[3] Rakhmiel said to him.

Peshe, Rakhmiel's wife, brought another plate and another small tin spoon to the table, and Zorekh the Community's remained with them for Sabbath. The next day, following the Sabbath afternoon meal,[4] Peshe said,

3. Molodowsky used the term oyrekh, meaning "a visitor or guest," usually a poor person invited to spend the Sabbath in a strange town.

4. The Hebrew term Shaleshudes signifies the late afternoon meal (literally the third meal of the day) on Sabbath.

not really asking her husband, "Reb Zorekh, if it's God will that we are alive next week, I shall make a better Sabbath afternoon meal."

And so, week in and week out, Zorekh the Community's kept the Sabbath at Rakhmiel the Dyer's house. The shtetl, Grudi, figured that Rakhmiel the Dyer, who was a poor man, and who, on top of that, supported his sister's orphan (she went barefoot in summer), now had a steady guest coming for Sabbath. On Thursdays, the miller added another scoop of flour to Peshe's sack—for their Sabbath guest. The butcher threw in an extra rib— for their Sabbath guest. And the market woman, who sold fish, added more weight to the scales—two little fish—let it be for their Sabbath guest. Rakhmiel the Dyer thanked God, that now he was a respected householder in town with a steady guest for Sabbath.

Rakhmiel the Dyer's means increased. Each householder, when he needed some clothes to be dyed, would remind his wife: Take the work in to Rakhmiel, he has a steady Sabbath guest.

The other dyers were envious of Rakhmiel, but they never said harsh things behind his back: God sends to him, so he has.

People on their own began calling Zorekh the Community's Reb Zorekh, and no one could say if he was a man of substance who took care of the town, or a poor man who went around with an alms box. They always saw him climbing on the roof of the synagogue or on the Talmud Torah, repairing a broken shingle here, a chink in the wood there. Many of the concerns of the community now fell away. Reb Zorekh looked around for whatever wanted repairing, where he might be needed, and all was done at the proper time. The glass panes in the synagogue were always repaired and shining for a holiday. The walls of the poorhouse, sagging all these years, were reinforced with planks, the windows were caulked with putty, and secured against the wind. The poor people were comforted when Reb Zorekh the Community's brought them a tin pot on a tripod for boiling tea. "Now there's a real person for you," they said, "a someone who sees to the needs of a poor guest."

And for all of Grudi, it was clear that what the community couldn't do, they could rely on Reb Zorekh to do it for them. When someone in town was sick and a sitter was needed (a person who sits the night voluntarily with a sick person), people knew that Reb Zorekh would come. No one had to ask him. He would come on his own. The poor people who had a hard time paying the fees, would push their children: "Run to Reb Zorekh!" and Reb Zorekh, who sat each day at a table in the study house for the afternoon prayers, taught the very small boys to read Hebrew aloud. He never acted like a melamed. He didn't force the children to learn and he didn't punish them: but when a child came and sat down next to him at the table, he opened the prayer book and bade the child: "Recite."

Many years passed. The children grew up, and the old people grew older. When Rakhmiel married off his sister's orphan, who had been reared in his house, Reb Zorekh the Community's provided the wedding supper for her. He placed two small cups of coins on the table, coins that he had taken from his own box and said these words to Rakhmiel the Dyer: "I have leaned on your table every Sabbath. Many, many Sabbaths. You've had an extra burden because of me. Now I want to take care of the wedding-supper for Shifra, whom you raised like your own child. Don't cause me grief by refusing me."

In Grudi, people soon found out that Reb Zorekh the Community's was providing Shifra's wedding supper, and when the time came, over half the town went for the blessing over the bread[5] and to deliver mazel tov. It was a community supper. And the wedding presents that people brought were enough to furnish a house with goods.

The young unmarried girls of Grudi envied Shifra her wedding presents a little, but no one had a harsh word to say.

"She's an orphan, and if it was meant for her, she deserves it."

Reb Zorekh the Community's died suddenly. He was found lying, broom in hand, in the courtyard of the poorhouse. He had fallen down when he was clearing the snow by the poorhouse so that its guests could make their way to the door.

In town, people said that Reb Zorekh the Community's had an espe-

---

5. The author used the term *makn b'motzi*, which means "to make the blessing over the bread before the meal itself begins."

cially peaceful death[6]—respectfully, they said that he "passed away," as one says for very important people.

When they picked up the body, Rakhmiel the Dyer tied a rope around his waist, tucked up the bottom of his coat, and finished the task of clearing the snow from the courtyard of the poorhouse that Reb Zorekh the Community's had not had time to finish.

The entire town came to the funeral. The people shuddered when Rakhmiel the Dyer arrived with the broom of Reb Zorekh the Community's in one hand and the bucket he had used for washing the windows of the synagogue in the other. People stepped aside for him, as though he were carrying a Torah scroll. Rakhmiel the Dyer, who had never once given a funeral speech, stood by the head of the casket of the deceased, and spoke to him just as though he were still alive: "Reb Zorekh, you brought light into our lives and revered the spirit of simple hard work. The twigs of your broom were like the branches of the *lulav* over which a blessing is made to the Lord, God of the Universe. And the tin bucket that you used for washing the windows of the synagogue was like King Solomon's golden vessels that gladdened and cheered the people of Israel. May your merits be a credit to all of Grudi."

The Jews of Grudi didn't forget the yortzeit of Reb Zorekh the Community's. Each year for the yortzeit, a person was called up to be the "Community's," and for an entire day he did the work that Reb Zorekh the Community's used to do for the shtetl Grudi. Each householder hoped that he would be chosen to be the "Community's." For this honor, he paid two groschen to the community, not any more than two groschen, so that it could be done by the richest man or the bitterest poor man, as was Reb Zorekh the Community's himself.

6. The Hebrew phrase *mise binshike* translates as "a death with a kiss," but a kiss from the breath of God; that is, an exceptionally peaceful death.

Appendix

· · · · · · ·

The following words and phrases appeared in English in Molodowsky's original Yiddish text. To avoid giving them undue emphasis in this English translation, they were not set off in the text, but for those interested, they appear here, listed alphabetically by story.

Brothers: First Lady, surprise party

The Brothers: slack, bargain, taxes, imported, domestic, sale, "will you please give me?"

Charter Members: taxes, funnies

The Crow: furnished room, sale, chewing gum

The Divorce: lunchroom

Do-All: customer, "thank-you," chain store, moving pictures, chewing gum, sales, connections

Elaine: boy friend, business, "All right"

Eliahu Zalkind's Bookkeeping: All Wool, mister, donations

Eternal Summer: junior high, the old people, date, hello, with love, "I assure you"

Family Life: yardstick, darling, "Yes, Sir," "Sure," "Hot coffee," salesman, radios, televisions, exterminator, broilers, headaches, damages, "Cheer up," "Good-bye."

Friendship: "Yes, the young people," grandpa

A Fur Coat: lollipops, extra, pay day, lunchroom, Bye-bye

A Glimmer of Youth: all right, funnies, magazine, boss, foreman, teddy bear, radio, electric broiler, vacuum cleaner, orange juice, washing machine, drugstore, movie actress, business, funnies, magazine

Gone . . . .: customer

Herschel Eisenbold: Sir, Mister, Affiliated

Home for Passover: sticker, bill, ranch house, barbeque oven, beautician

In a Jewish Home: government job, darling, drugstore

In a Living Room: funny, magazine, living room

"The Kretchma": quarter, dimes, stop, paper

The Lost Sabbath: vitamins, lollipop, "come here," nothing, please, starch, "I'm here"

Luck: honeymoon, foreman, boss, "Hey," movie star, designer, Style B, styling the season

Malkele Eshman: modern advertisements, first class

Married Off: doll, permanent wave, tickets, lobbies, choreography

On a Day of Rest: ambition

The Queen: queen, honey, chicken sandwich, tips, deposits, business, terms, management, "please," "What do you think, Philip?", checks, camelhair, station wagon, pin-up girl, sun parlor, strict, truck driver, "All right," valet, strict

The Rashkovitcher Wedding: vacuum cleaner

The Rich Man from Azherkov: tenants, loan, mortgages, receipts, dispossess, surprise parties, roof garden, income, overhead, junk shop, climate

Sholem Moishe: refugees, stands, tenants, "All right," anniversary, zeroes, hello, "What's the matter with you?", "What are you talking about?"

The Son-in-Law: wax paper, Mom, please, "He is right," "Nice day, isn't it?" "Yes, it is a nice climate," "A climate is a permanent . . . ," pass the exams, young people, hot dogs

Sylvia: shuttle train

Unhappy Celebrations: hikes, department store, beauty parlor

A Wedding: honeymoon, stainless, public school

Glossary

. . . .

aliyah: Literally, "to go up," often meaning to settle in Erets Isroel. It can also mean to go up to the *bima* to recite blessings.

bar mitzvah: A boy's rite of passage, held when he is thirteen, in which he assumes his religious responsibilities.

beit midrash: A house or place of study, especially for the study of sacred texts.

bima: The front of the synagogue, usually raised, where the Torah is kept.

britzka: An open carriage with a collapsible hood.

bris: The rite of circumcision for an eight-day-old baby boy.

bubbe: "Grandmother," a term usually connoting warm affection.

cheder: Literally, "a room"; the place where young boys go for religious study.

cholent: A nutritious dish of meat and beans, traditionally brought to the town baker, baked in his oven overnight on Friday, and served (without reheating) on Saturday.

chuppah: The four-poled canopy under which the bride and groom stand during the marriage ceremony.

dayen: An assistant to the rabbi, a person of learning who is accorded much honor.

Erets Isroel: The land of Israel.

Erev Pesakh: Erev is literally the eve of any holiday; *Erev Pesakh* is the night before the holiday begins, when the searching for crumbs of leavened bread takes place.

folkshul: A secular Yiddish school for children, often run by or affiliated with the socialist movement.

gabbai: An official of the synagogue; a trustee who handles monies.

Gemore: The part of the Talmud that comments on the Mishnah.

groschen: A small Eastern European coin worth about three cents.

Gut yom-tov: Traditional wish meaning "good holiday."

hamantashen: A three-cornered cookie stuffed with a fruit puree served at Purim.

havdolah: The ceremony at sundown on Saturday evening, signifying the end of Sabbath and the beginning of the new week.

Kaddish: The prayer for the dead, usually said by a son. Hence, one's son is often referred to as "my Kaddish," a son being the guarantee that the Kaddish will be said properly.

keyn eyn hore: Literally, "no evil eye." This phrase is used as a charm to ward off the evil eye or bad luck.

Kiddush: The blessing said over wine.

klezmers: Musicians.

kretchma: A Jewish public house or inn in Eastern Europe.

kugel: A pudding, usually of noodles or potatoes.

latkes: Potato pancakes traditionally served for Hannukah.

landsleit: Those people who came to America from one area, usually a specific shtetl, in Eastern Europe, and who, once in America, founded and belonged to a benevolent society, known by the name of their shtetl. *Landsleit* members took care of each other, organized the different societies, and provided various activities.

landsman: A member of the *landsleit,* or a person who has a connection to others from his shtetl of birth or that of his parents.

l'chaim: A toast, "to life."

lehavdl: To distinguish; specifically, to make a distinction between the sacred and the profane.

l'shona tova tikoseyvu: Literally, "May a good year be inscribed and sealed for you"; the traditional wish exchanged on Rosh Hashanah.

lulev: A palm branch that is carried and waved during the ceremonies in the synagogue on Sukkos.

matzo: A cracker made of flour and water; the unleavened bread of Passover.

matzo water: The best water; used for making matzos.

mazel tov: "Good luck"; a phrase usually offered as a congratulation, sometimes ironically.

megillah: The Book of Esther, read in the synagogue at Purim. The term is sometimes used ironically to refer to a lengthy document.

mekhutonim: The in-laws, or family of the bride or groom, and the relationship of these families to each other.

minyan: A quorum of ten men needed to say prayers.

mitzvah: A good deed.

pareve: Food that is in neither meat nor milk; that is, neutral.

Pani: A diminutive of *Pan,* this is a term of respect in Poland, roughly equivalent to Mr. in English.

Reb: A term of respect, roughly equivalent to Mr., within the Jewish community, used to indicate a man's status.

rebbitzin: The wife of a rabbi, respected because of her position.

schlimazal: An unlucky person.

sefer, pl. *seforim:* A book, usually on a religious subject.

Shabbes: The Yiddish pronunciation of *Sabbath.*

shamesh: The beadle in a synagogue.

Shavuos: An early summer holiday, celebrating the first gathering of fruit and God's giving Torah to the Jews.

shikse: A disparaging word for a Gentile girl.

Shimenesre: The lengthy Eighteen Blessings said thrice daily.

shivah: The seven days of mourning observed immediately following someone's death.

shkotsim: Naughty gentile boys, sometimes used affectionately for Jewish boys; stinkers, brats.

shpielers: Comic actors who perform at Purim parties.

shul: A place for both worship and study; familiarly, a small synagogue.

sukkah: A wooden structure, covered with branches or palm fronds, built by each family for Sukkos, where the family takes meals.

Sukkos: An autumn holiday following the High Holy Days and lasting a week, during which a *sukkah* is built outside the house.

tallis: The black-and-white-striped prayer shawl worn by men.

Tishebov: The ninth day in the month of Ab. A day of fasting and mourning to commemorate the destruction of the temples in Jerusalem.

treyf: Unclean, filthy, polluted, not kosher.

tsimmes: A stew of meat, vegetables, and often fruit.

yortzeit: Literally, "a year's time"; the observation of the anniversary of a person's death.

yeshiva: An institution of religious learning for older students.

yikhes: One's family's pedigree, parentage, or ancestry, and the pride one takes in it.